Praise for The Skin Artist

"*The Skin Artist* is the complex saga of a young man's search for his own identity on the dark side of the New South—it's hard to believe this is a first novel. Hovis has created an old-fashioned morality tale set against some of the most garish manifestations of the Sunbelt."
—Lee Smith, author of *Dimestore* and *Guests on Earth*

"Out of America's age of information, image, tattoo, and Adam and Eve eroticism comes a tightly written novel about addiction, family, and religion. *The Skin Artist* is at once both smooth-deep literary and fast-eddy suspenseful. George Hovis's first novel—it never slows down one iota—is an extraordinary debut."
—Clyde Edgerton, author of *The Floatplane Notebooks* and *Raney*

"George Hovis displays a world we know and try to turn our gaze from. But the story is too powerful, the forces of destruction too strong, and we readers watch, hypnotized, as the descent gathers friends, lovers, and family into its vortex. Can such dark passages lead to hope?"
—Fred Chappell, author of *Dagon* and *As If It Were*

"Equal parts psychological complication and harrowing action, a pull-no-punches tale of one man's reckoning with his mistakes. An unforgettable read."
—Leah Stewart, author of *What You Don't Know About Charlie Outlaw*

The
Skin Artist

Share Your Thoughts

Want to help make *The Skin Artist* a bestselling novel? Consider leaving an honest review on Goodreads, your personal author website or blog, and anywhere else readers go for recommendations. It's our priority at SFK Press to publish books for readers to enjoy, and our authors appreciate and value your feedback.

Our Southern Fried Guarantee

If you wouldn't enthusiastically recommend one of our books with a 4- or 5-star rating to a friend, then the next story is on us. We believe that much in the stories we're telling. Simply email us at **pr@sfkmultimedia.com**.

SFK
PRESS

The
Skin Artist

George Hovis

1-21-20

To Kevin,

Mary says, avoid
the ink!
I say, do as
you please.

G H

To Clyde
(for the gift of your voice and years of patient mentoring)

"I had come into a place mute of all light, that bellows as the sea does in a tempest. . . . The infernal hurricane that never rests carries along the spirits in its rapine . . . hither, thither, down, up it carries them; no hope ever comforts them, not of repose, nor even of less pain."

—Dante, *Inferno*
Translated by Charles Eliot Norton

Part 1

1

When his neighbor cut the seal on a new bottle of Baby God, Bill held out his glass. He moved his body into the last of the sun, its thin warmth, and turned to watch the dogwoods glow. The bourbon burned sweet, finished long. So, why this unrelenting sadness? He hadn't earned this funk. Through the French doors, Bill watched his wife hurrying around the kitchen. Too cool out here for her skin and bones. He could tell Anthony anything—Maddie wouldn't hear. And he had to try to talk to somebody.

For two weeks, almost every night, Anthony had been coming over in the evenings. He said his wife was working late at a new job. Sometimes Maddie would fix dinner. Or Bill would grill steaks. Anthony always brought the overpriced bourbon, some brand neither of them could pronounce. It had aged in oak barrels since God was a baby, so that's what they called it.

Nine miles to the north, downtown Charlotte shimmered against a purple sky. The Queen City. With a sky this clear, those skyscrapers piled themselves on the horizon. The days were finally starting to warm, and the smell of damp earth, combined with the ringing of peepers, took Bill home to the sticks—which only deepened his funk.

He started by complaining to Anthony about the house; the new green paint on the shutters had provoked the ire of the homeowner's association. Whenever he had a dispute with the homeowner's association—about the color of the shutters, or the clothesline he wanted to string up in the backyard to save electricity, or the chemicals he didn't want sprayed on his lawn—his wife always sided with the homeowner's association. Anthony grumbled agreement about "those fascists" and refilled Bill's tumbler with Baby God.

"There's other stuff, too," Bill said. "Bedroom stuff."

Anthony nodded and waited for him to go on. They had propped stereo speakers in the windows and had classic Springsteen turned up loud. *Darkness on the Edge of Town.* They both knew the words. Maddie was after him to get rid of all that vinyl. But in a house this big he didn't understand the necessity of compact discs.

How could Bill explain their problems to another man? He started by parroting what Maddie had told him on multiple occasions in the plainest language, how it wasn't about *him*; it was, rather, about *her* and *her* body image and *her* inability to feel sexy when she went to bed with him. He knew he was supposed to empathize, that somehow it was his fault—this diet she was on, her new obsession with high-impact aerobics, how she had dropped nearly thirty pounds and was now dangerously thin. Scrawny. Skinny legs that were pitiful to look at.

"Well, you can see for yourself, can't you? The woman is in trouble, and if you say so much as 'How about a doughnut?' she gets tight-lipped and icy and asks how anyone who pickles himself in bourbon every night could have the nerve to question her diet."

Bill was in mid-sentence when she opened the door and stepped out onto the deck, hugging herself and turning her back to the breeze, shivering.

"Are you guys going to stay out here the entire night?"

Anthony started joking with her, bellowing along with the record in a voice that took all of Springsteen's darkness and turned it into Maddie's laughter. Bill clawed in his shirt pocket for a Marlboro Light. That lilt in her voice. The only time they were civil lately was when they were around other people. He chugged the rest of his bourbon, inhaled the cigarette until the dizziness from the nicotine on top of Baby God made the horizon tip abruptly away from him.

Goose pimples rose on her bare shoulders, and it wasn't even that cold out. She wore a new pageboy haircut that broke his heart. He still ached for that face to look on him with kindness, with approval.

Her skin glowed from their trip to Myrtle Beach the week before Easter. Though they had not actually spoken of it, that week had been a clear signal that their marriage was in trouble. He had adjusted to the silences at home. But stuck together for seven days straight, those silences had begun to suck up all the breathable air, whether in the cramped hotel room or out beside the roaring surf. She had lounged in the sun with a paperback, hadn't even looked up from her book to make eye contact during their few brief conversations, and he had gone for long walks on the beach, stayed gone for an hour at a time. Pocket a flask, catch a buzz, and enjoy the view through green lenses, the sand sticky as lime sherbet tugging at his heels, the beach spreading out wide and open like a long par five, filled with hundreds of women lined up in rows, melting beneath the sun, the oil shimmering, dripping off of them. It would be September before he had another vacation, and he couldn't bear the thought of spending the whole summer in air conditioning, in a white shirt and tie, while his tan faded to the color of skim milk.

Maddie and Anthony were talking about towns in New Jersey, the state where both of them had grown up. Bill suddenly regretted telling this lawyer so much about his marital problems. Maddie said she had apple pie and a pot of coffee inside, and Anthony rubbed his hands together as if to warm them. Bill said cut a slice for him, he'd be there as soon as he finished his cigarette. But when he stubbed the butt out in the ashtray, he lit another. Baby God was empty, so he cracked the seal on a bottle of Jim Beam and sloshed it into the glass.

He walked to the corner of the deck so that the house blocked the glare of the security lamp. He stood in what passed for darkness and squinted up to see a few stars peeking out. Nowhere in Eagle's Pointe was there a tree over ten feet tall. The developers had clear-cut the land, bulldozed away the topsoil. They'd ripped up all the wild growth by the roots and plopped down as many half-million-dollar homes as they could fit per acre. One good thing, their house was built on a rise with a view of the city. There were too many streetlights to see much of the stars, but they enjoyed a clear view of downtown Charlotte. And there in the center of that hump, twenty floors taller than the rest, shone the crown of the new NationsBank Tower—lit up like a birthday cake. Its image whispered nightly to Bill that there was someplace else he ought to be other than this suburb—other people he ought to be partying with. Some of his frat brothers lived in Charlotte, and occasionally he would join in a foursome for a Sunday morning round of golf, but it wasn't the same. They couldn't talk the way they had in college. Now their talk was always somehow connected to money. His brothers had turned into a bunch of yuppies. And maybe he had turned into one, too.

Sometime later he found himself in the backyard walking among the dogwoods, their sweet, fecund scent; he wasn't sure what time of night it was. The music had stopped. These blackouts were plaguing him more and more often. He stepped up onto the back deck and heard Maddie and Anthony inside laughing. Anthony was doing one of his impersonations, President Clinton introducing himself to Ms. Lewinsky. It seemed too late for Anthony to still be hanging around, but maybe it wasn't so late after all. Bill stood in the shadows and strained to hear. Their conversation was muffled by the window panes, drowned out by canned laughter from a neighbor's TV. Through the glass he saw them sitting at the dining room table together, like husband and wife. Anthony talked nonstop and every so often reached out a hand to place on top of her wrist. She smiled at the touch, leaned forward. They both burst into laughter.

One of the straps kept falling off the tanned point of her shoulder, and she kept languidly lifting it back up. A string of pearls lay against her collarbones. Her eyes spread wide with life. Earlier, Bill had told Anthony that she had starved all the meat off her bones. But, no, not entirely. On such a lithe body, her breasts made two nice handfuls right there in Anthony's face, and he was talking right at them. That smile on her face, the one Bill had come to believe he would never see again, yes, that one—there it was. It made something glow inside of him, glow and rise hot to his moistening eyes.

2

The next day at work lasted forever. New rumors had spread about cuts in middle management—maybe cuts all the way down the line to product development and even quality control. He made his morning rounds, stopped by the employee break room beside the lab. It was a social call. The white coats shot him worried glances. Worried for him, or for themselves? Henry sat in a corner, working his way through a crossword puzzle and the day's first pack of cigarettes. Graying hair ran greasy and long down past the collar of his lab coat, which was splattered with ink. Supposedly he had done a tour in Vietnam.

"When are you going to let them wash that thing?" Bill said, forcing a smile, the way he did every morning. And, as usual, Henry just glowered back through a haze of smoke. This ritual exchange seemed to ease the tension in the break room. If Bill could get through the day pretending his wife wasn't making love to a man who lived at the end of their cul-de-sac, then they could all keep right along pretending their careers were built upon a solid foundation.

Back in his office, he took four Advil for his head and dialed home again. Nobody answered. She should have been back from her morning class an hour ago. The thing to do was to drive home and wait for her. Confront her. Just get it out in the open, all of it. But then Max asked again for the report on the new dispersion equipment, and, the next thing he knew, it was past seven o'clock that evening when he called home for the fourth or fifth time and left a message telling her not to wait on him for dinner. She and Anthony could eat without him. He didn't even try to mask the sneer in his voice. Giving her permission, encouragement even, a window of opportunity. Plenty of opportunity. *If that's what you want, go for it.*

By the time he got away from the plant, the sky had lost most of its light, but the air was still warm enough to put the top down on his Mercedes. He needed to feel a breeze.

Riding the Interstate southward, the thought of her infidelity made the city present itself. There towered a new hotel where before all he could recall was an unbroken tree line. Billboards advertised fine dining, gated prefab paradises, gyms to help him lose the flab, the best in care for heart or cancer. What a glorious place Charlotte was to live and die. He slowed down to watch the curve of a half-finished overpass glide by above, lit up by high wattage. Names of streets he had never traveled. So he picked one. At home his wife could be panting into the neck of their neighbor, while Bill decided to take an exit, just to see where it led.

MANY CITY MILES LATER, at a hole-in-the-wall called the Double Door Inn, he eased the Mercedes into a space beside a row of Harleys, their chrome reflecting neon light from the beer signs that crowded the windows.

Inside, he squeezed his way through bodies lining one long hall, pool tables in the rear, a bar near a makeshift stage. Between songs, a band tuned their guitars. The slapback bass thumped so loud Bill could feel it against his body. He watched a woman across the club at the pinball machine. Covered in tattoos. Jet-black hair down her back. Every time she slapped the flipper buttons, that mane swung like a pendulum.

True grits in biker boots and frayed denim vests. Bankers in black T-shirts, faking it. And Bill in his suit and tie, one of the roughs. On the dance floor, an old sober couple in gray pigtails, boogie-woogying. The band invited other dancers to join them, but apparently the crowd was waiting for a state of deeper intoxication. Bill waited with them. He drank three draft Heinekens and a shot of Pepe while the dance floor slowly filled. One acrobatic couple cleared a space in the middle. Swing, that was the craze. Bill watched the tattooed woman make her way over to the swingers and then begin swaying her hips. Black mini-skirt. Ink of every color blanketed the pale skin of her legs and the arms she held loosely above her head. Everybody in the house watched her dance, even if they tried not to. She moved with the grace of a snake. And as long as Bill kept his eyes on her, he found he could forget his wife's smile, the one he'd witnessed last night through the picture window. Dark eyes darkened by heavy mascara, her aquiline nose was maybe too large for some, but not for Bill. He liked a woman with a nose. He liked her deep cleavage and the way she moved her hips, which helped him to stop thinking about Maddie and how the thick bristles of Anthony's mustache might feel against every part of her body.

Bill ordered another shot and settled deeper into the place he had claimed at the bar. The singer's pompadour bobbed up and down with the rhythm he picked out on that big hollow-body, driving heels of dancers into the floorboards. She gyrated her hips in front of his guitar, both of them covered in tattoos. Maybe his woman. Lucky fucker.

Beer lights blazed in the mirror behind the bar. Bill tried to catch the bartender's eye. Two men pushed their way into the space next to him. His age, mid-thirties, slicked-back hair, one of them had a pack of cigarettes rolled up in his T-shirt sleeve. All muscles and confidence. They were talking no-load mutual funds. Bill tried to follow their talk, but this was Maddie's language, not his. When he turned back around, there she was, that woman, close enough to make him spill his drink, that silky black hair pouring down her back, leaning over the bar with her ass cocked up and swaying to the drums. She caught him staring—grinned at him long enough to make his heart race, to forget all the muscle and mutual funds he himself had thus far failed to accumulate. Then she turned back to the bar and caught the red-headed bartender by the wrist, pulled her close over a puddle of beer, and planted a wet kiss on her lips.

Ample flesh. Ample curves. His eyes drifted to her belly, bared beneath her crop top, pulsing to the rhythm of the slapback bass. A soft biscuit. Maddie worked so hard to eradicate this most erotic padding. A belly like that would scald you, would raise blisters. Surrounding her navel swarmed a spiral of blue tentacles. On her bare shoulders a tree on fire.

What if he offered to buy her a drink? Or complimented her tattoos? Was that a fish wrapping around her fleshy thigh? What if he allowed himself to return her smile or even to ask her name? What she did for a living, for fun? All the while enjoying a drink here at this shiny bar. Then maybe when he arrived home later he wouldn't splinter into a million pieces as he walked through the front door.

He reached for his wallet, waiting for her to look his way again, when he caught a whiff of men's cologne and felt a hand tug at his shoulder.

"Bill Becker! How about this, everybody! My buddy Bill!"

Bill gripped the edge of the bar and looked up at familiar blue eyes. "Kent?"

"In the flesh."

The woman took her beer from the bartender and hurried away into the crowd.

"Buy you a drink?" Kent offered. He reeked of cologne, and Bill was disturbed to recognize it as the same brand he himself had worn in college. Polo, in the green bottle. Who wore cologne anymore?

"Uh, no thanks," he said. "I've got one."

Kent had added more weight in the past five years, and a full head of hair. But any Gamma would recognize that face, even strangers might, since his picture had appeared in the news—first his photograph above the words "Missing" and "Kidnapped," then a week later the video clip of Kent being handcuffed and led into custody, this just after he had come back to the border from Mexico to turn himself in. At the time, the fraternity alumni association hadn't yet noticed the funds missing from their bank account.

"How you getting along, buddy?" Kent laid a hand heavy with jewelry on Bill's shoulder and left it there even after Bill inched away. "You're looking good," he said. "Nice tie! You must be coming from the office."

"Yeah. How about you?"

"Oh, hell no. I work for myself these days. I just dress sharp when I go out. The ladies like it." Bill let Kent brag a while about his new business. Kent sold steaks and pork chops and seafood door-to-door. He had a portable deep freezer on the back of a pickup and he carried his meat out through the country to people who couldn't get to the store—or, who preferred not to.

Bill stared at the mound of blonde hair where Kent's bald head had shone like a polished egg. And that loud tie against the pink dress shirt. And the rings and the gold chains that glowed against bronze skin. He looked like a shorter, pudgy version of the Nature Boy Ric Flair, the professional wrestler who had put Charlotte on the map, long before the Hornets were even a gleam in George Shinn's eye. Even in college, Kent had indulged such outrageous taste in clothing. Bill hated to think it, but that bad taste was the result of growing up dirt poor. Kent and Bill had both grown up out in the country near Hailey Creek, less than a mile from each other, but the country still showed in Kent, no matter how hard he tried to hide it.

Bill let his eyes slide away into the crowd and over to the band. What did you say to someone whose life everybody knows has fallen apart?

For no apparent reason Kent let out a boom of laughter. "You're the last person I expected to see out here," he said. "How did you talk Maddie into turning you loose on a weeknight?"

"We're separated." Bill tried out the words to see how they sounded. They sounded like a lie, which reassured him somewhat. But Kent turned instantly into a mush of consolation.

"Oh, damn. Man!" Kent started massaging his shoulder, and Bill wished he hadn't told that lie. He thought about taking it back, but already Kent was deep into the history of his own divorce. Bill searched for that tattooed woman in the crowd. Kent had once been a close friend, even before college and the fraternity. They had spent summers together as Boy Scouts. They had shared a tent, even. Bill remembered this and Kent's habit of engaging him in long, heart-to-heart conversations. It was late, and Maddie would be wondering what had happened to him. Wouldn't she?

"Those were some hard years," Kent said. "After Mexico, and then Cindy leaving me. People treated me like a leper. I could have flopped over on my back and given up. And, by God, I'll tell you something, I'm a stronger man now. I've done my time. I can come into this bar and I can walk over to you and shake your hand. I can buy you a beer without hanging my head."

"Why don't I buy you one? I need to sober up and drive home." If other fraternity brothers happened to come into the Double Door and see the two of them together, Bill knew that it probably would not look good for him. He waved the bartender over.

When he saw foam rising in Kent's mug, Bill ordered another round for himself, as well.

The band was doing a surf guitar tune, and a bachelorette party had taken over the dance floor. They formed a circle around the bride-to-be, who shook her booty in time to the theme song from *Hawaii Five-0*. She looked a lot like Maddie—tall and lank, same pageboy haircut. It was her last night of freedom, and she was advertising to the crowd that she intended to live it up. She lifted a leg into the air and balanced on one platform sandal while she did the twist. Maddie was a good dancer, too; it was how they had met.

The bartender brought the beers, and Bill reached for his wallet. He didn't have to drink it. Maybe if he didn't, and he drove home now, he could talk to her, before it was too late. He took a sip of foam, turned around, and Kent was gone—over by the dance floor, his pink shirt plunging through the crowd. Bill waited till he saw him talking to her, that tattooed woman. What the hell was that about? Bill lifted the mugs high and followed in Kent's wake, pushing and weaving through sweaty bodies.

He got there just as she was standing to leave. He offered her the beer he had brought for Kent, but she said she was late for work. Her voice was hick city. She didn't look country at all.

"So, come watch me," she said indifferently to Kent, her eyes darting all around, everywhere except at the man she was talking to. "Bring your friend here."

"Lucy dances at The Jackpot."

Bill nodded, recalling the billboard advertisements up and down I-77. She met his eyes in a long, direct exchange. When she spun around and headed for the door, he felt his buzz start to unravel. The music was too loud. All the energy in the club turned to noise. Bill glanced at his friend and knew he felt it too. They both stared at the door. One last flash of that bright ink, and she was gone.

The band left the stage for a break, and Bill set the beers down at a table behind a heating duct, a lousy view of the stage, but he didn't plan on staying for the next set. They sat down across from each other.

"I need to tell you something," Kent said. "About those years. After my friends dropped me and my wife kicked me out." The booming car-salesman joviality was gone. Now that they didn't have to shout over the band, Kent settled in for a drunken confession. He lit a Camel. Bill grabbed the pack and stuck one in his own mouth, leaned across the table for a light.

"I learned a lot about myself," Kent said. "Most people don't know what nastiness they're capable of."

Bill nodded absentmindedly and said sorry but he needed to call home real quick. He turned in his seat for privacy and pulled out his mobile phone from the inner pocket of his suit jacket. He was still getting used to this thing, the idea that he could push a few buttons and talk to anybody in the world, even his wife. He dialed home and waited but heard nothing, not even a dial tone. The screen went blank—dead battery again. Damn, the thing wouldn't hold a charge.

"Most people live out their lives in some fantasy world," Kent said. "They have some fantasy twin do the things they wish they could do. You know what I mean?"

"Why did you ever come back?"

"From Mexico?"

"Yeah."

"Well, for one, I didn't speak Spanish." Kent laughed at some private memory. When the fraternity's alumni corporation had elected him treasurer, he said, he had never planned to steal, but his house payments and Cindy's credit card bills and his own credit cards all added up. "I just thought I would borrow a thousand, you know, and then pay it back. And then it was two thousand and then three—" And finally thirty-four thousand dollars, which had bankrupted the fraternity and forced them to close the chapter at Carolina.

That was five years ago. Bill remembered sitting in that

meeting of the alumni corporation and the brothers turning to look at him. He was the one who had brought this fat boy into the fold, back in college when he had preached to them about democracy and character and how a brotherhood should be more than a group of good-looking rich boys trying to make it with good-looking rich girls. These days, he saw the brothers only occasionally—golf outings, the homecoming game in the fall, maybe a wedding. Anyway, they had tried to put it all on Kent, but the chapter had been suffering from a range of problems: low membership levels, low grades, a lack of permanent housing, drugs.

"Y'all asked me to turn my pin in," Kent said. "And I honored that. I guess I don't deserve to be a brother, after what I did. But I ain't ashamed anymore. I paid the money back, Bill. And now I can walk up to you and shake your hand. I can buy you a beer."

"Yeah, that's what you said."

"Tell you what, buddy, let's chug this backwash and head on to another place I know. You up for it? You don't got a curfew anymore."

Bill stared out across the crowd packing in close to see the band, which had now returned to the stage. The club was filled again with the blare of sax and guitar twang, booming bass, an eardrum-rattling snare. He needed to go home, but he was too drunk now to drive. He looked around himself, at the partners on the dance floor, at the band strutting around the stage staring into their microphones, at the waitress, her tray covered with empty glasses, not even trying to smile now as she forced her way through the rowdy crowd. He wished he hadn't stopped here tonight. He needed to find a way to contact Maddie and let her know where he was.

As soon as he and Kent stepped outside, Bill felt his head lighten. The parking lot was dark enough to see a few stars. Lucky stars. There was a pay phone, occupied.

"Listen to that Harley roar! Yeah *man!* That's enough to make fifty sound like the new twelve."

The biker, the one in leather, no helmet, did not seem to care for Bill's commentary. Kent took Bill by the shoulders and guided him back toward the now-empty phone booth. Inside the folding glass door, the air smelled of perfume and cigarettes. Bill unwrapped the coiled metal cable, slipped in his change and dialed the number, heard his own voice asking him to leave a message, promising him that his call was very important. He said some words that came into his head, something about meeting an old friend and how he needed to sober up. He started in on the story about Kent turning himself in to the border patrol, asking if she remembered seeing it on the news. Then he realized that the beeping on the line indicated the voice recorder had ended and the tape had reset.

He placed the receiver in its cradle and saw through the glass that Kent was waiting. What had he seen down there in that desert? Something that had made it possible for him to come back and reinvent himself. He had started his own business, bought a brand new head of hair, survived divorce and the scorn of friends. Down at the depths of alienation and self-degradation, he must have found some bedrock.

Or maybe he was only faking it.

3

B ill came to life with the buzz of a giant insect droning in his ear and two voices, a man and a woman, arguing. "You're making your money," she said. "He paid you good money. You act like you're doing me a favor, when it's me that's doing you the favor by bringing you the business."

"Please. Don't put yourself out for me. If it's absolution you came here for, you find a strange way to go about it, bringing your sugar daddy drunk to my doorstep."

"He ain't my sugar daddy."

"He didn't seem that drunk at first. There was a time I wouldn't work on drunks. And even if I need the money, I still don't need it that bad."

"His money's as good as—"

"It's just that I can't tell much difference among the soulless anymore, whether they're drunk or sober. It's like telling the difference between two opossums or two Japanese beetles, or two common house-flies, or two paramecia, or—"

"Niall, stop it."

"Well . . . he looks human. But we shouldn't jump to conclusions."

Bill fully awoke to the smell of hospital antiseptic. He lay on his back staring up at God and Adam, their outstretched fingers about to touch. The man of clay lazed dull and clueless of the change about to take place. Bill felt a pain in his chest that balanced the pain in his head. A hand smoothed across his scalp, and a woman's face loomed before him, her straight black hair brushing his shoulder. Tattoos. Somehow familiar.

A tattooed man sat on a stool and slumped against the wall. Something shiny buzzed in his hand.

"How'd you sleep, sweetheart?" The woman stood over him, a living comic book. That foothills twang in her voice, he'd definitely heard it before.

"Who are you?" His tongue stuck to the paste in the roof of his mouth.

"You embarrassing sonofabitch." She laughed. "I been telling Niall all about you, the funny things you say. And then you wake up and ask me my name."

"Niall?"

"I'm Niall." The guy straightened. Rows of studs in his ears gleamed in the bright light. His skin was covered with blue arabesques even denser than hers.

Bill lifted his head. Posters covered the walls and ceiling. The air was choked with rubbing alcohol and noise from a transistor radio. He leaned forward, and his skin peeled away from the chair.

"Where am I?"

The woman laid a hand on his shoulder and the black hair fell into her eyes.

"You're in hell," the man said, his lip lifting into a snarl of laughter. The silver thing he carried flashed in the light. "When I started on you," he said, "I thought you were half sober. I usually don't work on somebody who's polluted, especially virgins."

Bill looked down at his chest, a blue and bloody mess. "Oh my God."

"It'll look better after it heals," Niall said.

Right there on his chest, surrounded by a pink berm of proud flesh, the tattoo was recognizable as a blue butterfly, spreading its wings, ready for flight. One wing nearly finished.

"It's going to look fine." The woman smoothed her palm down his arm.

The man flipped a switch and the silver machine buzzed, loud and metallic, the insect Bill had been dreaming. Blue ink dripped, and the needle buried itself in the loose skin around his nipple.

"Wait a minute!" He squirmed beneath the pain.

"Tender around the nipple?" the woman said.

"I tried to talk you two out of working up to the nipple," the guy said. "I knew if he slept through this part, I was going to have to call an ambulance."

Bill gripped the chrome rails of the barber's chair. "How much would it cost me to take it off?"

"I'm not in that kind of business."

"The nipples were *your* idea," she said. They both started laughing.

"I don't remember," Bill said.

"Well, shit, don't fret about it. It ain't the end of the world." She pressed a lukewarm cup of coffee into his hand.

"I better not. Better not drink this."

"You need something to eat with it?"

"Better not." He looked down at the line of fresh blood and ink. He passed the coffee back to her, turned his face away, felt his eyes grow hot. To be here was bad enough. To start boo-hooing like a baby in this den of iniquity, that would be more shame than he could stand. "You're the dancer, aren't you?"

"There you go."

"How'd we get here?"

"Well now. That's a long story."

"God almighty."

"You pissed Kent off and he left you at the club, and then . . . well, like I said, long story."

"If it hurts too bad," the man said, "we'll stop and take a break. Tell you what, I need to get a smoke."

"Yeah," Bill said, "do that. Really. Maybe we should stop and think about this."

Niall lit a cigarette and stepped out onto the parking lot. Occasionally a car roared past. It was that time of night when every other car is a cop. Bill wondered if Maddie was sleeping or up worried, calling the police looking for him. Had he remembered to call?

He dug his chin into his sternum and angled his eyes down at the blue mess.

"How you doing? You all right?" The woman let her hip press against his shoulder. She laid her palm against his cheek, his neck. "You're a little bit chilled."

"How much blood have I lost?"

"Not more than a gallon."

"How much do I owe that guy?"

"You paid already. Niall only takes cash up front. Don't you remember?"

"No."

"We stopped by the cash machine." She grinned. "You paid Niall three hundred."

"God almighty."

"You got a deal, honey. He's the best." She sat back on the stool Niall had vacated and picked up the tattoo gun. She flipped a switch and brought the buzzing gun close to his bare chest.

"You want me to finish you?" She brought the gun down to her crotch and ground her teeth at him. "Oh hell. Don't cry," she said. "I ain't going to touch you. Niall would kill me. There was a time he let me apprentice, but nowadays he thinks he's too good. Works on a couple of musicians, half-ass local celebrities, and suddenly he's Leonardo da Vinci."

Bill could see Niall framed in the doorway, smoke spiraling from his cigarette, a neon sign filling up the one tiny window—TATTOO—vertical, buzzing red. The woman took a pencil out of her purse and scribbled what she said was her work schedule on the back of a purple flyer.

"Listen, I got to go." She folded the paper and eased it into the pocket of his pants. "I'll see you around—when you come back to the club." She put her hand against his cheek and left it there while she stared absentmindedly out the door.

"Yeah," he said. "See you around."

When she turned her bare shoulders to him, bare shoulder blades, covered only by spaghetti straps, recognition came. That tree on fire, its leaves a hundred flames. Coiled around its trunk, running down her spine, a red serpent, grinning at the woman and man holding an apple.

She walked out the door, and then he felt alone in this place. There was a lot he knew he ought to remember. His stomach growled. He should eat something. His chest had been shaven clean—that hair Maddie had, once upon a time, loved to brush her fingers through. What a fright. He let his head fall back onto the foam. On the walls, tacked to the ceiling: bleeding moons, blazing suns, hieroglyphic runes, every possible variety of ancient-looking shit, naked women—angels, mermaids, winged succubi—every kind of insect, drooping daisies, Kama Sutra lovers with intertwining body parts, sketches of anything you could possibly want. Polaroids of finished tattoos, satisfied customers smiling, intimate body parts on display. It wasn't too late to get the hell out of here. Find a cab. Deal with this half a tattoo later when he was sober enough to think. Where was his car? He ought to call Maddie, but what could he say?

The artist stepped back inside and sat down on the stool next to Bill. He was a short man, but somehow larger than his stature.

"Well then, are we ready for round two?"

"Look." Bill tried to hide his desperation. "What's your name? Niall?"

"That's right."

"Look, Niall, I don't know how I wound up here." He tried to laugh. He needed to get this guy talking. Needed to stall him. He stared at the tattoo gun on the table and still felt the burning in his flesh. He needed to get up, find his clothes, and leave—now.

"Of course," Niall said, "if you've changed your mind, it's your body. You should never even consider a tattoo unless you've given it a lot of thought beforehand."

Bill stared at the pattern of wings on the wall, two dragonflies mating. "I didn't know tattoos could be so realistic," he said, trying to establish some human connection. "Who'd you learn it from?"

Niall picked up the tattoo gun. "I don't want to sound like a complete egomaniac," he said, "but I don't know of anyone in the world doing what I do—the stuff I'm known for."

"Like what?"

"Hindu iconography. Renaissance figurative work. Animal studies, nature studies, Native American. Celtic work. There are a lot of people doing Celtic these days, but as far as I'm concerned, they all suck."

"Is that right?"

"Their lines aren't parallel or flowing, their compositions are stilted and have nothing to do with the body they're on. About ninety-nine percent of all the Celtic work I've seen is what I would call a failure. Just mass-produced crap. When you're talking about a six-thousand-year artistic tradition, there's no excuse for garbage."

"I see."

"So, what is it? Stay or go? I have another customer in an hour."

Bill imagined the confrontation with Maddie, that moment when he would unbutton for her. The only thing more humiliating than an accidental tattoo would be half of one. Plus, he'd already paid. He nodded and braced himself for the needle.

"The Celts and the Picts tattooed themselves extensively." Niall's words fell in rhythm with the pressure of the needles. "The Picts were named for their tattoos."

"Weren't they the ones who painted themselves blue?"

"It was *not* paint."

"Well, not paint, but—"

"Oh, I've read history books when I was young that tried to tell me it was paint. Right. They've got their bodies over there preserved. It's embedded deep within the skin. There's all kinds of historical rewriting and propaganda." The artist looked up, ink dripping from the tip of the gun.

Bill hadn't meant to piss him off. The needles burned. Maybe it was better not to try and make conversation. Just get it over with.

"I never knew tattooing went so far back."

"At one point in history, tattooing was taken very seriously, as well it should be, because it's strong fucking magic and not simply about looking good at the club. But few artists these days are practicing magic, at least not consciously. There are very few *human beings* left who practice magic—as long as you don't count crap like Wicca, which isn't magic. It's just mass-produced garbage designed to elevate somebody to the top of a social circle. More like Hollywood. If anybody in Wicca or one of its New Age spin-offs knows anything at all, it's only the people at the very top. The people in covens are nothing but pawns and workhorses and batteries to draw power off of when need be, and to be chucked when they are no longer needed."

Bill forced a laugh. "Wicca sounds a lot like corporate America."

"In a nutshell," Niall said, "*real* magic, no matter what tradition you're drawing off of, is about manipulation of the electromagnetic structure that all life and all matter are an expression of."

This was more than Bill needed to hear so early in the morning. The sky outside had turned gray, and the birds in the city had grown manic with song. He laid his head back against the foam and tried not to concentrate on the pain.

"Thousands of years ago," Niall went on, "when our species was young, nearly everyone practiced magic. When the planet supported only several hundred thousand humans, there was enough soul to go around—back when everyone was in touch with the diversity of life on the planet. Original sin had nothing to do with sex—that's just a lie the church tells us. Original sin? Raping yo' Mama, the Mother Earth—that was when people turned away from hunting and gathering and took up food production. What comes next? Population explosion, the plague, industrial agriculture, junk food hell, consumerism, nuclear and biological warfare, genetic engineering, technology run amok, climate disruption. The apocalypse. Everyone knows it's only a matter of time before we destroy ourselves."

Bill wiped the back of a hand across his forehead. A chill shot through him. He gestured toward the pictures on the walls. "I don't see any other butterflies," he said. "Have you done this one before?"

"I could do this one in the dark." Niall wiped away the excess ink. "No offense. It's harmless, a very benign mojo."

Bill felt the needles cutting along the line of his rib-cage, pressing hard against bone.

"Who's the guy with the flames shooting out his ass?" he asked.

"That's a woman."

"Oh. Looks like a man."

"She's tough. A real tattoo groupie. She loved her ass."

"How about this one in here earlier?"

"Lucy?"

"Yeah."

"What about her?"

"Who did her tattoos? You?"

"Yeah, that's my work. Most of it, anyway."

"You two a couple?"

"I've never known Lucy to be part of a couple. We made some plans once. She was going to come to New York with me. Before her habit for nose candy got so nasty . . . and then she got mixed up with guys like you. What do you do? Wait, let me guess. Middle-management for a multinational corporation. Light industry, maybe? Either that or auto sales."

"Packaging industry. I work for Imminent Ink, Inc." Bill laughed again, but Niall didn't appreciate the humor. If Bill was going to sit here half naked and listen to a lecture about the ancient roots of this monstrosity taking shape on his flesh, the least this guy could do was laugh at a joke.

"There's money to be made stripping," Niall said. "More than there is in this line of work, that's for sure. And there's even more to be made in her off nights, if she decides she wants it. She'll end up cut open in some hotel room. Or face up in her own puke."

"Is she like that?"

"Why? Are you interested?"

"I was just asking."

Niall thumped the gun and frowned. It was nearly finished, a patch of blue, right at his center. The antennae flowed up his sternum and the wings spread downward following the shape of his ribcage. A terrifying sight.

"Damn," Bill said. "Not bad." He tried to keep his voice from shaking. "I like those shadows under the wings."

"Yeah. It raises the image off of the skin."

It would take some getting used to. It would forever change the way he thought about himself. Nothing but the picture of a butterfly, and it had that kind of power.

"I really ought to get out of this business," Niall said. "Most people only want a tattoo when they're down and out, or when they're horny."

"I bet you meet a lot of interesting people."

"Are you familiar with the Biblical concept of the Guf?"

Niall turned his transistor radio off. He slouched on his stool and seemed irritated, as if this piece of information ought to cost extra. "It's a room in heaven," he said, "where the soul energy is kept, and there's only so much to go around."

Bill said he had seen a movie about that one time. With Demi Moore in it, maybe. When the Guf was empty, there would be no more souls to pass out, and the Rapture would begin.

Niall laughed. "No," he said, "it's simply why so many people out there don't fulfill most of the requirements of being fully human. With a world population now in the billions—"

"So that's where all the sociopaths come from."

"Not just the sociopaths but, like, the mindless hordes of people who do nothing except live animalistically—getting up, going to work, feeding themselves, fucking, and going to bed. That's not what being human is about. Human beings are luminous creatures who move in and among time and space, taking care of the planet they live on."

"So what do you do when one of these soulless people comes in asking for a tattoo?"

Niall let the gun drop into his lap. "Oh, I usually accommodate them. Work up a harmless mojo, a butterfly or a unicorn or something. It drains me." He sprayed cleanser on Bill's chest and wiped it off. "I'm finished here." He spread an ointment across the tattoo and covered it with a piece of cellophane. "You need to keep it covered for two or three hours. Two or three days with the cream." Niall handed him his shirt and tie and a page full of instructions. "It needs to stay moist while it heals. And it needs to breathe."

The sun was coming up, and the shop looked dingier in natural light. Bill glanced down at the tattoo beneath the layer of salve and cellophane. It seemed smaller now. Uglier. Plain.

"I know, it looks like raw hamburger," Niall said. "But once it heals, it'll clear up. The lines will get a lot tighter and cleaner."

Bill pulled the T-shirt over his head. He held the dress shirt up, wrinkled, ruined with beer stains. He slipped it on and then clumsily worked his fingers along the row of buttons. He wrapped the tie around the collar and tied a loose Windsor.

"So I should use this ointment every day?" he asked.

"That's right."

"I'm supposed to use this cream," he said. "But then . . . when did you say—"

"It's all in those instructions."

Bill stood up from the chair and tucked in his shirt, feeling the room spin. But he knew better than to sit back down. He had to keep moving. At least for this one day he would have to pretend nothing had changed. Hanging on the peg by the door he found his suit jacket. It smelled like a frat house floor.

"So," he said. "Just keep it moist?"

Niall was busy cleaning his equipment. He had spread everything out neatly on a towel in front of him and was now loading it into the autoclave.

"Yes," he said. "Just keep it moist."

4

Bill did not feel much like a luminous creature. Every step buried the ax deeper into the back of his skull. The early morning traffic had started to clog the streets. Carbon monoxide. If he ever decided to end it all, this intersection would serve that purpose—just stand here and breathe deep. He looked back at the buzzing neon TATTOO in the window and saw a wooden sign above the door with the name WAY OF THE FLESH spelled out in tiny naked Buddhas. This corner offered a clear view of the crown above the NationsBank Tower. Bill lifted his aching head to watch the flag flapping way up there. Down here, no breeze stirred. Only an invisible fog of car exhaust.

He had not attended church regularly since high school. He was open to nearly any notion concerning the origin and nature and purpose of the universe. And, still, at this moment he felt terribly estranged from something, which for lack of a better word he called God. He became gradually and then suddenly aware of the odor of human excrement. With a start, he noticed the man lying in the bushes, not five feet away, clothed in rags, deep in some form of unconsciousness. Bill shuffled toward the other end of the lot and flagged down a yellow taxi.

The cabby was an older guy who didn't talk. He was listening to NPR. Bill gave him directions to the Double Door, and then he closed his eyes and spread himself out on the torn vinyl of the back seat. The driver took turns too fast. Bill needed to lie down someplace. Independence Boulevard was already busy with traffic. The silver dome of the old Coliseum rose above the trees like a giant flying saucer. They made it to the Double Door in no time. Sure enough, there was his Mercedes waiting for him. It was a miracle in this neighborhood that somebody hadn't slit the convertible top to loot his stereo.

He recalled very little of the previous night, and right now he wanted to keep it that way.

Leather bucket seats, anodyne for the trials of modern existence. He pulled out into the traffic and, despite the throbbing in his head and the roaring in his gut and the dizziness that enveloped the whole car, he took pride in his ability to keep it between the lines. When he finally got off the interstate, he breathed easier. One thing about the suburbs—better air. Thick with the smell of newly mown grass. The sun rose above the horizon and sprayed its rays across the manicured lawns and the dogwoods exploding pink and white.

When he pulled into the driveway, a wave of nausea swept over him. The chemical van was parked there, and around the corner of the house he saw the man in a gray uniform with the canister strapped to his shoulders spraying the back lawn. Bill hurried to the front door, trying not to breathe in the chemicals rising from this unnaturally green grass. With a trembling hand, he sifted through his ring of keys. As much as he dreaded facing Maddie, he had to get inside the house and stop breathing this poison. He fitted the key into the deadbolt, turned it, pushed the door. It stopped against the chain lock. He pushed it again then pressed the buzzer, knocked hard on the wood and waited.

She finally came and lifted the chain latch then turned back into the house without speaking, without even making eye contact. In a thigh-length business skirt and a silk blouse, she was dressed for her advanced accounting class, one of three courses she was taking to complete her M.B.A. Her high heels clicked along the hardwood as she hurried back to the bathroom. She clutched a hairbrush in her fist like a club. Bill smelled fresh coffee, bagels toasting. Hunger gnawed at the empty space expanding inside.

From the bathroom doorway, he watched her brushing her cheeks, applying foundation. When she leaned into the mirror, the silk blouse tightened against her back, showing the ridge of her spine, rows of ribs through the thin fabric. She drew on eyebrows, pouted her lips and pushed them against a piece of tissue.

He tried to remember her before this anger. When they had dated, earlier in their marriage, before they'd moved to Eagle's Pointe, her organizing energy had found its proper channels. He had blamed Eagle's Pointe, but maybe it wasn't the neighborhood to blame. Maybe it was simply him. He had done this to her. And weren't the last twenty-four hours ample proof? Crazy jealous because she smiles at a neighbor, he had abandoned her here and gone off on a bender that very nearly ended all benders. He was lucky to be alive. He had always thought of himself as a decent person, but maybe he wasn't decent.

"I guess you're wondering where I've been."

She looked into the mirror at him, and he looked back at her reflection. They held each other's gaze that way, waiting for something to happen. He was trying to find the right words for an apology, but instead of words all that came was this choking self-loathing.

He unbuttoned his shirt and pulled it back to show the tattoo protected by Vaseline and a layer of cellophane. He tried to grin but his grin wilted. She didn't even seem to see the tattoo. She looked back at herself in the mirror and started applying mascara, lifting her lashes upward with quick, angry strokes. Then she slapped the brush down on the counter and abruptly turned around to face him with her arms folded over her chest in what seemed a self-protective gesture.

"I want you to leave," she said. "Today."

"What?" She had threatened as much before. His binges. His chronic inability to pay her attention. And now here it was. "Honey, I'm sorry," he began, tentatively peeling away the edge of cellophane to have a peek at the proud flesh around the edges of the wings.

"I honestly don't know how this happened. I had a long day at work and needed a drink, and then I met this friend—Kent Dempsey. You remember Kent? He was my fraternity brother, the one that bankrupted us. Anyway, we had a couple of drinks, and the next thing I knew I was lying on my back staring out at Adam and Eve." He forced himself to laugh, hoping it would be contagious. His knees shook beneath him as he stepped forward and extended a hand. She recoiled.

"Don't touch me," she hissed.

"What?"

"Why do you keep pretending? If I disgust you so much." Her face twisted into a tortured grimace. "A thick-nippled boy? Is that how you see me?"

He took a step backward and steadied himself against the door jamb. He tried to speak but couldn't form a word. The hammering in his skull intensified. He knew a lawyer who needed a major ass-whipping.

Sobbing hiccups rose in her throat, but she choked them down. He moved toward her, but she slid by, carefully avoiding any physical contact, and hurried out of the bathroom. Her heels clacked down the hallway and then he heard the echo of their bedroom door slamming shut. He stood looking at himself in the mirror, the blue thing under plastic on his chest. He was still standing there when, some minutes later, the bedroom door opened and she brought him a change of clothes and deposited them on a chair in the hallway. She had composed herself, but she would not face him. She stood out in the hall, and he kept staring into the mirror at the tattoo.

"If you have any compassion," she said, "you'll leave here today and not make me see you again. I'll stay away from the house tonight. After work, you can come by and get what you need for a few days. After that, maybe sometime next week, we can decide about further arrangements. In any case, I can't go on living with you."

He turned and met her gaze. "Oh, God. Maddie, come on, baby. Please. Anything I might have said to Anthony was just a lot of drunken hot air. Nothing to take seriously. Sure as hell not intended for you ever to hear."

She turned away and marched back to the bedroom and this time locked the door. He followed down the hall and addressed the thick maple wood.

"Now that I look back," he shouted, "I see how he was leading the witness. Hell, I never would have taken the stand in the first place, if you hadn't invited that scumbag over!"

The sound of TV news—some entertainment show— came blaring through the door. He picked up the fresh clothes off the chair and carried them back to the bathroom. When he found he couldn't look at himself in the mirror, he walked back down the hall again, but all he could hear was the TV. He stepped into the living room and stared out the window, down the street toward Anthony's house at the end of the cul-de-sac.

Outside the window a gray shadow slid into view. The man with the poison canister strapped to his back. He moved slowly across the lawn, sweeping the long metal stem back and forth.

Two nights ago, standing out in the dark, looking in at the two of them sharing coffee and pie, the way their hands had touched, the way they had laughed; Bill had been drunk, but he had seen what he had seen.

He walked down the hall and tapped on their locked bedroom door.

"Hey," he said. "Honey. Please, let me in. Can we talk? Please?" If she insisted on his leaving, then they should suffer this break with no secrets—maybe even some plan for reconciliation. Maybe, if they could only talk, get everything out in the open, if both of them could be totally honest, she would see how unfair she was being, asking him to move out of his own home. If he could touch her. If they could cry together. If she could skip her class and he could call in sick to work and they could spend the day together. He tapped on the door again. The noise from the TV erupted, talking heads at maximum volume, their smart voices breaking with static. He pressed his fingers to the maple wood and felt the angry vibrations.

Back in the bathroom, he let his clothes drop in a puddle. He picked up the shirt and studied the beer stains, the stench. He wrapped one end of the ruined shirt around his fist and used it as a whip to punish the towels hanging neatly from the rack. He whipped the walls, whipped the shower curtain. Plastic buttons rattled against the mirror glass.

He tossed the shirt into the corner and made himself breathe more evenly.

He reached into the cupboard for his razor and shaving cream. He lathered his face and surveyed the shelves lined with Maddie's various beauty products. Skin cleansers, moisturizers, eyeliners, blushes, bases, soaps made from beeswax, from goat's milk, from special Tibetan herbs with natural antioxidants designed to prevent aging. Two whole shelves devoted to hair products, packages with supermodels and their half-smiles. The air here was permeated with dozens of perfumes, constituting Maddie's own special smell. Once upon a time this perfume cocktail had been the smell of her sex that enveloped him, utter intoxicant, balm to all life's sorrows. Now, it was the smell of her kicking his ass out on the street.

He pulled the razor along his face and watched his hand tremble in the mirror. His stomach felt awful, and just looking at the toilet made him want to try to relieve the pressure welling up inside. But he wasn't a puker. He hadn't done that since his college days. He finished shaving and then stepped into the shower. When the water hit him in the face, he remembered from the page of instructions that he wasn't supposed to get the butterfly wet yet. He stepped back and smoothed the cellophane against his chest. Still tender there. Turning sideways, careful to stay away from the spray, he reached for the spigot and redirected the stream lower so that it struck his genitals, which he lathered with soap, rinsed, and then lathered again.

5

As soon as he made it to work, two hours late, Bill checked his voicemail and got a message from his boss, Max, asking him to stop by his office. When Max left a message, he always made sure his voice radiated optimism, even if he had bad news. But this message was full of pauses and apologies.

The thing Bill had claimed not to fear had finally come to pass, and it was much more of a blow than he could have guessed. Max paced back and forth across the plush carpet cursing Imminent Ink's new management. He cursed NationsBank, which had financed the buy-out and was, according to rumors, heavily involved in the company's downsizing. He told Bill that he had always considered him much more than a very talented technical manager. Bill had been his right-hand man, almost like a son. He'd always assumed Bill would follow him in the role of plant manager. And then Max explained that he needed him to clean out his desk before the end of the day.

Bill took the photograph of Maddie and his Rolodex and left the rest. When he got home, the house was empty. He checked the refrigerator door where she usually posted notes. He checked the answering machine, but the one message was from a bill collector, a polite but firm voice warning of possible legal action. The mortgage would at least be paid for three more months, the payments taken directly from his paycheck. Some severance package, three months' pay.

He took off his clothes, put on a fresh T-shirt and crawled into bed. He slept heavily and did not dream, and when he was finally awakened by the phone, he realized that it had been ringing for some time.

"Hello! Hello!" he said, hoping to hear Maddie. Maybe an opening. Even her anger could provide a new start.

"Hey there, Big Time." Kent. And in that unnaturally cheerful voice, Bill heard the fake tan, fake hair, the ropes of gold. Kent said he was calling to see what was going on tonight. Bill looked outside and saw that it was already night.

"I'm sleeping," he said.

"Shit, on a Friday? Son, what are you talking about? I thought I might be able to talk you into going out and seeing a little hoochie coochie."

"Not this time. Sorry."

"It'll do you good. Come on. What do you say?"

"I really can't make it tonight." He said goodbye and lay back in bed, looking up at the dark ceiling. He hoisted himself out of bed and felt drugged. His movements came slow and labored. His head hurt. He got dressed then went to the kitchen and filled a tumbler with ice and bourbon. He drank that down and refilled it then went to the bathroom and peeled off the layer of cellophane covering the butterfly. The skin was still tender, and he probed it with fingertips to make sure it was still moist.

He sat down in the living room and turned on the TV, which he almost never watched. That was Maddie's thing. But since she wasn't here—where was she?—he felt the need to turn it on. The house seemed too quiet without it. Some kind of talk show. Her program. Good enough, these talking heads, the next best thing to her actual presence. The phone rang, and he ran to pick it up, but when he answered, he heard a click and a dial tone.

He breathed deep the scent of potpourri Maddie had placed in crystal bowls. That's when he remembered her request. Command? She would stay away tonight so that he could pack the essentials. She wanted him gone. He sank into the sofa and cried. Deep, wracking sobs. His eyes burned with tears. When was the last time he had cried?

After he'd cried himself out, he stepped out onto the back deck. The night air washed over him, fetid scent of dogwoods already starting to drop their blossoms. He stared across the back lawn at the view of Charlotte's skyline in the distance. This always helped. He felt his breathing settle, leaving a familiar numbness. So long as he kept his eyes on that tower and all that wattage, those cold lights burning across the miles, he could keep his mind from fragmenting. He took long, slow breaths, struggled to center himself. Then he went back inside and started packing a suitcase.

BILL CHECKED INTO AN ECONOMY HOTEL off the interstate, halfway to the city. Not part of a chain. THE HORNETS' NEST was printed in simple block letters against a white glowing rectangle. No logo. So that's how they could get away with it. A free country. There had been hornets long before there were basketball teams named after them.

In the back parking lot stood a row of transfer trailer rigs. Diesel engines purred at idle. The blue light of TVs flickered through the high cab windshields.

On the second floor, he walked down the balcony to his room. The traffic noise from the interstate was louder up here. A big truck rumbled by and he felt the vibration rattle up through his knees. He could see overpass construction lit up like Hollywood. The lock on the door was the old kind that used a key instead of a card. He went inside with the one suitcase and looked around at the cramped space. A dripping faucet echoed from the bathroom. Water damage discolored the ceiling above the bed. Not the kind of place Maddie would ever stay. Neither would he, if it were some-body else's nickel. But he had no idea how long she would ask him to keep away. And he wasn't sure how deep his credit was these days. Pretty thin, maybe, even though they'd recently increased the limit. He pulled off the ratty bed spread to reveal sheets that *looked* clean, then slipped off his loafers and stretched out. The room reeked of stale smoke, so he lit a cigarette to freshen the air. The TV next door was coming through the wall loud and clear, so he turned on his own TV and went to the bathroom mirror and unbuttoned his shirt. He touched the tattoo and it was tender still. Around the tips of the wings he noticed patches of black dots where the blood had clotted and scabbed.

In his suitcase, he found the page of instructions. With warm, soapy water, he washed away the scabbing. He dug around in the wad of clothes in his suitcase until he found the ointment Niall had given him. He worked the cream into the skin in slow circles.

At the McDonald's across the street he bought a late supper, which he ate in the room.

THE NEXT DAY HE SLEPT till nearly noon. He called the house for Maddie but got his own voice on the answering machine again. The rest of the afternoon he slept or watched TV. At five o'clock he bought a Pepsi from the machine down the hall and mixed it with Jim Beam. He called the house again. He left three messages asking her to return his call. She had his mobile phone number, but he gave her the listing for the Hornets' Nest Inn, as well, because his phone battery wasn't holding a charge.

Several times that evening, he checked in with the front desk to make sure no one had called. The next morning, he got a recording of Maddie's voice instead of his own. She sounded more cheerful than he thought she ought to.

On the way to Eagle's Pointe he stopped at a supermarket florist, the only kind open on Sunday, and bought a dozen roses, pink with baby's breath.

The house was dark. Peering through the garage window, he saw the shadow of Maddie's BMW. He knocked, waited.

When he tried to unlock the door, the knob was different, the brass shinier. And, sure enough, his key wouldn't turn. He walked around to the side door of the garage and then around back to the deck and the French doors off the kitchen, but, of course, those locks had also been changed.

He walked down the street and climbed the front steps to Anthony's house. He waited, banged on the door again, and stood there fighting down the anger. Parked in the driveway next door was the chemical van. Bill detected the acrid poison in the air. From inside the house, footsteps drew near. Anthony's wife answered the door. A compact woman, she was dressed in a black suit, like she had just come from work. She explained that Anthony was away on business. Boston. He would be gone until the middle of next week. She seemed reluctant to provide this news and then offered him a formal smile, as if waiting for him to reciprocate by telling her what he knew. But he felt equally stingy with his information, what little of it he was sure about.

On his way out of the neighborhood, he glanced at his house, wishing he could get inside for a drink, and reluctantly conceding that Maddie and the homeowner's association were right: the green shutters did look like puke.

Rush hour. The viscosity of interstate traffic was thickening. With the top down, the buffeting wind deafened him, the exhaust fumes bitter on the tongue. He wove his way through cars, going eighty, eighty-five—as if he were in a hurry to get back to the Hornets' Nest. Up ahead, the exit for Billy Graham Parkway—that was the way home, that other home, out in the country, where his parents probably still waited for him to turn away from his "fast city living" and rejoin the fold. How appropriate that the highway bore the name of a televangelist.

He pulled into the drive-through at McDonald's for a Big Mac combo before driving across the street to the Hornets' Nest.

He stuffed a handful of greasy fries, already cold, into his mouth, then sweetened his Pepsi with a generous splash of Beam and settled down on the bed to watch Oprah and eat his Big Mac. He stared with malice at the grimy phone on the bedside table, wishing he hadn't left his new mobile phone in the car with the top up. Who knew it would fry the battery? He dialed Maddie and hung up when he got the recording. He thought maybe he ought to phone his mother and tell her what was happening, rather than have her call Maddie and hear the news. But he didn't feel like having to try to explain, having his mother ask him for the hundred-thousandth time if he had been going to church. And, worse, what if his father answered the phone?

Another day came and went. He drove to Eagle's Pointe again just to stare at his home's darkened windows, to grip the door knobs and push his old key into the new locks. He imagined her in Boston, honeymooning by the duck pond, walking the Freedom Trail.

Back in his hotel room, every time he picked up the grimy receiver, the beep on her answering machine grew longer.

He watched the pink swelling fade. Each day the lines in the scales of the wings became clearer and tighter, exactly like the artist had predicted.

THE NEXT DAY WHEN HE drove out to Eagle's Pointe, the sky was fading to dusk, and every light bulb in the house blazed. This was it, finally, a chance to see what was left worth salvaging. Maybe down in the dregs of their relationship, gold worth cherishing. It had to start with his own apology. No recriminations. On the seat beside him lay the pink roses, their petals only starting to brown and wither. In his head, he was rehearsing one of several speeches he had planned. He would begin by telling her that he loved her. He would apologize, but not in the old way, the apology that was not really an apology but merely hang-dog hostility. No, he would make her understand that he had decided to change his life, starting with the drinking and his neglect of her. Then he would find a way to tell her about the loss of his job.

He eased the Mercedes into the driveway, cut the engine. When he opened the car door, he heard Maddie's laughter. Such a cheerful sound, like the lilt in her voice on the answering machine. How strange, he'd nearly forgotten the sound of his wife's laughter.

On the back deck, framed by dogwood blossoms and the edge of the house, she bent double, hugging herself around the waist, trying to hold in laughter. She wore a sundress, his favorite, covered in petals white as the dogwoods. The sheer fabric caught the breeze around her ankles. How beautiful Maddie was. When she straightened up, she shuffled her feet to music Bill could now hear, smooth jazz, or what he always used to call "white jazz" just to get a rise out of her, but today he welcomed those saxophone trills as the sound of coming home. She moved her shoulders up and down, swayed her hips to the rhythm.

Bill set a foot out onto the driveway, reached for the roses and felt the prick of their thorns. He stood and watched her dance. He had always loved watching her dance. He never missed the opportunity to join her on a dance floor, just so he could watch and know she danced for him. When he saw Anthony step into view and lay a hand upon Maddie's shoulder, Bill felt the shock start in his throat and ooze its way down. Anthony took her free hand in his and twirled her. How easy they seemed with each other. Then Anthony started clowning around, did a little mincing shuffle step, which sent her into another fit of laughter. Bill pulled his foot back into the car and slammed the door. She turned toward the noise. He cranked and revved the engine and returned their stare, a part of him saddened to watch her smile be replaced by the face so full of darkness he had come to know.

Do not give in to rage. Breathe. He eased the Mercedes out of the driveway. But when he backed into the street, he turned left, aimed the long silver bullet toward the end of the cul-de-sac at Anthony's brick home. He stomped the accelerator. Bracing for the impact, he sped through the gears before jerking the wheel sharp to the left. Rubber squealed. Tires ripped at pavement. He buried the accelerator to the floorboard. The car spiraled through two doughnuts, vertigo overtaking him. Determined to plow through asphalt. Drill down to bedrock. His head banged against the side window. The fender grazed a mailbox. He straightened the wheel and lifted his foot from the gas. When the car jerked to a stop, it miraculously sat in the middle of the cul-de-sac.

By the time he made it to the community gate, he was driving under the speed limit. When he turned onto the main road, he opened his window and tossed the roses in a ditch.

THE MIRROR IN HIS HOTEL room had grown dingier during his week's stay. Backsplash from the sink, soap scum. His fault. He'd left the DO NOT DISTURB sign up the entire week. He never had liked strangers invading his space. He dabbed the cream on the tips of his fingers and rubbed it into the skin. It had been six days now and maybe he didn't need to keep it so moist, but he took comfort in the ritual of rubbing the cream into the blue skin. Under normal circumstances he would have been contacting laser surgeons to discuss the cost of removal. But here in this cheap hotel room, without a wife or a home or a job, the tattoo brought him comfort. His only responsibility, caring for it while it healed. Rubbing in the cream, watching the hair grow back, following with his eyes and with his fingers the now familiar patterns that defined the wings, the whorls of movement, the blue currents flowing upward, the cast shadows to suggest the illusion of flight.

6

That weekend, as Kent led him through the lakeside bachelor pad, Bill found himself wavering between laughter and begrudging admiration. Kent was a man who threw his considerable bulk forward through life, plunging onward, as if he knew that if he stopped too long to deliberate the merits of a piece of furniture, he would end up renting a basement apartment from some eighty-year-old widow, where the walls were already decorated with prints of wagon wheels and tin-roofed barns out to pasture.

Maybe the king-sized waterbed with the red satin sheets was a bit much. Did the lava lamp on his coffee table clash with the Indian headdress, its feathers fanned against the wall? Yes, the half-gallon bottle of Polo cologne did dominate the bathroom. All this phallic aggrandizement no doubt provided a thin covering for trauma better handled in some twelve-step program. But who really knew the best way to rebound from a failed marriage and public defamation? My God, the man had been led away in cuffs from the Mexican border.

Kent finished the tour with a look of mild embarrassment. "I keep thinking maybe I'll rip up this carpet and put down hardwood floor." He didn't seem comfortable until they found themselves in the kitchen and he began the preparations for dinner. Kent filled his foot-long pepper mill with fresh peppercorns. That's when he told Bill that he had invited two women to drop by and join them for dinner.

"Whoa! No, no." Bill fumbled for the car keys in his pocket. "I am not ready to meet other women, even if Maddie is having an affair."

"There's nothing wrong with meeting people," Kent said, stirring the pasta sauce that bubbled on the range, tasting a spoonful and grinding in extra pepper.

"Who are they?"

"Just some girls I know. We ran into them last weekend. You don't remember?"

"Where?"

"Alice was kind of sweet on you."

"Where did we meet them?"

"Well, never mind. Leave, if you want to. But you'll miss out on the rib-eye, and my special rub." He shrugged. "So, you said you finally managed to talk to Maddie?"

"Last night." Bill poured another glass of wine and swallowed half. "She threatened me with a restraining order. Lots of legal language I didn't understand." He stepped to the sliding glass doors that overlooked the marina and Lake Norman sprawling out blue into the distance.

"I still can't believe you told your personal problems to a lawyer," Kent shouted from the kitchen. "You must have been desperate for company."

"Yeah, I guess so."

"Actually, I know a lawyer you might want to talk to. The guy who represented me when I got divorced—"

"I'm not ready to do that."

"You better be ready—to talk to somebody. I'm sure she is."

"For free."

"What's the difference between a lawyer," Kent said, "and a species of blood-sucking eel that lives in the slime at the bottom of that lake out there?"

"I give up."

"No difference."

Bill cracked open the patio door to hear the yelp of gulls and the ping of halyards against aluminum masts. Maddie had moved into the guest bedroom maybe two months ago, complaining that he snored when he drank, telling him as clearly as she knew how that if he wanted to save their marriage, he would find a way to get sober and pay her more attention. On one of the last nights they had shared a bed, she lay propped against her pillow watching a show about a couple who in forty-eight hours transformed their home and their lives. "Don't you think it's sad," he'd said, "how all it takes is a camera to make these people believe their own performances?" She reached for the remote and switched the power off. "At least they have that," she'd said, turning away from him in the dark.

"You need to relax, brother." Kent placed his big hands upon Bill's shoulders and started kneading the tense muscles. "Stay up here for the weekend. By the pool. Son, the women come out in droves. Independent women who own their own homes. Divorcées who sold out in small towns and moved up here where nobody asks any questions."

Bill glanced over the balcony rail at the brown bodies lounging around the pool. Beyond, a dock stretched into the channel, the masts of sailboats rising toward the sky.

"I'm serious," Kent said. "You should spend the weekend. Stay the whole week."

"And lose my room at the Hornets' Nest?"

"Hell, you're welcome to move in with me, if you want." Kent let his eyes drop to the floor. He wrapped his ringed fingers around his wine glass, swirled it, and took a long swallow. "Until you get your feet under you. We're old friends. It's the least I can do."

The lake breeze freshened, and Bill breathed deep the air that seeped through the crack he had opened.

"You know what you ought to do?" Kent laid a hand heavy with gold upon Bill's shoulder and waited for Bill to guess his big secret. He raked at his fake blonde mane for dramatic effect. "You ought to come work with me."

"Selling meat?"

"Sure."

Bill glanced at the Indian chief's headdress mounted on the wall. "I'm not ready to get out of inks just yet. I still have friends in the industry."

Kent pushed the sliding glass door all the way open to let in the breeze. "Don't you ever think about working for yourself?"

"Yeah, but—"

"I didn't say work *for* me. Work *with* me. I'll make you a full partner."

"That's very generous—" Bill tried to imagine himself riding around in that pickup with Kent every day, peddling meat out of a deep freezer strapped to the bed, driving through the country looking for the trailer parks. Born and raised country poor himself, Kent knew exactly how to talk to those people. Bill could imagine him walking up to their doors carrying a pre-wrapped rib-eye in one hand and a swordfish steak in the other, loudly proclaiming that the Steak Man had arrived.

"You would be surprised how much money there is in steaks." Kent waddled back over to the range and stirred the bubbling pasta sauce. "And *you* decide about taxes."

Bill had let a week slip by without making any effort to find a new job, not even calling one of the several head-hunters he knew. The challenge would be to find a position with a comparable salary. He had too many debts to take a cut. But didn't he deserve a break? Hadn't he earned it?

"You'll never know true freedom," Kent went on, "until you give up working for The Man."

They stepped out onto the patio and Bill felt the sun warm his face. It lit up Kent's Hawaiian shirt, the ropes of gold around his neck.

"I been thinking about throwing a party." Kent hesitated. Suddenly, the Steak Man lost his sales pitch. "Well, I been thinking. I mean, I got plenty of room here."

"What's that?"

"Maybe get some of the alumni together. You reckon any of the brothers would show?"

"Hmm. You never know." Bill didn't want to encourage him. He didn't want to have to spell out the permanence of Kent's exile from the brotherhood. He shaded his eyes and followed the coastline out of the harbor and around to the next point.

"When I drove out here this evening," Bill said, "I took the long way around by Crook's Landing, or what used to be Crook's Landing. They've changed the names of the streets."

"I bought in less than a year ago," Kent said, "and already my property value has shot up twenty percent."

During their childhood, a campground had sprawled across the tip of the next peninsula. Bill reminded Kent of the many overnighters they had spent there with the Boy Scouts. Now it was completely developed. Condos. Million-dollar homes surrounding a golf course. After waiting until Charlotte had grown wealthy enough to declare itself a world-class city, the electric company that owned most of the shoreline cashed in. They gave the boot to the hillbillies who had squatted by the man-made lake in rented travel-trailers and mobile homes. In less than a decade, those summer campgrounds disappeared to make way for the bankers and pilots and doctors and race car drivers—and for the Steak Man with his new head of hair and his own piece of paradise.

The doorbell rang, and Kent chugged his wine. "We just act normal," he said, "like it's a normal date."

"Come again?"

As the women walked in the door, Bill hurried to the kitchen to refill his wine glass. He clawed in his pocket for his Marlboro Lights. The blonde walked straight up to him. In a red shiny dress wrapped as tightly as cellophane around a candied apple, she slid next to him, letting her hip and thigh rest against his. Mechanically, he laid an arm across her shoulders, against her tanned skin moist with lotion.

"You don't remember me, do you?" she said, grinning. "You were pretty trashed." She said her name was Alice and that she was looking forward to knowing him better.

He drew deep pulls on the cigarette. She languidly reached for it and took a long draw then passed it back. She laid her head against his shoulder and he pressed his face into her bleached hair and breathed in the oil of her scalp.

In the doorway, Kent was deep into negotiations with the other date. That woman, the one covered in tattoos. Lucy? The one from the other morning. The sight of her made the skin on his chest prickle. Kent slipped a wad of cash into her palm and closed her fingers over it.

"I said we can't stay past nine," she complained.

"I tell you what," Kent mumbled, "don't *plan* to leave. Just take it easy and have a good time."

"We both gotta dance later. We're going to be late as it is." Lucy put his money in her purse and walked into the kitchen with her friend. Lucy wasn't as dressed up as Alice was. In jogging shorts and a backless halter top, she looked like she had come from a workout. The tattoos shined bright against her pale skin. She was showing a lot of skin, and Bill had a hard time looking away.

"Ladies, we have a fine meal planned for this evening." Kent turned the corkscrew into a new bottle. "That Beaujolais is a good light wine, if you like something fruity. But this here Merlot is exquisite." Listening to Kent's voice practically caused Bill physical pain. When Kent started describing the combination of herbs in the seafood linguini, Bill prepared to excuse himself. But Kent never gave him an opening. He went into great detail about the ingredients of the rub on the rib-eye, and Alice pressed herself more firmly against Bill's side.

It was Lucy who finally interrupted, asking for the bathroom so that she could go "powder her nose."

"Honey," Alice said, "you *better* wait on me."

Kent watched them disappear around the corner. He leaned back on his heels, swirling the wine in his glass and sniffing nervously at it.

"Look," Bill said, "I appreciate the trouble you've gone to. But I can't be here."

"No, no, no."

"I really need to go."

Kent refilled Bill's glass and then his own. "See what I mean?" he said. "Most women have never had a man who knows how to cook for them. They can't handle it."

The pride in Kent's voice softened Bill's resolve. Kent raised his glass in a toast.

"It's really great to see you again, buddy."

Bill raised his own glass, and the easy smile came back to Kent's face. Bill said, "To a man who knows how to treat his women."

"To me and you, buddy." Kent let his glass ring against Bill's.

"So," Bill said, "I guess Alice is my *date?*"

"Yeah. God, she's gorgeous, ain't she? I saw how she warmed right up to you. You like her?"

"Well, sure. But like I said, I'm not able to do this sort of thing."

"What you got better to do? Hang out in the hotel and watch TV?"

"I mean, I guess I'll stay for dinner, and like I said, I appreciate—"

Kent shushed him, and the two women came back into the room, laughing.

Alice stepped close to Bill at the sink and laid her head against his shoulder again. She reached a hand to the back of his head and pulled him in for a long, wet kiss. Her mouth on his, her eager tongue. She turned her back to him, resting her shoulder blades against his chest and pressing her ass into him, until, against his will, he felt himself stiffen. God, how long had it been since a woman had wanted him? He wrapped his arms around her waist and glanced down at her face. He saw there a familiar blankness. It was the look he must have had himself those times when he had tried to stop drinking and found himself parked in front of the ABC store with nothing on his mind. But when he gazed over Kent's shoulder at Lucy and caught her staring back, recognition passed between them—a night they had shared, which Bill could not remember.

"I told Alice about your tattoo," Lucy said.

"Show me." Alice worked her fingers along the buttons of his shirt. He felt her fingernails brushing against the newly healed flesh. This was the first time anybody had seen it since he had removed the cellophane. A fuzz of hair had already started to cover the blue wings. Alice pulled open his shirt and laid her palm against the tattoo, spreading her fingers through the new hair.

Lucy walked over and gently pushed Alice aside. "I usually have myself a laugh when I see one of Niall's butterflies." She leaned in close to study the detail. "But this looks good on you." She gazed up into his face, and he saw deep wells of intelligence in her eyes.

Kent stood by the stove stirring the sauce a little too vigorously. "Bill," he said, "why don't you go on downstairs and start the grill. I'll get the meat ready."

BILL GRABBED A PAIR OF BINOCULARS he found by the door. As he descended the stairs, he saw the front end of his Mercedes. He was still sober enough to drive. He brought to mind the image of Maddie in her sundress, laughing, smiling into the face of that scumbag lawyer. Had they been using the guest bedroom, where she had slept of late? Or the master bedroom?

He picked up the bag of charcoal Kent had left beside the grill and started placing the briquettes. Above him on the stairs, footsteps. Long legs covered in ink.

"So," she said, "you see me in your dreams at night?"

At a loss for clever repartee, he stared dumbly up at her.

"You still don't remember anything about our night together?" she said.

He shook his head.

"I knew you were drunk, but damn." She took the binoculars from him and pointed them across the channel.

"Maybe you could help me remember," he said, his tone more suggestive than he had intended.

"We talked till three in the morning," she said. "until we ended up at Niall's shop. I told you about my sorry childhood. Well . . . part of it."

"I wish I could remember," he said. "I'm sorry." Maybe that's all they had done, talk. Surely, if there were more, he would remember.

A gust of wind hit them in the face. The dust devil, full of grit from the parking lot, spiraled past them, whipping her dark hair. She shielded her eyes, and he wiped at his own. When she turned to see him studying her, he smiled. If booze had erased the memory of their night together, some sweet tinge of that intimacy remained.

Bill took out his pack of Marlboro Lights, and she bummed one. They stood in the shade of the condo, on the slab of concrete, and looked across the lawn to the channel dredged for boat slips. She pointed the binoculars at a rust-colored sloop motoring toward the open water and a gray-haired woman standing on the bow attaching a foresail to its stay.

"That lucky fucker, Kent," she said. "What I'd give for a place up here. I've got to get out of the city."

While her eyes were focused elsewhere, he couldn't help but look at her translucent skin and the ink buried there, shining in the fading light of the sun. He glanced down at the blue wings on his own chest, where Alice had unbuttoned him. A quick glance was all it took to tell that his butterfly and her ink work were performed by the same hand. Leaves from the burning tree on her back, caught in a breeze, followed the curve of her shoulders over her breasts and beneath the fabric of her halter. She set down the binoculars and smiled.

"I bet you thought that butterfly was your idea, didn't you?" She turned around to climb the stairs then looked back and said, "You better light the grill."

7

Their meal was everything Kent had promised. Kent dimmed the lights and lit candles and kept the wine flowing while they listened to New Age piano music on the stereo. He produced the foot-long mill and ground pepper onto their salads. He managed to serve four plates of pasta and later four steaks, while each steamed hot from the grill. Lucy left most of the slab of beef on her plate. She said she didn't like to be too full when she danced.

After dinner they moved to the living room and Kent sat next to Lucy on the sofa. He eased back into the cushions and patted his big belly, made bigger still by that garish shirt and its print of bright red poppies. Bill and Alice settled into plush chairs placed in opposite corners of the room. Alice sat staring vacantly at the Indian headdress on the wall above the couch.

"Is it real?" she said.

"It's as real as you want it to be." Kent spread his arms out so that they lay along the back of the couch. He let his ringed fingers rest on Lucy's shoulder and nervously ran the other hand through his fake blonde hair. After an uncomfortable silence, Kent did what Bill had been dreading: he suggested that Bill and Alice go check out the view from the docks.

"Actually," Bill said, "I'm sorry, but I need to leave." He nodded at Alice, at Lucy. "It's been great."

On his way down the stairs, Bill realized he was too drunk to drive. Maybe in an hour, after he got some air. The wine was heavy in his gut, mixing with that red meat. He stopped by the grill, still hot with charcoal, and picked up the binoculars he had forgotten there. The harbor lights reflected off still water. The storm clouds had blown away leaving the night clear and oppressively calm. He lifted the binoculars toward the sky, hoping to see beyond the glare of security lights.

"Hey there!"

He turned and watched her clomp down the stairs.

"I thought you said you were leaving."

"Yeah, I'm working on it."

"I had to get out of there, too. I don't know what Kent was expecting. Well, he can kiss my ass. He's not getting his money back." She puffed a cigarette, and the smoke floated on the still air in front of them. "You probably think we just empty our heads and disappear from the room."

"Look, I'm sorry I don't remember anything about that night."

"You remember how we stopped by my apartment? Which is something I never do—take men back to my place."

"I guess I ought to feel special."

"Hell yeah."

"Was there anything in particular I *ought* to remember?"

"You mean did we have sex? No, we did not. I did let you show me a game."

"What?"

"*The close game* you called it."

"Really?"

"That's what you said."

It was something Maddie had taught him, back when they were first dating. He stepped closer to Lucy and she didn't move. He came another step nearer, waiting for her to step away. He brought his face toward the nape of her neck, her shoulders covered only by spaghetti straps. Her perfume, sweet beneath the haze of cigarette smoke.

The second time he and Maddie had met, at the home of a mutual friend, she had led him onto a cement patio not unlike this one. Before she ever let him kiss her, Maddie made him see how close he could come without touching. She taught him to linger there and focus his senses, just as he did now to this other woman, straining to hear the rhythm of her breathing, watching Lucy's chest rise and her breasts flatten against her halter top, making his own breath come and go with hers.

"You helped me organize my CD collection," Lucy said, still facing away from him and letting him look at whatever he pleased. "We sat on the floor like two teenage girls. You made me laugh, which is saying something." She put the binoculars to her eyes and pointed them up at the dark sky.

Despite the glow of the security lamp, there were a few bright stars. In the dim light, Bill studied the Fall of Man, the story unfolding across her shoulder blades, down her back: every orange leaf bursting into flame, every green leaf a seeing eye, the serpent, his wicked grin descending the tree, dividing Adam and Eve, the pair meeting only at their fingertips, sharing the fruit. These first parents were covered in tattoos, his blue body suit, and hers . . . hmmm . . . her back, which she turned toward the man, bearing the same tree, the same couple, in miniature. Eve's hair fell across the tree, long and glossy black like Lucy's.

She moved the binoculars away from her face and looked back at him.

He placed his hands on her shoulders and pulled her in, but she prodded him with an elbow.

"You got to follow your rules, remember?"

"Sorry." He took his hands away.

"You like what you see?"

"I never thought I cared for religious art, but you've changed my mind."

"You like that, do you?"

"Makes me hungry."

"Is that right?"

"I'm craving fruit." The points of Lucy's shoulders were so close. Her breasts, right there. He wanted to bring his lips down to touch. To taste.

She said she was looking for a little fuzzy galaxy, and Bill knew the one. Ever since she was a girl, she said, she always liked to see that galaxy and know there might be life so far away.

"The Pleiades," he said. "Not a galaxy. Star cluster."

"Yeah? Where did you learn that? College?"

"Boy Scouts."

"You were a Boy Scout!"

"Cub Scout, too. That's where I met Kent."

"Figures."

He told her how he and Kent had grown up camping together—and having older Scouts throw firecrackers onto their sleeping bags, dump water under their tent. The older boys were always bad to pick on Kent, maybe because he was a butterball.

"I'd forgotten," Bill said, "how I owe Kent for my first anatomy lessons. He taught me what a vagina is."

"Did you two play doctor?"

"Well. No."

"He didn't show you your vagina? He should have done that."

"I thought girls had what I had. Until Kent brought over a *Playboy* magazine and then *The Joy of Sex*. I was in the fourth grade. Can you believe it?"

"I've heard stranger things."

She looked back up at the sky. "Niall says there's aliens out there watching us. Controlling us. But I don't believe that. Do you?"

"With magnets. Battery operated. Very large and powerful, battery-operated magnets."

"You don't like Niall, do you? You might want to think twice then about getting another tattoo."

Bill laughed. "I'm a one-tattoo guy. Kind of like I'm a one-woman man."

She shot him a glance, that signified what? He really, really wanted to touch her. That line, why had he said that, if he didn't mean it? She didn't seem to believe he meant it. He absolutely did mean it. Which begged the obvious question. Maybe he was only using her to help flush Maddie out of his head—all that pain, anger, fucking betrayal, all that failure. Maybe Lucy could use him in some similar fashion. No need to belabor the question, it would just ruin something good. Maybe something very good. Standing this close to her, he could swallow air again without fear of choking. He breathed in her healing balm.

He put his hands around her waist, and she stepped away. She turned to face him, then looked down at her watch.

"I need to leave," she said.

"Aww, really? Don't go." He reached for her hand, and she let him hold it. He brought her fingers to his lips. Tobacco. And salt.

BACK IN THE CONDO, KENT and Alice sat at opposite ends of the sofa watching breaking news about the scandal at the White House. The special prosecutor had unearthed new evidence about the President's affair with the White House intern. They showed a photo of the young woman and the President together at some official ceremony.

Alice slumped down on her side of the sofa, feeding herself peanuts. Kent leaned forward toward the TV.

They showed the film clip of the President denying the affair, the same one they had been showing for weeks: "I did *not* have sexual relations with that woman." He pouted, his face stern, his bottom lip stuck out like a little boy who knows he's been caught.

"He shouldn't have lied," Bill said. "He should have told them to mind their own business."

"What makes you so sure he's lying?" Kent said.

"Oh, come on," Lucy said. "Don't be so damn gullible. Look at that face."

Maybe because he had voted for him, or because they shared the same name, it was a hard segment to keep seeing over and over again, and to know that if they could take down this big man, what might happen to Bill? What secrets was *he* hiding, even from himself? Tonight, with these women here, how would he feel if Maddie knew about this?

"Serves him right," said Lucy. "And I was starting to trust the man."

Alice wanted to watch the rest of the news, but Lucy was anxious to leave. She said they were already late for work. They both kissed Kent on the cheek and thanked him for the meal. Alice rotated her hips and made Bill promise to come watch her dance. Kent was busy with the stereo remote control, his stubby finger repeatedly jabbing a button that didn't work. The women got their things, Lucy found her leftover steak in the fridge, and Bill walked them to the door. He shared with Lucy what he hoped was a meaningful glance and then watched her and Alice tramp down the stairs and step out onto the parking lot. Lucy's car, a white Corvette, looked brand new. For some reason, he had expected her to drive a beater. He saw her ease down into the driver's seat and pull that long leg inside.

The sound of her muffler disappeared over the hill and he closed the door and shuffled across the carpet back to the living room.

Kent was slumped down in the sofa, balancing a glass of wine on his belly. Bill eased himself into a chair across the room and began putting together an apology over the TV news. Empty wine bottles littered the coffee table.

"I order a case of this stuff every year," Kent said.

Bill spun a bottle in his hands and read the label. He wanted to ask Kent about Mexico, that foreign place, where Kent had not even spoken the language—the burning sands, flea-ridden motels.

"You dog." Kent gave him a grin of the defeated. "I should have known you would end up with my date."

Bill watched Kent toss back the wine. He set his own glass on the coffee table. He wanted to stay awake tonight. Maybe in an hour or two he would be sober enough to drive them both to Charlotte and watch Lucy dance.

"Listen to me." Kent pointed a finger accusingly. "If you make love to her, she's going to teach you humility. I'll make you that promise."

"I'm not making love to her."

Kent laughed and belched and then breathed unevenly. He rose from the sofa and beckoned for Bill to follow him over to the balcony. He reached for the binoculars still strung around Bill's neck. They stepped out into the night and Kent leaned over the railing, pointing the binoculars out toward the lights at the tip of the far peninsula.

"Some time or other," he said, "you and me ought to go see if we can find that old campsite."

The lights on the far point defined a familiar coastline. With a little imagination, Bill could almost see the beach where they had pitched a tent. He could see two Boy Scouts lying in the dark, admitting for the first time their secret crushes and constructing together their bright futures of marital bliss. Everything either boy had known of intimacy with girls had been imagined together while staring up at tent canvas and the shadows thrown by pine trees in moonlight. By now, Bill realized, they each should have found a mature and lasting love, and he wondered what shared inadequacy or inertia had held them back. When he and Maddie had married, they had made plans and fulfilled those plans with surprising efficiency. His career had taken off in ways he had never expected, partly because she had convinced him that he deserved to succeed. So what had changed? His drinking had escalated, but the booze was a symptom. He had blamed Eagle's Pointe for some deeper discontent. And then when his marriage hit a shoal, he had jumped overboard instead of bailing water. Well, maybe it wasn't too late.

Kent stepped inside and came back with a fifth of Knob Creek. He pushed a snifter into Bill's hand.

"I need to slow down," Bill said, setting the glass on the coffee table.

"You snaked me," Kent said, pushing the glass back into his hand. "The least you can do is help me drown my sorrows."

"You never did say—how did it go with Alice?" First Bill sipped at the shot and then downed it and held the glass out for Kent to pour another.

"We watched TV." Kent held up three fingers in the Boy Scout's sign of honor. "You know me, I've got to *feel* love for a woman before I can make love to her. I can't ever pretend."

8

The next day, Bill drove back to Eagle's Pointe. Maddie's threat of a restraining order—she couldn't really mean that. He needed to see her, and she wouldn't take his calls. If he had to, he would camp out in the backyard. If he had to, he would find a way to break into his own home.

The lights were on, and when he rang the bell, she answered the door. Clearly, she wasn't happy to see him, but she did let him in and even put on a pot of coffee.

"I've been meaning to call," she said and settled herself into a chair at their dining room table.

"You have?" he said hopefully, glancing out the French doors to the bird feeder on the back deck. A squirrel sat perched there, digging with its claws and tugging out clumps of seed.

"There's so much business we need to go through, but in the short term, I want you to be able to claim your things."

"I was hoping we might have a chance to talk about us."

"Us? Bill, come on now. There hasn't been an *us* for a very long time. So why are you suddenly pretending there is. Is it simply to hurt me?" She pushed back her chair, putting distance between them, as if she were afraid of him.

"Hurt you?" He had never touched her in violence. He would never do such a thing.

"I can't believe you would blame this on me," she said. "I have waited and waited so long for you to show that you care anything at all about me, about us, and now when I finally believe I am worth being loved, you want to take it away."

He had rehearsed this moment, preparing himself to radiate calm, kindness, understanding. But the smell of the coffee changed his mind. She left the room and returned with two cups, hers with a dash of milk, his black. Her teaspoon chimed against the edge of her cup, and he sipped his, thinking how different this shared cup of coffee was from the coffee she always served Anthony. Bill felt his own gloomy silence in painful contrast to the other man's boisterous laughter. She clearly did not want him here, that much was plain. He stared out the French doors at the deck where he had seen the two of them dance. He thought of the spare bedroom upstairs, where they had, no doubt, continued their dance.

"What's going on? I at least deserve to know. How long have you been involved with him?"

"I am not going to have this conversation."

"Oh, you're not? How fucking prudent. What else has your legal counsel coached you not to say? What else has he done for you, pro bono?"

"He has helped me box up your clothes, your record collection. Anything else you want to take, I'll make arrangements for you to come get."

So Bill hired a U-Haul and rented a storage unit on the edge of the city. He cried again, behind the Hornets' Nest, by the tiny, rust-stained pool. He cried so hard that two little boys in wet swimming trunks with frogs printed on them stared at him in alarm. And then he went back to his room and started thinking about the rest of his life.

The worst part of being unemployed was finding ways to fill the hours of a day. He could not force himself to eat another Big Mac. The cheese had started to taste like plastic. He imagined he could taste growth hormones in the meat. He had arranged a meeting with Max at Imminent Ink. A closed-door deal. The old man was supposed to have a lead on a new position for Bill with another company. Maybe even a promotion. *Maddie, dear, I'm in a better place now. A new start.*

Why was he still doing that? What a knee-jerk suck-up, even in his head. Always had been. *Stop it.*

When he finally rose from bed, he made himself leave the TV alone. A hot shower. Once he put on a white shirt and tie, he felt like this was something he could actually do. After he got out of the Hornets' Nest and on the road, it was just another day driving to work.

His parking space near the front entrance was empty, so he nosed in. Right next to Max's long white Chrysler—a company car that had come to symbolize for Bill the enormous waste of American consumerism and litigation. Imminent's automotive coatings division had sold Chrysler a batch of white paint that failed the automaker's accelerated aging test—*after* Chrysler had painted two hundred sedans. Crush a hundred sedans. Enter legal team. Settle out of court. Merry Christmas, middle management. It was a mark of dubious distinction to drive one of those white Chryslers with the paint peeling around the back bumper. And still, how Bill had envied Max that distinction. No monthly payments. Between Bill's Mercedes and Maddie's Beemer—on top of all that other debt—they were drowning. Even if their marriage had crapped out, they were united in debt.

In through the glass double doors up front. Past Sarah at the front desk, busy on the telephone but smiling a sympathetic hello. Down the hall past Shipping and Receiving, without bumping into anyone. Left toward the labs and walking the gauntlet. Through Quality Control, past the rotogravure lab, where white coats stood over benches mixing together new ink formulas. Less than two weeks ago they had all worked for him. Like dominoes, they looked up from their work, smiled, offered some awkward greeting.

He took the long way toward Max's office, through the factory and its web of piping. The main production area was ringed by a high mezzanine, mixing tanks suspended toward the factory floor like giant silver udders, reeking of toluene and acetates and any number of other organic solvents. While most managers and office personnel and even lab techs avoided the heat and grime of the factory—its foul air, its taint of pigment on every surface—Bill had always felt at home out here. At some deep level, he liked these people better. He waved to the uniformed workers up on the mezzanine. He smiled at Dory as she glided by on a forklift. Her gold tooth sparkled as she returned his smile.

At the back end of the factory he walked into the maw of the dispersion room, into that oceanic growl, pigment crushing mills vibrating your ankles, rattling your knees—where he had first made his mark, back when he would get his hands dirty with grease and ink, doing work his father could respect. But that work was a long time gone. He had been a paper pusher for years. And now, he was an unemployed paper pusher.

He stepped up to an ink vat and rested his elbows against the steel rim, took his place there between Jerome and a new hire. The backs of their blue uniforms darkened with sweat. The three of them watched the red stream, bright as blood, trickling from a hose and pouring into the bottom of the vat.

"What y'all got planned for the weekend?" he asked, recognizing the hillbilly twang that came into his voice whenever he stepped into this factory heat. The voice he was born with. He'd rather they think him a hayseed than a yuppie. And, yet, whenever he opened his mouth out here, he sounded unavoidably white. Why was it that the only black people in his life were people he worked with? And why did most of them work in the factory, rather than in the lab? These were questions he had conveniently avoided asking.

"You coming back to join us?" Lamar rested his elbows on the steel rim between Bill and Jerome.

"We been missing you out there, boss," said Jerome. "Don't have nobody to keep O'Kelly off our backs."

"O'Kelly," Bill said. "What has that asshole done?" He didn't work here anymore; he could say what he thought.

"Sheee-it," Jerome said and shook his head. The better part of valor.

They both watched the production manager stalking through the other end of the factory, clipboard in hand, clip-on tie hanging askew, permanent scowl on his face. A hot-headed cracker, O'Kelly's browbeating management style bothered Max less than Bill had always thought it should. Like overseers before him, O'Kelly descended from a lower class of folk.

O'Kelly marched their direction, and the men dispersed, even Bill. Lamar, an ink sample in hand, joined Bill, and they tramped back toward Quality Control.

Together with Max, Lamar had taken it upon himself a decade ago to groom Bill for management, teaching him the lessons a man like Max would never know or care to learn about factory work and factory people. Lamar was a very handsome older man, even with the pink scars covering one side of his face and neck and the unnaturally thin and spotty afro. Twenty years ago Lamar had single-handedly saved the plant from burning to the ground. He was still a walking reminder of the ever-present dangers of fire, a lot more effective than the ubiquitous safety posters covering the factory walls. His uniform and the red bandana he always wore around his neck hid the worst of the damage, but everybody knew the scars were there. Bill followed the older man past the fire door, which, like Lamar's bandana, was the color of flames. Reinforced metal, big as the side of a house, the fire door rested on wheels, in case there was a need to close it in a hurry and protect the warehouse, the labs and offices.

"Rough night?" Lamar said, sniffing.

"What?"

"I smell a party."

"How the hell can you smell booze on my breath above all these solvent vapors?" Bill said, suddenly nervous.

"I could smell you ten feet away."

"That's my new aftershave."

"Damn! That shit smells just exactly like Jim Beam." Lamar straightened the bandana around his neck and sauntered off toward the lab.

MAX WAS ON THE PHONE, but he gestured for Bill to come in and take a seat. Before he stepped in on the maroon carpet, Bill, out of habit, lifted his feet and checked the soles for spots of ink. The old man swiveled in his chair to show Bill a profile. He always enjoyed an audience. His silver hair shined against the perpetual tan from weekends on the golf course. His sleeves were rolled up to his elbows like he was ready to get down to the day's business of talking his ass off. After Bill had waited ten minutes, Max finally settled the receiver in its cradle, only to offer Bill a glib and empty greeting, and then answer another call.

Bill let his eyes play across the golf trophies and plaques on the walls. Max still needed him, that much was obvious. Who else was going to run interference with production? Who else was going to spend time out there in the factory every day and ask about wives and children and second jobs and actually be interested? There was nothing—not toluene nor acetate nor even ammonia—that could stink up a factory like insincerity. Worse even than unconscious condescension. Bill straightened his tie, pushed up on the double Windsor. Not only the familiar workplace, the familiar people—like Lamar always said, "Come on now, talk straight"—Bill missed his position in this pecking order, the buzz of paternalism.

Out the windows to the right the flat magnolia leaves rattled in the breeze. The magnolias stood in a line across the front of the plant, like a fortress, blocking the view of the factory from the highway, the white blossoms perfuming the air with a heavy syrup. Bill picked up the trade magazine from Max's desk and flipped through its pages, feigning interest. After fidgeting for twenty minutes, waiting for Max to get off the phone, he began to suspect the old man was intentionally putting him off.

This chair had a deep ass groove that felt all too familiar. He slumped down in the chair, let the leather soles of his loafers slide out across the plush carpet. He could just stretch out here and take a long nap. Instead, he pushed up on the armrests, felt a little lightheaded as he got to his feet.

THE ASPHALT BURNED through the thin soles of his loafers. It was going to be another scorcher. Early May and they were predicting almost ninety; maybe Niall was right about the planet warming. Bill put on his shades, put the top down on his Mercedes and drove to I-77. Nothing to do the livelong day, so he rode that main artery north past the Hornets' Nest and took the exit into the heart of the city, past the city college where young women wandered the sidewalks with their book satchels and their retro short skirts and knee-high vinyl boots that had come back into fashion. His mobile battery was still dead, so he pulled into a convenience store to use the telephone, and when he got Maddie's answering machine, he didn't bother leaving a message. The telephone booth commanded a clear view of the NationsBank skyscraper towering above the trees on the other side of the road. He stood there holding the receiver in its cradle, looking up at that tower and the crown on top.

After a short drive to the parking garage and a two-block stroll, he found himself at the base of the tower. In contrast to the airiness of nearby glass-and-steel skyscrapers, the NationsBank building looked solid, built of stone, and not just veneer. Sixty stories—he stood and counted. He stood on the sidewalk and read the bronze plaque giving the building's vital statistics. Every day of the year, the building consumed nearly three hundred thousand kilowatt-hours of electricity.

The people rushed by him on the sidewalk oblivious to the monolith rising above them. For a better view, he backed through pedestrian traffic to the edge of the sidewalk, his back against the roar, standing within the flowing river of exhaust. Sixty stories up there, the red, white, and blue flapped in the breeze. He leaned against the stinking breeze of speeding, honking cars and looked up, willing himself to forget his problems. For the moment, at least, he forgot his vendetta against NationsBank, how they had bought the mortgage to his house and down-sized him out of a job, how they were on their way to owning the lion's share of the state. All around him, bankers swarmed to get a bite to eat during their lunch hour, and he felt that he belonged here among them. Bathed in the warmth of the swarm, himself just an anonymous cipher. There was something comforting in that. "Man swarm," wasn't that what the writer called it? Wolfe? At Carolina, Professor Felps had made them read it, *You Can't Go Home Again*, still the longest book Bill had ever finished.

He spent the lunch hour in a coffee shop, reading the newspaper, getting wired on fancy coffee, admiring the beauty and efficiency of businesswomen in their suits. His eyes lingered a little too desperately on one tall woman in line. She wore her hair short like Maddie. A little wider in the hips, but so long as she didn't turn around, Bill could make certain mental adjustments that allowed him to believe he was looking at his wife. Simply to feel himself this proximate to Maddie gave him a lift he hadn't been able to extract from his latte. She had said they were through, and no doubt she was right about that, but he still longed for her. Almost before he had time to duck behind his magazine, Bill saw an old friend step inside the coffee shop and stand in the back of the line, smacking his trousers with a rolled up paper, probably the money section. Before his career in investment banking, Blake had served as Bill's pledge educator in Gamma Omicron. Gray pinstripes. Not a blonde hair out of place. Bill and Blake belonged to the same country club, and whenever their paths crossed on the course, Blake suggested a double date. Bill was in no mood today to explain his current employment status, let alone his marital status, whatever that might be. As soon as Blake stepped up to the counter to order, Bill slipped out onto the sidewalk and into the heat.

He tossed his latte into a trash can. What if he took a ride out to Eagle's Pointe, tried one more time to make amends? But she wouldn't be home; she had classes the rest of the afternoon. And if he did care for her, he had to respect her wishes, which were clearly not to see any particle of him.

He walked on down Trade past the parking garage. Three blocks he walked, then made a left, crossed over into a cluster of nightclubs, including one façade of dark glass and black doors with the loops of neon tubing over top that jolted him with recognition. That neon sign, even without an electric current, let him know he had been here, and recently. THE JACKPOT, it said, and he knew tonight the gray tubes would blaze to life: purple nudes swarming a pot of gold, red cherries dangling over top. He hurried along the street, let the hill take him down into further degrees of seediness, past overflowing dumpsters, a syringe in the gutter, until he came finally to Arlington Avenue. And then it wasn't far until he saw more familiar neon.

Niall was busy with a customer, and for a second Bill thrilled at the possibility that it might be Lucy. But this woman was younger, a blank canvas, as it turned out. It was her first tattoo, and she was equal parts nervous and excited. Long, unruly brown hair, olive skin. Her jean shorts were pulled down to her knees, and Niall had just placed the stencil of a unicorn on her left cheek. Bill didn't have anywhere else to be, so he stayed to watch. The walls were dingier than he remembered. Natural light, choked with dust motes, illuminated posters as faded as the blue ink covering Niall's forearms. Taped to the ceiling, even the Sistine Chapel was still covered by centuries of grime.

Eventually the young woman pulled up her jeans, paid, and left Bill alone with Niall. Bill found himself reclining in his T-shirt, smelling disinfectant soap where the artist had shaved and now sponged the inside of his right forearm. Niall ran a bar of Speed-Stick deodorant across the spot, applied the stencil, and then the gun buzzed and once again the needles pierced Bill's flesh.

Niall brooded in the foulest of moods. He said he didn't have to justify anything. His customers were the ones who came asking for the butterflies and unicorns and sunflowers so that they could look cool at the club. How did you explain magic to the soulless, anyway?

"I could be a real whore if I wanted to be," he said. "Most of the people I know in this business are nothing *but* whores. They have no notion of responsibility."

Niall wasn't unattractive—if you could get past the tattoos, the crew cut, all the metal in his ears and tongue (and probably in other, less conspicuous places, too). But it was hard for Bill to imagine him ever achieving whore status. If anything, he simply wasn't tall enough.

"I guess giving a tattoo must be pretty erotic," Bill said, relaxing into the needle's cutting, thinking of Lucy and feeling a twinge of jealousy. Niall had penetrated flesh on almost every part of her body.

"It's the closest thing to sex you can do with your clothes still on."

"Uh huh." Without knowing why, he had to go through this one more time, this time sober. Not that he exactly believed Niall's line of bullshit, but there was no denying how that butterfly on his chest had kept him grounded through some rough days.

"The level of trust involved between tattoo artist and client," Niall said, "you usually only find in a marriage. And, unfortunately, most artists I know routinely violate that trust. I know magicians who are even worse. And since I do both, I'm under an immense burden of responsibility."

What a load of crap. Bill could sit and listen to him talk for hours. "Bad magicians? They make human sacrifices or something?"

"So to speak. Manipulating other people for sex, jobs, just plain kicks. Every magician goes through that stage, because the world doesn't prepare you for the kind of power you grow into. But once you open your eyes to the phenomena happening around you and realize that you are not simply in the middle of it but that you are, in fact, the cause of it, you either have to accept responsibility for your magic or just become one evil bastard."

Ever since he was a boy, Bill had wanted to believe in magic, the possibility of another world lying immediately beneath the visible. But even then he had known it all to be make-believe. And somehow, between fraternity parties, he had managed to learn enough physics and chemistry in college to understand that the colors you saw in the world had nothing to do with magic—they had everything to do with molecular structure and wavelengths of light. Still, as he gazed down at the tattoo gun etching the tender flesh on the whiter side of his forearm, the swollen pink berm rising around the half-finished carrot, it was easy to believe that anything was possible.

"Explain this to me," Bill said.

"What? Casting a mojo?"

"Yeah, you know, the magic."

Niall set the gun down and took a drink of his water. "You are not your body," he said. "It just happens to be the car you're driving right now. You could chop off huge chunks of it, both your legs, both your arms, as long as the basic generator is still there, you will keep that structure coherent. Your personal electromagnetic field doesn't have to be confined to the body. You can extend small pieces of it, large chunks, the whole thing. That's the basis of all magical traditions, the idea of projecting parts of the self. Chunks of electromagnetic energy. I've seen magicians move large objects across the room without moving a muscle."

"You've seen this?" Bill tried not to smile.

"It happens all the time. But those sorts of things tend to make you stick out like a sore thumb. You end up with no friends, no business contacts. Nobody wants to deal with a freak like that. People fear that kind of power." Niall sprayed the needles with alcohol. He had finished with the orange, and now he started working in the black outline, the detail right down to the veins that corrugated the sides of the long root.

"The average person can't tell the difference between his own electromagnetic field and someone else's." Niall leaned in close to Bill's forearm. "There are people out there," Niall said, "people being manipulated right and left who have no idea that the thought that just popped into their head is not their own."

"Whoa there." Bill forced a laugh. Suddenly he was acutely aware of the needles piercing his flesh. "You make us all sound like a bunch of computers being programmed. Manipulated? By who?"

"You call them gods. Let's just say that we're living on a very important piece of real estate. Certain parties have been interested in this little planet for a long time now, and they're getting ready to cash in. There are things floating around out there that do not have your best interests in mind." He raised his eyebrows knowingly.

"So what does this have to do with tattoos?" Jeez, what the hell had possessed him to let this freak engrave his flesh again? Sitting here listening to some crackpot with a shaved head and earlobes full of silver, with a dumbbell sticking through the middle of his fucking tongue.

"In our world," Niall said, "language has nearly lost its ability to signify. It's just noise. Art is just commodity. And, sadly, so many of these kids use tattoos to commodify *themselves*. Marks, shapes, sounds on a physical plane act as resonators, act as magnets, distribution points, batteries for electromagnetic energy."

Bill looked down at the bleeding carrot and thought of the NationsBank Tower, its sixty stories and the glowing crown on top.

"Thousands of years ago in early mystical cultures," Niall said, "they all believed the same things: there are certain marks you don't make unless you are ready to move mountains. And with tattooing you're breaking the skin. I can use magic to help or hinder people to whatever extent I want. The skin is a protective barrier in every way. When you start cutting into the skin, you can do ten times the magic work in half the time."

Bill looked again at the spreading blood. "So what if the tattooist is just some grease ball named Pork Chop—"

"—who specializes in rebel flags and Harley Davidson emblems—"

"—it still has an effect?"

"Of course. Even if the artist isn't actively engaging in a ritual at the time, it still can act on a metaphysical plane and alter someone's reality for good or bad."

"But with less predictability?"

"Usually the result is utter chaos. I'm very careful in my work, and even I have accidentally ruined lives. And sometimes not accidentally." He launched into a history lesson about ancient traditions of tattooing, and Bill lost track. "They didn't start bleeding from the hands," Niall said. "Unless you're just reading King James. If you read the Greek and Hebrew, they merely tattooed themselves. *Stigmata* is a political mistranslation of tattoo. The early followers of Christ would tattoo themselves with significant imagery because they were being hunted down like dogs. Back then, no one would have dreamed of tattooing a religious image on himself that he didn't believe in."

Adam and Eve standing beneath the tree. Damn, there she was, right there all along, tacked to the wall, the glossy color photo of her back. Mixed in with a Milky Way of Polaroids. In her photo, proud flesh, pink and sore, ringed the fresh tattoo, the green and orange leaves, eyes and flames. That tree, its branches flared like a peacock's spreading fan, bursting into flame. He leaned forward to study the photo. Just seeing her skin, even this simulacrum of her skin, and on public display, eased the hurt that gnawed away inside, replaced it with something sweet.

Niall had fallen silent, his lecture ended. And Bill was supposed to feel what? Guilty that he was a nonbeliever? Niall put the finishing touches on the carrot. He sprayed cleaner on Bill's skin and used a paper towel to wipe away blood and ink. Then he spread a film of ointment across the image and covered it with cellophane. Well, if belief was beyond him, Bill *could* pay attention. The bleeding tattoo. That was his blood. Spreading in a thin film. Capillary action. He felt the pump in his chest, its reliable beat, felt the breath rushing in, easing out.

"What made you pick this one?" Niall said. "We should have talked earlier. I'm sorry. I was preoccupied."

"Well, I don't know. I just liked the way it looked."

"This mojo suggests multiple implications even on a logical level. The carrot is both phallus and a source of better vision." He smirked. "It's a good choice for you. Maybe it will help you wake up, open your eyes, and pay attention to the person you're fucking."

"That sounds like powerful magic. And to think I almost picked the rutabaga."

"I did a tattoo for someone very close to me several months ago. A shaman's mask, placed on her lower thigh. A combination of Navajo and Japanese traditions. Two faces, one inverted beneath the other, a mirror image of sorts. The problem—which I should have foreseen—was that the world saw the smiling face, while she always saw the scowl."

"Lucy." Bill grinned.

Niall showed his surprise, before he turned away and began sorting his equipment.

"And you think," Bill said, "that it changed her somehow?"

"One-hundred-eighty-degree change in personality." Niall switched off the power supply and slumped down into a chair across from Bill, staring at him suspiciously. "That one tattoo dropped her into a nightmare of substance abuse. Obsession with money. It made my life pure hell. Yeah, I would say it had an effect."

"Don't you think you're being too hard on yourself?"

"Well, it wasn't just the mojo. Of course. She could have used it for better or for worse. It was the combination of the design, the placement, and her personality that was wrong. I should have been more careful. I misjudged. I thought she was stronger." He began straightening his equipment again, placing his inks very neatly in rows on the shelf.

"What about Adam and Eve?" Bill said, nodding toward the photo of Lucy's back tacked to the wall. For some reason, it was important to him that this tattoo be an original. "Did you copy that from a painting?"

Niall lifted his eyebrows. "I do not *copy* paintings. Inspired by dozens of Renaissance figures, sure, okay—and not *just* Adam and Eve—but you won't find that image in any museum."

"Was it her idea? Or yours?" They stared together at the photo.

"I like to believe it was a collaboration."

Bill studied Adam's blue body suit and then scrutinized the blue scrollwork running down Niall's arms, up his neck. Similar, but not the same. That was a relief. Good to know Adam bore no great resemblance to his maker. No metal studs in those ancient ears. And Adam was large, heavy with muscle. Earthy.

"Whose fault do you think it was?" Bill asked.

"Come again?"

"The Fall, I mean. They say Eve got a bad rap."

"Well, according to Milton—my reading of Milton, anyway—their disobedience was necessary." Niall stepped over to the photo and removed the thumbtacks. He gently smoothed the wrinkled borders flush against the wall and replaced the tacks. "You take two strong people," he said. "It's like two strong magnets rubbing together. They generate a big ol' electric charge. Take one strong and one weak, and it's not even worth the trouble." He stepped away from the photo and walked over to lift the lid off his autoclave.

"Magnets?" Bill said. "Battery-powered magnets?" He tried to joke but could not help examining his love life with Maddie. Was there something weak in him, something broken, that had failed to make her feel sexy?

"As a species," Niall said, "we have forgotten how to have sex properly a long time ago."

Bill began buttoning his cuff, hoping the tattoo wouldn't bleed and ruin the shirt.

"And without that knowledge, we are extremely vulnerable as we approach the millennium, confronting beings of a far superior intelligence, who are pursuing an information coup that will essentially degrade the human species to a state of bestiality."

Bill thought again of that mighty tower and the flow of suits along Trade and Tryon, of that strip joint just blocks away and the neon sign, which, within a few hours, would blaze with light.

"By eliminating the centerpiece of human resistance— sexual communication—these intergalactic beings have virtually already succeeded in their quest for total occupation."

"You're saying that I'm having sex *wrong?*"

"What most people consider sex," Niall said, "is little better than two dogs hooked together in the middle of the street. Men are not designed to fuck for five or ten minutes, spill their load, and then fall asleep. It's just not the way it is. The human male body is designed to have orgasm after orgasm without ejaculating, for hours and hours, upwards of six hours at a time, until you start to rub yourself raw."

"Good God! How often?"

"Every single day. Ejaculation is for having babies, nothing more. After coming fifteen or twenty times without ejaculating, you reach a point where your consciousness expands beyond yourself. You literally *become* your partner. It's the most reliable way to learn to project yourself. It's *the* way for a couple to bond together. On top of that, it's one of the most efficient ways to build up energy reserves—energy that can be used for business, art, or magic. Have you ever felt an orgasm come through to your fingertips?" Niall asked. "It's *really* good."

Bill felt confused. How much sex was enough? How much was too much? And how did a person do it for six hours without thinking about what they might like to eat for supper?

"So let me get this straight." He stood, waiting until the artist looked up from cleaning his equipment. "I am not my body. But I've got to learn to use my body. To be free. I've been focusing on this thing." He pulled up his shirt to stare at the butterfly on his chest. "I've been failing so long, feeling caged in. My life's totally fucking falling apart, if you want to know the truth, and I know you don't, but this butterfly thing here, it's been trying to tell me something, if I will listen. And what I think it's saying is that I am not doomed." He stared across the room at Lucy's skin, and at Adam and Eve, wearing body suits of ink. "I can act. I am, in fact, free."

"No, no, no, no." Niall smirked and shook his head. "It's not like that. It would be easier, wouldn't it? Freedom of the body? Freedom is an abstract human concept." He picked up his pack of American Spirits and walked toward the door. "It takes practice. And discipline." His words came now like a chant. Bill focused on the voice that was lost in the glare of the sun. The artist stood in the doorway sucking on his cigarette, his features shadowed, turning his head to blow the smoke outside into the white heat of late afternoon. Standing in the bright rectangle, a silhouette speaking. Sunlight burned around the dark outline of his short, wiry figure, the fuzz on top of his head, the rows of hoops tugging at the earlobes. "It takes discipline," the voice said. "Self-control. The willingness to lose yourself. Most people are so distracted by their own materialism that they don't have time for sex, at least not the kind of spiritual sex I'm talking about. That shit will turn your world upside down. If you do it enough and you don't close your eyes to the phenomena that start to happen in your life, then the next thing you know, you *will* be a magician—whether you want to be or not."

9

Hell of an upgrade from The Hornets' Nest. Like the billboards said, The Ambassador Suites Hotel was a place where two adults could disappear from the world for a long weekend without leaving the city. Eight floors towered into the sky on the edge of town, a miniature of that monolith holding downtown pinned to the earth. The guest book said it was built after the Roman model. A hexagon. The rooms opened onto inner balconies that were stacked in eight concentric rings overlooking the courtyard below. Way, way down there, the Romans were at brunch, surrounded by a fiberglass replica of ancient ruins, ivy-covered columns. Greenery everywhere. Planters overflowing with ferns, begonias. Sunlight filtered down from the eggshell at the top of the tower. Pretty impressive, really.

Leaning over the rail of the top-floor balcony, Bill and Lucy could see down to the ruins, where the people sat at glass tables with their buttered croissants and their mimosas. Sunday morning casual. High above them, he and Lucy wore matching plaid pajamas. She stepped back into their suite for another bag of chips and her cigarettes. Why did it bother him that she smoked the same brand as Niall? Niall said American Spirits were healthy, because they lacked the chemicals found in corporate-produced tobacco. Had she bought into that load of crap?

"We should go downstairs for brunch," he said. The chips from the mini-bar were four dollars a bag and brunch downstairs was complimentary. Then he laughed at his own stinginess, trying to save a dollar when this weekend was costing him hundreds. He watched her light a cigarette. They had a smoking room, and housekeeping had already warned her about smoking out here on the mezzanine. A weird place to hang out, but she liked it, said she felt cramped up staying too long inside the room.

"I don't feel like getting dressed up," she said.

"Me neither." He pulled her close, brushed back her hair and buried his face there, spreading his lips and tasting the salt on her skin.

"What do you reckon we would have to do to get thrown out of here?" She leaned over the balcony and spat through the air, trying to reach the fountain down below.

"You want to be thrown out?" He thought of the stares the night before when they had checked in, him with a patch of cellophane plastered to the side of his neck covering his new blue rose, her in a tank top and a miniskirt that showed off a body covered in ink.

Out here on the balcony in pajamas Bill was again aware of the stares. Older couples. The muted outrage of the women. Their husbands' feigned indifference. What was so outrageous? Pajamas in public? His special gift to both of them for this special weekend. Lucy did look young in the pajamas. He hadn't thought to ask her age. Maybe he should have done that. Maybe now he would rather not know.

"How old are you?"

"Twenty-seven. I'm how old my mama was when she had me. You ain't got any children, do you?"

"No."

"Don't you ever worry?"

"Why?"

"That you might not be able to."

He laughed nervously. "I've never really tried."

"I worry about it sometimes." She pushed the stub of her cigarette into the soil of the planter hanging from the balcony rail then opened the bag of potato chips and started eating chips one after another. "Not that I'm planning on having children. But still . . ."

"We could try to make a baby." He slid a hand up the back of her pajama top and felt her skin, still warm from the bed. Neither of them had washed, and her body smelled of sex.

She playfully elbowed him, below the belt. "I hate it when men talk nonsense."

"I mean it." He grinned down at her, glad that she had demanded he use a condom, but nevertheless intoxicated with the possibility of her womb swelling with their child. "It's been so long since I've felt this way," he said.

"What, fatherly?"

"Yes."

"You didn't want to have kids with your wife? What was wrong with her?"

"Maddie was great. Is great. And, yes, we did talk about it. Had talked about it. Talked. But we were going to . . . wait. We both . . . well, she . . . I mean *she* . . . I'd rather not talk about her. Actually." Since the moment he had slid his Visa across the marble countertop in the hotel lobby, Bill had managed to forget about Maddie and her lawyer. But now he was visited by remorse. So what if she was in another relationship? Did that alone give him license to move on? And was that what he was doing? He had seen them dancing. What more had he wanted to see? To catch them in the act? Is that what he had wanted?

He let his hand slide down Lucy's back over the soft fabric of her pajama bottoms. He turned her in his arms so that her back rested against his chest and both of them could enjoy the view from the balcony. He hugged her into him and looked out across the hotel's Eden of trees and ornamental ferns and patches of pink and red blossoms. He slid a hand beneath her pajama top and let it rest on her belly, soft and smooth. He gently touched her navel ring, pulled her tight and felt the strong urge to love her that he would not suppress. He would not let his love be cheapened by the recollection that at its basis was an economic exchange. He would put out of his mind any memory of the fluttering bills she had collected beneath her garter, strutting across that stage while she undressed herself to Eddie Van Halen's guitar riffs. Money, he believed, had helped ruin his marriage, and it would no doubt ruin this love, too. But not yet.

He and Maddie had argued over money from the start. Their problems ran deeper than differing attitudes toward saving and spending. He would be the first to admit he'd been a tight-wad, until Maddie had broken him. But, in the habit of *being* as a form of economic exchange, the idea that you ought to get exactly as much as you give, balance the spiritual ledger, he'd been as guilty as Maddie. More so. He hadn't been ready enough to lose it all. But he felt ready now. Why not?

He pulled Lucy tight and felt his erection pressing into her. "You make me feel holy."

"I ain't never heard it put that way before." She smirked.

"I feel like I could tell you anything."

"Why? Because I'm a freak?"

"No, no, you're not a freak. *I'm* the freak. Remember. It's my turn."

She laughed and fed him a potato chip. He spat it onto the carpet and went for her fingers.

She laughed again and crumpled up the empty bag and tossed it at his face. He kept chomping at her fingers, at her hair, her nose. He would gobble her up.

"What you said." Her face went blank. "You know, I feel like I could tell *you* things."

"I could tell *you* things."

"I'm serious. You seem like you would be a good listener."

"Yes. That's me. My mother taught me manners. I'm a very good listener." He brought his face down to hers, and she stepped back.

"Do you want to hear something?" She shook a cigarette out of her pack and stood there with it between her lips. "About when I was a kid?"

"Yes, tell me about your girlhood." He moved in close again, brought his mouth down to hers. "Feed me the words," he whispered, and she removed the unlit cigarette and opened her mouth to let him inside. After a moment's reluctance, she stroked his tongue with her tongue. So soft. To be let inside her like this. Here by the railing, in public. Flannel soft, and soft under the flannel. He backed her against the railing and pressed himself into her. Even as the housekeeper in her uniform pushed the cart of towels past them, he kept kissing her. When the woman had gone, he stepped back to look at Lucy. Still holding her hands. The gurgling of the fountain. The calypso music, floating up eight floors from the courtyard, steel drums, the quality of light filtering down from on high, the smell of this woman—all elements magically balanced.

"I'm sorry," he said. "You were going to tell me a story."

"What?"

"From your childhood."

"It's nothing."

"No, you had something to tell me. I want to hear it."

She lit the cigarette she was still holding. "Maybe another time." Somebody official-looking from the hotel, maybe a manager, was rounding the mezzanine in their direction, and Lucy palmed her smoke. "Come on," she said. "I'm tired of being on display."

They walked back into the room and she locked the door behind them. They sat close together on the side of the bed and, after she had finished her cigarette, she let him kiss her again. He couldn't get enough of her mouth. He wanted to swallow her, but she pulled away. She smoothed the black hair away from her face and leaned in to try again. She met his tongue with hers in the space between them so that her tongue flickered nervously against the tip of his.

He hugged her close and pulled her down onto the mattress. He brought his hand up underneath her pajama top and felt her heart racing. She broke free and stood from the bed, went to her purse by the TV.

"I'll be right back."

"Where are you going?"

"I'll be just a minute." She stepped into the bathroom. He heard the light switch click, the fan whir.

"Don't do that. Why do you have to do that?"

"Fix yourself a drink," she called.

He stared at the half full bottle of Beam there beside the coffee maker. He looked away. Trying to cut back, he was determined to wait until happy hour before he started.

When she came back from the bathroom, wiping her nose on a tissue, she brought her stage show with her. She began loosening the buttons down the front of her pajama top, taking her time. But that glassy look in her eyes—she was gone, not even in the same room. His heart sank a little. Before, when she had wanted to talk, what was it she'd been about to tell him?

She stepped over to the window and pulled the sheer curtains together, softening the light.

"Do you want me?" She stepped close, and he reached for her skin, pressed his face into her soft belly.

"How bad do you want me?" she said.

"I want to eat you up."

She pushed him hard, so that he fell back onto the mattress. She slid her feet along the plush carpet, finding the groove that was playing inside her head. He sat up and watched her dance, watched her close her eyes and sway her head from side to side, watched her belly rise and fall with her breathing. She opened her eyes and saw him staring. She turned her back toward him and kept dancing, easing the plaid pajamas off of her shoulders, letting the top slide down her arms, revealing the burning branches of the tattoo that covered her back, the Tree of Knowledge, on fire but unconsumed. Its limbs spread across her shoulders, followed the edge of her scapulae. She dropped the pajama top to the floor, and he saw the couple standing beneath the tree, Eve handing the apple to her mate. Lucy kept swaying her hips, lifting her arms above her head. When Bill noticed what appeared to be Adam's erection, he felt the swelling of his own. A trick of perspective, the tree's root system connected to the man. Niall was damn good, good with technique as well as ideas, composition. But Bill did not want to be thinking another man's thoughts. Not now. Adam's root—did Lucy even know? She glanced back at Bill to see him watching her.

"Come here." He reached out and grabbed the elastic band of her pajama bottoms. She batted at his hand and grinned, kept dancing. She wrapped an arm around her breasts and turned to face him, still swaying her hips.

"I want you," he said.

"I haven't finished my dance."

"It's my turn to dance for you." He stood to hold her, and she let him pull her to the bed. They undressed each other, and he started kissing her arms, her shoulders. He brought his tongue down her spine, following the trunk of that tree, all the way down. He crawled beneath her and moved his face down between her thighs, kissing until she moistened and then began moving her hips in a rhythm that quickened with the rhythm of his tongue. He breathed in hungrily, letting his body relax beneath her, letting her weight rest upon him, watching her face far above, her lips pursed together in a mixture of pleasure and struggle approaching anger, hearing the breath going violently in and out of her, and her grinding into him, harder and faster until she pressed firmly against his face and then rested, rolled off of him, and lay on her back with her eyes closed, while he put his lips to the film of perspiration covering the tentacles wrapped around her navel, moving his mouth upward to her breast and the swollen nipple and then up to her cheek, flushed with color, and hungrily kissing her mouth and her forehead.

She waited while he fumbled with the condom.

"Okay. Okay. Okay." She repeated the word quietly to herself, as he eased inside.

"Lucy? Are you all right?"

But she didn't seem to hear him. Her eyes were closed, and trance-like she kept repeating the word. "Okay. Okay."

"We can wait. If you're sore."

"Just do it!" She grabbed a fistful of hair at the back of his head and pulled him deeper into her.

Her back arched and her lungs filled and her mouth opened wide as if she would cry out.

He stroked her cheek. He moved the hair away so he could see her better. A pink blush like a rash spread across her cheeks and her neck and chest. Her eyes were open, and he looked into them, succumbing to an adoration that was complete and consuming, leaving no residue of himself that wished to be separate.

"Are you gonna take all day?" She rolled over onto her stomach and reached back to guide him.

He could see the side of her face still, her mouth still open wide, and he watched her feel every thrust. When he felt himself ready to finish, he collapsed onto her back, resting, not wanting to finish so early, wanting to stay with her, and slowly he picked up her rhythm and then felt the waves paralyze him, so that he had to stop and rest, rest and feel her movement, without finishing, without having to withdraw. She coaxed him to finish, but he shushed her and cooed sweet things into her ear.

Time passed. They were both covered in sweat. His attention moved back and forth between her face—God, how he adored this woman—and the face of Eve, the piece of fruit she handed to her mate, both of them staring at it, a puzzle.

The limbs of her tree shook, burst into flame, opened their hundred eyes. It happened exactly the way Niall had said it would: wave upon wave spreading through his body, until he was not aware of himself as separate, until he could think of nothing but staying inside her, spending the afternoon keeping this same rhythm.

"I'm sorry," she said, pulling away, rolling onto her side. "I'm too sore. Sorry."

"*I'm* sorry," he said.

"Maybe we can try again later."

"It's okay. More than okay."

She turned her back to him, and he let his body spoon next to hers, feeling the film of sweat and the heat trapped between them, thinking how she was just the right size. They were of a piece. Her knees curved where his curved. He felt the arches of her feet resting on top of his. He buried his nose in the nape of her neck. She turned to kiss him. Then she reached gingerly toward his neck and ran a finger across the film of ointment covering the blue rose. She sat up abruptly and leaned close to study the tattoo.

"It's healing," she said. "But you need to go wash it again. I see some spots of dried blood. You don't want it to scab."

"I can't believe I let you talk me into this."

"You were the one who picked it out."

"I know." He trembled. "I mean I can't believe I let you talk me into putting it on my neck." He reached up and felt the sore skin, then he laced his fingers into hers.

"It's badass," she said. "Something to remember me by."

"I'll be wearing shirts with collars from now on."

"Honey." She gave him a quick peck on the lips. "It's going to show above your collar."

10

Three days passed quickly. They would wake late and make love and then lie in bed snacking, watching TV, until Bill would get up and pull the curtains open to look outside at the sun already high in the sky and the blue water in the swimming pool down below. From the eighth floor, the pool furniture and sun umbrellas were toy miniatures.

Their suite was spacious and comfortable with a bedroom separate from the main living area. There was a kitchenette, which he had stocked with half a dozen liquors, beer, cold cuts, fancy cheeses, fresh fruit, ice cream in the freezer, and she ignored it all and kept munching on those greasy snacks from the mini-bar.

They spent the afternoons by the pool. By evening he would already be drunk when she drove them to The Jackpot in his Mercedes. Kent would be waiting for him with a table. Neither Bill nor Kent held back when they tipped their favorite dancers. They blew through money. He was already bored with the striptease, but tipping was the only way to start a conversation. The other dancers knew how gone he was on Lucy. "Sweet Bill," they called him. When Lucy found her way over to their table, Bill made Kent put up his wallet. It was one thing to see her dance on stage, strutting along that runway, but he couldn't watch her out here in the crowd, squatting in some greaseball's lap. Later in the night she would sit at their table wearing her gown, until somebody came over with a twenty-dollar bill. He told himself it was her job. He told himself that she could shake her flesh all night long—she would still be going home with him.

On Sunday when they woke at noon, he talked her into staying with him through the middle of the week. She wouldn't have to dance again until Wednesday, so he would have her to himself. They spent the early afternoon by the pool, her sitting in the shade of an umbrella, while he stretched out beside her in the sun.

"It's a good thing you got mostly blue ink." She spread sunscreen across the tattoos, first the butterfly on his chest. He winced when she came to the blue rose on his neck. The tenderness had gone, but the idea of it was still so new.

"Blue ain't nearly as bad to wash out as other colors," she said. "If I laid out in the sun the way you like to, my colors would turn dirty by the end of the summer." She dropped the tube in his lap. "Lube up your carrot," she joked. "Orange is bad to fade." She sauntered back over to her chair under the umbrella. "And you shouldn't spend so much time in that chlorine water."

He looked over at her skin shining in contrast to the turquoise bikini. She reclined in the shade with the magazine propped in her lap and the sunglasses and headphones blocking out the rest of the world. He stretched out a hand to rest on her leg, and she dropped a hand on top of his without looking up from her magazine. It was enough to have her beside him, to remember the love they had made for days on end. His favorite thing was to have her in the pool with him, to lift her knees around his waist and make out in the shallow end when no one was watching.

They had developed a language to talk about money. Gifts. Loans. She needed help with her rent. She had a credit card bill to cover by the end of the day. Her Vette needed transmission work, and the mechanic was demanding cash in advance. On Wednesday, after their sixth night together, after he had run up one of his cards to its limit, he found himself squatting in the shallow end of the swimming pool alone, trying to account for all his debts. A breeze had freshened and now rushed through the tops of trees across from the parking lot. He could not bear the thought of parting from this woman, and she would bankrupt him if he wasn't careful.

Feathery clouds in the upper atmosphere stretched across the sky, the early signs of the severe thunderstorms predicted for the evening. Already the sun was a fuzzy copper spot that cast weak shadows on the white cement. He stepped out of the pool and walked dripping wet over to her chaise lounge, where he let the water pour off of him onto her skin.

"Stop it," she said, irritated at his playfulness.

He took one of her hands and tried to lead her toward the pool, but she pulled free.

"I'm ready for our afternoon nap." He grinned. "A little quality time."

"I'm sore today." She lifted her shades and dropped the magazine beside her chair. "I'm sorry," she said. "I can do something else for you." She stretched out her hand and mechanically stroked his leg.

He leaned down and kissed her on the forehead then sat beside her chair watching the cement darken with water. "We don't have to do anything," he said. "You know? I'm happy just to lie beside you. We could actually take a nap."

"You say that now." She flopped over on her belly, threw a towel over her head.

On her back, Adam and Eve stared at the apple, puzzling over its meaning. Adam leaned toward her, rigid with longing. But Eve's body twisted toward the edge of Paradise, where—only now did Bill notice—the thick and unruly undergrowth clogged her path.

"I was wondering." He wasn't sure how to bring this up. What happened when you fell in love? How did the two of you negotiate a change in your relationship? "I was wondering what things are going to be like between us. After our honeymoon."

"So that's what this is?"

"I think maybe we could have something."

"What are you talking about, exactly?"

"You've been good for me. You've helped heal something broken. And I think I could be good for you." He didn't know the right words for what he was thinking, how for a long time now he had been toying with the idea of getting sober, and maybe she had, too, how the two of them might be able to help each other do that. Instead, he said, "I don't mind giving you things. But I need to know you feel something. I haven't heard you say anything." He waited for her to answer, at least remove the towel from her face. He waited. "I think I'm in love with you," he said. He lifted the towel so that he could at least see her reaction.

"You think so?" She rolled over on her back, stared blankly up at him.

"What's changed?"

"You honestly expect me to fall in love? You want me to pretend we're some kind of newlyweds out here? And then when you get tired of me, you go back to your wife? *Please.* I like you, Bill. We had a good time together. If it wasn't me, it would have been some other whore."

"Okay. We'll give it time. I know you've had some bad experiences. We'll just give it time. I'll show you. Okay?"

She looked away. But the coldness had disappeared from her face. She was upset. He had gotten through to her.

The night before at dinner he had pestered her to tell him the story of her childhood, and she had finally opened up. He had reached across the linen tablecloth to take her hand in his while she kept her eyes fixed on the centerpiece of flowers and let the words spill out. She said she'd never really known her father, which hadn't bothered her so much. All she had ever wanted was her mother's love, and probably she was still waiting. Then there was her mother's boyfriend. Ex-boyfriend. At this point her confession hit a brick wall.

Her breathing grew ragged. Tears welled in her eyes. And despite how Bill stroked her hand, tried to make her feel safe to talk, she was done. Instead, she reached in her purse for a photo, a Polaroid taken when she'd turned fifteen. "The summer of the mohawk," she said. The way her black bangs hung down in her face and the ragged locks spiked on top her head, the way dark stubble covered her scalp, it looked like she had done it to herself. She straddled the banana seat of a bicycle with chopper handlebars. And the look on her face was the same look she got on her face now whenever she got a head full of snow and strutted out onto stage. Gone. But somewhere inside, under siege, defiant, waiting to be found. Bill hadn't been sure he was in love until she'd showed him that photograph.

He squatted in the puddle of water he'd made by her chair. "What do you want to do tonight?" he said. "We could do whatever. See a movie?" He took her hand in his and rubbed it.

"My Vette's still broke down. I don't know when my friend will have it fixed for me. So I'll need your car again. I need to run an errand. And I need some money."

"How much? I'll tell you the truth, I'm starting to run low. I'm going to have to cut back. Three hundred through the first of next week? Will that be enough? And, look . . . oh God . . . I'm sorry if you've done anything with me you didn't want to do. I don't want you to feel that way. I mean it. I don't expect anything." He stroked her hand and watched her face for some sign. "I only want you to stay with me."

"Thanks." She squeezed his hand.

"So where do you need to go? I can drive you."

"You don't want to go where I'm going," she said. "I'll be back in time for supper."

A jet roared overhead, shaking his world to pieces. "Who is he?"

She frowned. "What do you think I am? Lord! I wouldn't fuck somebody else on our honeymoon. I just need to run an errand."

He sat by the pool and watched her walk across the parking lot toward the hotel lobby. Her ass twitched side to side, covered by the tiny bikini, as she moved gracefully away from him. It was possibly a huge mistake to let her take his car, and he wondered whether his insurance would cover her in the case of an accident. Upstairs she would find his wallet and the keys. She might not return. He didn't know where she had come from or possibly even her real name. He knew her only as Lucy from The Jackpot, this helpmeet on whom he was utterly gone. She could leave with his Mercedes and the rest of his cash and the credit cards, and there was nothing he would do to try to stop her. The cloud cover was thickening, and the sun cast its pale light upon his damp body. The wind chilled.

He waited nearly two hours by the pool for her to return. After dark clouds blanketed the sky and he had finished the bourbon in his flask, he reluctantly rode the elevator and entered their suite alone. He made himself a fancy drink, a whiskey sour with a slice of orange and maraschino cherries. Then he walked into the bedroom and told himself he could not put off any longer the thing he had been dreading.

In damp swimming trunks, cold in the air conditioning, a beach towel thrown around his neck, he sat on the bed and flipped through the cards of his Rolodex. He finished the whiskey sour then poured a highball glass of straight bourbon and drank half of it before dialing the first number. He'd replaced the battery in his phone, which had cost a small fortune, and that helped his confidence, connected him to his professional self. He heard his own voice speaking too loudly, his business voice, the one he had not used in over three weeks and that now surprised him as this other Bill Becker whom he had forgotten.

So humiliating, each time he was forced to explain how Imminent Ink was restructuring, cutting back middle management. Especially difficult to explain his situation to Imminent's suppliers. He imagined them grinning on the other end of the line. *Salesmen.* High-tech hucksters whom he had enjoyed the luxury of snubbing, men whom he had always called back at his convenience. He could picture their blossoming grins, their asses sinking into swivel chairs, searching for that spot of deepest relaxation, letting him talk, letting him spill out the details, waiting for his confidence to crack. He listened to the rumbling of distant thunder and watched the fifth of bourbon make its way toward empty. The fog in his head thickened each time he heard *Bill, I really don't know of anything at the moment, but I'll keep my ears open. If I hear of something, guy, I'll get right back to you.* The cheer in his voice sounded progressively more absurd. Each time they put him on hold, he would stare down at the butterfly on his chest and feel the severing of another tie connecting him to the old Bill Becker.

He took a shower. He cleansed every orifice thoroughly. He washed the grime from beneath his fingernails, thinking how his father had always carried the stain of the earth—its clays and black oil—under his nails, between the ridges of his fingerprints. But that was a healthy stain. Bill scrubbed at the ink buried in his skin until the flesh reddened.

He dressed and found that the light in the room had darkened. Outside the sky had filled with black clouds. He sat mindlessly scrolling through the file cards, his head dizzy with numbers. He lifted out a card at random, stood to pace back and forth across the room, with the phone in his hand, staring at the card, trying to muster the confidence to dial that number.

Standing in the doorway between the two rooms, he looked out the far window at the storm. Downtown Charlotte was being pounded by sky-to-ground lightning strikes, and there, centered in the window, enlarged by an optical illusion of the frame, stood the NationsBank Building, a lightning rod towering above those around it. The glow from the crown dispersed through the soup of clouds that eddied by, a beam pouring through the dark.

The room lights blinked off. A thunder clap exploded overhead. He sloshed his drink on the carpet and dropped the phone. God almighty! That was close. He looked up at the ceiling—the eighth floor might be the wrong place to weather this storm. For a moment he stared out the window at the shining tower in the middle of the storm, and then he turned away, shut himself in the other room away from that view. Turned on some lights. Turned on the TV just to have some noise.

Then the door opened and she walked in. Her white halter top was soaked and her pink nipples peeked through. He started telling her about the five-star Italian restaurant he had picked out for dinner, but she ignored him. She headed straight for the mini-bar, pulled out a Diet Coke and a bag of potato chips, then slumped down in the corner, facing the TV.

"What happened?" He eased down on the floor beside her and took her limp hand in his own, rubbing it a lot more vigorously than he would have if he had been less intoxicated. Wet bangs stuck to her forehead, and gooseflesh covered her shoulders.

"I hate driving in the rain." She handed him the car keys and picked up the TV remote.

"You're freezing. You want to change clothes? Get warm? Let me fetch you a towel."

"I'm fine."

He snuggled close to warm her. She kept cramming potato chips into her mouth.

"You shouldn't ruin your appetite," he said. "You'll like this place."

"I ain't hungry." She set the chips on the table and began flipping through the channels.

THE NEXT FEW DAYS were bad ones for both of them. He went with her each night to The Jackpot, and he drank so heavily that Kent would help him to the Mercedes and leave him there so that he didn't pass out inside the club. Back at the hotel parking lot she would wake him and help him stumble to the elevator and down the walkway to their room.

Cloudy days. Instead of swimming and lounging by the pool, they sat cramped up in the suite. By noon each day, he started drinking and calling the remaining numbers in the Rolodex. He didn't want to leave the room in case someone called back. He understood how superstitious that was. Now that he had a mobile phone, he could take a call by the pool just as easily as indoors, but for some reason the pool felt unlucky. All she wanted to do was lie around smoking cigarettes and drinking diet sodas while she stared blankly at the TV. If he insisted on going out for dinner, she would sit across from him playing with her food, sulking. He tried to draw her out again about her childhood, about her mother and her mother's boyfriend, but Lucy only shook her head. The one time they made love, she lubricated herself and just flopped over on her belly.

She became fascinated by his mobile phone. After she went into the bathroom the third time to make a call, closing the door behind her, he stood outside the door and tried to listen. When she stepped back out again, he confronted her.

"Who is he?"

"Marvin."

"Who's Marvin?"

"He's just a guy back where I grew up. Sells me blow."

"Oh."

"He's in a dry spell."

THEIR SECOND SUNDAY TOGETHER, they woke to bright light pouring through the curtains. When Bill pulled them open, they saw a cloudless sky, and since no one would be calling he decided to spend the morning by the pool. She asked to borrow his Mercedes, and he tossed her the keys on the way out the door, without even bothering to ask where she was headed.

Later, he lay half asleep in the sun on a chaise lounge when he felt a shadow fall across his face. He opened his eyes and there she was leaning over to kiss him, their first real kiss in days. She slid her tongue into his mouth and then let him into hers.

"I'm sorry I've been such a bitch." She took her spot in the shade with her magazine and her headphones and he moved his chair next to hers so he could watch her tapping her fingers and nodding her head in time to the music he couldn't hear. Her fingers rapped the chair's metal tubing so hard that it chimed. This new energy—so that's where she had gone. Her dealer out in the sticks. Ah, Lord. Should he say something? She'd bitten his head off the last time he'd lectured her about the dangers of her addiction. She'd called him a drunk. "I'll quit when you quit," he'd said but was relieved she hadn't called his bluff. And today they were both already high. He was on his third drink. He needed to slow down. The ice cubes had melted and the Pepsi was flat. He reached out and took her hand, brought the fingers to his lips.

That night they took a cab to a Mexican buffet and drank margaritas. Without even trying, he was making her laugh. They went back to the hotel and danced to disco in the lounge. Every time they got bored with a song, they rode the elevator to the top floor so he could mix himself a drink and she could "powder her nose." Sometime after last call, they were the last couple to leave the dance floor. Glowing with exhaustion, they went upstairs and took off their clothes.

She said she was still sore. He said not to worry. He told her she was a good dancer. They lay with their arms and legs twined together until finally she fell asleep. He held her like a treasure and let the currents of sleep pull him into her wake.

ON MONDAY HE GOT HIS first positive response from the many phone calls he had made. He set up an interview for that Wednesday afternoon. It was a marketing position, so he had his doubts, but he told himself that, at this point, diversity of experience might be exactly the boost his career needed.

First he tried a cosmetic base, but that only made his skin itch and did little to hide the blue petals, the blue fangs. They went to the mall and he tried on five white shirts before finding one with a collar high enough. Tuesday, he got a haircut and they drove to see her mechanic, who had finished repairing the transmission in her Vette. That night he took it easy on the booze. Wednesday, he and Lucy awoke early and lay propped up on the pillows talking about the days ahead. He tried to nudge the conversation toward the prospect of a shared future, but she resisted and told him instead about how she wanted to save up enough money so she could quit dancing and move away from the city—or, maybe stay in the city and open up her own tattoo parlor.

"I didn't know you did tattoo work."

"I told you—how I apprenticed with Niall, until I got tired of him always bossing me around."

"Are you an artist? I mean, besides tattoos?"

"I told you about that, too."

"Painting? Drawing?"

"Be nice to me, and maybe sometime I'll show you my etchings."

They made love long and tender. He was sure to take his time down low, kissing her until she came and then pushed him away. They ate lunch in the room and still he had ample time to shower and dress. He was studying himself in the long mirror on the back of the bathroom door when she came up from behind and smacked him hard in the seat of his pants.

"You spend more time primping than I do."

"This is a sales position. I have to look perfect." And he did look perfect. That neck was still solid; he only wished for a defensive line to prove it. His tan had never been deeper. His skin glowed in contrast to the bright white shirt. The red stripes in his tie added the right splash of color to the conservative gray pinstriped suit. He practiced his smile. He brushed his teeth three separate times in an attempt to scrub away the tobacco stains. This job would be a chance to recreate himself. It was the kind of change any really successful businessman had to consider at some point. Otherwise, you were too easy to pigeonhole. Unless you had a Ph.D., you were going to reach the upper levels of technical management only as an accomplished generalist, and this had always been his strength. Like his daddy, a jack-of-all-trades.

It probably was not wise to arrive at a job interview with the convertible top down, but he was deliberately trying not to react to negative energy. When he pulled into the visitors' parking lot and turned off the engine, he glanced in the rearview for one last look at his collar line. Niall's words about "casting a mojo" came back to him—you could use it for "business, art, or magic." He could still feel the pressure of Lucy's body against his and yearned to be with her again. He ran a hand through his hair and walked toward the front doors of ICB Chemical. He pushed against the glass but, catching his reflection, checked his smile, then paused long enough to pinch his collar on both sides and tug it up another inch.

11

At ICB, the polished mahogany table was so large it took up half the room. The director of marketing and his number one salesman sat across the table from Bill, swapping golf jokes. The three of them lounged in plush chairs and nodded their heads in agreement with every opinion expressed. This conference room was the kind of space that always put Bill at ease. He'd grown up in the country, far away from such ostentation. His parents had skimped and saved and "made do" not out of necessity but out of spiritual orientation. They had squirreled away every spare dime, investing it in land. Their eighty-two acres were an irreducible fact of Bill's world; he had grown up in those woods, possessing them acre by acre. So, a conference table like this one, intended to impress him with its size, looked puny by comparison. Gazing down into the surface so smooth he could see his own reflection, Bill let his tongue run wherever it wanted to go.

Without exactly divulging any of Imminent Ink's trade secrets, he talked *around* those secrets enough to let these two gentlemen know he was ready to share, after they tied the knot. The more he talked, the more his confidence inflated. Marketing people were always impressed by anyone who had spent time in product development, or who had direct experience with manufacturing, and Bill talked both languages.

"One thing that really impresses me, Bill," the marketing director said, smiling, leaning across the table, "is your loyalty. You were with Imminent since you graduated college. These days it's hard to find a man who will spend a decade with one company."

Bill smiled and relaxed in his chair, confident the job was his if he wanted it. Then the director's eyes dropped from Bill's, dropped maybe ten inches to a spot just below and to the right of his chin.

HE LEFT THE TOP DOWN when he drove back across town, sucking down one beer after another. Bottles clinking in the floorboard, the stereo blasting. *Goddamn white trash*, he thought. *What have I let her do to me?* He drove south past the exit for the Ambassador Suites Hotel. He stayed on the interstate until he had left the city and arrived at his suburb on the south side. He chugged the rest of his beer before coasting around the corner and pulling into his driveway, wondering whether Maddie would be home and whether she would possibly consider letting him inside to talk. Just get everything out in the open and figure out where the hell they could go from here. Friendship? Something, anything! He was willing to accept her relationship with Anthony, well, maybe, so long as he could still see her.

The grass in the front yard was going to seed. What a scandal. He could imagine the rising hiss of whispers passing from house to house until all of Eagle's Pointe was drowning in static. The mailbox was jammed full, so he sat on the front steps and took the pile into his lap to sift out his own, nothing but bills and junk mail. For the hell of it, he tried his key. Still a different lock. Oh, well. He peered through the garage window and saw that her BMW was gone. Her semester was over, so she had no commitments. She could be anywhere. He considered walking down the street to see if Anthony's wife was home, find out whether Anthony was out of town again, but just now Bill wasn't ready to interact with the public. The look on that marketing director's face, the shock mixed with confusion, Bill could not stop seeing it. Then how coolly the man had ended the interview, all the while pretending not to see what he had seen.

Bill stuffed the mail back into the box and got out of there. Once on I-77, he drove north toward the city. Hell, he could just spend the whole day driving back and forth. He watched the Hornets' Nest Inn slide by, and when the exit for Ambassador Suites approached, he stepped on the accelerator. He slapped the rose on his neck, smacked the flesh until it hurt. But it wasn't fair to blame Lucy. He'd done this to himself.

Up ahead he saw the exit for Billy Graham Parkway, and the hymns cranked up in his head—*Precious Lord, take my hand, lead me on, help me stand.* He turned on his car stereo, punched the buttons until he found a wailing guitar, and still the pressure of the pipe-organ built in his brain. He gritted his teeth, stomped the gas, but at the last minute, his foot dropped from the pedal and he felt the Mercedes changing lanes, gliding off to the right.

So he answered the altar call. He rode the Billy Graham Parkway to I-85, then flowed with traffic heading west. He stayed in the passing lane and listened to the engine hum. The NationsBank Tower haunted his rearview; in the waves of heat rising from pavement, downtown flickered in the distance. How long would it take NationsBank to erect a second tower, for them to finance a third, a tenth, a hundredth skyscraper? Total metastasis. The bull couldn't run forever. There would come a reckoning yet. Bathed in neon, it was easy to believe yourself free, to live for the moment, but he was headed toward a very different landscape: mill houses covered in vinyl siding, tall chimneys standing alone in fields decades after the homeplace burned, the ghost of pig shit on the wind years after the sty succumbed to a sea of kudzu—everywhere reminders of past generations and their claims on you.

At the water's edge, he left Charlotte's outer limits, crossing over the wide muddy river that flowed between a "world-class city" and the hinterlands. Every night of the week in some comedy club downtown, an asshole on tour filled in the blank of his generic redneck jokes with the name of Bill's family's county seat, even though a fair portion of Charlotteans had grown up in Gaston County and had fled across this river in the middle of the night. They'd fled under cover of darkness from some hick town and its collection of textile villages, fled across the river looking back over their shoulders until they made it to the safety of a cul-de-sac in some cookie-cutter housing development with a name like Heather Downs or Oakwood or Eagle's Pointe—where they were so sure that their lives must be larger now.

Somehow, everybody else in Bill's family had resisted this temptation to flee. Maybe they had never felt it. Even the cousins who had gone away to college hadn't gone far, and then they'd come home, rejoined the fold. Ten generations of farmers and mill hands had lived in this county before him. And here he came, the skin artist, molting before their very eyes, warping into a shape they would not even recognize.

The farther west he drove, highway turned into byway. Development appeared less frequently, in dense clusters followed by stretches of forest.

Finally, there it was. At the far end of a pasture, surrounded by towering oaks, stood his parents' house. He smelled wood smoke. It was too hot today for a fire in the hearth. He'd seen his grandpa keep a fire going in May, complaining that he couldn't get warm. But Bill's parents weren't old yet, were they? Not so old that they had given up on grandchildren. When his first marriage had fallen apart, they'd acted less surprised than he'd expected. So, this time no doubt they would just nod their heads at the inevitability of his failure.

Bill's senior year in high school his teetotaling father had started riding him about drink. Those arguments had driven the wedge. Then in college came the tectonic shift. They drifted on their respective continents toward opposite poles until, Bill's junior year, Daddy survived the removal of his colon, followed by the horrors of chemotherapy. Except for several weekend visits, filled with long stretches of silence and lots of shared TV, Bill spent that semester getting drunk on keg beer at sorority mixers and promising himself that one day he would go back home and find a way to reconcile with his old man.

But he had not returned. Not really. And he did not stop now. He could imagine them gathered in the living room around the TV, his mother reading the Bible, his father staring at the tube and thinking about God knows what. And Wesley, the good son, still there among them, living in that cottage in the woods like some bachelor hermit, working by their sides in the summer vegetable garden, hunched over a cassette recorder, transcribing the voices of old timers telling stories from days of yore.

Bill wanted to stop for a visit. He wanted to be in the same room with his parents, with his little brother. No big expectations. It would be enough to breathe the same air, just to take in their shapes, their voices, for an hour or so. But he had been drinking. Worse: drinking and driving. They would surely smell it on him. And they would ask him questions he was not prepared to answer.

A mile up the road he pulled over onto the grassy shoulder. He stopped long enough to gather the bottles out of the floorboard and toss them into the ditch. What would they say if he did stop? He stared into the rearview and tugged his collar down to see the blue rose tattooed on his neck—all of it: the wilting petals and the serpent coiled around the thorny stem, its diamond head peeking up through the center of the blossom.

[To learn more about the history and practice of tattooing in America, the Double Door Inn, and other Charlotte landmarks, visit Southern Fried Karma's YouTube channel, Fugitive Views.]

Part II

12

Wesley could have explained to his mother that he needed to finish the chapter he was busy drafting. She would have understood. She took pride in the fact that he was writing a book about their people, built upon stories he had heard them tell. A narrative history, he called it. Maybe this book would somehow make up for the many ways he routinely failed them. For example, when his mother showed up just now asking for what would amount to an hour of his time (even though she said "fifteen minutes") to help her string twine for her green beans, he was ashamed of the fact that he resented her request, that what he most wanted this morning was to be left alone.

Her tomato vines had already grown knee high inside chicken-wire cages. Their astringent aroma filled her garden. But she'd gotten a late start with her beans, which had just started to send out runners. Wesley passed the ball of twine between two cables, weaving a Jacob's Ladder for the beans to climb. His mother worked across from him, bending over a patch of radishes.

"There's a covered dish supper at the church tonight," she said. "I don't know if you have time—"

"I won't get home from the airport till nearly seven. They've got me working extra hours."

"Well, if you want to just drop by, you could come in and fix yourself a plate to take with you. Nobody would care. They'd be happy to see you, even for a minute."

"I don't think I'll make it." He tugged on the twine, pulling it taut, until she hobbled over and asked him to leave it looser. She took the ball of twine from his hands and demonstrated.

He could tell she was in pain, kneeling down on arthritic knees. In the morning light filtering through the pines at the edge of the garden she looked even older than usual, white skin corrugated with wrinkles, age spots covering the backs of her hands, despite how careful she'd always been to protect her skin while gardening by wearing a straw hat and one of Daddy's long-sleeved shirts that swallowed her whole.

"You want me to pick those radishes? It looks like your arthritis is bothering you."

"I'm fine. You string that twine for me and it will be a big help."

Wesley did not know how to have an open conversation with either of his parents. He considered himself a good listener, which was an asset in the many interviews he had conducted with distant kinfolk and with other old-timers in the community. All he had to do was keep his mouth shut and most old people would gladly spill out their life stories, even intimate details. But that same reticence only produced decorous small talk in his parents. He had learned some years ago from his granny that before he was born Mother had lost a child, a little girl, weeks before she was due. Mother had never mentioned a word about it. And he'd never found the courage to ask. Maybe this early loss was the reason she worried so much about his working around "those big airplanes."

When he'd been very young, barely out of diapers, Mother had been diagnosed with breast cancer. He grew up seeing her scars. As a child, when he had glimpsed her leaving the shower, he saw nothing of her body save those two thick, pink, puckered lines across her chest. It was a rare glimpse, but just knowing the scars were there, beneath her clothes, frightened him. As a little boy, he had worried that something might happen to her, but she had assured him that there was nothing to fear. Taking a tomato in her hand and turning it to show him a dark spot on the blossom end, she said cancer in humans was just like a little rotten spot on a tomato. And just as she sometimes did to salvage a tomato, the doctor had needed to cut out a little extra flesh, more than he had originally expected, to make sure the rotten spots wouldn't spread. It was a precaution.

It was only many years later, after Wesley returned home from Gardner Webb College, that she told him more details of the surgery, how the doctor had also, as a precaution, removed her womb. When Wesley asked if it had been a hard choice, she said no, she had never even considered taking the chance that her two boys would be left alone in the world without a mother. But he already knew this, had always known it. As a child, Wesley had understood those scars to signify motherhood. In his child brain, he had conceived gender in the simplest and most brutal terms: if you were a boy, you had to go off and fight in a war when you grew up; if you were a girl, you had to undergo the trauma of childbirth and then bear those scars on your chest. After giving the matter a lot of thought, he had decided it lucky to be a boy.

Standing across the bean row, Mother announced, "I called Maddie again last night."

Wesley jerked the twine taut and waited.

"She thinks Bill is still living out of that motel, but she doesn't know for sure. The Hornets' Nest, I think she said. She wasn't very eager to talk to me. I keep thinking I should try harder to get in touch with him, but I don't want him to think I'm prying, tracking him down."

"Why bother?"

"A mother has to keep up with her young'uns, no matter where they stray."

Wesley had almost said no when Bill had asked him to serve as best man the second time around, to stand beside him at the front of the church and listen to the minister's pious pronouncements, which Bill completely ignored while he grinned down into the face of his new bride, oblivious to anything but white lace framing perfect cleavage.

"I could have told you it wouldn't last." Wesley wove the trellis and watched a red-tailed hawk hovering on the breeze over the corn patch.

"I thought maybe this one *would* last," she said. "I hoped so, at least."

"Bill don't know how to care about anybody but himself."

She didn't answer. She kept moving right along the row of radishes. And Wesley regretted mouthing off. Better to keep his opinions to himself. When he did speak, he had a bad habit of overstating his positions.

"How about you, Wesley?" She shuffled over to help him tie off the end of the bean row. She reached through the latticework and took the twine from him, and together they wove the next section of trellis.

"What about me?"

"You have your eye on anybody special?"

He had to give it to his mother, she did occasionally surprise him with her directness. How the hell could he answer such a question? He was nearly thirty years old, too old to discuss his love life, or the absence of one, with his own mother.

She tossed the twine over the cable and he caught it. "Wesley," she said, "I know you don't like me meddling, and if you're not interested you can just say so."

"What's that?" He passed the twine back.

"Well, one of the women in my circle at church has a niece who's single. And from what I understand she is a very attractive and very nice—"

"Mother," he interrupted. "I'm not interested."

"Well, I didn't say get *married*. Just meet her. There's nothing wrong with meeting people."

"I meet people." Actually, he didn't, not outside of work,

and that was the problem, but he was not so desperate yet that he would let his mother set up a blind date.

"I don't mean to meddle. It's just that she came back into town, and I thought maybe—"

"You want me to help you side-dress the corn? I can bring the tiller over for you."

"No, you go ahead and do your thing. I know you're busy with your book. I can get the rest of this." She tied off the trellis and dropped the ball of twine in her apron.

"I don't mind helping—"

"I'm fine," she said.

"All right." He watched her hobble over to her patch of Swiss chard. She wouldn't stop, no matter how bad the pain in her joints. And he felt like a jerk for walking away and letting her do the rest alone.

13

Lucy lit another cigarette and leaned out over the rail. What a hive of arrogant assholes, buzzing all around her. So judgmental. Fucking spoiled rotten. Green vines trailed down eight floors. Smug punks down there waiting in line for their happy hour. Their women acting so pure, like they'd never put out in their lives. Fucking whores. What if she jumped? What if she arched her back and swan-dived right into that fountain way down there? She'd soak every single one of them.

Everything was brand spanking new. This brass rail, not a smudge, not a single fingerprint but hers. At the front desk when she and Bill had checked in, Lucy had asked if the Ambassador Suites was hiring, and the woman pretended like she didn't even hear her. The little bitch. They probably wouldn't hire her, would they? Probably not. Not even to vacuum? Not even to swab toilets? Fuck that. Minimum wage to swab toilets? No, thanks. Even standing behind a desk all dolled up, standing there like a prize, she wouldn't make the kind of money she was making in room 810. Bill was good-looking. Hell yeah, he was. Smart, too. Polished like a river stone. He had more money than he had sense. Never mind how phony he sounded every time he got on the telephone. *Hey, guy! Hey, guy!* Fucking phony. Spoiled rotten. Anybody who got attached to him was in trouble.

Bill had a bad-ass ride, though. Sweet and sleek. It reminded her of the Miata convertible she'd driven until she'd gotten behind on payments and then the jerks repossessed it, just like they were trying now to repossess her Vette—if they could only find it. Good luck with that. She liked Bill's constant attention, that sweet look in his eye. He knew how to put the sugar in sugar daddy. And the dinners, this gorgeous room, fancy cheese, fresh fruit, cold cuts, anything she wanted, twenty-four seven. She was his pampered baby. Damn straight. And by the way he used his tongue, you would think *she* was the one paying.

He had saved her ass. Bailed her out of a real bind. Creditors calling. Talking about fines. Even jail. Knocking on her door. Knocking on the peeling-paint door of her ratty-ass apartment. And not just creditors. Middle of the night, somebody stalking her—she couldn't guess who— some man from The Jackpot. Some man who had paid her twenty dollars for a lap dance and now felt like he owned her, body and soul. Maybe not just one man. How many? Let them try to stalk her here. Good luck with that, motherfuckers. That trail had gone stone cold. Safe here. Safe as Sleeping Beauty in her fern bower. What the fuck was a "bower"? Something like this vertical cave, green vines falling down, down into the earth. Hell yeah—splash every one of those punks.

Sleeping Beauty. Lucky bitch. Deep sleep in the forest primeval. Just sleep and breathe. If Lucy could slow down on the blow, maybe she could sleep again. That's what Bill said. Fuck him. What did he know about her sleep? Like he's going to waltz right in and fix her problems. She was glad to get rid of him for a bit. Always watching her. But where was he now, though? He said he'd be back three hours ago. Late. Later than he'd said. Could be gone. What if he was? After two weeks, she was getting used to ol' Bill. Getting to the point where the sex didn't even bother her so bad—except that he wanted to fuck forever and never finish. "Trying to become a magician," he would say and then laugh about it. She could kill Niall for putting that idea into Bill's head. That stupid Tantric shit. Nothing a woman ever thought up, that much was certain. Yeah, she was getting used to Bill. Not his drinking. And not the way he had started carping about the money he was giving her. Or riding her ass about the blow. Never should have let him watch. As tight as she was with her blow, when she was flush and had her nose full, she sometimes wanted to share the buzz. "Just taste it," she'd said, offering that sweet, sweet tingle. He'd walked out of the room. Like she was trying to corrupt him. Ha! Corrupt him! Fucking drunk. Who was he to lecture her about her habit? Of course, he was right. She had to give it up. Couldn't keep riding this fast car. Bound to end in a ball of flames, right? So what. Not the worst way to go, a ball of flames. Pour on the gasoline.

But what if she *could* slow it down, just a little? Step by step? She could do that. Couldn't she? Get her shit together. She had this little cushion of dough now. That was a start. She had nearly paid off her medical bills. Bill had helped her turn a corner, and she was grateful. Even if she couldn't bring herself to say it, she owed his ass. Bill had helped her avert catastrophe maybe. At least this vacation, that was something. A start maybe. One day—she'd leave Charlotte behind. Get herself a nice little place in the country, lakeside, like that fucker Kent. Kent had set himself up. Yeah, Lake Norman, that was the ticket. She'd take Cassie with her. She and Cassie were always talking about moving to the lake. Just bullshitting, but still it didn't hurt to dream. They could both get a job tending bar. Take up painting sunsets, right? Pick up her brushes again. Why not? That skinny motherfucker, Niall. She had let him draw all over her, when it could have been, should have been, her own work. She could learn to work that machine. Niall was the best. Hell yeah, he was. Got her higher tips. Still, it wasn't her work.

She had to give up the nose candy. Yeah, had to. She had thought this hotel would be a good place to quit. A fresh start in a nice clean room. The last hustle. But Bill was the wrong person to quit with. Everything about him, everything but his words, said, *Get high, baby, as high as you can get.* If the two of them had to stay sober together, it wouldn't work out, not for a night. They were play-acting. He bought her clothes, fine, sexy things. They got dressed up and went out and spent gobs of money. Living the dream. Somebody's dream.

She stubbed out her cigarette in a potted plant. What a view. Those people down there had been born sleeping in fancy hotels like this one. They didn't even notice. She had to dance tonight. She couldn't let herself forget. Leaning out over the balcony rail, she caught a scene unfolding on the balcony below. A girl, awkward but pretty. Damn, so pretty it hurt to stare. Fourteen? Giving her parents a fit. Walkman, baggy jeans, pierced eyebrow. Ears full of metal, almost as much metal as Niall. Her parents, dressed to the nines, home from dinner. They were trying to get her to come into their room. No dice. Their baby child, bopping her head to the music on her Walkman, turned her little back, leaned over the balcony rail toward the fountain below.

"Why don't you just, like, leave me alone?" the girl said. "I'm not hurting anybody out here."

"What is it you're wanting to do?" the father said.

"I told you. I just want to hang out. Just leave me alone. Go watch your stupid TV."

Daddy-O looked at his wife then back at the girl. He glanced up at Lucy, and she stepped away from the railing.

"Okay," he said. "You can *hang out* for exactly ten minutes. Then I want you inside with us."

The girl didn't answer. Just kept bopping her head.

"Do you hear me?" the man said.

"I heard you."

Lucy listened to the door open and then close. Parents gone. Parents in retreat. Good. She glided along the balcony until she stood directly over the girl, who looked a lot like Cassie. That mop of red hair. A baby Cassie, she told herself, but, no, what she really saw, what she always saw whenever she let herself look at a girl this age—so confident, so full of her safe little rebellion—what Lucy could not help but see and crave so bad it opened a void inside that kept expanding until she was nothing but a hollow shell, a thin balloon filled with stale air and about to float away, was Lucy herself at that tender age. She followed the fluid motion of the girl's head bobbing to music only she could hear, and Lucy was looking at herself at thirteen, fourteen, so full of hope. There she was, her true self, what she should have been, a solid, flesh-and-blood girl, before her insides had been blasted to smithereens.

When the girl looked up, when their eyes met, it shocked them both. Lucy's breath caught. She smiled. The girl looked away, nervous. She looked up again, and Lucy started bopping her head the way the girl had done.

"What you listening to?"

"Garbage." She wore braces.

"They're cool. Which CD?"

"It's the new one." The girl moved the headphones down to her white throat. Such a pretty girl. Such pretty skin. Lucy leaned far over the balcony letting her body balance there. Letting her black hair hang down. The girl smiled.

"You try it," Lucy said.

"What?"

"Like this." She stretched her arms out like an eagle and balanced on the rail.

"You're crazy." The girl grinned.

"I know I am."

"I like your tattoos. That's so cool."

"Thanks."

"I had this, like, really cool karma ring picked out, but Dad wouldn't let me get it. They piss me off. They treat me like a kid."

"They probably can't help it."

"They're, like, so controlling?"

"They don't want you to turn into a freak."

"What?"

Lucy pulled out her cigarettes and lit one. She glanced around to make sure nobody was watching. Like Bill was always telling her, this wasn't a designated smoking area. She hot-boxed it. The girl stared.

"You want one?"

"Sure."

"You shouldn't smoke."

"So?"

She tossed a cigarette down. "You need matches?"

"Nah. I think I'll just save it for later. If my Dad caught me, he would be, like, bugging me all night."

A door opened below, and then there was the man's voice. "Who are you talking to out here?"

The girl turned. "Nobody."

"It's time you came inside."

"Aww, Daddy!" The girl stepped away from the balcony. The door closed again. Lucy leaned over but couldn't see. Gone. She flicked an ash over the balcony rail and watched it fall. Down below, the fountain gurgled. Steel drum arpeggios took wing. Her skin stretched taut, ripe to bursting. She jammed a thumbnail into her elbow and pulled down to her wrist. Unzip herself. Pink-line. Make the blood come. But no blood came. If she could bleed off this pressure, this lightness of being, this heavy hollowness, this memory of all she had lost, this failure of her mother to be a mother.

She fished in her pocket for the plastic card, slipped it, slid it, reversed it, slid it, Jesus, what was wrong with this fucking thing! Green light flash and in. The TV was still on. The door to the mini-bar was open wide. In her purse, she zipped the pocket open, the little safe pocket. Empty. What? The countertop. The TV. There by the telephone.

Bill's Rolodex. Bill's stuff. Bill's stuff scattered everywhere. Her shit too. New clothes scattered over the bed. Price tags still on. Half-empty potato chip bags. Magazines. Suitcases! So many zippers. So many pockets. Goddamn all of these fucking empty pockets! Bureau drawers. Calm down and pull open the drawers, look under her underwear, his underwear, his neatly folded T-shirts. Back to the purse. Who had been messing with her purse? The maids? Bill? She turned it upside down over the bed. Everything fell out. Cigarettes. Tampons. Lipstick. Condoms. Birth control pills. Perfume. Somebody's business card. But no rock. Not a trace. Not a sign.

She searched the kitchenette. The bathroom. The glasses with the paper caps, the tiny bottles of shampoo and conditioner she had been hoarding in her suitcase. She looked in her bag of toiletries and there it was, damn, exactly where she had left it.

The thick little bundle, the plastic baggy soft in her palm. Razor blade. Short brass straw, cold between her fingers. Compact mirror marked by the residue of pleasure. Eightball all to herself. Thank you, Bill, honey. Let the heart find its rhythm. Settle down. Plenty of stuff and plenty of time. Thick. A thimble full.

She opened the bag and inserted the edge of the razor blade. Three white lines. She worked the blade, sifting for chunks, chopping. Fine as dust. Fine as her Ma Maw's snuff. She licked the tip of a finger and stuck it into the bag; enough here to indulge herself. She rubbed her finger across her gums. Numbness spread. Fat, full lips, yes. Dried blood in the left nostril still. Right side was the right side. The straw fit her hole. Cold. Sniff like snuff. Ma Maw snorted snuff. Sniff. Just a little sniff. Yes. The tingle spread across the back of her throat, seeped and spread. Numbing sweetness. She inhaled again and then, before her nose clogged, she snorted the third line. Magic number. Breathe deep. Taste that sweet stuff.

Brighter lights, powder-soft bulbs. Above the mirror in a line, like a movie star's dressing room. Even the bathroom was high class. A whirlpool tub. She had soaked herself that afternoon till her fingers had turned to prunes.

She pulled up her shirt and rolled her belly, watching the blue tentacles wriggle. Belly-dancer. Hell yeah, she was a star. Open wallets gaping like graves. Like bleeding wounds. Fives. Twenties. Every blue moon even a Ben Franklin in her garter. She loved to embarrass a man in public. Some girls fawned over them. She wouldn't do that shit. She would degrade herself as much as it took just to see them writhe. She would taste herself. Make them taste it, if that's what it took.

Couldn't keep dancing forever. Twenty-seven, halfway to twenty-eight. End of the decade starting to show. She struck a match and watched it flare in the mirror. Funny to watch women age. Especially dancers. The surface of skin. Sagging tits a terror? Really? When always, right there at your elbow, the possibility of a violent end and then an eternity of hell fire. How could you not believe in hell, after the way people treated each other? Some people deserved to burn in hell. Forever. Did she? Even if it wasn't her fault—and maybe it was her fault—she had already burned for what felt like forever. And it was how long? Thirteen years? Barely half her life. Such a short time really. What if she had to burn like this forever? To be alone and apart from God and everybody who might have loved her—forever? She struck another match and this time lit a cigarette, blew smoke against the mirror. Who you looking at, huh? You looking at somebody? Why can't you even look at yourself?

Niall didn't believe in hell. Lucy would be the first person to say Niall was crazy. But he was smart. He had managed to think up a whole different version of the universe, as complicated as any you had been taught to believe in. So she had let him draw on her, pictures of God's creatures, including His masterpiece, and pictures of shit that did not exist anywhere in the known world except on Lucy's body. Alice had been trying to sell her on this guy she knew. Alice never used the word "pimp." She used the words "protection" and "tired of this shit." The same guy from the club had been following them both. Alice said they needed somebody to watch their back. Two dancers had been cut loose when their pimp came around causing trouble at the club. If Big Sammy found out you were hooking, that was your ass. She had her cushion of money, and Bill was the last man she was willing to take money from—outside the club. She was through with all that. Done. The telephone rang again. Let it ring. How could he find her, huh? No way. No way in hell. Her mother had sworn she hadn't seen him in eight months. Sworn that they were through. Tried to apologize after all this time. Broke down and cried about it. Demanding forgiveness. Played the birth card. Just because she had given Lucy life didn't earn her forgiveness. Didn't earn her shit.

She tossed her cigarette into the toilet. Dizzy. She turned on hot and cold to fill the tub. If she didn't watch herself, she would be too fried to dance. And she had to dance. Runway baby. They all wanted her. Dollar bills lined up against beer bottles all down the line. Even with the spotlights hot, blinding, she felt their eyes on her. Hungry eyes. Searching eyes. Probing eyes. She looked over their heads, because if she looked down, she saw only him. The joint crawling with him, him swarming the stage, him opening his wallet, him waiting for her to take off the dress and show some skin. Mama said he should not have bought her the dress, warned that he would spoil her. Or, in her mother's tongue, "spile her." And that's exactly what he did. Spile her. She was spiled. Rotten to the core. The first man to pick out a dress for her, to tell her she was pretty. Mama's boyfriend, not hers, but what was wrong with him telling her she was pretty? Stupid whore. You found out, didn't you. Huh? Say something. Pretty? Is that why you covered yourself with ink? Because you wanted to be pretty again? Or because you didn't want another man to see you the way he did? Don't lie. Huh? Don't lie. Don't lie! *Stop lying, Lucy!* That's what Mama said. *You liar. You whore.* And every time a man touches you, every time he looks at you, every time you take off a dress for them all to see, it's like that first time when he made you. Tell the truth. Did he make you? Did you stand there petrified? Did you trust him? Every time now you compound that first mistake with endless mistakes. Nothing but one whole lifetime of fuck-ups. You whore. Whether he made you a whore or saw the whore you already were, does it matter? Huh? Either way, you're still a whore.

"Lucy!"

In the other room the door slammed. Behind her the tub spigot gurgled.

"Lucy!"

Shit. He was here. His voice coming her way. She watched herself, frozen in the mirror. If she didn't move, he wouldn't find her. If she didn't move, it wouldn't happen. Wouldn't be real. She could forget about it.

"Lucy! Are you here?"

She had to move. Because if she didn't move?

She stepped to the door, pushed it closed and locked it. She let herself slump against the sink, let herself breathe.

"Lucy?" The door knob rattled against the lock. The door pushed against the jamb.

"I'm taking a bath."

"There's half a damn dozen bags of potato chips out here you've opened and ain't even touched."

"They get stale."

"They stopped me at the front desk. They said they've

been calling the room and nobody would answer." The doorknob rattled again. "Are you gonna open up?"

She could tell by his voice he was drunk.

"They said my credit's shot. All three cards maxed out." His voice changed. Laughter and sobbing. Muffled by pillows? She reached into the tub and turned off the water then stood by the door, listening. A long silence, and then when his voice came again it was close.

"You don't have any of that money left, do you? The money I gave you?"

She stepped away from the door, stared at the toot on the counter, thought of her purse out there on the bed. If he touched that money—money she had worked for, money she had earned the hardest way possible!

"Well, they said we have to leave. We've got exactly one hour to pack our shit and clear out of here."

"I'm sorry." So this was it. Vacation over. The bathroom lights were adjustable, and she turned them down until the tile glowed softly.

"Where are we gonna go?" His voice was on the move. Her purse was on the bed, in clear view. But she couldn't go out there.

"We could stay at your place," he said.

She hesitated. "Uh, no, I don't think that would be a good idea."

"Why not? You paid the rent didn't you? I gave you money for the rent."

"I paid the rent."

"You afraid to ruin your reputation? Afraid I'll run into your other men?"

"I don't take *men* there!" She let her voice soften, let it be the voice he wanted to hear. "You're my man."

"Sorry." He was very close now, right outside the door. "We'll think of something."

She saw the doorknob working against the lock.

"Why don't you open the door?"

"I need to take a bath. I'm gonna be late for work." She looked away from the mirror, slipped off her shorts, her top, her underwear. She stepped into the tub and eased down into the water. Warm.

"I could take one with you."

"You should have thought of that four hours ago."

"Sorry. I had to blow off some steam. You didn't want to see me after that interview. I had those fuckers in the palm of my hand, and I dropped them."

She lifted water from the tub and poured it over the top of her head.

"Well, hell. I didn't really want to work for those assholes anyway. Yeah, I guess it's just as well. Jeez, I've got to work for somebody. I've got to go back down to the unemployment office tomorrow, tell them I've been a good boy."

She rubbed shampoo into her hair, breathed in the smell of strawberries. She turned on the spigot to add hot water. "I can't hear you!" she shouted.

"You're going to be late."

She turned off the spigot and scooted forward to stretch her body out beneath the water. She folded up a washcloth to use as a pillow, her hair darkening the water around her shoulders. She saw her body broken in the hotel lobby, her blood spreading in that gurgling fountain.

"Lucy?"

"Yeah."

"You're going to be late."

"I know!"

"Well, I didn't know if you knew."

"Are you going with me?"

"You know I am. I want to be there when they start pawing you. Those bouncers might not be quick enough."

"What?"

"I don't want anybody else touching you! They can look all they want but, damn it, when the night's over, you're going home with *me*."

I don't want you telling your mama. You hear? You hear me?

"Lucy?"

"What!"

"I wish you would unlock the door. I just want to be able to see you when I'm talking to you."

"I'll be out in a minute."

"Do you have any cigarettes?"

"Look on the bed." *Your mama wouldn't believe you anyway.*

Outside a commotion. Voices. Men's voices. She hugged herself, stared at the locked door.

"Hey hey! Party party."

"Hey, Lucy!" Bill shouted. "Kent's here. He's going to drive us to the club."

She bent her knees and let her head sink down below the surface of the water. Water filled her ears, but she could still hear their voices. And the water was too cold. A chill spread up from her toes, her corpse cooling. She reached for the hot tap. Felt it pour warmth around her toes and fill her submerged ears with its gurgling churn, drowning out their voices. *Don't tell your mama. She wouldn't believe you didn't want it. Because you know deep down you wanted it.* Hair floating about her face. Heat spreading up around her legs, but her legs and arms kept their chill. Last breath poured out. She sank into the churn until only the tips of her breasts, the top of her face, were bared. If she didn't move, nobody would know she existed. Water rising higher. So high it floated her body until it seemed she had no body. No weight in this world.

14

Some early-bird neighbor was busy with a chainsaw. And every time the saw idled, there was the twittering of a finch or a sparrow or whatever it was right outside the window, making enough racket in its tiny throat to rattle Bill awake even without the chainsaw and the squawking jays and the distant, endless barking of a neighbor's dog. It was the rooster crowing that finally made Bill open his eyes and acknowledge that something was badly wrong. This purple paisley sofa, soft but moldy—he could feel it in his lungs. He lifted himself up to sit and take in the room cluttered with books, a sink and a stove even older than the sofa. Brother Wesley's cottage. Oh, Christ.

In the next room, he heard snoring. He fought back the dizziness as he stood and shuffled toward his brother's bedroom then pushed aside the flimsy curtain hanging in the doorway. God almighty, this was not good. Three bodies squeezed tight into that double.

Lucy lay in the middle. Wesley and Alice perched precariously on either edge of the bed, facing her. Alice, that Barbie doll, she was the one calling the hogs, snoring so loud she nearly drowned out the sound of the chainsaw. Lucy lay on her back with her hands folded just below her breasts. Bill stepped closer to see the fluttering behind her eyelids and jealously wondered what she might be dreaming. Her black hair fell across her face and the pale, ink-marked skin of her shoulders. She had on her top, thank God. They were all dressed—up top. He couldn't see below the quilt. Wesley lay deep in sleep with his face pressed against Lucy's elbow. Sir Studly. All that weight lifting, damn, little brother had grown some muscle. Arms the size of Bill's thighs.

The chainsaw revved again, closer than Bill had thought. He stepped through the makeshift curtain back into the kitchen-slash-living room. What a mess. Wesley had covered the walls with handwritten notes, family trees, taped right to the sheetrock. The kitchen table was a sight. Empty beer bottles crowded around Wesley's computer. An ashtray had been turned over onto the shag carpet. An empty potato chip bag floated in the corner. The place reeked of stale beer and smoke. Somebody had thrown a party.

The whine of the chainsaw dropped to a low growl, biting something heavy. Bill cracked open the cottage door and squinted in the sunshine. He followed the noise of the saw up the hill through the woods until he sighted the old couple. His father was operating the saw. His mother, who was short and arthritic but determined, rolled the log on the ground and held it with her foot while Daddy cut into it. Fitting punishment, Bill supposed. She was a light sleeper. No doubt she had lain awake half the night listening to their party.

Hello, Mother, I'm home.

HIS FEET SWISHED THROUGH THE CARPET of brown leaves, and as he came closer, they both stood up straight and waited. His father let the saw idle until it sputtered and choked.

"Don't stop." Bill tried to sound cheerful. "I came up here to give you a hand."

"We thought that was your car," his mother said. "Who you got with you?" She nodded down the hill toward Lucy's white Corvette, its bumper almost kissing the Mercedes.

"A couple of friends."

"From the sound of your party, I'd say your brother don't need to meet the kind of people you been hanging around."

"Good morning to you, too, Mother."

"Well . . . have you had your breakfast yet?"

Bill laughed. This was always her way of making peace. *Feed the boy.* "Let me sweat a little bit first."

"What's that you got on your neck?" his father asked.

He took a step toward the old man and dropped his head to the side.

"What *is* that? A flower?"

"That's what it's supposed to be. A rose."

"Uh huh. I never seen a blue one."

His mother shook her head. "Now why have you gone and done such foolishness as that! That's a fad for teenagers, not a grown man like you." She wiped her hands on her jeans and said she would go ahead and get his breakfast ready if he wanted to take her place helping Daddy.

"Those friends of yours," she said. "They'll eat meat, won't they?" When she left him there with Daddy, he felt the guilt rising in his throat to choke him. It didn't matter what he said to Mother—they fought well together. But he and Daddy would only brood in silence.

Daddy seemed to have lost more hair, but the brush of his mustache was thick as ever, hiding his upper lip, so that the few words he ever uttered passed through the bristles like a sieve. Because Bill could not see the upper lip, it had always seemed to him that his father's words were disconnected from the person.

Daddy was bent over the saw, tightening the chain. "Why ain't you at work today?" he said. "You taking vacation?"

Hmm, there was that little matter. "They laid me off," he said. "Well, actually, they terminated my position."

Daddy's eyes flashed upward with alarm.

"It was a cutback," Bill said. "I wasn't the only one."

Daddy fixed his eyes upon him, and everything he didn't say registered loud and clear: *Did your drinking get you fired? Have you been laying out of work? Have I produced a drunkard? Worse, a son who is afraid of work?*

"Our company was bought out by a competitor," Bill said. "Middle management took a big hit. But, don't worry, I'll find another position. There are other ink companies in the region. I may have to move, but I'll find work."

"Well, layoffs happen," Daddy said. "Back when I worked for the cotton mill, there toward the end when the unions started coming in, you never knew one week to the next whether you would have a job. Now the work's all gone to Mexico."

Bill surveyed the family land that expanded around him—down the hill the field-sized gardens, and, stretching toward his parents' house, the pasture Daddy regularly bush-hogged. It must have been six acres of lawn surrounding their house—an ocean of green. This forest they thinned for firewood, stacked and split months before it would be needed. Growing up, he had simply taken for granted the immense effort required to manage, to inhabit, so much space. His quarter acre in Eagle's Pointe had always felt so tiny by comparison.

"If you're looking for work," Daddy said, while he primed the saw and pulled the cord, then fiddled again with the carburetor. "I could use a little help."

"Oh, sure."

"Well, I don't want to interrupt your plans, but so long as you're going to be visiting for a few days . . . I've got a house I'm trying to get in the dry. It's just me and Rodney. A third man would make it a lot easier handling those rafters."

"I'll lend a hand."

"We're going to be starting early."

"I don't mind."

"Well, I know how you like to sleep in." Daddy pulled the cord, and the saw whined then grumbled as the blade bit into the log.

As long as his brother kept his face hung down staring into his grits, Bill could joke and laugh and devour everything Mother put on his plate. She kept the platters moving around the table—eggs, sausage, bacon, grits, biscuits. She might raise hell later, but so long as they were seated at her table, no one would go without hospitality, not even women who dressed like Alice and Lucy. All that flesh and all that ink. Even if her every fiber strained not to show it, his mother was no doubt boiling with the blackest of rages over his effrontery to the most basic decency.

And yes, he did feel like a toad in Eden. Bill considered himself a fair judge of hangovers, and from the look on his brother's face, his labored movements with knife and fork, Bill could tell that Wesley was hurting. Rank amateur. As usual, Bill would take the blame. He'd been doing that his entire life. In fact, this readiness to assume blame had proven to be one of the major factors in his successful career. Whenever some project went awry, he was always quick to step forward and call it his fault. Amazing how much Max loved him for this one trait above all others. Max's golden boy. Until it came time to throw Bill under the bus.

Despite his mother's scraping of plates and jumping up to get something she had forgotten from the kitchen—butter, then milk and sugar for the coffee—it was pretty quiet around that table. Bill's brave face had faded. The concentration Wesley focused on his grits approached catatonia. Daddy seemed simply absent, not merely mute but otherworldly. Alice self-consciously picked at her food, stripped fat off the bacon. She knew when she was being judged. But Lucy had heaped a mountain of eggs and grits and meat onto her plate, and she was devoted to it. This hunger from a woman who Bill had had to coax to sample appetizers at a four-star restaurant, who had left half-eaten bags of chips around their hotel room. She chewed with bulging jaws, ripped at bacon with a fierce appetite. Finally, when Lucy had sated her hunger, she broke the tense silence. She talked like a hick, but the woman was shrewd. And as soon as she opened her mouth, Bill wondered where the hell she was taking them.

"Mrs. Becker, I just love your home. Wesley showed me your garden last night. The moon was so bright we didn't have any trouble seeing. Didn't even need the flashlight. I just love how you grow all your vegetables. It reminds me of my Ma Maw's garden."

Bill watched his brother's face sink perceptibly closer to his plate, but Mother's tone began to warm.

"Well, I don't know what all's in the cans we buy," she said. "But I know what's in the jars I put up myself from the gardens."

"Mrs. Becker, this is the best food I ever put in my mouth."

"Well, now, if I'd had time . . . if Bill had given me some warning . . . I might have—"

"How do you cook this bacon so crispy?"

"Well, I've started pouring off the grease when—"

"I just love it!"

The sight of Lucy fawning over his mother was the last thing he had expected. If Bill hadn't known better, he would have thought she were trying out for the role of daughter-in-law. But he knew better, had known from the start, even when he had pretended not to. In the last day or so she had cooled toward him again. Maybe it was simply the fact that he'd slept without her last night. He yearned to hold her, to press his mouth to hers and breathe in the breath she let out. What would happen now that his gold was gone, his credit shot? And what was that she'd said about taking a moonlight stroll with his brother?

She asked his mother a string of questions about her garden, her canning and preserving. Mother got quite technical about the use of a pressure cooker and then about the rise in the populations of nocturnal pests—deer and raccoon—which were forcing her to experiment with new methods of deterrence, most recently clippings of human hair.

"We saw some deer last night, didn't we, Wesley?" Lucy smiled.

"Where at?" Mother asked, sounding more resigned than alarmed. "Were they after the corn? I tell you what, it's getting near about impossible to have a garden."

Bill withdrew from the conversation. He sat stuffed, taking in his former home. The dining room walls were cluttered with the same bric-a-brac he'd grown up study-ing. Inspirational cross-stitch. A paint-by-numbers seascape Wesley had done as a boy, hung on the wall like fine art. Eager to disappear from the table, Bill didn't want to be the first one to get up. Then he noticed that his father was already gone. Without a word, Daddy had taken his leave, and the conversation had clipped right along without missing a beat. Daddy sat over in the living room, kicked back in his recliner, pointing the remote control at the TV.

"Here, y'all help yourselves to more," Mother said. "If you don't eat it, it'll just go to waste." There was a new intonation in her words that suggested she was preparing to adjourn the meal. She hefted the frying pan over Lucy's plate and let her rake out the eggs herself.

Bill scooted his chair back from the table, and Mother reached out a hand to clutch his. There was a firmness in her grip that startled him.

"Come with me a minute," she whispered, and he followed her to the kitchen.

While she busied herself at the sink, scouring egg scum off of cast iron, she inquired about his plans.

"Do you need a place to stay? I've been storing some old quilts in your room. I've piled bolts of fabric on the bed, but it wouldn't take half an hour to get it ready. You know we always have room for you. Not for your guests, but for *you*."

"Mother, I wouldn't dream of putting you out. I might need to sleep on Wesley's couch a few nights—"

"Wesley has to work. He don't need to be bothered with parties that last half the night."

"Understood."

"Well." She placed the frying pan in her drying rack and turned off the coffee pot. "If you're planning to stay with us a few days, you might fit in a visit to Grandpa and Granny. He's not doing so well. You might not get another chance."

"What? Why didn't you tell me?"

"I'm telling you."

This news was inevitable, wasn't it? Grandpa was ninety-something. Then why was it so hard to hear? And why hadn't Bill known, been better prepared?

"How's Daddy doing?"

"Fine."

"Okay. That's good. No signs, symptoms?"

"No cancer, if that's what you're asking." She opened the dishwasher and started lifting plates to the cupboard, making room for the breakfast dishes. Bill poked his head out the kitchen door and glanced at his father tilted back in his recliner. If Daddy were in pain, would he even say? He looked older, weaker.

"You want to help me clear the table?" she asked.

"Sure." He turned toward the dining room, then pivoted back toward his mother. She held a hand to her lower back as she leaned over the dishwasher.

"How's *your* health, mother?" he asked, and only when he heard the words did he register how much like an afterthought they sounded. She, too, had fought cancer, long ago. He had grown up taking it for granted that of course she had won, that the loss of two breasts was a sacrifice she had hardly given a second thought, so strong was her indomitable will. And he knew she fought arthritis every day, but because she had never complained whenever they did talk on the phone, he gave her suffering little thought. He vowed to correct that error. He could do better, and he would.

"Has your arthritis been flaring up?" he asked, watching her slowly straighten up from her stooped position.

"Oh, I'm getting along," she said. "It'll take a lot to kill me."

Just then from the dining room there came a burst of laughter. Lucy's voice rang clear and musical, and Bill rushed out of the kitchen to hear it more clearly, to see her shining face.

15

Bill watched as his granny stood on her toes to peer out the glass. The top of her white head appeared in the bottom pane of the door window. He and Wesley stood on the stoop and waited while she fumbled with a lock. After what felt like minutes, the door swung slowly open, and there was his granny, even more shrunken than he had remembered, balancing herself on an aluminum cane and staring up at him.

"Good gracious, look who's here," she said in a voice too hoarse for a woman who had never picked up a cigarette in her life. Bill stepped through the door and swept her up in his arms, what was left of her.

"You keep getting better looking every time I see you, Granny," he said. And he meant it.

"Oh." She smiled briefly. "The old gray mare ain't what she used to be. Come on in here, both of you. He'll be so glad to see you." Maneuvering her cane, she turned and led them across the room, skirting the brick hearth decorated with frontier fans made of turkey feathers. In the corner, Grandpa lay sleeping in his hospital bed, the patchwork quilt pulled up to his chin, even though it was hot outside, and hot inside the house, too.

"How's he feeling today?" Wesley asked.

"Oh, not very good. All he wants to do is sleep. It worries me so much, Wesley. If he would just take an interest in something. If he would watch a little TV. You know your mother planted that little garden down there for him and he just let the weeds take it. He don't want to leave the house. He'd stay in bed all day if I let him."

"Maybe he needs the rest," Bill said.

She looked up at him without speaking, as if she could not believe her ears. "It's what his mother done before she died. Just like Matthew, she wanted to lie in bed all day long."

Grandpa's bony hands clutched the metal rails as if he were afraid of falling. He labored for each breath, his mouth gaped open, and a deathly rattle floated out of him. White stubble covered the scaly dry skin of his cheeks. His ears were red and raw and prominent.

"Matthew!" Granny shouted to wake him. She took one of his hands in her own and patted it. "Matthew, the grandchildren are here to see you."

His eyes flickered open and he looked at them unseeing and uncaring, like Lazarus might have looked when he was snatched from the other side.

"Hey, Grandpa!" Bill said, picking up the hand Granny had dropped. The old man smelled bad, and it made Bill want to cry.

"Who are you?" he said, with a stubborn and confused and fearful look.

Bill laughed uneasily and released the old man's hand.

"This is William," Granny shouted. "You remember William!"

"Who!"

"Margaret's boy!" Granny shouted. "You remember! Wesley's brother!"

The old man nodded his head slightly. "You're the one in Durham, ain't you?"

"I used to be in Chapel Hill," Bill said. "I went to college there. I've been in Charlotte for the last ten years, Grandpa."

The old man shook his head. This was evidently a piece of information he had no need for—he made no connection to a Bill in Charlotte and it was not worth the struggle to put the pieces together. He closed his eyes and slowly lifted a hand to press against his forehead and smooth down over his face.

Granny spoke in a quieter voice, "He's been talking crazy." She picked a newspaper off of the ladder-back chair pulled next to Grandpa. "Here, have a seat, Bill. Visit with him."

The old man looked at Bill a long time, while Bill struggled to find some conversation starter. Finally, Grandpa broke the silence.

"I'm the oldest living man person I know," he said.

"Everybody he knew is already dead and gone," Granny said.

"That must be hard," Bill said, "missing your friends."

"All his brothers and sisters," Granny said. "Every single cousin, gone."

"I'm sorry," Bill said.

"You have to talk louder," Granny said. "He complains about his hearing aid. He won't wear it. I had your mother take it to the doctor and have it worked on and he wouldn't touch it after that. He won't let me handle *anything*. I tell him he ought to clean his teeth now and then. He just sets them on the side table by his bed, and the things are getting filthy. When I tried to soak them in the cleaner, he complained for a week. Said I ruint them."

"It must get hard sometimes."

"I try not to be ugly with him," she said in a lower tone, "even when he's ugly to me. I just tell myself it's not the real Matthew talking."

So this is what a marriage came to. Some reward for her decades of commitment. He thought of his own parents and the long stretches of silence they endured. He considered how he himself had already trashed two marriages in less than a decade, how he was ready to pledge himself again, to a woman he'd known for less than a month.

Granny told Wesley she had a book in the other room she wanted to show him. She struggled to rise from her chair. Wesley took her hand, helped her up, and steadied her while they walked to the den, the room where she kept her boxes of family records and newspaper clippings.

"I'm so glad you always take the time to visit him," she told Wesley as they left the room. "None of the other grandchildren come around."

Bill sat beside his grandpa who, wide awake now, stared vacantly toward the fireplace and the turkey feathers spread into fans. As a child, Bill had fantasized about taking those fans down, when no one was looking, and carrying them into the woods somewhere to see if he could use them to fly.

"Have you seen any interesting programs lately on TV?" Bill asked.

Grandpa nodded and continued to stare at the hearth, its firebox scoured clean. No more fires to be lit on those bricks. He and Granny were far too old to manage the wood, the flames. Instead, they'd cranked up the electric heat till it was hot as July. Out the picture window, Bill could see a cooling breeze in the trees. It was even harder than Bill had often imagined—reconnecting with his roots. The heat in the room was making a slick of sweat rise, dampening his shirt. Grandpa reached for the quilt and pulled it up to his chin. Bill reached a hand to help tuck the quilt, and Grandpa shot him an angry look.

Bill wished he had learned to pray. His mother had tried to teach him. Maybe prayer was the only thing that could break this paralysis. Even sweating didn't help. If he could, he would pray to their god to look down on their suffering and have mercy. He would pray for understanding, to know why bodies broke down, why they took so many years to fall apart.

After what felt like a very long time, Granny came hobbling back into the room. Wesley followed her, carrying a box full of papers, notes on family history. The two of them sat together on the sofa, comparing family trees. Wesley had always possessed a patience Bill lacked. Bill did remember one discovery he had made, sifting through those old family documents. He must have been in college already, home for break, when he had stumbled upon the photocopy of what turned out to be an estate sale, dated 1821. Among the ancestor's horde—an apple press, a tinder box and tobacco, a cobbler's tools, a box of nails, pigs, a pair of mules, a bay mare—there appeared three names. One wench, Sarah. One man, Tom. One boy, Ben, along with the prices, which Bill had forgotten. What had he ever been told about this scattered family? Nothing, ever. And the only person he had ever asked about it was Wesley, who claimed never to have seen the ledger. Worse still, Bill knew he himself had not been as bothered as he pretended to be by the enslavement of these three people, by the wealth from their labor and then their sale that had been passed down the generations. Did their suffering in any way touch him? Really touch him? In fact, wasn't there at least a part of him that had been titillated by the horror—glad to see his family's innocence shattered? But it was a knowledge he couldn't unknow, and every time at the ink factory when he met with Lamar about the production schedule or when he went out to lunch with Stuart from the lab or spent any time with his black friends on the factory floor, and he pretended no knowledge of that ledger of sale and those three lives, he knew that his co-workers knew. Even though they said nothing, they heard it, the blood crying up from the ground.

Wesley held a pile of handwritten notes stacked in his lap. Granny, sitting beside him on the sofa, kept adding pages to the stack. It was more than restlessness that made Bill want to leave Wesley here, to run out the door to his car and send a cloud of dust in his wake as he made it safely back to the hard-surfaced road and then back to Charlotte and the nearest liquor store to get good and drunk before he sank with relief down against the Naugahyde and felt the pain that was almost pleasure and saw the ink being pumped beneath his skin.

16

Always a burn barrel stinking somewhere. In the fading light, Lucy counted three separate plumes of smoke, polluting the purple evening with soot. Trailers packed so tight. Trailers on top of trailers. Her mama called them *mobile homes*, like that was less trashy, even though mama's trailer hadn't moved an inch since Lucy's girlhood and was rusted so bad it looked like it was about to go back to the earth. *Mobile* only inside Lucy's head; wouldn't never give her any kind of peace. She remembered how he always liked to sit on these front steps to smoke, blocking her way, how she always had to step past him to get in or out.

Lucy stood on the same steps, empty now. Three tiers of cement blocks. She wouldn't even be here if Bill hadn't dragged her out to his brother's home last night. Just getting out of Charlotte, watching Bill argue with his mama this morning, got Lucy to thinking about her own mama. Last time on the phone, Mama had said how her diabetes was progressing. What if she died out here, and they were still mad at each other? Maybe she was a shitty mother, but she was the only one Lucy had.

Her fist rattled against the aluminum door, until she heard Mama grumbling inside. When Mama jerked the door open, she stood behind the screen staring out into the dark, before she seemed to recognize her.

"Why, looky who's here," she said, like somebody else was lurking inside to hear and be equally surprised by Lucy's visit. If he *was* here, Lucy would walk right back out the door.

Before they could even get settled into the ratty 70s furniture, her mama was reaching for a cigarette. And since

Lucy had left her purse in the car (maybe that was a mistake) she bummed one. Menthol. Didn't Mama understand she was too old to keep smoking menthols? Poor old Mama. After he had left her, she must have lived off Twinkies. She'd gained at least fifty pounds. Her face puffy as rising dough. Heavy eyeliner. Some sort of hippie dress that fit her like a tent.

The news blared on TV, somebody else's catastrophe, and Mama reached for the remote to turn it down, not off. Lucy glanced down the shotgun hall, all the way to the end where that bedroom door stood wide open. Fuck! Didn't Mama even have the decency to close that door! She turned away. Too late. She had seen the shadows.

"Can I get you something to drink?" Mama said.

Lucy shook her head and glared at the shag carpet.

"You sure? I got some of that coconut rum you always liked."

"I'm driving."

"I thought maybe you'd spend the night. If you don't got to work. We'll have ourselves a little party, like old times. Just you and me."

"Like old times?" How could Mama be so deliberately dense? To sit there and pretend Lucy hadn't barely escaped this hellhole with her life. They'd been through this same trash last summer, when Lucy finally got her to admit she had chosen him over her own daughter. Mama had sat right there in that same recliner, her face slick with tears, saying how sorry she was, how she had no idea what an evil bastard he was, while that same TV blared in their faces. And now evidently all that coming to Jesus was ancient history.

"I wouldn't mind something to eat," Lucy said.

"What you want? My fridge is pretty bare, but I can probably scrounge something up."

"Anything. I'm starving."

Mama went to the kitchen and started banging cupboards. The kitchen and living room were the same room, divided by a little partition. She opened the fridge and stood staring a long time. Was it that difficult to sit and have a conversation with her daughter?

"Whatever you got," Lucy said. "I ain't picky. I ain't had nothing to eat since breakfast." How full she'd been, and now how empty again.

Finally, her mama pulled a frozen dinner out of the freezer and stood in her tent of a dress, her hip cocked out like a TV model, displaying macaroni and cheese for Lucy's approval. Lucy nodded, remembering the breakfast Bill's mama had fed her. Fresh eggs, crispy bacon, grits swimming in butter.

"I was kind of surprised to see you today," her mama said, popping the frozen meal into the microwave.

"Why's that? I said I would come, didn't I?"

"Well. That last time, you left here in such a huff." Lucy looked at the shag carpet and felt the anger buzz through her. "What do you want, Mama?"

"I just wanted to see my little girl. Damn. You always was so touchy. Everything I say pisses you off."

On the wall above the TV, Lucy saw herself evolve from an infant with chubby arms and legs to an awkward teenager, sporting a mohawk and heavy mascara. Then, older, her first tattoo, on her shinbone. *Cursed?* God, she hated that tattoo, and the artist who had done it. She was still trying to talk Niall into covering it up, but he said that would only make it worse. Across the wall, inside the cheapest frames money could buy—there must have been fifty of them—the entire family smiled out at her. Ma Maw and Pa Paw Wilson. All her cousins. Aunts and uncles. But it was her own face that dominated the room.

Mama had always said, *Rich people got their money, their status. Poor people don't got nothing but each other.*

What bullshit. At Bill's mama's house, Lucy had seen a few family photos, one portrait of Bill, one of Wesley, tastefully placed on furniture, but nothing like this fireworks display. Overcompensation. When her eye caught the studio portrait, the one with Mama's boyfriend in it, Lucy in her mohawk frowning there between the two of them, one happy family, the only thing she could do was point.

"What is that?"

Mama puffed on her cigarette, letting her eyes play across the wall. "Where?"

"Why would you still have that picture?"

Her mama's jaw clenched as she stared at the wall.

Lucy stood up, walked to the collage of photos, and reached high and lifted the frame from its nail. She carried it to the kitchen and opened the cupboard under the sink, tossed it into the trash.

Mama settled deeper into the recliner, her eyes taking on a hard look. What? Did she blame Lucy? Did she still think her daughter had lied? Hadn't they hashed that out last summer?

Lucy stepped out the back door and down a set of rickety stairs onto a concrete patio. There in the purple light of dusk, she stared at the backside of the neighbors' trailer and tried to catch her breath.

Next to the patio was a narrow patch of red clay her mama tilled every spring—the one spot between her and the neighbors where she got enough sunlight for tomatoes. A buzzing security light overhead shined down on half a dozen scraggly, blighted plants that drooped and tilted toward one another. Lucy thought about that other garden she had surveyed by moonlight, the one Wesley helped his mama cultivate: tomato vines tall and resinous, dark green with health, half an acre of corn and beans and squash and peas and okra and every sort of collard or kale you could think of.

"I see you're still driving that new sports car." Mama stood at the top of the stairs and pointed to the white Corvette, sparkling beneath the security light.

"Yeah, does that surprise you?"

The cherry on her mama's menthol glowed in the dark.

"Be nice," Lucy said. "And maybe I'll take you for a ride."

"Don't be a bitch."

"It takes one to know one." She wasn't going to let the old woman bully her.

"I just think you ought to save your money—or you'll end up like me, stuck living in a shit hole the rest of your life. I know you been talking about moving away from that apartment. And cashiers don't make enough money to drive brand new sports cars." Her mama nodded and raised her eyebrows, like she knew all about Lucy's secret source of income. Lucy had never mentioned losing her job at Food Lion—or her work at The Jackpot, let alone her moonlighting with men like Bill.

Somewhere in a trailer nearby she heard a woman screaming—"Fuck you! You lying asshole! I hope you rot in hell! I hope you fucking rot in hell! I hope you rot in *hell!*" The bullfrogs in the swamp out back started up their nightly orgy. That rhythmic croaking never failed to make Lucy feel unclean. She couldn't understand how some people were sentimental about frogs—their slimy, wart-covered flesh. Just because they had two legs and two arms did not make them cute. Those empty eyes. The incessant invitation to the other frogs—let's fuck, *let's fuck, let's fuck.* That dank swamp, one big cauldron of sex. Disgusting.

"Well, shit hole or not," her mama said, "I've managed to get behind on rent. And I thought if you're flush enough to pay for that shiny thing in the driveway, you might be able to spot me enough to cover this month."

It was not only the sound of those frogs but the smell of this place that got her down. Even when you weren't breathing soot, smoldering garbage, all kinds of flaming plastic, that swamp constantly belched its foul odor of rot, green scum of algae blooming thick as pudding.

"I ain't got any extra money just now." Lucy cast a glance at her car, glad she'd left her purse there. The windows were rolled up. She had locked the doors, hadn't she?

"I ain't asking for much," Mama said. "I just need enough to tide me over. I'm afraid the landlord is about to pitch me out in the street."

"And how is that my problem?"

"I'm your *mother!*"

"When it's convenient for you."

Her mama pouted in silence. Lucy made sentences in her head but managed not to say them. That rent-money poormouth was the oldest con in the book. Hell, she had used it herself. She worked *hard* for her money. Harder than anybody knew. As the dark deepened, the frogs croaked louder, every minute their number increasing. She climbed the steps and pushed past her mama.

She reached into the microwave and found the macaroni and cheese, grabbed a spoon from the silverware drawer. The kitchen table was covered in stacks of old *Cosmopolitan* magazines. She took her food to the living room and settled down into the sag in the sofa. When her mama followed her into the room and slumped down in her recliner, Lucy tried to ignore her. Mama stared angrily at the TV, luxuriating in her self-pity. Lucy reached beside her to turn on the lamp. She twisted the knob—*click, click, click, click*—why couldn't Mama ever replace a bulb? With the windows open, the frogs were nearly as loud inside as they were out there in the yard. She spooned the hot orange goop into her mouth, thinking how spoiled rotten Bill was, boo-hooing because he wasn't his mama's favorite, not understanding how a woman that strong had love enough to go around—maybe even to a stray like Lucy.

Almost as dark inside as out. Only the blue screen of the TV gave them some light. She couldn't help but glance down the shotgun hall, at that open door, a black hole, the long shadow reaching out to her. The frogs were finding their rhythm. No longer the spontaneous, solitary calls. Now all of them were grunting together, like the rhythm of those mattress springs when he had raped her, his groans and the croaks of those frogs synchronized. Her mother gone, the two of them alone in that room, as he forced her down on the bed, while the funk of the swamp spilled through the open window and she ground her teeth against the unbearable pain as he broke her, body and soul.

"Well." Mama shifted her weight in the recliner and leaned forward toward the TV. "While you're here, I'm hoping you can at least help me move some furniture around in the guest bedroom. Ma Maw's old chiffarobe is heavy. I tore up my back, and I can't hardly bend over, but I figured if you helped me slide it . . ." With a hand on the small of her back, Mama lifted herself from the recliner and started shuffling in her pink slippers down the shotgun hall. She was grumbling some complaint beneath her breath, but when she got to the door at the end of the hall, she turned and glared at Lucy. "Are you coming?" she shouted. "Or do I have to move it by myself!"

Lucy felt the cheese thicken in her throat, choking off her air. How could Mama not remember? Of course she remembered. Lucy could hardly bring herself to look at that door, let alone enter the room.

Misshapen bodies glistening in the night. The bladders in their throats swelled with air. Slick with the muck of that swamp, they crawled out onto the banks and sat hunched over, eyes wide open reflecting back the emptiness all around them.

17

Bill had already taken a couple of drinks. He rode shotgun in Wesley's rusted pickup. They were headed west, deeper into the sticks, exactly opposite the direction Bill had proposed.

"I've got no interest in Charlotte," Wesley said. "Other than earning a paycheck."

It amused Bill that his little brother handled luggage for an airline that would fly him all over the continent free of charge, and Wesley never left the tarmac. Bill tried his mobile phone again, but there was still no signal. Little point, Lucy wouldn't be home this time of evening. Chances were she would already be occupying a bar stool, while the Double Door started to fill with regulars. She liked to stop by the Double Door on her way in to work and flirt with that bartender—what was her name, Cassie?

"Why don't we grab Duane and go check out a band," Bill said. "Didn't Duane use to play in a country band? Guitar, wasn't it?"

"Where is it you're wanting to go so bad?"

"I know this hole in the wall you'd like. Ever been to the Double Door Inn?"

Wesley shook his head.

"I'll teach you to shoot a little pool, a useful skill."

He only wanted to talk to her for fifteen minutes. The way they had parted that morning, those little pecks on the cheek she'd given both him and Wesley, what was that? When she'd gotten in her car, she hadn't even bothered to return his wave, hadn't even looked at him when she'd driven away from Wesley's cottage.

Black Snake Road. The pines crowded in so close, the bends coming so regular, Bill had utterly lost his bearings. Might as well throw breadcrumbs out the window. But Wesley knew the way. From what Bill gathered, Wesley drove out to Cousin Duane's farm house near about every Friday night.

All afternoon, after leaving Grandpa and Granny's house, Wesley had brooded in silence, and now behind the wheel, staring out at the curving snake of a road, the anger finally came spilling out.

"So you basically just need a place to stay," Wesley said. "This is not an intentional visit. You're not really concerned with the fact that Grandpa is struggling for his last breaths, or that Granny is there watching it."

"That's not true. Or fair."

"If your boredom wasn't already plain as day, I believe even Grandpa couldn't have missed it when you made that snide comment about his mother's diary."

"I just wanted to see him laugh."

"Did it work?"

"No." Bill was still haunted by the sight of his grandpa's grizzled chin, his heaving chest. In order to tear his eyes away from his grandfather's dying, Bill had walked across the room and lifted the stack of photocopied pages from Wesley's lap. Great-Granny Porter's weather diary. An entire decade of daily temperatures, records of rainfall and occasional snow. Beyond such careful attention to weather, the pages held no other commentary on her life. So typical. Whenever Bill spoke to his parents on the phone, seventy percent of the conversation related to the weather in all of its repeated though infinitely varied patterns. Why was real intimacy so elusive? Maybe the weather was enough. Maybe it had to be.

"Another thing," Wesley said, thumping the steering wheel with the palm of his hand. "I still can't believe you're asking me for money. Haven't you saved *anything?*"

"It would be very short-term."

"If your credit is shot, do you really think it's a good idea to run to Charlotte and throw away more money on over-priced drinks?"

"You're right, brother. I just figured we might have some fun tonight." How could he explain his desperation to see her, if only for fifteen minutes, to buy her a drink before she went to work at The Jackpot. He couldn't afford The Jackpot's cover. It wasn't just the money; that place was killing him. Other dancers had their boyfriends sitting patiently out in that darkness. He couldn't do it. No sir, not him. Maybe if she called him *boyfriend*. What he *could* do was drive sixty miles round-trip to Charlotte without even knowing whether he would find her at the Double Door. Yeah, she'd be there, for sure, chatting up her girlfriend.

Bill saw his brother casting glances his direction. Something else was obviously on his mind. Wesley had just finished working out with the weights scattered among the weeds in front of his cottage, and the muscles in his neck were still engorged, taut as cables.

"Hang out with Duane tonight," Wesley said, his tone shifting to reconciliation. "You haven't seen Duane in how long?"

"I don't know. Three years? Four?"

"He makes a pretty tasty scuppernong wine. You'll like it." Wesley smiled. "It's free."

"Yeah," Bill said. "It'll be good to see Duane." Here was another chance to forge a meaningful connection to family—a cousin his age, without that huge generation gap. With Wesley as a guide, they'd surely discover common ground.

"So this girlfriend of yours," Wesley said, staring out at the road.

"She's not my girlfriend," Bill said, careful to keep the

tremor out of his voice. Simply acknowledging the fact made tears swell in his eyes.

"Really?"

Bill studied his brother, remembering the sight of him in bed that morning pressed against Lucy's side, the way she wouldn't hold Bill's eye at breakfast, the itty-bitty peck on the cheek before she drove away.

"They don't touch her, right?" Wesley said. "I mean, she takes her clothes off up on a stage or something. She can probably just pretend they're not even there."

How easy it would be to take that steering wheel and jerk the truck off the road, feel the truck slam into the pines. Bill placed a hand on the rose tattoo, still tender, held his hand pressed there firmly. Sometimes Wesley's innocence, his need to be the good son, filled Bill with a rage that frightened him.

As soon as Wesley pulled the pickup to the side of the carport and shut off the engine, Bill could hear the voices of tortured souls wailing in anger. He looked up at the old farm house. It took a moment for the voices to resolve themselves into their constituent parts: from the backyard pen, hounds were baying, and from within the home a couple shouted curses at each other. He hesitated, then stepped out onto the grass and followed his brother toward the back steps.

"I don't know if we should intrude," he said. You could hear them through the windows, through closed doors. Even the nearest neighbors, a hundred yards away, must have heard the fight raging inside.

"They're always like this," Wesley said. "Lately, anyway. Since Crystal started working third shift." Wesley tramped up the steps, opened the screen door and walked into the house without knocking or looking back, and Bill reluctantly followed.

Inside the mud room he looked down and saw a long-haired

gray cat lying on her side and a mass of tiny kittens swarming around her belly for milk. When he stepped through to the kitchen, Duane had Wesley wrapped in a bear hug. Duane was even bigger than Bill remembered from high school, the young tackle he had always trusted to bust through a defensive line and drill a hole big enough to drive a station wagon through. Duane released Wesley and came over and shook Bill's hand in both of his.

"Good to see you, Cuz!"

Crystal stood slumped against the sink holding an unlit cigarette to her lips.

"Good to see you both," Duane said, slapping Wesley and Bill on the shoulders. "How's your mom and dad?"

"Fine," Wesley said.

Bill began formulating a response in his head—older, cancer-free so far as anyone knew, his mother's arthritis seemed worse, just like Daddy's hearing—but Duane was already opening a cupboard and digging for coffee he accused Crystal of hiding from him.

"Why would I hide coffee?" she asked. The cigarette shook in her trembling fingers as she cursed the lighter she couldn't get to work. From her other hand dangled some kind of old-fashioned cudgel, a short, straight stick with a smooth round plunger at the end. She followed Duane with her eyes. One look at her face and Bill could tell this was the wrong place to be.

Duane was their first cousin, but apparently he had been more like a big brother to Wesley, in Bill's absence. Based on what Wesley had told Bill, the only social life he enjoyed now was coming over here on Friday nights to sit and watch TV with Duane and Crystal or accede to Duane's wishes and turn off the TV and just sit and listen to Duane talk.

"I'm so glad y'all came by," Duane said, laughing. "You might have stopped Crystal and me from murdering each other."

"Don't count your chickens," she said.

"That's why I love her," he said. "Because she knows how to fight."

"It's all a game to you." Her voice trembled. She looked at Bill. "I can't take it anymore. I'm too tenderhearted." She rubbed at her shoulder, kneaded it, smoothed the hand down her triceps.

Duane laughed. "Crystal, you're about as tenderhearted as Godzilla. You're just like me, rough as a cob." He walked over and hugged her to his side. She pushed him away, but his hand got caught in her auburn hair.

"Stop it!" She disentangled herself. "Why do you always have to show off in front of company? You can't just act like nothing happened."

What had happened, according to Duane's retelling, was that when he came home from the NAPA store, already pissed because the part he'd ordered for his tractor hadn't arrived, Crystal was sitting on the kitchen floor with a brand new microwave oven when not a damn thing was wrong with the old one.

The box and Styrofoam padding sat on the counter beside the microwave. Its touch pad was so full of buttons, it looked like the console of a spaceship.

According to Duane, when he had complained about the two gallons of raw milk spoiling in the fridge, milk she had promised to churn into fresh butter, Crystal had grabbed the dasher out of the churn and threatened to dash out his brains if he said another word. At this punchline, Duane threw back his head and hooted with laughter, poking Crystal in the ribs until even she broke into a grin. Duane took the dasher from her hands and replaced it in the churn sitting in the corner. His whole performance seemed rehearsed.

"Y'all churn your own butter?" Bill asked. The churn, its weathered boards, looked like it hadn't been used in a hundred years.

"Not yet," Duane said. "It's part of our master plan."

From what Wesley had told Bill, Cousin Duane had set about pursuing the agrarian ideal of their grandpa. Duane wanted to produce at least ninety percent of the food and beverages they consumed. He was between jobs, so they were living off Crystal's paycheck. She worked late nights in home health care. Meanwhile, Duane stayed home and tended their garden, kept bees, bred dogs, and made scuppernong wine. In the fall he always tried to get a couple of deer for the freezer. He was thinking about raising hogs.

By the time Crystal finished her cigarette, the conversation had veered back toward argument, this time over the question of whether she was going in to work tonight. Crystal suffered from severe rheumatoid arthritis, and the long night shifts had placed her body on the rack.

"Call in and tell them you can't get out of bed," Duane said.

"We need the money," she said and continued to massage her own shoulder.

When she started discussing their budget, Duane took it as an accusation that he wasn't contributing to the household. He threw open the cupboard doors to display shelves crowded with the jars of honey and tomato sauce and green beans he had put up from last year's harvest. Even Bill could hear that what Crystal really wanted was sympathy, for Duane to shut his mouth for once and listen to her talk about her pain.

Bill smelled coffee grounds. Across the room, Wesley held up the bag he had found deep in a cupboard. He spooned coffee into a filter, oblivious to the storm gathering.

"Y'all sound like you need to get out and have some fun with each other," Bill said.

"We never go out." Crystal stared across the room at Bill like a woman held hostage.

He averted his eyes. The last thing he wanted was to intrude into this domestic dispute.

"Come on and ride with me and Wesley to Charlotte," he said. He painted a picture for them of a scene that would cure all their woes, dancing to live rockabilly music, keg beer that never stopped flowing, pinball, pool tables, a house full of strangers to lose yourself in.

"There was a time I loved to dance," Crystal said. "But these days the arthritis is eating me up."

"You want to taste something good?" Duane said. "Cuz, you don't have to ride all the way to Charlotte." He winked at Wesley. "Y'all follow me. Crystal, where did I put that flashlight?"

"I don't know. It ain't my job to keep up with your stuff." She turned to leave the kitchen, and Bill saw the hitch in her gait, the way she kept a hand on the counter for support, like a woman twice her age. From the darkness of the next room she stood watching, and Bill could see her cigarette glowing. "I hope you ain't planning to get drunk tonight," she said.

"You just smoke your cigarettes and drink your Cheerwine," Duane said. Big as a horse, Duane had a temper. He was a man who could do terrible harm to a woman. He led Bill and Wesley on a tour, showing off his new garden tiller, the load of wood he had split and stacked to dry inside the carport. A chorus of bellows went up from the chain-link fence, where hounds leapt into the air, fighting for position. Duane led the way with a flashlight to his garden behind the house. There was nothing to see but red mud turned over in furrows, but he stood there pointing with his flashlight, showing where he had planted okra, corn, beans, squash, and cucumbers. Duane showed them his compost bin and the scuppernong vine and his peach trees. Around in the front yard, he shined his light into the branches of a fig tree covered with marble-sized green knots.

He bragged about Crystal's preserves and promised to give them a sample later.

"How about that drink," Bill suggested.

Duane nodded and smiled. "Follow me, boys." Shining the flashlight out in front of them, he led the way back around to the side of the house, where he swung open the plywood hatch that led to the crawl space. A gust of cool air poured out, bearing the tang of iron. Duane shined the light down in the hole, then crouched low and disappeared inside. Wesley ducked low and followed. Bill dangled a penny loafer over the edge and felt it sink into mud. He looked down at his slacks, his white shirt, and pulled his foot back out. He ducked his head into the black hole and said, "I don't think I'm dressed for this."

Duane poked his head out, smiling, and shined the light in Bill's face. "It's the perfect temperature under here year round," Duane said. "Perfect place to age wine."

"You live in the best of all possible worlds," Bill said.

"Well," Duane said, "if you've had it easy your entire life, this might not seem like much. But it's my paradise, and I love it."

Why was it people only ever heard the irony in his statements? Bill also sincerely meant what he'd said. To live here near his people, to live off the land, who could want more than that?

"I'll wait inside," he said.

"Suit yourself."

This whole project was beginning to seem a little farfetched. Rediscovering his kinfolk, getting in touch with his roots? There in the driveway, Wesley's pickup sat in the dark. Wesley had left the keys in the ignition. Nearly a full tank of gas. Hell, he could hop in and go. Five-dollar cover at the Double Door. He could manage that plus a round of drinks. If he left now, he would get there before Lucy went in to work, and who knows, maybe she even had the night off. All he wanted was fifteen, thirty minutes to talk, just to see her and figure a few things out. To smell her perfume, to hold her hand. That little peck on the cheek this morning after breakfast still stung. That was less than Bill had gotten from Alice—she had hugged him tight, like a sister, like he actually meant something to her.

HE FOUND CRYSTAL ALONE IN the master bedroom sitting on a high mattress in the dark. She was watching TV and holding a heating pad to her shoulder.

"Come on in." She sat up straight on the bed and set the heating pad beside her on the pillow.

"So you decided to stay home?"

"I don't know." Her eyes wandered absently across the room back to the TV. "I still ain't called in—but I guess I probably should."

She moved the ashtray so he could sit at the foot of the bed. He climbed up on top and crossed his legs. They shared a cigarette while he began adjusting his plans: too rude to take Wesley's truck and go.

"So, it's your shoulder that's bothering you?"

"Shoulder. Hips. Back. Knees. It's eating me alive."

"Ouch."

She grabbed the remote control and turned down the volume on the TV, so that the screen flickered in the darkness. Some cop show was on. In an aquarium against the wall, fluorescent blue rocks and orange fish glowed brighter than a neon beer sign.

"People don't believe how painful rheumatoid arthritis can be," she said.

"I didn't realize you could get that so young." He thought of his mother, although hers was something different.

"Lots of nights I don't feel like leaving the bed, let alone going to work and wrassling some old man to the toilet."

"You shouldn't—"

"I'll go to pick up a cup of water, and it feels like my arm is going to break off at the socket. The other day my shoulder swelled up so bad, I couldn't lift my arm to put on deodorant. Duane, he tries to understand, I guess. But he can't know how bad it is. I try not to complain."

She seemed embarrassed to have said so much. There was an awkward moment of silence during which they both stared at the TV flickering in the dark.

"Hey, would you mind doing me a big favor?" She directed his attention to a cloth bag on her dresser, and he got down from the bed. It was something her mama had stitched for her, she said, a simple flannel sack full of rice inside, and it worked so much better on her pain than the electric heating pad, but she didn't like to keep getting up to stick it in the microwave.

"If you don't mind," she said. "About ninety seconds."

He stepped back through the rooms to the kitchen, looking and listening for Wesley and Duane, wondering if maybe they were still under the house. He placed the heating pad inside the new microwave and then stood staring at all the buttons, wondering which ones he was supposed press. He settled for the button labeled POPCORN and started counting to ninety. The coffee pot was full and cooking. Beside the stove there was a door ajar and a Lazy Susan inside. Bill spun the turntable, loaded with bottles of oil, honey, vinegar, until he found a Mason jar half full of a clear liquid. He opened the lid and sniffed. Strong stuff, even without bringing it to his lips. Just a sip. Whoa! Pure corn. One shot of that would set him right. Yes, it would. But that would mean goodbye, Charlotte. Goodbye, Lucy. It was a crazy plan anyway, absconding with Wesley's truck. Plus, Crystal needed somebody to talk to. He took a long pull from the jar then replaced the lid and returned the jar to the Lazy Susan.

Inside the microwave, the bag of rice was steaming. He held it by the corner and headed back toward Crystal when he had second thoughts. One more shot would fix him. He revisited the Lazy Susan. One long pull. Another for good measure. Like a river of fire pouring straight to his core. In seconds, his brain began to ignite. Walking back through the living room, he admired the furniture, a matching sofa and love seat, covered in maroon velvet. He admired the ability of his feet to make contact with the floorboards and convey him back to the bedroom.

"Did you get lost?"

"I might have cooked it too long." He held the bag by the corner and laid it on the bed. "Sorry about that."

"Look in that top dresser drawer over there and bring me a sweater."

He brought her a gray wool pullover and she wrapped it around the heating pad. He helped her stack the pillows and settle back with the heating pad behind her neck.

"I see Duane let you sample his shine."

"Uh, yeah. Pretty good stuff."

"You should be careful. It's stronger than you think."

"Yeah." He took his place at the foot of the bed and watched the rocks in the aquarium glow. Orange fish floated, immobile, staring at each other, barely flapping their fins.

"I'm leaving him," she said. "I can't stand it anymore. I want somebody who's going to treat me the way I deserve to be treated." Her voice was plain, sincere, and full of hurt. "Every night he drinks himself blind and then rants and raves, expects me to be his audience, when I just want to rest."

Bill nodded to himself in the dark and thought of Maddie, what all she had endured.

"I like your tattoo. A snake in a rose. What's it supposed to symbolize?"

"Whatever you want. I guess I was sort of drunk." He rubbed his neck. "If I had it to do over, I sure as hell wouldn't let somebody talk me into putting it right there on my neck."

"Whose idea was that?"

"Some woman's."

"I see." She laughed. "What love makes us do."

Crystal's voice reminded him of Lucy's. That same twang. She had him scoot closer then flicked the lighter and produced a flame she brought next to his neck.

"You wouldn't believe the things my ex-husband tried to talk me into."

"Like what?"

"Mmm mmm." She laughed, shaking her head. "You wouldn't believe it."

"Well? You going to keep me in suspense?"

She propped herself up from the pillows and looked out the bedroom door through the living room and out toward the front porch where Duane and Wesley now sat smoking cigars. The smoke floated in through the screen door, along with Duane's voice. He kept up a steady stream of talk, and Wesley sat there quiet, an attentive audience. Had they missed Bill yet?

"Hold on a minute." Crystal got up off the bed and rummaged through a dresser drawer and brought out a video tape that she pushed into the VCR. "If Duane knew I was showing you this, he would kill us both."

She climbed back up on the bed and sat beside him. On TV they watched what looked like a family cookout. Crystal, a few years younger and with shorter hair, sat in a lawn chair holding hands with a heavy-set man who wore hot pink shorts that exposed his hairy thighs.

"That's Victor," she said. "My ex."

"I like your hair better now." How nice it would have been to reach out and stroke her long, unruly hair. Dark red as a river in flood.

"I shouldn't be showing you this." She pushed the fast forward button on the remote control until the scene changed to an interior shot, a living room filled with modern furniture, all chrome and leather. "I miss that house," she said. "And that Jacuzzi." She pushed fast forward again, and when she pushed play she was on the screen, dancing to some Duran Duran song, wearing nothing but high heels and a sexy black bra and French-cut panties. Tanned skin. Long shapely legs. In high heels, Crystal stamped out an angry rhythm on the hardwood floor, a jaunty tap dance syncopated with a *thump thump* from her heel like a big bass drum. Occasionally the man behind the camera would suggest some movement. He wanted more striptease, but Crystal ignored his instructions. She wore a mask of indifference and changed her routine in her own good time. She threw out her hip like that old 70s dance, the bump, and then she would grind her pelvis in a slow circle. Whenever she turned around for the camera, the bra straps framed a strong, slender back, and the high-cut panties exposed half her ass cheeks, as firm as any Bill had seen at The Jackpot.

"Damn, I was in good shape. Back before my arthritis got bad."

Bill thought maybe he ought to excuse himself, go find his brother. And, yet, he could feel how Crystal needed him in a way Wesley and Duane did not.

"You're a good dancer," he said.

"Yeah, I was the dancer in my family."

"We ought to all go out dancing," he said. "I know this place called the Double Door. They have live music. Always a dance party."

"Is that where your girlfriend is tonight?"

"Hmm. Busted. You'd like her, I know you would. Yeah, I'd like for the two of you to meet."

"Duane don't ever want to go nowhere."

"Let's not give him a choice."

"Good luck with that. Plus, I do have to work."

On TV Crystal was tugging at the straps of her bra and letting them slip over her shoulders. She kept teasing the camera, all the time wearing that same pout. "That's about all I better show you." She pushed the fast forward and the TV picture changed to another family gathering.

"Maybe when you get to know me better," he joked, "you'll let me see the rest."

"Victor wanted to make other tapes, too," she said. "He wanted to set up the camera in our bedroom. I wouldn't let him." Her voice broke, and she cast her eyes down at the cigarette smoldering in the ashtray, shame clear on her face. "I'm worried he may have hid a camera without my knowing. He was always doing stuff like that. Before we split up, I found sex tapes he made with other women right in our living room."

The screen door slammed and they both turned as Duane came clomping in from the front porch. In two seconds he was standing in the doorway holding a beer and staring at the two of them sitting on the bed in the dark.

"I see she got you to watch her smut tape," he said.

"I didn't show him any dirty parts."

"I really wish you would get rid of that thing."

"It's mine," she said. "I like to be able to see what I looked like when I was young and in good shape."

"You like to show it off," he said. "Bill here is my first cousin. Don't you think it's sort of tacky to show my cousin a movie of you stripping?"

"I didn't let him see me stripping!" She grabbed the remote and switched the TV off then eased down from the bed and hobbled over to the closet. She violently shoved a bunch of hanging clothes out of the way and picked out a blouse.

"Crystal, what are you doing?"

"I gotta get ready for work."

"They said you don't have to go. You just need to call them. I bet you never called."

"Well."

"How you plan on getting there?" In the aquarium light, Duane's features looked even harder. You could tell they were cousins: the square chin, the Porter eyes. But Duane's features were more sharply cut—a heavy brow and a sharp beak that had clearly been broken more than once. When they were kids, Bill had always aimed for that nose.

"I wish you would have said something," Duane said. "Before I started drinking."

"Bill said he would drive me."

Bill glanced at Crystal, as if to explain he was in no condition, but her eyes were locked with Duane's in a fierce struggle.

Duane turned to Bill. "Are you sober?"

Crystal stretched out a hand to wrap around Bill's wrist. She stepped closer, settled on the side of the bed next to him. He felt the warmth of her, felt her body weight communicate itself through the mattress.

"Yeah," he lied. "I'm sober." He hadn't meant to get involved in these people's lives. The only thing he had wanted tonight was to find Lucy and let her help him believe his love wasn't entirely in vain.

Duane looked down at him and then over at the TV. "I don't reckon my own cousin would snake me." He finished the beer and tossed the empty bottle into a metal trash can. It crashed against a bed of empties. He stared across the room at Crystal. She wouldn't turn around, just kept sorting through her closet, angrily rejecting blouse after blouse.

Duane clomped back toward the porch but stopped with a hand on the screen door, letting it squeak open and then ease shut. He turned and slowly shuffled back toward them till he stood in the shadows outside the bedroom. He grunted curses underneath his breath. Then, measuring his words like an old-fashioned orator, Duane announced to them, "Goddamn the man that ever invented the camcorder."

18

Wesley had so many questions, but before he could come up with the right words, Bill had passed out on the sofa. He snored louder than Daddy's saw mill, like he was about to rip the sofa in half. One leg falling over the side, a Nerf football clutched to his chest, his other hand gripping the fifth of bourbon on the coffee table.

If Bill wasn't Lucy's boyfriend—and he claimed he wasn't—what exactly was the nature of their relationship? The way he had danced with her, the way she had let him grab her ass and pull her close, suggested a certain intimacy. But maybe a woman who stripped for a living held different attitudes about physical proximity. Maybe it was only dancing, after all. But that big blue butterfly, and that thing on his neck. Wesley took the bourbon from his brother's hand and replaced it—what was left—to the cupboard. Then he let the screen door bang shut behind him and stepped outside to sit on the cinder block steps. Summer was here again. Manic cicadas sang high in the trees. Through the woods, across the pasture, his mother's bedroom light shone. Every night when he worked late or was visiting Duane, she listened for his screen door to bang shut. That was her way of knowing when he arrived safely home. And every time he heard it rattle against the jamb, he was aware of her hearing it two hundred yards away through the night.

Maybe Bill was right about the family property. They weren't farmers. Eighty-two acres were more than either of them would ever need. Certainly Bill had as much right to it one day as Wesley. All Wesley wanted was enough for a home and a garden. That ten-acre piece around Uncle Olin's old lot, the Porter homeplace, he'd always had his eye on that. He had always just assumed that one day Daddy would help him build a home there, maybe right over the original foundation stones. But no need to get the cart in front of the horse. First, he needed a wife. Any time he tried to love a woman, it took him forever to get comfortable with her. And they never wanted to wait. What a shock this morning, flesh against flesh. His head so thick it was a part of the room. Her right there beside him in bed, like a gift from heaven—or hell—strange and beautiful, still deep in sleep, her hand thrown across his chest, skin that screamed for every bit of his attention, skin that wouldn't leave him alone, even later when he sat at his mother's breakfast table. Even now.

Much of the previous night came back only in washes of color, fragments of sentences, parts of songs. His brother's grinning face at the cottage door like a ghost out in the darkness, and women's laughter. Then the door swinging open and two women, solid flesh, moving across the floor in spiked heels and evening gowns cut low down the front. Lucy was dressed in black silk, with those tattoos up and down her arms. "They're in show business," Bill had explained and then walked straight to the kitchen, rifling through the cabinets until he came up with four Mason jars that he set on the table beside a bottle of tequila.

She had sauntered right over to where Wesley sat hunched over his computer and plopped herself down on his lap. He remembered that first contact of their flesh, where her gown gaped open and the backs of her thighs rested against his knees as she placed her tattooed arms around his neck and leaned back to smile at him. "You writing me a love letter?"

He'd tried to explain his work, nervously going on and on about the commercialization of agriculture, the emergence of the textile industry, the erosion of subsistence farming culture, and all the while she played with his hair.

"Bill never said you were so cute."

"Don't get too attached to him," Bill warned.

"He wouldn't have to sleep in *my* bathtub," Alice said.

There had been dancing, first the women loosening up together, and then Bill cutting in to try to teach them both how to shag. And then sometime later, after the booze was working hard in Wesley, her trying to show him how to salsa, saying, "Just move your hips, you feel salsa in the hips, feel it?" until she finally gave up on him and he sat alone in the corner watching her and Bill grinding their hips to the music.

By the time Wesley found himself alone with her, while she scanned the trail ahead with a flashlight and they stumbled down the hill past his watermelon patch, through that stand of poplar trees with their bat-shaped leaves, and then up the ridge to the old Porter homeplace, he might as well have been walking on the surface of another planet.

Lately this had become a familiar feeling. It seemed the more he discovered about the history of his people and this spot of earth they had inhabited, the more displaced he felt.

What skills did he possess that anyone needed? He had a strong back and could lift heavy bags from a tram to the belly of an airplane. But he could not tan leather or milk a cow or fix machinery or shoe horses or make pottery. All the many tasks he had heard old people describe in detail— which he had tape-recorded and then transcribed—he could not do one of them himself. Never mind plowing a field with a team of mules, which Grandpa had done at the age of ten—never mind that; Wesley could not even drive a tractor. Whenever he tried, one of his parents would be there in front of him, afraid he might hurt himself. "That tractor is temperamental," his mother would say. He had probably never fully appreciated the blow to his manhood of watching his sixty-four-year-old mother climb up to the driver's seat of that tractor to plow a field under.

No matter how hard he worked out with the weights, or how much overtime he pulled toting luggage at the airport, he never felt that he was gaining mass. Even when the evidence was there in the mirror, or from the comments of coworkers, he felt like the same little boy covered in baby fat who had tried for years to muster the courage to fight back against Bill.

He went to check on his brother, still snoring on the sofa. Wesley pulled him up by the shoulders and helped him stumble to the bedroom where he flopped down in the middle of the mattress. Wesley rolled Bill to one side and then stretched out beside him, pulling a pillow to his chest to feel the weight, imagining it was her weight pressing him deeper into the mattress. When the sawmill in Bill's nose and throat started grinding again, Wesley stuffed the pillow over his head, and when that didn't work, he got up and moved to the sofa.

LATER THAT NIGHT, after he had lain sleepless listening to his brother snore from the bedroom, trying to focus instead on the cicadas purring in the trees, he heard a car pull up outside and then Preacher crawling out from underneath the cottage, barking like mad. He lay there thinking maybe it was Duane. Duane had been pretty upset about Crystal going into work and Bill driving her. Wesley waited for the knock, rubbed at his eyes, and slipped on a T-shirt and shorts. He shuffled to the door and looked outside for the headlights. Only darkness. He stepped out onto the cinderblock steps and let his eyes adjust, then he saw the ghost of a Corvette. He felt the panic rise as the white door swung open and she stepped out.

"I'm sorry," she said, standing there by the driver's side. "I didn't mean to wake you up. Did I wake you up? I only wanted to sit out here a while. I was visiting my mama, yeah, and then some friends in the country, and it's a long way to Charlotte, and I thought maybe I could spend the night out here in my car, in this bucket seat, which is almost like a bed. If you don't mind."

"Well . . . why don't you come inside."

"Do you mind?" She reached through the driver's window for her purse and then carefully stepped across the muddy ruts. He propped the screen door open for her.

"Did you want to talk to Bill? Good luck." He nodded toward the sound of ragged snoring from the other room.

"Actually, I was hoping for another invitation to breakfast." She barked a laugh. "Your mother's cooking is the best food I ever put in my mouth. I've been thinking all day about that crispy bacon crumbled in those creamy grits. You don't, by chance, have a cigarette?"

He walked into the bedroom and found Bill's carton of Marlboro Lights, empty.

"Fuck," she said. "I really need a cigarette." She looked around his cottage, everywhere but in his face. "Nerves. I've got the nerves. I'm so fucking wired." She sat on the sofa and pulled off her clunky boots, then sat there with her legs crossed, swinging a foot. Those fishnet stockings covered her legs and all those tattoos.

He went to the refrigerator and found an open bottle of Duane's scuppernong wine. "Here," he said. "Good for the nerves."

They clinked tumblers and she drank a long swallow. She smelled of cigarettes and perfume, honeysuckles running riot over the ashes of a family homeplace.

"I feel bad coming out here and getting you out of bed." She rifled through her purse, shook her head, and got up to walk around the room, like she needed to burn off the energy.

"It's okay. If you need a place to stay, I can roll Bill out of bed. I don't think he'll notice."

"I'm not going to be able to sleep tonight."

"Well, hang out. I haven't been able to sleep either."

She stepped to the entrance of the bedroom and moved the curtain aside to let the light fall in on the bed where Bill lay snoring. Wesley felt a stab of jealousy.

"It still surprises me," she said.

"What's that?"

"Your brother being so willing to cover himself in ink. Everything he has to lose. One of these mornings he's going to wake up and hate my guts."

"Why did you do it to *yourself?*" Wesley asked and then was sorry he had. He surprised himself sometimes with these stupid outbursts.

She shot him an angry glance. "You don't like my tattoos?"

"I do. I mean, like you said, it's a commitment."

At the screen door Wesley's dog stood and whined to be petted.

"Preacher!" Wesley said in an admonishing tone.

"What did you call him?"

"Preacher. My mother always thought I'd be a minister of the Gospel, said her family had produced a preacher in every generation. So, I didn't want her to have to go without."

"That's funny."

"Preacher Claude is his full name, after her uncle."

"Can I let him in?"

"Better not. That long hair gets filthy. Preacher is an outside dog." Mother had impressed upon Wesley from an early age the idea that dogs and cats lived outside.

She walked past his computer, over to the wall where he had taped the collage of family trees.

"All these your cousins?"

"Probably. If you trace it far enough."

"That's amazing."

If that was sarcasm, he ignored it. "Yeah. If you let yourself study those charts very long, it's pretty mind-blowing. The hundreds of connections."

"I can't imagine your people and mine are related. Mine don't have a homeplace, unless you count a mobile home."

"Didn't you say you're from Gaston County?"

"No, but close. Near Crouse."

He nodded. Maybe it was coincidental—the coal black hair, her sloping nose, the fair skin like his mother's. Underneath the tattoos, she looked a lot like his mother's people. He felt the tug of kinship, of likeness seeking out likeness. He asked about her parents, her grandparents, but didn't recognize the family names.

"I could tell you a little about my mother's boyfriend," she said. "And that would tell you all you need to know."

"What's that?"

She shook her head and stepped over to the screen door. He had said something to upset her. What did she need, want? Space or his presence? Was he, could he be, any sort of comfort?

"Last night," she said. "Was it last night?"

"What's that?"

"When you took me on that walk. Over to your dead uncle's homeplace."

"*Great* uncle. Olin. Yeah."

"I've been thinking all day how peaceful it is there. Under the moon."

Then it wasn't just him, she had felt it, too. The two of them sitting in the grass in the middle of the old foundation stones, all that was left after the demolition, after the lumber had been carted away. Their own mini-Stonehenge. Those many hours he had spent with the scythe and the wheelbarrow, the push mower, clearing the site, little had he known the reason—until now.

"You're a good listener," she said. "All those old people talking your ear off, and you *care* about what they tell you."

"Some pretty fascinating life stories—"

"I'll bet you could listen to me, if I needed to tell something about my past."

"Yeah, of course."

"My totally fucked up childhood."

He waited for her to say more, but she turned away and stared out into the night.

Wesley stood up from his chair, stood and watched, before shuffling over to her side. Her breathing came ragged, and she pressed her face against the mesh of the screen door. Maybe she needed this moment to herself. He moved a little closer and patted her back in a friendly way, then he let his hand move across her shoulders and slowly pulled her into him. Outside, high in the trees, the cicadas purred a lullaby. He held her loosely and rocked her back and forth. She looked up at him with the eyes of a cornered animal, if an animal could add blackest shame to rage. He wanted to tell her it was okay to talk. He was there to listen. It was okay to cry. But he just held her and waited.

She turned again and reached for him. With both hands she gripped his arm and held onto him as if for dear life. He felt himself unconsciously flex. He wanted her to feel his strength, to know that he was a rock she could cling to. He looked down at her sharp knuckles. Beneath her nails digging in, his biceps grew huge. She buried her face in his chest. With her trembling against him, he was a giant. Like a watermelon in July, he could feel his entire self swelling, taking on size and mass before his very eyes.

"You should spend the night," he said into her ear. "You can have the bed all to yourself. I'm fine on the sofa. I can put Bill on the floor. It's a soft bed." Usually he was a listener, not a talker, but he could tell she needed him to talk, so he gave himself over to useless palaver, just sounds meant to soothe. "It's quiet here at night. You've got the cicadas ringing in the trees. No streetlights."

When she finally responded, her voice was steadier. "What time does your mama serve breakfast?"

It was a question that shouldn't have been so hard to answer, he knew that, but he was stunned into silence. He could not find his voice. And before he did, she stiffened and stepped away from him. Brushing the hair out of her face, taking deep cleansing breaths, she gathered herself, then stepped across the room for her boots and her purse.

"Tell her I said hello. Your mama. Tell her that was the best food I ever put in my mouth."

19

Sometime later that night or early the next morning, Wesley sat on the cinderblock steps of his cottage and stared up through the tree limbs to the fragments of constellations shining through. He didn't know their names; astronomy was his brother's thing, but Bill had once showed him a few of the shapes that Wesley sometimes still was able to recognize. Wesley had been up and down from the sofa for hours without sleeping. His brother's snores droned on from inside. Up in the oaks, the summer's first cicadas purred together at exactly the same pitch, one choral voice, hollow and resonant. They filled the woods.

His hands still remembered the touch of her skin, her body shaking in his arms. Why when she asked about breakfast had he frozen? It was just breakfast. Up on the hill the lights were off, but that was no guarantee that his mother was sleeping. He ran his fingers along his dog's back, patted his rump, scratched behind the ears. He knew how to bring that dog to ecstasy. Unconsciously, he searched through Preacher's blond coat for ticks. He pulled off half a dozen, swollen with blood, and tossed them as far as he could into the dark.

Preacher heard it first and set in to barking. Wesley saw it moving toward him before he heard the quiet rattle of gravel under its belly, a curved line zigzagging across the drive. There was something about the sight of a snake curling along the ground that made you want to catch it, even if you were afraid. He had touched snakes. He had even handled tamed ones, but the last time he had caught a snake from the wild he was eleven years old, when Bill had lifted the tail of a sleeping king and had forced him to grab its head.

The light from his cottage shone out across the drive enough to tell that the snake was solid black and maybe three feet long, moving slow. He knew he could not hesitate and that he would have one chance, that he must reach directly for the head.

Cool like he remembered. Surprisingly smooth, and coiling around his forearm, constricting with a force that would make a rodent's heart stop from fear. Wesley felt his own heart pounding in his throat. He held the head trapped in his fist, maybe too tightly, and walked to the light of his doorstep to see this thing he had caught writhe about his forearm. He felt his own pulse, rapid against its constricting body, and thought how nature shows on TV had not prepared him for this moment. He held the head firm, but stroked its belly and watched the lidless eyes and flickering tongue. He stood in the light of his doorstep and watched for probably ten minutes while the black knot pulsed around his wrist, until finally it seemed to wear out, and then gradually he relaxed his grip, letting go a bit, but still holding on, while they both got used to each other. No hurry. He couldn't get to sleep now, anyway. He stood there under the stars, watching and waiting, until eventually it seemed as though the coils around his forearm were no longer something alien but, rather, a part of him. Familiar and comforting. Like a lover's slow, tight caress.

20

When Wesley's mother woke him early the next morning, Bill lay still snoring on his side of the bed. Mother stood at the screen door waiting until Wesley got himself dressed. She said she only needed him for fifteen minutes to help mulch the tomatoes. It was hard for her to bend over that far.

He spread the sheets of newspaper and covered them with hay while she gave him an update on Grandpa's decline. She told him about the church homecoming that weekend, wondering if he would be free to set up tables and chairs. And then she asked the question he had been expecting.

"Who was your company last night?" She stood above him, while he sprawled on his hands and knees pulling the bricks of hay apart.

"One of Bill's friends."

"Which one? One of those women?"

"Yeah. Lucy."

"I never dreamed he would do this. I'm going to have a talk with him. It's one thing for him to impose on you and keep you up half the night with his wild talk and his drinking. He kept *me* up. I could hear him all the way up the hill. That's one thing, but for him to bring those women down there. Did he take your bed?"

"Mother, it's not like that. Last night, Bill was asleep. She came to see *me*."

"I see."

"We just talked. She's had it rough. She just needed somebody to listen."

"She's the one that's covered herself in those tattoos?"

"Yeah."

"Mm hmm. It's a pity. Such a pretty girl." She dropped a pile of hay and he spread it over the newspaper. "You be careful, son. Don't you let that brother of yours lead you into places you don't need to go."

"Mother, all I did was listen."

"Mm hmm."

But, of course, she hadn't talked, except to ask for breakfast. Why hadn't he offered to cook her breakfast himself? He knew how to fry an egg. But it wasn't his food she had wanted. What was it his mother had that he lacked? Or his brother? Women looked at him, but as soon as he had to talk, something always changed between them. He saw it happen at work and even in casual exchanges at the supermarket.

"Oh yeah," he said, tasting bitter bile in his throat. "She wanted me to thank you for breakfast."

"What's that?"

He turned away so that his mother wouldn't see him scowl. "She said it was the best food she ever put in her mouth."

21

Bill pounded nails until his ears rang. He made such a racket with the hammer that he almost forgot his father's frown when Bill had showed up two hours late for work. He had wanted to say, "Listen now, old man, a volunteer sets his own hours," but he had seen Daddy staring at the rose tattoo. Four years in the Marines and Daddy had made it out with clean skin, without an anchor or an eagle or the name of a woman.

The three of them sweated together under the sun now high in the sky. The pine skeleton of walls supported half a dozen rafters waiting for a roof. It took the three of them to manhandle and then nail down the rafters: Daddy and Bill and Rodney, Bill's blind cousin, part of the Porter clan. Earlier that year Rodney had lost his driver's license and then his warehouse job when his poor eyesight had deteriorated to the point of legal blindness. Building this house, Rodney said, had saved his life. He had always wanted a house of his own but never thought he could afford it, and when Joe Becker offered to deed him an acre of land and help him buy the building materials, even offered his skills free of charge, it was the most generous thing anyone had ever done for him. Bill's father had been there with him from the digging of the foundation, to the laying of the block, the framing. All morning long, Rodney sang Joe Becker's praises.

By the time they stopped for lunch, Bill could feel the sunburn on the back of his neck, and he had sweated out most of his gloom along with last night's bourbon. His mother brought them Pepsis and burgers from Hardee's, and when he stepped to the back of the lot to take a leak, he pulled the flask out of his nail apron and sweetened his Pepsi.

The air was saturated with the smells of drying cement, sawdust, red earth broken by a bulldozer's blade. That red Piedmont clay.

He turned around to study the skeleton of pine studs framing the walls, a simple, functional design, so different from the collection of bizarre angles that made up any one of the computer-designed houses in Eagle's Pointe. Daddy had built dozens and dozens of them from the ground up. Back in the seventies he had seen the boom in Charlotte for what it was: his ticket out of the cotton mill. Even to the most humble man, *general contractor* had to sound a lot better than *lint head*, and the change let him be outdoors while doubling his income. With or without a crew, he could do it all: from surveying the lot, to laying the blocks of the foundation, to all of the carpentry and plumbing and electrical work. They were skills any bright and industrious man with the proper teacher could learn. And Bill could not help but consider how the skills he himself had spent the last ten years acquiring seemed dishonest and insubstantial by comparison. Instead of *building* something, instead of sweating and wielding a hammer out in the sunshine, he had learned how to *communicate*. In any situation he could determine exactly what needed to be said, *how* it needed to be said, whether to a new customer or to a group of rank-and-file employees, or to his boss, or his boss's boss. He wasn't worried about finding a new job; there would always be a place for him in the Information Age. But he could never think of the right words for the man who straddled a ladder on wobbly legs, his aging daddy who went deafer with every stroke of the hammer.

Mother left the men to eat their lunches, and when his father bolted his burger and climbed the ladder to measure off spaces for the rest of the rafters, Rodney moved closer to Bill and spoke in a whisper.

"It ain't none of my business," he said, twirling his hammer. "And, look, I'm the last person to tell somebody what to do." His blind eyes drifted toward the sound of Bill's father on the ladder. "But I wouldn't let Joe catch that on your breath. I know from talking with him, he don't hold with drinking on the job."

"Just a little pick-me-up. That's all. Rough night, you know."

Rodney grinned and nodded. "Yeah. I know."

Bill felt the anger burning him again. It wasn't more than a half pint of whiskey. He could knock that back and smile through the rest of the day. But he saved it. He wandered over to the truck and shuffled through the glove box for a jawbreaker from Daddy's stash. Maybe lemon-lime would cover the booze on his breath.

After the jawbreaker dissolved and left his mouth sticky, he switched back to whiskey and tried to wash the slime of sugar off his teeth. He rationed it out, so that every time he descended his ladder to take a leak or get a drink of water from the spigot at the well house, he would sneak a shot and climb the ladder with doubled stamina—until sometime around the late part of the afternoon when his legs started to go out from under him and he found himself holding onto the rafters to keep his balance.

He pounded the nails. Four strokes of the hammer was all it took. Sometimes three. One summer during his childhood—he could not have been older than ten—he had been helping Daddy lay down shingles and then the ridge cap on a new roof, and he had accidentally dripped black tar on his legs. He remembered the smell of gasoline on a rag when Daddy washed off the tar. When Bill looked down and saw the color of his skin changing from brown to pale white, he jerked back and shouted for Daddy to stop. "It's washing off my tan!" he said, and Daddy let out a roar of belly-laughter, then explained that it was only the dust of red mud from where Bill hadn't taken a bath. Bill held still, letting Daddy dip the rag in gas and then rub off the spots of tar, watching his tan wash away and leave those lily-white legs. Even at that tender age he had been vain about his skin.

He pounded the nails, keeping up with his old man now. Three strokes and on to the next.

"Bill might be helping us build his house next." Daddy's grin spread wide around the bush of his mustache. His joy showed in his eyes. He spoke to Rodney, but Bill knew Daddy meant it for him.

"I hope he don't mind living in a house built by a blind man," Rodney said.

"He probably needs something bigger," Daddy said.

"Not me," Bill said. "Right now the only thing I need is six feet to lay my head."

"Well, when you and Maddie get back together. There's a nice spot on that pasture over that way." Daddy pointed. "Over above that stand of white pines. You know where I'm talking about?"

"Yeah." He remembered. *All this will be yours one day*— those were the unspoken words he heard his father say. All his life, Daddy had labored for his family. And these eighty-two acres satisfied him only because he would be able to pass them on. Nothing would make Daddy happier than to help his sons build homes on family land, homes where they would each settle down with a woman and children.

"How's your hands holding out, Ace?" Daddy smiled down at him. "You might ought to wear gloves. Your hands'll blister if they're not used to a hammer."

"They're okay." He looked at his red palms, at the blisters rising beneath the skin, and he felt the pain he had been numb to. That pet name, *Ace*, he hadn't heard it in years. He wished he knew how to let Daddy show tenderness, when he chose to, without Bill flinching.

"You need some more nails? Here you go." Daddy came toward him with a box of nails, and Bill froze. He could have climbed the ladder. He could have taken them from his daddy's fist, but he stood still and let the old man pull the apron open. Rodney must have heard it from twenty feet away, the sound of the big sixteen-pennies thudding against the empty flask.

He only glanced up at his father's eyes to see the confusion giving way to profound disappointment. Then Bill climbed the ladder and began pounding the nails. His face burned. His head swam. But he kept pounding nails, focusing on the angry rhythms of three hammers. Even when Rodney tried to joke and draw them out, there was nothing left for Bill or his father to say. They worked for maybe another half hour, until Daddy stepped down his ladder, wiped his forehead on a towel covered with sawdust, and said they would quit early.

Bill carried his step ladder to Daddy's truck. He pushed the base of the ladder into the bed, all the way to the cab. He went back for the box of nails and collected the three hammers. He carried them to the truck and then asked Daddy what they would leave and what else they would take home. He carried the circular saw and the extension cord. He carried the chalk line, the square, a power drill, the tape ruler, and a gallon of paint. That made the end of Daddy's list. Quitting time. He knew he needed to set things straight, but how? Daddy didn't care much for empty apologies.

He stood out in front of the truck and watched Rodney feel his way to the passenger seat. "That's all the tools, Daddy. Unless you need me, I'll just walk on home. I've been wanting to walk back through those woods again. I want to see how much that stand of white pines has grown."

"Come here a second."

As a child, Bill had been spanked once at home, by his father with an open palm. After that, Daddy had never tried it again. They were not violent people. They were not genteel, but they were gentle.

Daddy looked down at his work boots and crunched a piece of candy between his teeth. "I appreciate your helping us out today. That was the hard part, lifting them rafters." Bill followed his glance back to the skeleton roof, just waiting to be covered with plywood and shingles. "I can't pay you the kind of money you're used to making," Daddy said. "And you're too old for me to tell you how to live your life." He looked Bill square in the eyes. "But I've never been able to work with a drinker. If you show up here tomorrow, I expect you to leave your liquor at home."

22

Bill sweetened his Pepsi. The bourbon was ice cold from the cooler. Another inch, two. He put down his book after reading the same paragraph over for the third time. It was nice just to sit back in the sun and relax, look out toward the main channel at the sails swelling full of wind. Thinking about his life was so much easier out under the sun, where even the most painful decisions were softened by the smell of lotion and the intermittent breeze and the constant heat on his body.

Two women sat together upwind of his smoke, with their legs dipped in the shallow end while they watched their children playing Marco Polo. Deep tans, those moms probably did a lot of babysitting out here. According to Kent, there were always women here, every day of the week. Even with the extra pounds, the brunette wasn't bad looking. Not bad at all. From behind his sunglasses, he kept an eye on her and thought maybe when she looked up from her son, she was staring back through her own shades. He thought of carrying a drink over to her. But, no, they looked like the kind of women who would be frightened by a man with tattoos. Still, having them close by helped ease the heartache—his encounter with Lucy last night at The Jackpot. He had borrowed money from Wesley without explaining why. He'd sat alone at that table in the purple light, waiting for her to wander over his way. She'd seen him and kept her distance. He waited for her to finish a lap dance, and then he took her by the elbow and asked for five minutes of her time, just to talk, just so she could tell him what was going on. Please.

"Nothing," she said. "Nothing is going on."

"Is there another man?"

She shook her head.

And, then, remembering the other morning at the cottage, "Is Wesley—" but she had already turned away.

He had to put that woman out of his mind. Just lie back in the sun, puff the stogie, and release every ounce of negative energy—Lucy's snub, Maddie's disappearance from his life, all the debt, Mother and Daddy's disappointment, the non-existent job market, and this string of bad dreams he'd been having. Last night he'd dreamed he was helping Daddy shingle the roof they had started, and his daddy had walked along the ridgeline to Bill carrying a bucket of tar. He'd handed the bucket and a spatula to Bill and said tar was good for cancer, that he ought to take care of that one on his neck. When Bill felt his neck, he found the rose had infected and was now growing a cancerous lesion. And when he looked up, he saw the same cancer on his daddy's neck, a blue rose, its petals swelling to monstrous proportions. Then, suddenly, there stood his brother, his mother, his cousin Rodney, all with grotesque protuberances swelling from different parts of their bodies. This morning over his hangover coffee he had asked Wesley if he ever worried about cancer.

"No, can't say as I do," Wesley responded.

"Mother and Daddy?"

"They've been clean of cancer, both of them have, for nearly half my lifetime."

"Mother got it so young."

"Well, that's the way with women and breast cancer sometimes. I often wonder if she regrets letting that doctor cut her to pieces. She did it for us, you know. She didn't want to risk you and me not having a mother."

What worried Bill was how some people said cancer often responded to some singular event, some particular stressor.

It could even start with an individual who brings chaos into your life, compromises your immune system, rearranges your cellular structure.

HE SAT BY THE POOL long after the two women had taken their children home. The sun had dropped behind the trees bordering the pool, and he had to move his chair to keep the light on his body. It must have been six o'clock when the black truck with the deep freezer in the bed pulled into the parking lot. He set his cigar down and stuck his fingers in the sides of his mouth and whistled. He jumped up and waved his arms in the air.

Kent walked up wearing a tie and a long-sleeved shirt soaked through with sweat down the back and underneath his armpits. Bill had a bourbon and Pepsi ready for him.

"I wish you would've called and told me you were coming," Kent said. "I've got somewhere to go tonight." He fidgeted with his tie as he told Bill about the Society meeting. The Society for Creative Anachronism was a group of people who dressed up like medieval knights and ladies. "They're historians," Kent said. "But they're more than that. It's all about honor and chivalry. You leave your own identity behind and take on a new one."

"It sounds like *Dungeons & Dragons* to me," Bill said.

"I'm thinking about joining."

"Well, whatever. But do you have to go tonight?" He handed Kent the half-smoked cigar. "Try that. Cuban seed," he lied.

"Not bad," Kent said, a cloud of white smoke spiraling away in the breeze. "How's the family?"

"Better off without me."

"Okay?"

"I thought maybe we could grill a couple steaks," Bill said. "Sit out here by the pool, drink some beer, maybe play some poker. And then if we don't get too drunk, we get dressed up and hit The Jackpot. It's Thursday night, brother. The weekend is here!"

He saw Kent hesitate.

"Is there enough bourbon in your drink?" He fingered a wedge of lime and squeezed it into Kent's cup. "Man, you need to take off those clothes. Come out here and relax with me."

"Well, I've got an hour or so before the meeting. I need to get the meat inside."

"I'll help you with that." Bill swallowed the rest of his drink and tossed his cup into the cooler. He put on his shirt and his flip flops. "I've made a decision. Listen, you've got to help me celebrate tonight. I've made a life decision. If your offer still stands, I'd like to be partners. And if you think you could put me up for a while. Not every night. Just, say, weekends and maybe Thursday nights. Maybe some Wednesdays. Just to give little Wesley a break." He took in the scene around him. He breathed in deep the smell of chlorine water and burning charcoal. The sound of a stereo blasting classic Beach Boys carried across the lake from a boat at anchor. The water in the pool was bluer than the sky above.

"You're sure about this?" Kent smiled and loosened the knot in his tie. "Damn, boy, you've been in the sun. You're brown as a fresh turd."

"Yeah." Bill held up his palm and waited until Kent slapped it high five. "I'm sure. I've been lying here thinking all day. Just call me Steak Man, Steak Man."

[Visit Fugitive Views, Southern Fried Karma's YouTube channel, to discover more about the struggle for civil rights in Charlotte.]

Part III

23

While disco thumped on the stereo, Bill stared out the tinted glass at passing shadows. Miles and miles of dark countryside, an occasional porch light. When they at last came to the edge of Charlotte, something approaching *esprit de corps* had settled over the foursome, huddled together in the leather gut of this beast. The stretch limo was top-of-the-line. Full bar. Kent had spared no expense. Bill watched him fill Duane's glass with ice, pour gin on top, add a splash of tonic, a slice of lime. Wesley, who usually drank in extreme moderation, was sucking the booze off ice cubes and holding his glass out for more. Only Bill abstained. Cut glass decanters. Probably cheap stuff in fancy bottles, but who cared? Bourbon, scotch, gin, vodka, tequila, rum—the big six. Every kind of mixer, sweet Vermouth and bitters, maraschino cherries—all of it free—and here he sat perversely sober, in charge of his little brother. It was bad enough to drag him along to The Jackpot; Bill couldn't stand the thought of Wesley watching him belly flop into that cesspool. Actually, he had been toying with the idea of visiting an AA meeting, just to check it out, something Maddie had been suggesting for years.

Duane kept begging the limo driver to change the music, but the man understood little English. He kept nodding his head in rhythm to the beat and saying, "Is good? You like?"

Duane asked again about the occasion. "Why the stretch limo?"

Bill and Kent exchanged a look.

"Let's just say," Kent replied, raising a toast, "we're celebrating international travel."

It certainly wasn't Bill's place to say any more, to explain how five years ago on this day Kent had returned north to the U.S. border and surrendered himself to the authorities, how every summer he celebrated the anniversary of his time in Mexico by throwing a week-long party, his own private Mardi Gras. And tonight was Fat Tuesday, the grand debauch. Kent kept telling them all how the party was on him, so don't hold back.

Wesley smoothed his hand across his hair and looked into the mirror above Bill's head. Only then did Bill realize his brother's hair wasn't simply wet from the shower, but that it was slicked back with some kind of product.

Maybe it was simply the result of his self-imposed sobriety, but all these signs of life—the electronic music, the drink, the rough humor of men—felt forced and sad, an unnecessary redundancy. He watched Kent's cherubic face as he danced in his seat to the loud disco. Kent had to know they were coming to the end of something, and not only Mardi Gras. Those first nights Kent had dragged him to The Jackpot had been a revelation Bill was still trying to untangle. But to keep returning? The idea of Mexico had never been to set down roots there.

The limo driver pulled up to the curb beneath flashing lights: neon nudes dancing around a pot of gold, red cherries raining coins. Kent led the entourage. After paying their way, he held open the heavy door padded with black leather. Across the darkened room, men sat at tables like cattle, their noses pointed at the woman dancing on stage in a silver thong. Bill watched Wesley stop just inside the doors, like he had stepped into wet cement. Kent took him by the elbow and kept them all moving toward the stage. A group of men were standing to leave.

"We'll get the front row," Kent said.

"Good," Bill said. "Maybe we'll save some money." It was a lot cheaper than paying for table dances all night long.

"I told you *I'm* paying."

The tall, blond dancer slid her bare feet across the stage and tossed her hair in time to Guns N' Roses' "Paradise City." Bill took his seat on the aisle, next to his brother, beneath a blaring speaker mounted above the runway. Already the bass was hurting his ears. Duane had put on a white dress shirt to match the Becker brothers, and the three of them glowed purple in the black lights. Bill knew what was coming. Eventually those women would have their paws all over Wesley.

Kent brought them a round of Coronas with lime wedges shoved into the long necks. Bill passed his on to Duane. He jealously watched his cousin, double-fisted, chug one and then the other. It was just beer. Damn, couldn't he even allow himself a beer? They were sitting along a runway that extended from the main stage into the audience, and on both sides dollar bills, creased lengthwise, tilted against brown bottles. Proceeding one man at a time, she would stop and dance, stare lovingly into his eyes, caress her breasts, run a palm along her open thighs, whatever it took until the man leaned back, satisfied, and lifted the dollar up into the air, where she raised the garter and let him slide it next to her skin. What an awful lot of work for a dollar. Still, those dollars added up. Bill checked his wallet. Selling meat door to door was generating cash flow, but not enough to waste.

"Where's your girlfriend?" Wesley mumbled in his ear. "I thought she was supposed to be here."

"Girlfriend?" The joke had grown stale. "Lucy will show up when she gets good and ready."

"You reckon Crystal will ever speak to any of us again?" Wesley said.

"I told her she could come." Duane shrugged and tried to look unworried. "She's probably on the phone with my mama now."

Bill hoped not. If Aunt Rachel found out, so would his mother, and then she would be all over him for dragging little Wesley along. Screw that, Wesley was a big boy, he could make his own choices. But Bill couldn't forget the look in Crystal's eyes when that limo had pulled into her carport, its eight cylinders purring. Only then had Duane explained where they were headed. Bill had just brought Crystal a rice bag warm from the microwave for her knees. They were all sitting around the kitchen table sharing a pot of coffee when Kent had knocked at the door.

Next on stage was a skinny young woman in a floral print bikini, a top hat, and a tuxedo coat with tails.

"I can't believe the young'uns they let up there." Duane laughed and raised his beer in a toast to the dancer on stage.

Okay, you were not supposed to acknowledge out loud the age difference. Cousin Duane had never understood the distinction between things you said and things you just thought privately to yourself.

"She hurts my periscope," Duane said.

"Behave," Bill said.

The women danced to an eclectic playlist: Donna Summer, Def Leppard, Garth Brooks. They wore teddies in every color of the rainbow, long gowns, mini-skirts.

Wesley leaned close and asked again, "So . . . you think she's dancing tonight?"

On the other side, Kent eased his head in close to hear Bill's answer.

"How should I know?" Bill said. "You've slept with her more recently than I have." Every day that she refused to return his calls, the memory of her dark hair spilling over his brother's pillow pissed him off a little bit more. And *had* they just been sleeping? The benefit of doubt was wearing thin.

At the top of the hour, a fog machine poured smoke across the stage. Into those perfumed vapors, angels descended from on high. Every dancer in the house paraded along the catwalk and in her heels tramped down the stairs into the club. They mingled and flirted, waiting for men to pull out the big money and buy private dances. They flocked young Studly. Wrapping their feather boas around Wesley's neck, they gyrated and pirouetted, they belly-danced. After Wesley kept sitting on his hands and staring dumbly up at them, they floated away on the thumping bass line, the strobing lights.

Kent leaned across Duane's lap and squeezed Wesley's knee. "You're the man tonight."

"They're a lot friendlier than I expected," Wesley said.

"They really take to you!" Kent fished out his wallet and told Wesley to take his pick.

"So where's Lucy?" Wesley asked.

Kent gave him a worried look.

"Who's this Lucy I keep hearing so much about?" Duane had brought them shots of Cuervo from the bar. Bill tortured himself with a long inhale of the spicy tequila but set the shot down on the edge of the stage in front of his brother. Duane tossed his shot back then grinned and produced a flask from his pants pocket.

"One-hundred percent Lincoln County corn," he said and refilled his own glass. Kent made him put the flask away. He said he had too many friends here to get thrown out. *Friends?* Had he actually used that word? It seemed important to Kent that they recognize him as the master of ceremonies. It was his party. He flagged down a waitress and ordered them another round. Duane brought out the flask again, and when Kent tried to wrestle it away, Bill eyed the room for bouncers. He wondered where his wife was at this moment. She was still his wife, though she refused to speak to him. It was only a matter of time before the papers were served. The others hardly noticed when he took his leave and made his way over to the bar.

Behind the bar, tiers of booze. All those pretty shapes, all those colors. The bartender knew him well, and when Bill ordered a club soda, Jimmy raised an eyebrow.

"I'm babysitting." Here at the bar, out of the glare of the stage lights, he was able to survey the crowd with a modicum of dignity. There were the regulars, but at least half The Jackpot crowd came for special occasions: bachelor parties, buddy reunions. No doubt theirs was the only group to celebrate a man's incarceration, the handcuffed hero returning from Mexico. Bill watched an empty table near the stage be claimed by a new group of young men. Mid-twenties, barely out of college. Well groomed, sporting expensive ties, they looked familiar. Fuck, this could be bad. They were the right age, same as the class of Gammas to whom Bill had been forced to break the news of the chapter's closing and why: because his friend, the man Bill had nominated to serve as treasurer of the alumni corporation, had embezzled his way to their bankruptcy. It was hard to tell for certain under the strobe lights, but with any luck they weren't Gammas. They were just a type.

On the other side of the stage, Kent was standing and waving at a tall redhead in a long sequined skirt. Green sequins. The mermaid. When she sauntered over, Kent pointed at Wesley. Duane and Kent pulled their chairs aside to give her room. She started swishing side to side, and the sequins sparkled beneath the strobe. Bill was having a hard time seeing his brother, but he could see Kent and Duane just fine, staring from the sidelines. By the time she was down to her G-string, the strobe shut off, and in the purple light Bill could see Wesley plain. He sat wide-eyed, gawking up at her, his cheeks flushed with blood, his cherry popped. One more piggy at the trough. It was Kent who stepped forward with the twenty to slide beneath her garter.

Let them have their fun. Bill stayed at the bar and nursed his club soda. He counted the minutes till closing. How much money had he thrown away in this joint? He had allowed himself to sink into the worst sin imaginable, what his parents had instilled in him to be a crime against oneself worse than infidelity, worse than drunkenness—he had fallen into debt. And he had fallen in deep. Probably even had creditors this very minute trying to locate his whereabouts. No way his work with Kent—*Steak Man!*—would pull him out of the hole he had dug.

"Hey there, stranger." Alice slid into the spot at the bar by his side and laid an arm around his shoulders. She pulled him in for a sideways hug. "You looked like you could use it."

"Does it show that bad?"

"You look like your hamster died."

He tried to smile.

"Do you like my outfit?" She flounced about in a French maid get-up: black silk, white lace trim, tight in all the right places. Like Alice herself, her outfit was probably the least imaginative in the joint. But it was sweet.

"You wouldn't have to clean my toilet," he said.

She swished the feather duster in his face. "You never give me a chance."

"I like you too much." And it was true. Ever since that first night at Kent's, when she had made his barometer rise, something had clicked inside him. Instead of lust, he felt protective of Alice. Brotherly. He'd never had a sister, not one who lived. "I haven't seen Lucy tonight," he said. "Is she on the schedule?"

"Everybody's crazy about Lucy. I'm worried about her. She's been missing work, showing up late." They shared a Marlboro Light, and Alice caught him up on the lives of other dancers. Bill told her about the little celebration Kent was throwing himself.

"My number's up." She forced a grin, then popped a piece of gum in her mouth and began working it to death.

"I'll be out here rooting for you."

"You're a sweetie-pie." She teased his nose again with the feather duster then headed backstage.

After Alice left, he pivoted on the stool, stared down into his club soda, and felt the weight of his funk settle itself again over his shoulders. He forgot to watch her dance. On the TV above the bar the Braves were taking the Mets into extra innings.

Jimmy wiped the bar down around him. When he came back with a shot glass full of some colorless liquor, Bill felt his blood pressure rise.

"What's this?"

"From a friend. I told him you were babysitting." Jimmy turned back to the bar, and Bill glanced toward the stage. Under the purple light, Kent was sliding a bill along the thigh of a biracial dancer who went by Ebony, one of several dancers Bill knew who were putting themselves through college on tips. He scanned the length of the bar, empty except for a fat man sitting in the shadows at the other end. Bill stared down at the shot, then wrapped his fingers around the cut glass. He lifted it to his lips. Peppermint schnapps, the last thing he would ever order. Kent knew that. Still, that tingle wasn't half bad. He got Jimmy's attention and ordered another. Not half bad. On the TV, the silent crack of a bat, then Shea Stadium on its feet. Bill imagined the roar, the Wurlitzer arpeggios. He swiveled on his stool to stare at the stage. The dancer was working the young turks. Where was Bill's crowd? Wesley? Then he saw them. Duane was on his feet, then falling across the men in the next row back. A table tipped and beer spilled. Two men, cursing, stood to challenge Duane, who, oblivious, kept stumbling toward the bar.

When he arrived, Duane sank down onto a stool and laid his head on the backs of his folded hands. The new bartender eyed him warily. Bill didn't like that guy. Matt, was that his name? All muscle. He'd been promoted from the front door to the bar, but he didn't know shit about mixing drinks.

Bill laid an arm across Duane's shoulders and said into his ear that he couldn't pass out here. "The limo is parked down the block. Let me help you find the way."

Duane shook his head and asked if he could borrow Bill's mobile phone. He needed to call Crystal. He needed to see if she had taken her medicine.

Duane had trouble operating the phone, and so Bill offered to dial the number for him.

"I think your battery is dead." Duane kept punching the buttons.

"Let me see that." Bill grabbed the phone. "That's a brand new battery!" But it was dead.

Duane started cussing modern technology a little too loudly, and the bartender kept eyeing him while he poured drinks. Bill helped Duane back toward the stage. There he found Kent also very deep into his cups.

Kent held up a meaty palm, and Bill gave him the obligatory high five. Kent's bought head of hair was slicked back with sweat. A red flush covered his face. He looked like a heart attack in the making.

"What you say we give them a round of the Glimmer Twins?" Kent grinned, belched.

"Let's don't and say we did." Back in their fraternity days, when the party broke up in the wee hours, the DJ had always played "Can't Get No Satisfaction," and the die-hards who had partied till the bitter end would link arms and sway back and forth, kicking their legs and shouting the words in unison. Bill looked across the stage, but the lights in his eyes kept him from seeing much of those young guys over there. Nothing more than their bright ties.

On the other side of Kent, Wesley leaned back heavily in his chair, a beer dangling from his hand. But his eyes were alive and alert, watching a new dancer take the stage.

Tanned and wiry with muscles, she performed all sorts of acrobatic stunts involving the pole. She found her way over to Wesley, dropped into a backbend with her palms on the stage, and pumped her pelvis right in his face.

"She is nothing if not flexible," Bill said, punching Wesley in the shoulder. Wesley didn't flinch. His concentration was impressive. He had needed something, the little hermit. He'd become an ingrown toenail, his own sex cutting into himself. Bill knew that problem, cock and balls with no love object in sight, turning in on his own body, looking for an orifice.

Above rock 'n' roll blasting through the speakers, Bill heard the bell at the bar and tasted the ghost of peppermint in his throat. Last call. He had some catching up to do.

By the time he got there, he had to muscle his way toward an empty stool. He leaned toward Jimmy, but Jimmy ignored him. Bill pulled the last ten from his pocket and waved it at the new bartender. That's all it took.

"Give me two shots of Barton."

The bartender raised an eyebrow—nothing left for a tip? But he brought the shots. Setting two shots on the bar was an opportunity to flex his muscles. Not as big as Wesley, but he would kill Wesley. He turned to wait on another customer, and Bill wasted no time. Sweet as molasses. Heavy on the oak. Notes of peat and fishnet stockings. Now the world was feeling right again. He worked his hands into his pockets. Keys. An empty wallet. Not a single dollar bill. Not even a quarter. A third shot would set him right. Maybe Kent would spot him.

A chorus of hollers and whistles drew his attention back to the stage. Lucy's tattoos shone under the purple light. Her silky black hair fell down across an emerald camisole, and she held a feathered mask to her face. Even from back here at the bar, he could see her eyes framed by the mask. She danced to spooky music—Prince, maybe. She worked her way around the stage, looked at each man, marking him, her movements swift, abrupt, like a praying mantis. It was all so theatrical, more than a little ridiculous. Still, at the sight of her, he tasted bourbon-flavored acid reflux. He might need to find a place to get sick.

With other dancers, the first song was a freebie. Men waited for tits before they tipped. But they were already crowding the stage, holding up money. Bill's wallet was empty, even if he could bear to push his way into that feed trough. And he couldn't bear it.

The second song was faster. Lucy's garter filled with dollars. She had discarded the mask. She slid her bare feet in quick three-step circles on the floor and moved her hips to the grind of a rockabilly guitar. It was a dance for two. She slipped a camisole strap off of one shoulder and let the other find its way off as she danced. He'd seen this routine often enough, didn't need to see it again. The silk slid down until it hung from her breasts. She slipped it off and let it pool around her feet. Those plump breasts. She touched them, offered them up. Dancing at the edge of the stage, she ran her fingers along the inside of a thigh and did not stop at the border of her G-string.

A change was taking place. Bill had seen it happen here plenty of nights before. It had been a lounge emptying itself of men who were reaching the frustration of that late-night state somewhere between drunk and hungover, a time when they pry open their wallets and can't believe how much money they've spent. But with Lucy onstage, suddenly anything was possible. She moved in a way that made bouncers nervous. The crowd cheered and clapped and shouted dirty words. Dollar bills appeared along the foot of the stage.

She rode the brass pole. The other women had danced around it, climbed it, rubbed themselves against it. Everything they insinuated, she made explicit. What they pretended, she manifested. Men kept leaving their tables and filling the seats up front. She wrapped her flesh around the pole, buried the brass in her tender core. She wasn't dancing now. Bill watched her face. She held the pole in one hand and leaned back, her chin dug into her sternum, the long hair flowing free. She was biting her trembling bottom lip, eyes closed, frowning in her struggle.

There was one special morning Bill liked to remember, their first full day at the Ambassador Suites, when they were wearing matching plaid pajamas and drinking virgin daiquiris together. They had been to Way of the Flesh the night before, and the blue rose on his neck still burned. They were standing at the balcony rail, listening to the calypso music floating up eight stories. He held her soft body, made softer by the flannel pajamas, and she did not resist. That was the morning he had decided he loved her.

"I'd like her to ride *me* like that." At first Bill didn't see the man, just the glowing tip of his cigarette resting in the ashtray. "Most of these boys have never witnessed anything like her." It was the fat man from the end of the bar, now overflowing the stool next to Bill. "My God, that negligée she took off," he rattled on. "That's what tears me up. My old woman tried to wear one of those and, damn, it looked like a Halloween costume."

All at once Bill saw the tattoos that blanketed the man's skin, up and down his arms, wrapping around his neck. He was ugly with ink and deeply tanned. His face was a mass of wrinkles, but he was probably not nearly as old as he looked. Fat as a toad.

"How'd that Schnapps treat you?" The toad winked.

"Schnapps?"

"You looked like you needed something. What you having?" He glanced at the empty shot glass in Bill's hand.

"Barton."

The toad fished out his wallet and waved for the new bartender. "Double shot of Barton for my friend here." With a quick glance at Bill's neck, he said, "I like the rose. What's that inside? A snake?" He leaned in close. "Yeah, nice work. Very nice."

Bill knew that etiquette required him now to repay the compliment by admiring the man's prolific tattoos, but the idea of addressing that skin with any kind of praise revolted him.

Lucy finished her dance to wild applause. She made a last round of the stage to collect tips in her garter, a chance for men to touch those thighs, to come close to that ink. Bill downed half the double shot and then made himself sip at the rest.

When Lucy turned to leave the stage, the men crowding near shouted for more, and the DJ spun another song, The Rolling Stones' "Under My Thumb." She turned her back to the audience, shifted her shoulders up and down, found the groove with her hips. Bill looked away, stared up at the TV, at the pitcher's arched back, the way his knee lifted before the wind-up.

"Listen to the Word of God," said the toad.

"What?"

"Under my thumb, that one there," the man said and winked. "First Timothy. Let a woman learn quietly with all submissiveness. For Adam was formed first, then Eve; and Adam was not deceived, but the woman was deceived and became a transgressor."

Bill turned and saw the Tree of Knowledge, its branches spreading across her shoulder blades in the purple light.

"I don't think we should be judged by our worst choices," Bill said.

"Some choices are fatal."

Bill turned and studied the man's ink work—fiery skulls and poker cards and naked women, down his arms, up the sides of his neck. Bill stared down at his own forearm, at the long, orange carrot. He thought of dirty needles, polluted blood. Niall said he always sterilized his needles. But he also said he had accidentally ruined lives. And sometimes not accidentally.

Bill made a move to stand, but the man placed a hand on his wrist. "You want to know what she's like?"

"Excuse me?"

"In bed." The fat man nodded toward the stage. "The painted lady."

"I gotta . . . I gotta go."

"She did whatever I wanted. If the price was right." He clinked his glass against the shot Bill was still holding. "She did it all, man. What you saw a little while ago, that ain't shit compared to what she's like once you get her in private."

"You're a fucking liar."

"Scout's honor."

"Fuck you!" Bill balled up the man's shirt in his hands. The fat man shoved Bill, who was still clinging to the shirt. Buttons popped. The fabric ripped along the shoulder. The man just laughed.

"You shouldn't be—" Bill struggled for words. "You shouldn't be telling lies about people."

The man jiggled with laughter. The new bartender came around the bar, his neck taut, his biceps flexed for action.

"What's going on here?"

The man removed his torn shirt, revealing rolls of fat covered in tattoos. "My friend has had a bit too much to drink." His gut quivered with his continuing laughter.

The bartender, his neck muscles swelling with blood, squared off with Bill, then he followed Bill's stare to the indecent spectacle of all that tattooed flesh, the man's sheer surface area, roll upon roll. No way she had done what he said she did. No way she had gone to bed with this toad. No way.

"Give him your shirt," the bartender demanded.

IN HIS WHITE T-SHIRT, Bill made his way toward his friends. They had moved to a table now, near the stage but with breathing room. Another dancer had taken over the runway. The bar rang out last call yet again.

"Is it time to go?" Wesley asked, in the voice of a child at the circus, a child who doesn't want to miss the elephants but has already eaten too much cotton candy and feels the onset of a stomach ache. Then, as an afterthought, and still staring toward the stage, he asked, "What happened to your shirt?"

Bill only shook his head and stared back at the bar where the man was pushing his fat arms into Bill's tailored button-down. Bill reached across his brother to nudge Duane. Duane's eyes were closed. His chin rested against his fist. When Bill nudged him again, his eyes fluttered open. Kent was staring at the floor, his face twisted with some dark emotion Bill was afraid to stir.

"See if you can help me get Duane up." Bill grabbed one arm and lifted, but it was like lifting a pile of mud.

When Lucy appeared, Bill let Duane spill back into the chair. He wanted to say something, but he couldn't even make himself look at her.

"Hey there," she said. "Did you have a good time, huh? Did you watch me up there? That was all for you boys." She was so coked up and into her show that she didn't seem to recognize them. She was selling hard, like Bill and Wesley were two johns she hadn't met before.

"Which one of you boys wants a dance?" As final proof of her intoxication, she had slipped into her thickest hillbilly accent, pronouncing *dance* so that it rhymed with *paints*. "Time enough left for one last *daints*."

It scared him to see her like this. She probably hadn't eaten. If she could get something in her stomach, that might help.

"You want to run out and get a bite after the show?" he said. "Kent hired this crazy-long stretch limo. We could make him take us to the Waffle House. You always loved to get some grub after you dance."

"You're a beautiful dancer," Wesley said, his eyes wide and worshipful. If possible, he was even more intoxicated than she was.

"Oh, you liked that, did you?" She stepped between Bill and his brother and started gyrating her hips. "You ain't seen dancing yet."

Wesley tilted his chair back on two legs and stared up at her with that innocent face, like he expected nothing but goodness and light.

"Let's call it a day." Bill grabbed his brother by the shoulder, but Wesley flexed his arm and fixed him with an angry stare.

"He wants to see me dance," Lucy said, and Wesley reached for his wallet.

"Let's put that away," Bill said.

"I want to see her dance," Wesley said, carefully inspecting the money in his wallet.

"Let's all go out and get some food in our bellies."

"You don't tell me what to do. I want to see her dance."

"Come on," Kent said, grabbing Bill by the T-shirt. "We'll wait in the limo." When Kent got his weight moving and he had hold of you, there was no resisting. Bill let his drunken friend guide him to the exit.

When his hand pressed against the padded leather, Bill turned and glanced back toward the table. In the glow of the purple light, Wesley sat straight up in his chair, like a man awaiting execution. He set his palms flat against his thighs. He flicked a tongue across his lips, a nervous tic that showed up whenever he was intent on something. Beneath the starched white cotton of his button-down, you could see his diaphragm working overtime, his abs pumping like a furnace bellows. Bill saw the teddy slip down past her shoulder blades, exposing that familiar ink. Paradise. Adam and Eve.

Then Bill was out the door, running full tilt along the sidewalk bathed in neon. Up ahead the stretch limo sat parked at the curb. In the distance the crown at the top of the NationsBank Tower sparkled like stolen diamonds, casting its tawdry light upon the entire realm of its dominion. Duane was staggering down the sidewalk with the dull, implacable purpose of a zombie. Kent stopped and leaned against the glass of a storefront window, his guts spilling in a puddle at his feet. That group of young men from the lounge strolled down the sidewalk in long easy strides, laughing at some private joke. Without so much as a glance, they made a wide arc around Kent and continued on their way.

Bill stepped up beside his friend and laid a hand across his shoulder. "How's it coming?"

"Sick."

"This is your big night."

"Huh? Yeah. Did you see her?"

"Yeah."

"Goodbye, Mexico." Kent retched again.

"Goodbye, Mexico," Bill said in a tone meant to soothe their pain.

"Party's over."

"Yeah. Party's over." Though he was only halfway to the drunk he needed, and though he was already thinking about the full bar inside the stretch limo, Bill felt the need to purge everything inside of him. It was a thing their fraternity brothers had done sometimes back in college—when one got sick, the other one got sick along with him. He stuck two fingers on the back of his tongue and pressed and pressed until he felt his gorge rise, and his guts flowed onto the sidewalk to mix with his friend's.

24

The boat rode at anchor. Out the cabin window, Wesley saw the gray sky turn blue. His head continued to throb from too much scuppernong wine. Since Bill had come home, it wasn't uncommon for Wesley to wake up hungover. When the upper rim of the sun sent its image across the water in one unscattered column of light, he watched the shapes on her skin reappear. She slept on her stomach, her black hair spilling out over the orange life jacket she used as a pillow.

While she slept, he focused on the skin beneath the tattoos, her shoulders pink with sunburn. All that ink, a second skin, it was just a screen designed to hide her from view. But he saw her plain. Exactly like she saw him. That first night they'd met, when she had waltzed into his cottage and sat down on his lap, she looked straight at his need, without judging. And so he wasn't about to be the one to start judging. He could hear his mother's voice in his head, all the reasons why he should not be lying naked beside this woman, beginning with her profession and the drugs and moving on to her involvement with his brother. He was determined not to listen to that voice of fear. He thought instead of two does he had observed at the edge of his watermelon patch one morning the week before. How graceful in their stillness. That's the way he felt with her—two perfect creatures about to discover each other this morning, when the world was once again new.

There would be baggage, sure, hers as well as his. How many years had Wesley gone without a lover? So many years when it was just him, and then Elizabeth for two short months. Maybe Elizabeth had gotten tired of having to park her car around behind his cottage whenever she spent the night. He had tried to explain that he wasn't trying to hide her from his parents, simply that he didn't want to put their overnight dates so boldly in his mother's face. Or, maybe Elizabeth had felt some deeper dissatisfaction; to say it plainly, maybe he hadn't been man enough for her. Two months of nervous intimacy, and then him alone in a room again, in his bedroom trying to evoke Elizabeth's spirit—no, not her spirit but her body, because it was *through* her body that he knew her spirit—closing his eyes and grabbing a pillow or a wad of covers in his arms and sniffing for a trace of her perfume and trying to pretend and then giving up. It wasn't working, trying to make believe she was there *beside* him, it just wouldn't work, until he felt *himself*, pressing his fingers into his own soft flesh that felt a lot more like Elizabeth than the pillow felt like her, until it was easy to feel her *inside* himself, her body inhabiting his own body. Pushing the pillow between his legs and grinding into it the way she would grind into him, until *his* movements were *her* movements, and he could see and feel her face getting hot there in the very same space where his face was getting hot, spreading his own legs the way she had spread hers, until he was Elizabeth making love to himself. And then it would be over, and he would be left with the shame and the worry over what was happening to him.

Full of the bourbon Bill had kept pouring, that night a week ago, Wesley had shared more of this history than he liked to remember.

"Ingrown toenail," Bill had said. "I know the feeling."

Burning with shame, Wesley had stumbled into the bedroom and thrown himself down on the mattress.

"Where you going?" Bill asked. "You quitting on me?"

He didn't answer. He lay still and let the mattress spin. And even then Bill would not stop talking.

"I'm just going to sleep in here on the sofa tonight," Bill said from the other room. "It's too hot tonight in that bed for both of us. Is this light bothering you? I'm just going to stay up a while longer. I'm going to stretch out here on the sofa. You know, the other night, I saw the way you and Lucy were looking at each other. You might not think I saw you skanking on my woman, but I saw it. Brother, you don't want to be messing with her—she's too much for you. You ought to start off in the shallow end. Wesley, are you listening to me? Wesley? Wesley! If you get the bed spins, put your feet down on the floor—sleep with your feet on the floor and it always helps."

Now sitting above her in the cramped V-berth, crouching low, Wesley watched Lucy breathe, ashamed still of his own impotence the night before. This morning, he was gripped again by a balance of desire and the urge to escape to wind and sunlight. Before she could wake up and see him, he quietly slipped out into the sun and retrieved his swimming trunks from where, under the light of the stars, he had lashed them to the furled mainsail. After dressing, he dropped to the deck and pumped out a set of fifty push-ups. That felt better. Better to feel the added size in his chest, his arms. When he crawled back into the cabin and scrambled forward to the V-berth, he sat watching her sleep, feeling his muscles slowly deflate.

If only he could have studied her lying asleep long enough, he might have calculated his chances. But she moved. She yawned and lifted her head. She opened her eyes, rolled over onto her back and laid her head back down on the orange life jacket.

"Morning," she said. She looked into his eyes for half a second and then away. She reached her arms up around his neck and pulled him down to her so that he felt her breasts pushing against him, her lips brushing against the side of his face, and her warm breath.

"How long have you been up?" She pulled the spinnaker sail they'd used as a sheet up to her shoulders.

He shrugged. "Not long." Why not say more? Why not come out and say how he had been sitting here, making up his mind to love her.

He lit the propane stove and heated water to make instant coffee, then sliced a cantaloupe into chunks and tossed the mess of seeds over the side for fish to nibble. They both left the cabin to sit in the sunshine. They sipped coffee, while he fed her chunks of cantaloupe. A pair of mallards swam up to the boat and begged for food; she found the empty bag of potato chips and scattered the crumbs on the water.

They spent the early morning lounging in the companionway between the cabin and cockpit, in the shade of the Bimini top. She was still getting her sea legs, and even though she was so graceful on land—and even onstage in those ridiculous heels—she walked cautiously around the boat with her feet spread comically wide. She had thrown on one of his extra-large T-shirts. It fit her like a dress. Still, he could not keep his eyes off her. Neither could any other man on the lake. Every single redneck on the water cut his throttle when he saw her.

"That pisses me off."

"What? Other men looking at me?"

"The way they stare."

"Are you a possessive lover, Wesley?" She opened a bag of potato chips.

"Come here." He pulled her tight into himself and felt his erection pressing against her thigh. Maybe if they went below and tried again, things would work out for him. But he was afraid if he pulled off his shorts and she saw him, he would shrivel again. No hurry, they had all day to get to know each other. He had food enough for two days. He would call in sick to work if she would, too.

He still could not believe his luck. That night at The Jackpot, he'd had the nerve to ask for her number, and she had given it to him. It took her three days to return his call. He had given up on her, then one evening after work he was lying on the bench press outside his cottage with three hundred pounds of iron and cement suspended above his chest when he heard the dinner bell outside his mother's house ringing the alarm. His mother's shouts carried to him across the pasture, through the woods, saying somebody was on the phone wanting him. He set the barbell in its slots and took off at a sprint. When he'd arrived, out of breath, and stretched the phone cord as far as he could into his parents' dining room, his mother had sat in the living room reading her Bible, pretending that she wasn't eavesdropping.

A breeze freshened and continued to blow throughout the morning as the sun climbed blue sky. He and Lucy talked about raising sail but never mustered the energy. It was too nice riding at anchor, with the bow blown first one way and then the other. The line stretched taut, the boat bucking to break free. He pulled her into his lap, and she kissed his nose, then hopped up and went below for the magazine she had brought. She came back topside wearing sunglasses and settled across from him and flipped through the pages of her magazine while he absentmindedly coiled the end of a line, practiced knots, and studied the tattoos that wrapped around her legs. Self-portrait? A fish. Starbursts. Some kind of face—a mask. He wondered if she had ever thought about having them removed. Laser surgery? When she looked up, he smiled. She put down the magazine and stared back a long time without speaking.

"Do you have a safety pin?" she asked.

"What's that?"

"And some ink? Blue works best. If you have a ballpoint pen we can cut it open."

She took her lighter and heated the tip of the pin to sterilize it. On the inside of his wrist she pricked him, pushed the ink in deep. It stung. He tried not to show it. One point at a time, she drew the outline of a tiny blue heart. She wiped the excess ink away and turned his wrist for his inspection.

"Wow. That was easier than I expected." *Permanent*, he thought with relief.

"One of these days I'm going to open my own parlor," she said. "Niall let me apprentice for a while, but he always wanted to tell me what to do. It was like I couldn't have a single idea of my own."

Wesley decided not to bring up the possibility of laser surgery. He looked down at the heart on his wrist and wanted to believe this one was special, that she hadn't ever done this before.

Along Big Island, pines darkened the water against the red mud banks. Higher up the slope, poplars revealed the pale undersides of their leaves to the wind that rushed across Wesley's face and washed away his hesitation. The wind blew away the voices in his head, voices that told of farming with mules, hunting with dogs that could follow a scent without putting their noses to the ground, sharecropping, hog lots in mill villages, textile strikes, livestock trading, a mule that wouldn't eat corn sold for full value and brought home dead and bloated in a wagon, chickens running headless around the backyard, possums kept in a cage and fed scraps until their meat was clean to eat, cotton-picking races and red raw fingers at the end of the day, gas rationing during the war, twelve grades in a single-roomed school, bedbugs, lye soap, maypoles, elopements, silent movies, a dozen different old-timers each remembering the first time they ever rode in an automobile.

Overhead, clouds moved swiftly, boiling in dark patterns. The western sky had filled with brown clouds lending the lake beneath them the color of dirty dishwater. But in the east, already clearing, enough blue showed through to turn the water to pewter, dense with texture.

"I could stay here all day," he said.

"Let's go for a swim."

He pulled her into him, but she was determined to swim. She slipped on her one-piece then climbed to the highest part of the cabin deck and stood by the mast. Without warning, she sprang into the air and performed a perfect swan dive. He jumped overboard after her. They treaded water beside each other, moving slowly away from the boat and toward the island beach. He swam behind her and tried to get near enough to reach out and touch. But she turned and kicked, moving away in one graceful stroke.

Two fishermen trolled along the near beach, standing with their backs to each other, casting from bow and stern toward the shallow water. They had their radio turned up loud, and he could hear the NASCAR announcer and car engines roaring. Lucy plunged her head below the surface and began a rapid freestyle. He followed at a slower pace, watching her crawl across the surface of the water. After swimming past a shoal marker and rounding the corner of the island, she turned to shout something he couldn't hear.

He exhausted himself trying to close the distance between them. At the beach on the far side of the island he watched her rise out of the water and walk up to the shore. She bent down to the sand then stood and disappeared into the pine trees bordering the beach. He sat in the shallow water, catching his breath, and watched her come back to the edge of the water. She held her face tilted upward toward the sky and ran fingers through her wet hair, working out the tangles.

Still panting, he trudged out of the water. He let his body lean heavily against hers, and then she let him lead her away from the beach into the pines. He smelled a campfire. Nearby, stones ringed a pile of charred logs and empty beer bottles. They walked toward the center of the island, navigating a narrow path between patches of poison ivy and across pine needles and the twigs that poked at the soles of their feet. Near the very center of the island, he showed her the spot at the top of the hill where they could look down across the small bay and watch their boat riding at anchor.

"What a perfect spot," she said. "How did you find it?"

"I know this lake pretty good." He cleared a place on a bed of pine needles for her to sit, then knelt beside her and began kissing her.

She asked who had taught him to sail, and he admitted that he had taught himself out of books. Books and trial and error. He kissed her again, and she stood to part the branches overlooking the harbor.

"What you see there?"

"Come here," she said.

Out in the main channel a tall-masted sloop flew an orange spinnaker that blossomed in the afternoon sun. He reached for her hand, and she sat back down on the bed of pine needles. While the lake water dried from their skin, she let him touch her gently, there where the pine trees filtered the sunshine. He tugged at the straps of her swimsuit, and she peeled it off the rest of the way. He studied the gooseflesh rising across her chest. Under the shadows of the pines, her colors looked deeper, indelible. He whispered to her that he wanted to make love to her. He pulled off his own swim suit.

"Come here and kiss me," she said, pulling him into her belly. He planted kisses on her navel, all over her soft belly, still cold and wet from the lake. He closed his eyes and buried his face in the pillow of her belly and tried to forget his frustration from the night before.

"Kiss me down there," she said, and he flattened himself on the ground so that the pine needles prickled his thighs and his groin.

"I want to make love to you," he whispered, even though he was flaccid, half-erect at best.

"Shh. Kiss me instead."

Earlier, in the lake, circling her while treading water, his erection had been firm and steady, but now that she lay back, inviting him to close the distance between them, he knelt over her and could only joke. "I'm waterlogged, I guess."

"It's okay," she said. "Don't worry about it. Relax."

The previous night there had been the excuse of too much wine and sun, but there was no reason for this to happen again today, except that he had feared it might. He concentrated on her body. He focused on one part of her at a time and let desire rise within him. He let his fingertips glide along a smooth thigh, one of few blank spots left on her body, down to the daisy covering her knee cap. He laid his face on her belly. He moved his lips across her chest, tasting her nipple, then up to her shoulder, he kissed his way along her collarbone and back down across her breasts.

This is like Mother's insomnia, he thought, how the more he tried not to fixate on his impotence, the more useless it seemed. Twenty-nine was too young for this to happen, before he had the chance to learn about married life, before he even had the chance to know what it was like to live with a woman, to sleep with her every night and wake up to her every morning. He had lived too long at home, too long inside himself.

"Kiss me down there," she said again, and he did. He buried the bridge of his nose in her furry mound and pulled the pillows of her inner thighs tight against the sides of his face.

It was soft and smooth and lightly salty, nothing like he would have expected. He breathed her musk in deeply and wrapped his arms around her legs and squeezed. Her thighs enveloped his cheeks and sealed both ears from the sounds of the woods. He did not hear the rustle of wind through the pines or the waves breaking on the shore. He did not hear the rapid, varied song of a mockingbird somewhere close and up high. He pulled her legs tight around his ears to shut out the world. All he knew were the rhythms of her body, her racing heartbeat beneath the breasts he massaged, and the way her abs tightened and then relaxed, tightened and relaxed again, as her back rose from the ground and then dropped back down, like a woman experiencing the contractions of childbirth. He kissed her down there for a long time. A cloud bank rolled in and the woods filled with dusk at mid-afternoon. The mockingbird wore itself out on a dozen different songs and then left the island for the mainland. The sun buried itself deep in purple clouds, and he had not yet left her thighs. Even after she was spent and could take him no longer, he kept kissing her.

25

It was a bad morning, not only bad for sales, but full of bad people. Rude, dangerous, poor. Usually Saturdays were their best days, but this Saturday was full of people who slammed doors in Bill's face, threatened to call the law, sicced dogs on him.

"I really hate selling to the trailer parks." Bill slumped down in the seat and put his feet on the dash.

"That's our best market." Kent pushed at Bill's feet and the truck swerved. "Don't do that," he said. Bill sat up straight and stared out at the country road.

"I've gone from flying the friendly skies," Bill said, "to riding shotgun beside Steak Man."

"You can quit any day you take a notion."

Bill knew he ought not blame Kent for the headhunter's lack of success, for the absence of managerial positions in packaging inks, nor for Bill's failure of nerve, his fear that his former career was an exception, that the future held a long stretch of unemployment broken only by jobs like this one. Worse still, on the radio, financial analysts were forecasting an overdue recession. The great expansion was an anomaly in human history, they said, one that had lulled too many people into complacence. He should have left Imminent Ink while he had the chance. It was impossible to find a job when you didn't have a real job. Every day he rode with Kent, he was sure he couldn't last much longer. He punched a button on the dash and the dire economic news gave way to a preacher's forecast of the apocalypse. Bill reached to change the channel again, but Kent grabbed his wrist.

"Wait. Let's see what he has to say."

"I know what he has to say. We're damned."

Kent had been showing an unsettling interest lately in radio preachers. His mother was after him to rejoin their church. One day the previous week, selling on the outskirts of Hailey Creek, Kent had pointed it out—some Pentecostal Holiness church made of cinder blocks. White blocks. Blood red windows.

After an hour with no sales, Kent said they would quit early.

"Amen to that," Bill said.

But when Bill asked about stopping by the Citgo for a twelve-pack of Corona before they hit the pool, Kent said he had other plans. The Society for Creative Anachronism was hosting their Summer Fair on Lake Norman and he was hoping Bill would join him for the festivities. When Bill groaned and began attacking the very idea of chivalry, Kent promised him not only never-ending taps of ale but also honey wine, just like Beowulf had quaffed in his mead hall centuries ago.

An hour later, Bill found himself sitting on a blanket, tankard in hand, gazing across a grassy sward at two opposing armies dressed in flowing capes and an assortment of impressively authentic-looking medieval helmets and armor. They were beating each other with sticks.

"Help me out here, will you?" Kent pulled on his do-it-yourself armor, a breastplate fashioned out of double-ply cardboard he'd salvaged from a refrigerator crate, covered in three layers of Berber carpet.

Bill set down his tankard and helped him fasten the loops in back. Already almost drunk enough to put the morning behind him, he made himself forget the face of every redneck who had stared down his nose while Bill stood on a pair of rickety steps and held up a pair of steaks, beaming a smile, desperate to make a sale.

He listened to the whack of wood on wood. The earnest grunts loosened his tongue.

"What a farce. Right out of *Ivanhoe*. These poor crackers pretending to be knights and ladies."

"It's role-playing. What's wrong with that?" Kent reached through his legs and took the length of rope Bill passed him, then secured it to the buckle at his waist.

"It's not real," Bill said.

"Honor, honesty, the sanctity of sex and romantic love." Kent was starting to work himself into a huff. "It's powerful. People still need that kind of idealism."

Apparently, some people still needed *Dungeons & Dragons*. Bill watched the battle raging over the field. Across the lake stood the two reactors of the McGuire nuclear station. Their domes rose into the sky above the trees. The water at this end of the lake was warm as blood. Still, why not let himself pretend along with Kent? The smell of roasting pork filled the air. The shouts of warriors. Applause for the archer who hit the bull's-eye.

Bill gestured with his tankard toward the reactors and their upside-down reflections in the water. "How are we supposed to pretend we've gone back to the garden with those things staring us in the face? It's a fake garden, like these costumed knights and ladies."

"Hold on there a minute. Every garden is something people cultivate. Like this lake—it ain't natural. Duke Power dammed it up."

"Exactly." Bill drank a deep draught of the mead. "What do we humans touch that we don't invariably turn to shit? We're not content to kill each other; we've got to kill the planet. Energy. Who has access? Who is being used? Who is most exposed to exploitation?"

"The Society is open for anybody to join. It ain't like college, rushing frats." Kent slid on a motorcycle helmet and fastened the chinstrap. Its red metal-flake sparkled in the afternoon sun. He had somehow fastened a metal grate in the front and duct-taped a plume of feathers to the top.

"In the Society," Kent said, adjusting the plume, "everybody starts out as equals. Nobody asks how much you make, whether you live in a mansion or a mobile home. We're all free to compete in battle for title and rank—"

"Freedom? Like my guru says, freedom is an illusion."

"Guru?"

"He's a nut, but sometimes he makes sense."

"The guy who did your tattoos?" Kent pulled on his gauntlets, heavy construction gloves he'd embossed with strips of carpet.

"Niall. He says we're unaware of how we're being manipulated by aliens. Like we're all part of some huge machine, being used by the machine to control each other, exploit each other for money, sex, status."

Kent let out a belly laugh and started doing a robot dance in his cardboard armor.

"Yeah, it's weird shit, involving electromagnetism. I don't really believe it. But there was one thing he said that has been bugging me. Something called the *replicator*."

"Replicator? What's that?"

"Some theory about the origins of life on Earth. According to Niall, our Garden of Eden arrived on an asteroid. All the DNA we still recognize today travelled across space to land here billions of years ago with the urge to colonize."

"Okay?"

"So every time you think you're in love, you're only doing what the replicator commands, following its imperative to propagate, to subjugate."

"What?"

"That's what he says. I know, it's troubling."

"What a load of bullshit."

"Still, it's been bugging me." What he had asked Niall was how he could square this replicator theory of sexuality with that malarkey about magic—using sex to attain enlightenment, an authentic connection to the world and others, to become more conscious of personal responsibility. Bill tried to explain this conundrum to Kent, but Kent waved it off.

"Two people who want the same thing," Kent said, "there's the magic. That's the only time we get to create. Here, help me fasten these greaves." He held lengths of rounded metal to his shins and waited for Bill to tie them behind his calves.

"Why don't you just say *shin guards*?"

"I'm trying to use the correct terminology."

"Ultimately," Bill said, "the question I've been asking myself is whether sex is a force of the garden—no, the wilderness—or a function of the machine."

"I could see how that might keep you awake nights."

"I'm serious."

"Well, what do you think? Which is it? Sex: Garden or machine?"

"I don't know."

"I wouldn't worry myself to death over it. I do know one thing for sure: there's love and then there's everything out there trying to kill it." Kent took off his motorcycle helmet and held it in the crook of his arm, like he was posing for a portrait. "And, brother, you and me have wasted a lot of time. That fucking striptease. You know, I been thinking a lot about Lucy. And Alice, too." His eyes dropped to his greaves. "I wish Lucy would get away from that hellhole. I wish I could get her out here to a tournament. I think she'd like it. She needs to get away from that city altogether."

Bill looked down at his own feet. Just hearing Kent allude to The Jackpot made Bill's face burn. "How much money you reckon the two of us blew in that place?"

"I hate to speculate."

"When I think of what I spent at the bar alone, damn."

"I regret more what we were supporting."

"Yeah, there's that." Then again, it was where he'd met Lucy. Bill looked away toward the nuclear reactors and focused on a lone sailboat with a big orange balloon of a sail puffing out in front of the mast.

"It's not too late to make amends," said Kent. He replaced the motorcycle helmet on his head and faced the soldiers mustering in the field across the gravel road.

"How's that?" Bill asked. He needed to know.

"Self control. Self sacrifice. Devotion and honor. They're values cultivated in battle. You should join us."

"I'm lacking armor." Bill swept a hand toward the refrigerator crate covering his friend's torso.

"Go visit the quartermaster. I'll bet he has something to fit a runt like you." Kent smiled through the metal grate.

"I still don't understand what this has to do with Lucy."

Kent pulled his rattan "sword" through the dirt, scratching out runes Bill couldn't begin to decipher. "I have chosen her for my lady," he said and lifted the stick in the air as if in salute. "Lady Lucy. Every time I go into battle, I fight for her honor and glory."

"Come again."

But Kent only let out a whoop in answer to the roars rising from the soldiers gathered together in a scrum. With chunks of carpet sprouting from his shoulders like wings, he shuffled across the road to join his comrades.

Left alone, Bill wandered in the opposite direction, across the field toward the music he heard coming from a stand of pines. Men in leotards and women in ankle-length dresses plucked old-timey stringed instruments. Dancers touched palm to palm and walked in circles, then changed partners and entered other circles. This was more Bill's style. He lifted the tankard and swallowed, felt the buzz go through him, wishing again he had a costume. Maybe he should visit the quartermaster and requisition a leotard.

He pressed to the back of a crowd of onlookers to watch the lords and ladies at their dance, so synchronized, like the intricate workings of a timepiece. One dancer in a purple dress looked a lot like Maddie. Page-boy haircut. Thin, she swayed to the music with a regal gait. When she spun palm-to-palm with her partner, he caught the flash of her cheek and a jolt went through him. She looked an awful lot like Maddie. This had happened to him several times since their separation, seeing another woman and swearing it was his wife. When this one turned again to the music, he saw that she was, in fact, Maddie. She changed partners again, and Bill recognized his neighbor. Anthony wore motley, a ridiculous patchwork outfit and a cap with bells. Ever the jester. Once upon a time, that's how Bill had wooed her, too—through humor. And dance. He watched her smile blossom now that she clasped hands with Anthony. Underneath the cap of bells, Anthony's mouth worked nonstop, and his eyes glowed with the fire of intoxication, or maybe only with love for Maddie.

Bill pushed his way through the crowd toward the dancers. When he bumped into Robin Hood, he swallowed the rest of his mead and traded the fancy pewter tankard he had bought for the cheap felt hat on Robin's head. It was too small, but Bill stretched it out until it nearly fit. He studied the dancers' movements, how the circles broke apart and reformed, how partners swapped partners, how the original pairs came together again and paraded down the middle of two lines. Just when Bill felt prepared to cut in, the musicians took a break. They propped their lutes against the edge of the little stage where they sat. A giant in a scraggly beard ascended a short set of stairs to the stage and announced the opening of the competition for the bardic arts.

Bill saw that Maddie was now standing alone at the edge of an open space of trampled grass. The dancers had scattered, and Anthony waited in the back of a line that wended its way behind a long table covered in white paper and kettles of soup and platters of meat.

"Hail, my lady," Bill announced himself. He wanted to touch some part of her—at least an elbow, a shoulder—but he knew better. He braced himself for her recoil, but instead, she smiled and raised a cup in toast. He sniffed. Mulled wine.

"What the hell are you doing here?" she asked, astonished, but not angry in the least.

"With a friend."

"Girlfriend?"

"No."

She wobbled ever so slightly. Evidently standing still was more of a challenge than fifteenth-century dance.

"I'm here with a friend, too," she said and grinned sheepishly.

"I saw."

"I always wanted to go to one of these fairs. I asked and asked, but you never wanted to go. And now here you are."

"It must be fate." Now that she reminded him, he remembered what he had thought was a passing phase, her obsession with that novel *The Mists of Avalon* and that King Arthur TV series.

"Oh my god! What happened to your neck?" She leaned forward, and he inclined his head for her inspection.

"Accident," he mumbled.

"Singular accident."

"Sometimes it's surprising how hard you can work at causing harm." He meant this as an apology, an effort to acknowledge what a lousy partner he had been, but she must have taken it wrong, because her eyes clouded with hurt and she looked away.

"What I wanted to say—" he began again.

"I've been meaning to call you," she said. "I'm sorry I've been impossible to reach. I just couldn't . . . talk."

"I understand."

"We do need to talk, though. We need to talk and put our heads together sometime, figure out some bills."

"United in debt."

"The mortgage is fine. I'm guessing you're still on the company payroll."

"My severance runs through next month."

"That's a relief—for now. But we need to talk. I've cut back, where I can. Lawn care. Anthony has been helping out with that, mowing, keeping the hedges trimmed."

"Thank him for me."

Her eyes dropped. "He's been a big help."

"I'm sure." He forced a smile. "I'm glad."

"I cancelled my gym membership. Started working out at home."

"You must be doing something right. You're looking good. Great." The dress clung to her lithe frame, tall and wiry strong. In purple velvet, she fit the part of royalty. Maddie had the kind of body other women could not see without envy.

She averted her eyes again. She would probably never believe he found her beautiful; he had too often expressed worry about her diet, her indomitable drive to be skinny. "Unnatural," he had once called it, one of the many statements he wished he could retract.

"So, we need to talk," she said again. "About the house. I'm on the job market. I've had a couple nibbles. A second interview next week."

"Congratulations. That's really great. I'm sure they'll hire you. Anybody would be lucky to have you."

"Thanks. So, about the house—"

"Let's find a time to talk. Later. I don't want to spoil your day at the fair." Indeed, he did not want her only memory of him this day to be haggling about money.

Anthony pushed through the crowd double-fisted with turkey legs. His arrival was accompanied by bells; he tossed his tinkling head and began chanting some strange tongue, what he afterward identified as the opening lines of *The Canterbury Tales*, from the General Prologue. He wrapped an arm around Maddie and she sank deeply into his side, laughing at the words, or maybe just the way he made them sound. Funny guy, always eager to entertain.

He passed her a turkey leg wrapped in a napkin and she buried her teeth in the meat in a way so out of character that Bill hardly recognized her as his wife.

"You should go get in line," Anthony said and smiled falsely at Bill. "The food's going pretty fast."

Bill was not going to be that easy to get rid of.

The bearded giant returned to the stage and explained the rules of the bardic arts competition. All original compositions of five minutes or less were welcome. Musical accompaniment was also welcome, as were stories, ballads, riddles, poems.

"I've got this thing whipped," Anthony said and smoothed a hand across the top of Maddie's head. Then, turning her in his arms, he began to declaim, loudly enough that those nearby stopped their conversations, so that even the giant on stage turned to stare.

"My mistress' eyes are nothing like the sun," he began. "Coral is far more red than her lips' red. If snow be white, why then her breasts are dun." He parodied the act of coldly evaluating Maddie and of being shocked and disappointed by what he saw. She laughed along. Bill was pretty sure he had heard this language somewhere before.

"They said it has to be original," he interjected.

When Anthony ended with words of reverent praise for his "mistress," loud applause went up from the crowd, and Maddie folded into him.

"I'm no bard," Anthony said to Bill, "only a fan of the Bard—and an admirer of the kind of real beauty Maddie shows me every day."

Cheater, Bill thought to himself. But he made himself congratulate Anthony on his recitation and smile at the happy couple. What hurt Bill the most, more than seeing how graceful they were dancing together, or how easy her smile came, was witnessing her tipping up the cup of mulled wine. She had never abandoned restraint that way with Bill, not in recent years at least, maybe because he'd always gotten so drunk that she had to be the adult in the room.

What he needed to do now was walk away with some grace and dignity, or at the least avoid causing a scene. He kept his eyes focused on Maddie's off-kilter smile, because if he looked again at Anthony, he worried he might throw a punch.

"I'm glad to see you're happy," he told her. "You're looking really great—just like the poet here said. If there's anything I can do, don't hesitate to call. And, yeah, I guess we should talk about the house sometime. You have the number to my mobile phone. Or you can always reach me through Mother and Daddy."

She nodded with what appeared gratitude that he wasn't going to cause trouble. He had never apologized for the mailbox he'd grazed or the doughnuts he'd ripped into the cul-de-sac in front of Anthony's house. The swirl of tire marks were there for them to admire every day as a warning.

"Well, my lady, fair thee well." When he walked away, all the questions he hadn't asked filled his head. Were they living together? What was going on with Anthony's wife?

The quartermaster sat at the back of a work van, its doors thrown open to reveal an empire's worth of armor and weapons and gewgaws. He was a squat fellow with mutton-chops and a bushy mustache. He wore a mail shirt and jeans and was busy grinding rough edges off of a curved piece of steel, which he kept measuring against a breastplate hung from a frame. That electric grinder, Bill was pretty certain it wasn't allowed in the Middle Ages. When the quartermaster hit the kill switch on the grinder, Bill asked about armor.

"Okay," the man said, as if already exasperated. "Chain or plate?"

"Uh . . ."

"Let's start with the torso. In plate mail, I have brigandine, cuirass, heroic cuirass, cuirass with faulds."

"Are faulds good?"

Bill resorted to pointing into the back of the van in order to express his preferences and generally nodded at whatever the quartermaster offered. He paid fifty dollars cash for the rental, nearly all he had left, so when the quartermaster requested a license to keep, Bill handed him the entire wallet. The man helped Bill adjust the straps, and then Bill peered through the helmet visor and set off at a jangling jog toward the smell of camp smoke and the noise of impending battle.

When Bill arrived, he found himself lost in the confusion of soldiers, all of them eyeing him with suspicion. Two armies were gathered on opposite sides of the field. He gravitated toward the army in greater disarray. An argument was spreading among the ranks there over how they should engage the enemy. Bill hovered at the edge of a circle of mail-clad soldiers long enough to gather that one faction favored advancing across the field in a phalanx, while others objected that a phalanx was rarely practiced in medieval warfare.

At the edge of their circle he caught the sparkle of red metal-flake. Kent stepped into view wearing the motorcycle helmet and refrigerator crate. Even that absurd spectacle failed to lift Bill's spirits. He was glad for the helmet; he didn't want anyone to see his hurt. He walked up and slapped Kent's carpet padding with as much gusto as he could manage. Kent took a step back. When Bill spoke through the visor, Kent raised his rattan sword in the air and roared a greeting.

"Damn, brother, don't you look fine! That quartermaster set you up right." Kent asked if anybody had prepped him for battle, and, seeing Bill's confusion, Kent began explaining the rules.

"The fight progresses according to an honor code. A blow to the leg and you're supposed to drop to one knee. An arm gets chopped off, and you fight one-handed."

His instructions became progressively more intricate. When Kent came to body and head blows, Bill lost track. Did he say two, or was it three hits, before his game was over?

"How many blows before I'm dead?"

"Any legitimately crippling blow is fatal."

Kent gripped Bill's helmet and lifted it, turned it. It was important that the helmet was secure. If it spun when struck, Bill could lose his vision. Kent adjusted the straps and padding and then, once Bill was satisfied with the fit, Kent demonstrated a significant blow, bringing his rattan sword against the helmet so that it rang Bill's ears.

"I get the picture," Bill said.

"We've got to get you calibrated. Let me demonstrate a legitimately crippling blow."

"That's all right. I get it."

The phalanx faction prevailed, and so Bill and Kent were placed side by side in a tight line of soldiers. The plan was to march across the field in time to the beat of a drum until they engaged the enemy. It was absolutely crucial to keep their shields aligned and overlapping.

The two forces opposed each other at a distance of maybe a hundred yards. Off to the side the referee chanted, preparing them for the start.

Bill could hear his breath starting to come fast and labored inside the tin can he wore on his head. The helmet felt too tight and hot. He worried the slit in the visor might not let in adequate air. He couldn't see very well. No peripheral vision whatsoever. The metal flange pinched his ears and dug into his temples. He glanced beside him at the motorcycle helmet on Kent's head, that thick cushioning inside.

But when the referee shouted his signal and the field erupted with a roar and he felt himself thrust forward to meet the army rushing toward him, Bill forgot about the way the helmet cut into his scalp. He thought instead of his wife and her lover, heard the bells jingling on Anthony's cap and Maddie's responsive laughter. Worse even than the fantasies Bill had indulged of those two rolling in bed was the sight of them so comfortable together, so friendly after these many weeks. Bill lifted his sword and roared with the other voices. He charged forward and felt a hand grab his shoulder and pull him back.

"No!" Kent shouted. "Stay in line! Keep your shield level with my shield!"

The other army charged pell-mell across the field, and Bill checked his urge to rush toward them.

"Listen to the drum!" Kent shouted as they marched. "When we close ranks, stay by me!"

Bill had to put her out of his head, accept this closure. He stared up at the intense focus in Kent's eyes. Was Kent thinking of "his Lady"? And how did this stupid battle in any way help her? Fighting for her "honor and glory," like she was some plaster statue. What Anthony had said about Maddie, admiring the everyday reality, who she really was, maybe that was Bill's biggest failure. Same thing with Lucy. He'd lined up at the trough with all the other piggies, slid his money under her garter. He saw the illustrated couple on her back, reaching for the apple together. Maybe that was their rebellion; like Kent had said, the only time we get to create. Bill could feel the feet of the opposing army pounding the earth. He could see their eyes now, crazed in their charge, drunken with blood lust. Always some kind of lust. Bill roared his own challenge and pulsed forward.

"Stay in line!" Kent shouted.

A tall man in leather armor hurled his body against Bill's shield. The shield wall splintered. In an instant, the war machine broke down. Kent and Bill were shoved apart, and Bill found himself alone, fighting for his life against a single berserker. Dark hair poured out of the man's silver skull cap. He swung a long pole in wide, angry arcs with terrible skill. Bill held up his shield to block but felt the blows to his side, his shoulder, his neck. His ring-mail hauberk felt like thinnest satin. *Thwack* across the helmet, and his head rang with pain.

He crabbed sideways while the berserker lunged. Bill ducked another blow.

He kept backing across the field wondering *When will I know I'm dead?* A single stroke wrenched the shield from his hands, and the next head blow drove him to his knees.

A warm stream trickled across his nose. On his lips he tasted blood. He licked at it. It was salty, like her. Hot and mineral, tang of her heart wood. The sap she had shared with him, pouring out of her core of pleasure. Thick with her inmost self.

26

Lucy didn't want to hurt him. A small part of her still believed Wesley might be the one to hear her story, hear it from beginning to end. He had showed her the drawer full of cassette tapes, containing dozens of voices—all those old and now dead people he had made talk. Maybe he could make her talk, too. But the more he sought to possess her, the more Wesley's eyes began to look like *his* eyes, those nights Lucy's mama had left her alone with him.

She had slept at Wesley's cottage several times over the past three weeks, on nights she wasn't dancing. Slept, that was all. Each time, he had asked her to park around back so his mother wouldn't see in the morning. The countryside out by his cottage soothed her nerves, helping her stay off the nose candy. And the money he'd loaned her had freed her from debts she had never expected to pay off. In bed, she would let him spoon next to her. Even though she knew he wanted more, he hadn't pushed. While she drifted off to sleep, he would lie awake stroking her back, massaging her neck, undoubtedly believing that if he kept it up long enough she would think of nothing in the world but loving him.

When he showed up at her apartment, she instantly regretted giving him her address. It was the day after she had taken down her old posters and painted the walls yellow. She hadn't gotten high in almost two weeks and had thought the worst was over—until he showed up, totally unexpected, standing there freshly groomed, the muscles in his arms ripped, like he had just done a hundred push-ups outside in the parking lot.

He opened the blinds and they sat staring at the lemon walls. She let him help her decide where to place the new prints she planned to buy as soon as she found a day job. The way his eyes followed her around the living room made the walls shine too bright, like they were radioactive. Underneath the single coat of paint, every ugly stain shone through.

She made him a snack, put a cheese Danish and a cup of microwave coffee in front of him so that, for at least a few minutes, he had something else to watch. He bolted the Danish and gulped the coffee, and then he sat back in his chair and smiled up at her. She shifted her eyes across the empty walls where there were not enough windows, thinking how if the apartment had more furniture maybe it wouldn't seem so lonely. Whatever comfort she found in Wesley evidently would not transplant but was rooted in the countryside around his cottage.

He went on and on telling her about the dead—some failed romance between a disabled woman named Frankie and his great uncle Olin. He walked around the room talking and she sat still. It was only the two of them trapped by four bare walls, and it felt like a prison cell. But finally she calmed down, told herself it was just withdrawal. She talked about her job search and her plans to give up dancing.

Obviously mistaking himself to be the cause of her decision, he offered to loan her more money. And, too accustomed to playing along, to habitually stroking men's egos, she failed to correct him. He got that crazed look in his eyes and started talking about commitment again. She could see the ledge he was stepping out onto.

"This is a nice apartment here," he said, and she could tell he was lying. "I like what you're doing with it." He fingered the blinds then stepped over to the table and pulled out a chair opposite hers. "But, well, I've been wondering if you'd ever consider leaving the city. There's that piece of land I showed you. Uncle Olin's old homeplace. It might not be much. But it's what I've got to offer. I've been wanting to build a house up there. Just needed to find the right partner."

She stared across the table at his earnest expression. These were not the words she had prepared herself to hear, and so the speech she had rehearsed stayed lodged in that part of her mind.

"Homeplace?" she said, and he nodded.

ON THURSDAY EVENING when she drove out to the country, back to his cottage, she kept arguing with herself out loud in the car. She had to talk to him, he was a friend. She wouldn't hurt him now. Not yet. But what he had offered was more real than any opportunity she would ever find. That land. They could have a farm, a garden full of vegetables every summer. Chickens. Goats? Her Ma Maw had kept both chickens and goats, and one time a milk cow. It wasn't the land itself she craved so much as the way the land anchored the people who inhabited it, who had lived there together as family for generations.

When she got off of I-85, she was so glad to be away from those streets choked with traffic. She rolled down both windows, let the breeze whip her hair.

The dirt drive in front of his cottage was full of ruts, and her tires spun in the mud. The last thing she needed was to get stuck out here. Underneath the oak he was lying bare-chested on his bench, working with a pair of dumbbells loaded with iron.

"You're early," he said, an embarrassed smile on his face.

"I'm hungry." She cut the ignition and rolled up her windows.

When she stepped out, he asked if she would mind parking behind the cottage, but she said she couldn't spend the night. He was still bent over the bench, feverishly pulling the dumbbells up to his sides, letting out a grunt each time he exhaled.

"I'll be through here in a minute," he said.

"Take your time." She slumped down on the ground beside him and rested her back against the tree. While he finished his workout, she lit a cigarette and felt the solidity of the oak at her back. He had a perfect, healthy body, covered in sweat—he could be a stripper himself, if only he could dance. He was one beautiful boy, and he had no idea how completely she did not want his sex.

He said he had one more set of reps. He was bent over pumping the weights when they heard a bell tolling in the distance. Through the woods and across the pasture she heard his mother calling from the house on the hill.

"Wesley? Son?"

"Yeah?" he hollered back.

"Wesley?"

"Yeah!"

She called to him in a voice only a woman who had grown up on a farm could manage, this same voice and maybe the same bell she had used twenty years ago to call her boys home from deep in the woods.

"What is it!" he shouted.

"I've got some leftovers up here! Green bean casserole! And some deviled eggs! If y'all want it for your supper!"

"That's all right!" he shouted, turning his face away from Lucy, stepping toward his mother's voice and calling loud, almost angry, "I've got enough! Thanks!"

"It'll just go to waste!"

"Green bean casserole might be pretty tasty," Lucy said.

He went inside for a shirt, and when he came out again he said he would be right back, but he barely looked at her as he turned and walked toward the house on the hill.

She heard the rumble of a big engine roar to life in the distance. Minutes later, Wesley's daddy came driving by the cottage on his tractor, headed for the cornfield down in the bottoms. He lifted a hand in greeting and kept chugging on his way. Bill was so worried about his daddy's approval. He couldn't see how the man's very presence, his quiet strength, was enough. Enough to *have* a daddy, a whole family, two parents still married after all these years. And here Wesley was offering her a chance to be a part of that.

She went through the motions one last time, smiled gratefully when he pulled out her chair and they sat down to that rickety dinner table covered in vegetables he had grown himself. Boiled corn, sliced tomatoes, fried squash, and his mother's green bean casserole still bubbling hot from her oven, smothered in melted cheese. She sat through dinner planning her break-up speech but could never find the right way to begin. Then she walked with him beneath the stars to the hillside with the crumbling chimney where he intended to build their house.

They sat facing each other on a quilt beneath the stars and drank his cousin's scuppernong wine while he told her about Uncle Olin's lonely old age and his mother's side of the family who had long ago farmed this land.

Later, at his cottage, she tried to leave. But somehow, instead, she found herself moving her car and then undressing and changing into a nightgown he had bought for her. She slid under the cotton sheet while he took his turn in the bathroom. She lay on her back stiff with uncertainty, the sheet pulled up to her chin. Too late to try to explain— to say her mother's boyfriend had raped her—when she was already lying in Wesley's bed wearing nothing but a satin nightgown. Then he lay down beside her and started touching her. His hands followed the paths they had learned, up and down her back and shyly across her breasts, and then up to her neck where he began pressing firmly to draw the tension out.

"Wesley?" she said with her back to him.

"Yeah, sweetheart."

She could simply lie here and he would let her go to sleep. "Wesley?"

"I'm here." He leaned over her, but she turned away. Her knees tucked into her stomach. Her fingers entered her mouth, grew slick with saliva.

"Lucy. Talk to me."

"I . . . I've never been lucky with boys."

"I know. I know, honey. You're having a rough time. Hey, it's okay. I don't mind waiting, I told you. Just relax. I'm here. Just go to sleep."

He held her tighter. She felt his muscles flex as he pulled her close. He started telling about a wild grape vine he had discovered behind the site of Uncle Olin's fallen-down smoke house. It was just words, meant to calm her nerves, and it was working. She listened to his voice and the chorus of cicadas chiming in the trees and somewhere out in the woods a whip-poor-will calling its mate. What if she said yes? Maybe there was a life to be made with him that she was only beginning to recognize. Wesley was not the partner she had imagined—and who was that? Certainly no man she had ever met. She could never be sweet on Wesley the way she had been sweet on, say, Cassie. But maybe she could be a different kind of sweet, because there was a sweetness in him that quieted the alarm bells ringing in her head. But the next minute, she felt his arms locked around her and she couldn't breathe. The thin sheet lay heavy against her body. Her skin was a piece of glass about to shatter. The ceiling fan whirred on high speed, and still the syrupy air choked her. She needed to leave.

"It's okay," he said. "Everything's going to be all right. You'll see. Just ride it out." He rocked her in his arms and kissed the back of her neck.

Maybe he was right about her panic. Maybe it was only the cocaine blues. Two weeks wasn't very long to be clean. But the hardest days were over, weren't they? They had to be over. A year from now she could be sitting in a rocking chair shelling beans beside his mother, helping her stretch a quilt into its frame, while Wesley came home from the airport and put on his overalls and climbed up on the seat of a tractor. Sex on the full moon, she could handle that, couldn't she? If she said yes, they would have to agree to a schedule ahead of time.

He spooned closer into her back. He kept putting his mouth on her, little, loud pecks all over her neck, the way a child might kiss. He rocked her from the hips. She felt the rhythm quicken, and then she felt his erection rise and press against her. Her own body picked up the rhythm, and she touched herself till the moistness came. She arched her back and pressed her ass into his erection. He started kissing her harder.

"Okay," she said. "Okay."

He moved his mouth down her neck and spread the little pecks across her shoulder. She reached for him and moved him inside her.

"Are you sure?" he asked.

"Yes."

He held both of her breasts in his hands, and while they rocked sideways together she stared out across the dark room, thinking how it wasn't fair to either of them. And, goddammit, she knew he was looking. She could feel him studying her like some exhibit. Why couldn't he close his eyes and feel the movement and know her body with his, this one time, without tormenting her with that hungry, childlike gaze?

27

Wesley lay awake a long time before he pulled himself out of bed. He walked to the sink and washed his privates again. She had left him sometime during the night. He had lain awake for hours, holding her, listening to her breathe deeply in sleep, and then when he awoke this morning she was gone—she had come in and taken his cottage away from him. It did not belong to him anymore. He turned on the radio, but the sound poured out thin and brittle. He went to the refrigerator and filled a glass with orange juice, but the juice smelled rancid. A void yawned open inside him, a deep longing for the boy he had been. He had married her, and he wasn't ready for marriage. He wanted his body back. He walked back to sit on the edge of the bed and pulled on a pair of shorts and a T-shirt. He was a stranger inside a body he did not recognize. He had pretended with her that he was a man. He stood and walked back to the sink, began washing last night's dishes. Through his kitchen window he could see the sun rising, and a figure hobbling in his direction. Mother.

If Lucy were only still here with him, or if the two of them hadn't gone all the way, if he had not spilled his seed inside her, then he might still feel complete and able to confront the stooped-over shape making its way toward his cottage door.

"Wesley?" She always cracked the door enough to shout his name, but she never entered without being invited. "Wesley? Are you up yet?"

"Yeah, Mother."

"I need some help this morning. I'm trying to string another row of beans, and you know I can't reach it. I just need a hand for fifteen minutes. Then I'll let you go."

He stood at the sink and listened to water from the spigot splashing down the drain. He watched his mother hobble back toward her garden. It was difficult this morning even to perform simple tasks like dressing himself. He found his sneakers and carried them outside. The screen door slammed behind him, and he sat down on the cinder block steps. He laced up his sneakers and watched a swarm of black ants tear apart a dying cicada. He leaned close to watch the wiry jaws dig into the meat. They would feed until nothing was left but a camo exoskeleton. A large, fine specimen, fat as a peach pit. Lying on its back, its wings fluttered in spasms.

He found his mother already busy in the garden, throwing the ball of twine up over the cable she was too short to reach. The tomato plants reeked. A jay perched high in the elm above and cawed. Two squirrels barked as they chased each other from limb to limb. He took the ball of twine from his mother and wrapped it around the upper cable. Down in the corn patch, Daddy was making laps with the tractor. The engine rumbled. Diesel exhaust carried on the breeze. This was the way his parents made a marriage of forty-one years work: they kept their distance, her working the vegetables closer to home, him laboring in the outlying fields.

"Remember my circle is having a little party for Granny and Grandpa tomorrow," she said, catching the ball of twine he dropped across the upper cable.

"That's right," he said. "Their anniversary."

"They're expecting you to be there."

"Who's coming?"

"Oh, just a few people."

He could imagine the church ladies gathered together in that old house, birds in a henhouse fluttering and hovering and pecking and fussing over the two old ones.

"I hope you realize what you mean to Grandpa and Granny," she said. "You're their favorite grandchild, the only one who visits them regular. Every time I'm down there, they're talking about nothing but Wesley. Granny's always looking for any excuse to get you down there and look over some old newspaper clippings she's probably already showed you a thousand times."

Wesley was tensing every muscle.

"They've been missing you lately."

"I know it." Maybe she would leave it at that, not force him to discuss how he had chosen to spend his time lately, and with whom. Her garden accused him—the tomatoes plump, the okra waist-high, the bean-vines spiraling toward the sun.

"You don't realize how much good it does them to see you. For a young person like you to show so much interest in them—it keeps them hanging on."

"I know."

They moved along the row of beans passing the ball of rough twine back and forth, weaving Jacob's ladder for the tender vines to climb. While she talked, he heard the apology in his own voice responding to her ongoing report of the heavy earth grinding along on its axis, slowing down toward some apocalypse when all the old folks and their old ways would disappear from the planet. As if he could do something to stop it from happening.

"Well," Mother said. "Did she spend the night again?"

"What's that?"

"That tattooed girl. What's her name? Lucy?"

He hesitated. "Yeah," he said. Here it came.

"She's been a regular house guest lately."

They worked a while longer in silence. He focused on the tractor rumbling through the corn patch and the squeak of bedsprings, homemade harrow, banging across clots of red mud.

"I don't pretend to understand everything you're going through," she said. "But I do know how a young man can be tempted." She measured her words out carefully in a voice meant to soothe. "I just want you to think about what you're doing. And trust yourself. You know right from wrong. Don't let your brother or anybody else lead you somewhere you don't need to go."

"Bill has nothing to do with it."

She nodded and waited for him to go on. "Well," she said, "I only want you to try and take the long view."

"Mother—"

"When you become a father, when you see your own child open his eyes, your whole world will change in a way you can't even imagine. What seems interesting now will terrify you one day. You need a woman that's reliable. You can't be the rock alone. It takes two."

"I know that."

"I'm just saying that a child deserves the kind of love and care you had."

"I know that."

"Well. I don't want to see you ruin yourself the way your brother has done. I want to see you—"

"Mother! How do you know so much about me? About what I need?" He let the ball of twine drop to the ground and roll between his feet. He took a step backward away from her and the trellis separating them. "How can you know? Shouldn't I know better than anybody else what's good for me, what I need!" He nervously eyed the garden all around them. He spread his arms out pointing for her. "Mother. Look around! There's a whole world out there."

He studied her squatting in the dirt, the blank stare on her face. Such certain judgment, like she knew everything, like she was God.

28

Lucy awakened to birdsong. And in the distance, the low rumble of his daddy's tractor. Beside her Wesley lay deep in sleep, his hairless chest rising and falling. Across the quilt lay his hand palm up, as if begging, and there upon his wrist spread the dim blue outline of a heart. She rolled toward him and laid her cheek on his shoulder. Last night had been rough. But last night was over. And now the morning glow crept through the window the way it had done every other morning she had lain in his bed. The sparrows sang the same pattern of notes. She watched the rapid movements of his dreaming eyes covered by the thin layer of skin.

In the kitchenette she took a plate out of the drying rack and carried it to the fridge. Hunger had woken her. She pulled out his mama's green bean casserole and rolled back the aluminum foil. She scooped out three spoonfuls and put the plate in the microwave, watched it cook, then switched it off seconds before the bell chimed. She didn't want to wake him.

Outside on the front steps, she sat and watched the fog dissipate while the sun lifted from the trees. She spooned the creamy beans into her mouth. Even better than the night before. This morning she wasn't rehearsing any speeches. Let speeches wait till tomorrow. Wait and see.

She washed her dish and still he lay deep in sleep. She slipped off the satin nightgown and changed into her blue jeans and a long-sleeved T-shirt. She stepped to his bathroom mirror and put her hair up in a simple bun. There, now she looked like any other farm girl. Not a trace of ink to alarm his mama. Even if she had staved off her hunger with the woman's casserole, she still had room for her bacon and eggs and grits. Her cinnamon toast. Of course, she didn't want to presume, but it didn't hurt to hope for an invitation. Every morning she spent the night with him, she kept expecting to be invited back to that table. It was only a matter of time.

Wesley had rolled over onto his side, but his breath still came slow and regular. She slipped on her flip flops and went back outside. Mornings were easier than nights, but still she had to keep moving. If she sat in one place for five minutes, her nerves flared up. Was it still cocaine blues? After staying clean for two weeks? Maybe this case of jangling nerves was just who she was.

She found the trail to Uncle Olin's. Wesley's dog followed. Preacher Claude, named after some dead ancestor. That was fucking funny. Wesley was slow to laugh. Too serious. That could be a problem. One thing about Bill, he had a sense of humor.

When she came to the footbridge across the creek, the dog let out a bark, as if in warning, and stood there waiting. She clicked her tongue. "Come, boy," she said, but he spooked. He turned and trotted back down the path toward home and his sleeping master. She climbed the hill alone and came to the building site, the ancient foundation, square blocks cut out of granite.

She picked out a stone and sat, felt its solidity radiate through her body. To the left lay the remnants of a smokehouse. To the right, a nice clear spot for a chicken run. Wesley wanted to build a traditional I-house, what the old farmers always built. When he talked about his plans, she saw them taking shape. She saw the site here filling with structures, teeming with livestock. She understood how, more than anything else, it would be their shared labor that bound them together. And in time, his mama would come to see her as legitimate. It *would* happen. Only a matter of time. Six days of creation, of new beginnings, the Bible said. Six days of labor, and then rest. When she had spoken to Niall about Adam and Eve, it was the tree that mattered to her—the Pentecostal flames, branches erupting into a new knowledge of reality. Starting over clean. He had made the man and woman bigger than she had imagined them. And she had always been bothered by the fact that they both held the apple. In her mind, the new beginning started with the woman's action, her choice. But now she saw it was something she could not manage alone. She needed a partner. Not only that, she needed his family. In time, Bill would come to understand this path. The father was easy. And the mother, well, she was inevitable. She babied her boy, that was clear, but now that Wesley had chosen Lucy and stood waiting for her to choose him in return, all Lucy had to do was say yes, and his mama would have no choice whatsoever. Say yes, and his mama's love would flow like milk and honey.

She stood and surveyed the lot, measured the perfect rectangle of foundation stones. If she turned her back on this paradise, the chance might never come her way again.

Her flip flops slipped beneath her on the way down the hill. She slowed her pace, careful not to twist an ankle. Crossing the creek, she heard her feet thump the planks of the footbridge. It felt good to be walking with a purpose. Her appetite had returned, and she was certain this would be the morning she accompanied Wesley up the hill to his mother's house for breakfast. Inside the cottage, if he lay still asleep, she would wake him and make a different speech than the one she had planned only yesterday.

But the bed was empty, unmade. The quilt his mama had sewn for him lay crumpled on the floor.

She let the screen door slam behind her and stood on the steps, scanning the woods. She heard voices. She looked up the hill toward his parents' house then down the valley toward the garden. Through the trees, she glimpsed movement. She walked down the garden path. Maybe she could lend them a hand. But she hadn't walked far before she understood something was wrong. And the closer she came, the more the woman's voice clarified itself into tones of anger, judgment.

Lucy slowed her pace, walked stealthily onward, and when she came to the pine woods, she waited there in the shadows. This was close enough to hear and to understand that the woman was talking about her. She heard Wesley's voice, too, talking back to his mama. Defending himself. Defending Lucy. But his words might as well have been hurled at the freshening breeze. It blew to her the smell of resinous tomato vines, spicy basil leaves, a garden she knew she would never again enter—because the wind carried also his mama's voice, telling Wesley that the woman he had chosen was of a class beneath them. Unfit. Unclean. Not worthy to mix with their blood.

29

Bill had regained consciousness in the parking lot— standing up. He hadn't yet sunk to the level of passing out in ditches. He would admit it had been a struggle. He remembered the palms of his hands against pavement, but not his belly. The bouncer at The Jackpot had gotten rougher than was necessary. Bill had simply tried to talk to him about human sexuality. He had posed his question— whether sex was part of the machine or the garden—and the guy had told him to go find a seat.

"I'm thinking definitely *machine*," Bill had told the bouncer. "The nature of the question itself inclines me to believe *machine*. Language is like computers, all zeroes and ones, all either/or. All virgin/whore." He pulled from his pocket a drink napkin bearing The Jackpot logo, silhouettes of naked women dancing around a pot of gold and the stream of coins pouring out of a slot machine. "See," he said. "*Machine!*"

He didn't remember walking to Way of the Flesh, but it was downhill, easy to find his way in even the most polluted state. The more curious question is how he had managed to convince Niall, yet again, to overlook his state of intoxication. Maybe he had seemed totally lucid; he couldn't remember. All he knew for certain was that now he had a very bad headache. Niall kept feeding him water.

Bill peeled his face from Naugahyde and stared out the open doorway. The sun was up high—he could tell by the glare on the puddles—which meant he would miss another day of work. Well, Kent was better off without him. Who wasn't?

Sometime in the night it had rained, and the air was soggy. He rested his face against the padded headrest and focused on the needles following the line of his shoulder blade, plowing furrows for its black seed.

Niall was in the middle of a diatribe concerning NationsBank's plans for demolition of the old Independence Building sometime today. Charlotte's historical preservation society had protested. Declaring the old twelve-story Greek Revival structure the city's first skyscraper, they had tried to have the date postponed, but NationsBank owned the property. And the bank wielded political power the historical society could only dream of.

"Will we be able to see it from here?" Bill asked.

"Oh, most definitely." Niall pointed toward the door with the buzzing tattoo gun. Bill craned his neck toward the light, followed the hand and saw the top stories of the old building above the brick square across the street. Granite columns rose up to a frieze filled with statues. What a shame.

Niall said the bank had flown in experts who planted explosives all over the structure. According to the news, it would come down in seconds.

Bill carefully lifted his head, squinting at the pain of movement. "So," he said. "I've been working on my magic."

"What?"

"Like you said." He made a flourish with his hand toward the open doorway. "Projecting myself."

"What a frightening thought."

"No, I'm serious. I've been doing like you told me. Meditating on my chi. You know, focusing on myself—"

"Magic involves more than self-indulgence."

"I know that. Hey, I am not my body, right? It's just like you said. Once I refused to close my eyes to the phenomena happening around me, I came to see how I was not simply in the middle of it but possibly the cause. And at that moment I became a magician."

"Right." Niall turned up the rheostat and the tattoo gun buzzed angrily.

Magic was proving a lot harder work than Bill had anticipated. When he'd heard Maddie's voicemail, he replayed it three times, listening for some note of affection. *Hi, Bill, it's Maddie. I'm calling . . . about the house. . . I promised to call, so that's what I'm doing. There are some other bills we should discuss . . . the credit cards. I've paid the utilities. . . . Anyway, call me. It was good to see you the other day.* This last line sounded like an afterthought. He returned her call and got her answering machine, this time not even her voice but synthetic words, a woman's, asking him to please leave a message. If it had been Maddie's recorded voice, he would have left the message, but he wasn't going to start talking to computers. That was almost three weeks ago, and Maddie hadn't tried to call again, which was just as well. Every time they did talk, it only seemed to further clarify how finished their marriage was, and right now he was having a hard time handling that kind of finality. Every relationship seemed to be reaching its terminus. He hadn't talked to Lucy in three weeks either, and during that time he had seen little of his brother, not since the day Wesley had called Bill's mobile phone to ask if he could stay with Kent that weekend; when Bill pried, Wesley had confessed that Lucy was coming over for dinner.

After spending a long time wallowing in rage and sorrow, Bill had finally confronted the burden of responsibility that lay upon him. Lucy had never returned his calls, even when they had dated. And so he had retraced his steps back to The Jackpot with the purpose of discovering, face to face, what her intentions were with his little brother. But she had never shown up, and after waiting for hours, he had ended up here.

"I'm nearly done," Niall said. "Just finishing up the shadows under the wings." One of the things Bill appreciated about Niall was how he narrated his work, inch by inch. Bill felt the wet sponge across his back, which for a moment soothed the pain. This tattoo was bigger than the rest. It felt like Niall had filleted his back with a dull knife. Bill wondered how much pain his father had felt after his colon was removed, after they stitched him back up. This was as close to surgery as Bill had ever come, and, yeah, it did feel like something had been taken out and something else put in.

He began to remember pieces of his midnight dialogue with Niall, how Niall had been finishing a tattoo for that rockabilly singer and said he didn't want to stay up the rest of the night, but something in Bill's monologue had convinced him. "I want it on my back," Bill had said, reaching over his shoulder and slapping his scapula. "Where only other people can see it. Because I've gotta learn to see myself through other lives. I can't keep blundering through lives, you know, leaving this path of destruction in my wake."

All the suffering around him: Maddie, his parents, Wesley, even Lucy. What he had called loving her was just more trauma—to both of them. He had nothing Lucy wanted, except money, and maybe his abject worship. So, he was waiting for some signal, clarity on how he could go about loving her without causing more harm. And if that meant turning her loose, getting out of Wesley's way, believing that his brother was capable of giving her the love he hadn't, then he wanted to bless that happy ending. But, damn, he couldn't seem to hold the blessing in his mind; it always evolved into a story of their suffering.

"How much longer?" Bill gritted his teeth. The pain burned hotter by the minute.

"I'm almost there," Niall said. "Just a little more shading, a couple lines I need to hit again."

When Lucy walked in the door, Bill looked up into her surprised eyes. She paused at the counter, nervously flipping through pages in Niall's portfolio, like some first-time customer.

"It's early for you, isn't it?" Niall said.

"I didn't really expect to find you here." She came around the counter and then saw Bill's back.

"Well, well," she said. "Look at Count Tequila."

She sprawled out on the couch in a long-sleeved T-shirt and jeans. Something about her looked different. Less goth. No make-up, for starters. Her eyes looked smaller without mascara. Her hair was pinned up in a bun. She stood and stepped close, studying Bill's back.

"Holy shit, Niall," she said.

Niall raised an eyebrow.

"I guess I never knew how much you had it in for Bill."

"He was the one who requested bones and bat wings."

"While you're at it, why don't you go ahead and etch the mark of the Beast across his forehead?"

Bill tried to laugh. "Is it really that bad?"

"Six six six."

Her presence made it very difficult for him to remain centered. The colors on her pale skin pierced him with longing.

"Where were you last night?" he asked, Naugahyde tugging at his jaw. "I waited for you at the club."

"I'm not getting on the schedule much lately. The boss is trying to teach me a lesson about missing work and coming in late. That's what he says. He can kiss my ass. I'm giving up dancing, anyway." She sat down on the sofa, grabbed the black vinyl at the top of her boot and began peeling. She pulled off both boots and sat barefooted. "I was at your brother's last night."

"I see. Well. Move on, that's what I say. Don't stay in a line of work you don't enjoy."

They stared at each other like strangers. But they knew each other well enough. The three of them had come to a standoff deep as blood kin. Even with this silence, Bill felt closer to these two tattooed freaks now than he felt to his own wife. Maybe it was time to disappear from Maddie's life entirely. Just snip that thinnest tether. And what then? Mexico? For weeks he had been expecting mail from a lawyer announcing some decision. Funny how when Lucy started blowing him off, he had gone back to obsessing over Maddie. But now that Lucy sat before him, in the flesh, he could bring himself to think of no one else.

The rumble of a dump truck out on the street shook the floor beneath them. Traffic was already bumper to bumper.

"You're still staying with Kent?" Lucy said.

"I guess so. I don't have anywhere else to rest my weary head. Since you're sleeping with Wesley." He forced himself to laugh.

"I ain't *sleeping* with Wesley. You can have your bed back."

"I thought you said—"

"I won't be going back there."

"What? It took you longer than that to get rid of me."

"Yeah, well, you're tighter with your money."

"You fucking whore." He shook his head, shame hot on his face.

"I was joking. God!"

"Sorry. I'm sorry. I didn't mean that."

Niall stood and laid the gun down on the counter. He grabbed a rag from his bench, wiped the sweat from his forehead, and walked outside.

She blew her nose and Bill saw the trickle of blood. She pinched the tip of her nose and tilted her head back. She wasn't high. He could always tell when she was high.

"Look, I didn't mean what I just said. I'm sorry. But Wesley, he hasn't had a lot of experience."

"Don't worry, I won't corrupt him any further. Your mama made sure of that."

"How are you doing?" Bill sat up and faced her. Why was the simplest thing so hard?

She shrugged. "I'm making it."

Bill wondered if there was a way to start over. Only when she sat here before him, the actual woman, was he forced to reckon with the reality of how completely she did not want him. One look at her face and it was clear. But she didn't understand how he had changed. What he understood now, maybe too late, was how the ink on her skin signified a lifetime of endurance. Every day, she had claimed the right to be. Not only her present, but her teen years, her childhood, it pulled at him across time. The stories she had told him and the ones that lay still buried inside her: the trailer park about to sink into the swamp, her mother's boyfriend who bought her the dress, the time she gave herself the mohawk haircut and ran away from home, the rusted Schwinn bicycle she modified with the chopper handlebars, the ramp she built out of plywood and bloodied her nose and fractured her wrist. He wanted to share all of that, to take away the pain and leave the glory. He wanted to hop on the banana seat of that chopper bike and peddle like a bat out of hell until his front tire hit the makeshift ramp while she stood and watched him hurtling through the sky, tumbling over the handlebars, falling in a broken heap, fracturing a rib, maybe puncturing a lung, just to show her what he was capable of.

Niall stepped back inside and took his seat beside Bill. He plugged in the gun but only held it in his lap. "I've got to get out of this business," he said.

"When are you going to fix that air conditioner?" Lucy asked.

"What are y'all doing for the Fourth?" Bill surreptitiously drank in her form, her whole living presence. She could still change the world merely by walking in and slumping down onto the sofa.

She shrugged. Niall put on a hick accent and said he planned to fly his rebel flag from the rear window of his pickup—maybe ride downtown to watch the fireworks while he listened to the final laps of the race.

"One of my cousins and his girlfriend are having a party," Bill said. "Out in the certified country. Pulled pork off the grill, maybe a sample of scuppernong wine. Maybe even some moonshine, if we're lucky. We'll just kick back and take it easy, catch a buzz. Maybe throw some Frisbee. You both should come." How nauseating, this dissimulation, this pretense that he was satisfied to be her friend, her social planner. But if it meant he might know when he would see her again, so be it. Plus, Duane and Crystal needed to throw a successful party, the bigger the better. They needed to see people having fun at their house, picking the bones clean, licking their plates, gulping down the last drops of Duane's wine. They had fought for too long in private—they needed desperately to come out into the world.

"Good luck getting Niall out to the country," Lucy said. "He's afraid to leave the shop. That's why he never sleeps, or if he does sleep, it's probably here on the couch. He's scared of crowds, and still he dreams of working in New York City. He's scared of flying saucers."

"I'm afraid of what people like you will do out there," he said.

"People like me?" She laughed.

"So, this buddy of yours," Niall said to Bill. "The Grail knight. You're doing this for him?" He made a flourish with his hand over Bill's newly inked back. "He must be some kind of friend."

"Well, it's not *for* him," Bill said, defensively. "His preaching gave me the idea." If the skull and bat wings were for anyone, they were, of course, for her, like the rest of his tattoos. But he couldn't come out and say it. Not here, anyway. Instead, he told them about Kent and the book of

Revelations, how Kent had already graduated from Grail knight to evangelist—"born again" in a little country church, out where he was raised. Pentecostal Holiness. Bill could tell that Kent was fed by it, but the constant sermons had gotten deep under Bill's skin, literally. The other morning, Bill had stumbled to his buddy's pickup truck, hungover to hell, just trying to hold down his breakfast. Kent had stood by the deep freezer holding a crate of steaks, staring at Bill wide-eyed, finally explaining how he could see a shadow cast over Bill—a gray shadow of sin falling over his shoulders.

"Spooked the shit out of me," Bill said.

"From your description, frankly, he sounds delusional," Niall said. He wiped Bill's back clean and said he only needed to make a few finishing touches.

"He says he's filled with the Holy Spirit," Bill said.

"No, I'm afraid I would have to say it's insanity."

"How do you know so much?" Lucy said. "Kent might have more soul than you think. He might have the real thing."

"I kind of doubt it," said Niall.

Bill felt a pang of betrayal. He should have kept his mouth shut.

Niall said he knew those kinds of people, that he had grown up around them and that unfortunately, when you inbred over ten generations and lived off of nothing but white flour, white sugar, and pork fat, the body simply did not work. And the brain, a key part of the body, was particularly susceptible to misfiring. When those people started rolling their eyes up into the backs of their heads and talking in tongues, it was because they had simply worked themselves up into such a frenzy that the brain was misfiring constantly. There was *no* magic going on there at all—except maybe in the form of less than friendly entities flying into a weak body they knew they could rape and destroy.

"It's so ironic," Niall said, "because the Bible itself talks about that sort of thing with great warning." Whenever Niall got so worked up, Bill worried about the straightness of his lines.

"There are things floating out there that do not have your best interests in mind," Niall said. "And these Pentecostal Christians think it's God flying into them." He laughed to himself. "And it *ain't* God. It's some extraterrestrial sonofabitch who's here getting ready to clear us all out so the real estate deal can go through." He sprayed cleanser across Bill's back and wiped it down with a paper towel. He peeled off his gloves and slumped back against the wall. "I hope it's scary enough for you," he said. "It's still going to bleed, but go ahead and take a peek before I cover it with salve."

Bill sat up from the chair and went to the mirror on the far wall. He turned and looked over his shoulder at the reflection of his upper back. What he saw made him tremble: a pair of bat wings, tier upon tier of skulls, evolving from toad to human, to demon, to . . . robot?

"Niall." The faintest snarl of nervous laughter spread across his lips. "That's something, all right. Look at it. I am the pale rider." He pivoted so that Lucy had a clear view. No solicitation. If she wanted to comment, then good. But either way, he would show her what he was capable of. He worked his arms so that the black wings covering his shoulder blades appeared to flap beneath a film of blood. Outside, a cloud passed before the sun and the shop went dark. He felt the shadow fall over his head, across his shoulders, down the length of his body, a gray haze he could see in the mirror, a gauze curtain separating him from everyone he had ever tried to love.

He was staring out the doorway, directly at it, when it blew. The Independence Building. For a fraction of a second before he heard a sound, he felt the tremor and saw the top floors shudder and crack. Then came the blast, unbelievably loud, and jagged lines forming along the white granite, the roar of stone grating against stone, columns buckling, the whole thing tumbling in upon itself.

Then it simply was not there.

[To learn about the demolition of Charlotte's historic Inde-pendence Building—and also to discover the first Declaration of Independence in the English colonies—visit Fugitive Views, Southern Fried Karma's YouTube Channel.]

Part IV

30

Bill pushed his head out the window so that the clean country air flattened the skin on his face and filled his cheeks. It poured through his open collar, washing away the lingering taint of cheap perfume, the bitter taste of strawberry lip gloss. If he was going to die, a high-speed car crash would be the way to go, much better than succumbing to the slow growth of some cancer.

"So they're still lovers, then?" Kent kept staring straight out at the road.

Bill pulled his head back inside the truck. "She's sleeping with him, I guess. She says she's not. But if she needs money, she'll be back over there." He sucked hard at the pint bottle of Beam and drew only air. He tossed the empty out the window, and when it crashed against the road sign, he felt his heartache ease a smidgen.

When Bill had probed, it was clear from the way Wesley brooded that he was licking his wounds, but he wouldn't say a word about Lucy. Mother, on the other hand, wouldn't shut up about her. Bill had offered to help her burn a brush pile. She stood there with a gasoline can and a box of matches, while she accused him of bringing home that "woman of the night" with the sole purpose of polluting his brother's body and soul. In her mind, Bill had ever been the enemy of innocence. Maybe so. But wasn't there something fascist about innocence?

Kent pressed his lips together, chewing on them. Probably an old habit, but one Bill had only recently noticed. And once he had noticed, it seemed like Kent was constantly chewing his lips, always clearing his throat to fill the silence, leaving Bill no interval of peace.

"I think we meet people for a reason," Kent said.

"What's that?"

"I think God puts people in our path for a purpose."

"Oh."

"It's not an accident the way I met Lucy. The Lord has good things in store for her. We have to believe that. Otherwise . . ."

It was early morning, but Bill was already fed up with the Holiness hoodoo. And that bald head; mortification of the flesh was one thing, but Kent was butt ugly without hair. He had paid a ton of money for that implant, and to shave it off for religious reasons offended Bill's economic sensibilities.

"I just mean," Kent said, "there is a reason we met. If there's not some overarching purpose, then it's all chaos. It's just appetite and contests of power and resources."

"Mm hmm. That's right."

"But how can you live with that? The world we see, the world that includes our desires, the Hindus call it *maya*. Illusion."

"That's not in the Bible."

"Don't be so sure. Look, friend, I'm trying to apologize."

"For what?"

"For leading you on a wild goose chase. But now I'm on to something real, and I want to share it."

"Buddy, I hope you won't take this wrong." Bill turned and stared at Kent's egg of a head. "I liked you better when you were guzzling beer and watching titties shake in your face. This puritanism is bad for you. I'm only telling you this for your own good, okay? At some point, somehow, the flesh will have its way."

"So you're saying I should do like you and try to have sex with my customers?"

"You're right, maybe that wouldn't be the best idea."

"You just went into that woman's home, and Lord only knows what you promised her. Every time we come back this way now, she's gonna be looking for you, and you're gonna be ducking down in the seat. Once you've had your way with her."

"All we did was kiss. She kissed me first! We felt an affinity for one another, okay? She got well kissed. *And* she got a free four-pack of prime ribs."

"You gave her a free four-pack! I'm taking that out of your pay."

"Good enough. I'm thinking this will be my last check."

"Fine by me."

They drove on in silence deep into the country, along a narrow road crowded on both sides by scrub pines standing so thick most of the lower growth was dead, bone-dry limbs, brown pine needles, the perfect kindling for a forest fire. She had lain back on the sofa and pulled him close, let him touch her wherever he pleased. He had felt the urge but not the love to back it up. So he left with promises to return when he got off work. But he would not return.

He wiped his mouth on the sleeve of his Polo shirt, and still he tasted her lip gloss. Nothing like real strawberries, just some cheap imitation. The idea of kissing Wilma had been to forget Lucy, but now all he wanted was to remember—her touch, her kiss, the way she teased him with the tip of her tongue, the smell of her perfumed skin, the briny taste of her, the soft padding of her belly, the ink all over.

"So," Kent broke their silence, "have you given any more thought to that profound question?"

"Which one?"

"Our sexual urges, where do they come from, the garden or the machine?"

"Nah, still working on that."

"I've got your answer."

"Oh, yeah, which is it?"

"Neither. It comes from a fell fire, a fire that would envelop the whole planet, spread to the whole universe, if

God let it. But He's not about to let it. Still, in the meantime, how much damage do you want to see your life do?"

"Oh, please, please, please, please! Tell me when church is over!"

"Carnal desire," Kent said, "is a degraded form of our longing for God."

"What?"

"Carnal desire—"

"If that's true, then what is sexual disgust?"

"Disgust?"

"Yeah, you know, when a woman wants nothing to do with you and has made that perfectly clear."

The veins flared across Kent's bald head. He fixed a hard stare at the road ahead.

"I wasn't talking about you. Me." No wonder Lucy hated him. How much had Bill paid for her pretense?

The truck hit a pothole, and instead of slowing, Kent stomped the accelerator. When they reached the bridge, the shocks bottomed out, and the crash exploded in Bill's ears. The whole vehicle lurched sideways like a ship in high seas.

"My God!" Bill shouted. "Can you slow down!" What he had thought earlier about preferring to die in a car crash—he hadn't really meant that. He didn't want to die.

Kent gunned it along a straight-away and then abruptly braked and skidded to a stop in the middle of the road. He shifted into four-wheel drive, turned the wheels hard left, and pulled off onto the grass.

There was a gas pipeline, a wide swath cut through the middle of the pine forest. Rolling hills. They bounded over a ditch and tore through mud until they hit grass again. Kent didn't explain. He stepped on the gas and they bumped along. Despite what the TV commercials led you to believe, Bill's buddy's truck really was not built for this kind of punishment. At the foot of the hill, the dark ribbon of a creek wound through marshland. They approached at high speed, hit a terrace, and launched skyward. They slammed down, slewed sideways, and entered the creek with a splash. Kent revved the engine, but they were stuck. There was a loud hissing and steam rising from the vents in the hood.

Kent's door creaked open. Without explaining himself, he stepped away from the truck, followed the creek upstream into the woods.

Bill got out and saw the front wheels mired to the axles. The keys were still dangling in the ignition, so he cranked the engine and tried to rock the truck loose. But the wheels only spun deeper grooves. He rolled down the windows and still the air in the cab was hot and foul. They could walk out and then hitch a ride. He glanced back at the freezer strapped down to the bed. How long before the meat spoiled? Fuck it. That was Kent's problem.

Bill checked his phone. Plenty of battery left, but no service. He waited for Kent to return until he got fed up with waiting.

After the glare of sun on water, the dark woods deepened his gloom. Not fifty yards in and the canopy had blotted out the sun. Oaks and sycamores stood tall along the creek. Kent could be anywhere. Bill stayed close to the water, and he hadn't hiked far before he saw Kent on his knees, his bald head leaning over a pool deep enough for swimming. The far bank was high, and it cast its shadow over the murky water.

Bill squatted by his friend. "Did I say something to piss you off?"

Kent shook his head and stared into the pond. "I just needed a little prayer time."

"Oh. Okay. That's fine. But did you have to ruin the truck?"

"The truck is the least of our worries."

At the far end of the pool a shadow shifted. Something disturbed the brown leaves that lined the bottom of the pond.

"I used to come here a lot," Kent said. "When I was a little boy. I was born up there in that trailer park. We lived there till I was nine."

"Where we sell? In that slum?"

"Yeah."

At the top of the hill perched the back ends of mobile homes. There was a barking dog and the smell of plastic in somebody's burn barrel. Laurel carpeted the hillside. And throughout that laurel hell lay scattered beer bottles, tin cans, plastic milk jugs, disposable diapers. People had just pitched their garbage. Bill shook his head. He felt tempted to call them trash, anyone who ruined a beautiful view like that. They were a cancer on the face of the earth. But, then again, there were people who might look at his marked skin and say the same thing. His shoulders itched with the ink of bat wings, the still healing flesh.

"You want me to leave you alone?" Bill asked. "Get your praying done and then maybe we can figure out what the hell we're going to do about the truck." It would likely take up the whole day.

"I led you into sin," Kent said. "I've been praying for a way to lead you out again."

"Gee, thanks." Bill skipped a flat stone across the water all the way to the far bank. Kent wanted him to be born again. Bill had already tried that magic—answered the altar call way back in puberty, when he had convinced himself he was going to hell because he couldn't stop masturbating. If he believed he could be born again, he would be the first to sign up.

"Tell you what," he said, "I'll wait in the truck. Take as long as you need."

"Bill."

"Yeah?"

"The wages of sin are death."

"Really?" Bill stepped over to a narrow rapids, where the

pond drained. Dehydrated from the bourbon, he wondered if the creek water was fit for drinking. "We ought to go out tonight," he said. "After we deal with the truck. They might have some new girls working."

"Don't even try to tempt me."

"Okay. Sorry. Jeez." New girls. Right. There was only one woman either of them had ever paid to see. "I'm going to walk back to the truck. You get your praying done, then let's make a plan." Together they would figure something out, like where to find a tractor or a towing service? At the very least, how to salvage the meat. Maybe this was it, the end of the line. They'd been Boy Scouts, frat brothers, strip club regulars, even Grail knights. But with this dark place Kent was headed, the time had arrived for Bill to stick out his thumb. He crawled over a fallen tree and began picking a clear path along the creek.

"Wait a minute." Kent came up behind and laid a hand on Bill's shoulder. When Bill turned around, Kent fixed him with a worried stare, like he could see how everything inside had grown foul with rot.

"There's coming a day," Kent said. "And it won't be long. The heavens will split asunder, and the Lord's going to come back to call his own. My friend, you need to get right with God." Kent swept a hand up to the canopy. His face turned purple. Veins forked lighting across his bald head. "It's time you got serious about the state of your soul. There's only one choice—between life and death. Don't put it off, Bill. Choose life!"

31

Wesley studied the blue heart on his wrist and then turned his hand over and tried to focus on something pure: the hollow pop of mallets striking croquet balls, around the house in the front yard, the shouts of three boys accusing each other of cheating.

He and Bill and Crystal and Duane sat together in lawn chairs arranged in a half circle. In the shade of the carport, they stared at the television Duane had brought outside for their Fourth of July celebration. "Pork 'n' Porn." It wasn't how Wesley wanted to spend his holiday, watching nasty home-made videos, while Bill and Duane got soused on scuppernong wine.

"Duane," Crystal said, nervous. "You shouldn't be watching this stuff with those little boys around here."

"I told them to stay away from the TV." Duane took a long swallow of wine and kept his eyes glued to the screen. "If their parents let them run wild through the neighborhood, that's their problem."

Crystal had just finished mowing the lawn, and the clean smell of mown grass would normally have lifted Wesley's spirits. Almost thirty years old, and he'd never actually sat down and watched porn, this most private act now made so degradingly public. That troubled him, of course, but what really troubled him was how this anonymous cock and vagina on the screen took him back to the night with Lucy. He recognized a fundamental sameness, same enough to make him stiffen now with desire and to hate himself for his desire. An extended orgasm rattled out of the TV's tiny speaker, and Wesley tried to make himself turn away.

"I couldn't stand it any longer," Crystal said. "For years I been worrying myself sick over these tapes." She sucked her cigarette down to the filter and glanced nervously at the sex scene on TV. "I never *let* him film anything indecent, but I don't know what all he might have filmed. I been worrying myself sick about it, so I finally had to do something."

She said she had considered bringing pornography charges against her ex-husband, based on the tapes he'd made of other women. But her cop cousin had cautioned against getting a bunch of lawyers involved. The embarrassment it could bring the family, et cetera. So that Wednesday, while Victor was at work, she had braided her long hair into a ponytail, slipped on a baseball cap, and changed the numbers on her license plate with blue tape. She drove right up to the house where she had once lived with him.

"It was easy." She grinned. "I knew he didn't keep all the windows locked. And, hell, as it turned out, he hadn't even changed the locks on the doors. It was like he was expecting me."

Duane aimed the remote at the VCR, and the tape whirred forward.

"I should have burned them," Crystal said, studying the many labels in the cardboard box. "Now Duane feels like he has to watch every single one."

"I want to see how you were before we met," he said. "Maybe I'll learn something."

"I'm not in any of these." The plastic cases clacked together as she sorted through them. "I'm pretty sure—"

"We'll find out, won't we?" One of Crystal's kittens climbed into Duane's lap, and he roughly lifted it and dropped it to the concrete.

Two of its siblings were wrestling in front of the TV. Wesley bent forward and tried to lure the black one into his lap. When she demurred, he scooped her from the concrete and cradled her in a palm, stroking her fur with the other hand, which she seemed to enjoy until, in a flash, she twisted her body and dug a paw into his flesh. Playful? Or cruel? He detached her claw and set her back down on the slab. The mama was nowhere to be seen. She was weaning them and so was keeping off to herself. It seemed like she was dropping a litter two or three times a year, and Crystal was always trying to give away kittens. Why didn't she go ahead and get the thing fixed?

"I ought to toss every one of those tapes in the burn barrel," Crystal said.

"You're not going to touch a goddurn thing," Duane shot back. "Not until I see them all. If you *are* in one of these films, we're going to sit right here and watch you."

Earlier, when Wesley had gone inside for a spatula, Duane's pistol had been lying on the kitchen counter. Tarnished gunmetal, probably old as the house. Wesley had replaced it in the drawer where Duane usually kept it hidden.

"Duane," she said, "if you plan to spend the whole day—"

"Shh!" He put a finger to his lips and glowered at her.

Until today, Wesley had never really thought Duane capable of violence. How deeply was Wesley implicated? Staring into the gaping abscess of their lives, he knew he had to own a part of that corruption.

Bill brought the wine from the cooler and offered to refill Wesley's cup.

"I'm good," Wesley said. One was his limit today.

Bill squatted by his chair and spoke in a whisper. "So, about that loan . . ."

Rent money. Where had Wesley heard this before? No sooner had they spent their first night together than she started talking about how she was two months late on rent. So smooth. Well rehearsed, no doubt.

"Yeah," Wesley told his brother. "I can help you out. What do you need?"

"Not much. And not long. I just, well . . . with the current situation . . ." Bill nodded toward the couple copulating on TV. "I'm not real comfortable sleeping at your place. And I guess I'm not invited." He fixed Wesley with a challenging stare.

Wesley reached for his billfold and pulled out a wad of twenties, passed them to Bill.

"Hey, thank you, little brother. This helps. Yes, it does. This helps a lot."

"Anytime."

"Hey, you doing okay?"

"No complaints."

"Mother and Daddy?"

"They're making it."

"Grandpa? Granny?"

"Look, if you care so much how everybody is doing, come around and see for yourself." He got up and walked over to the grill to try to give Crystal a hand. She couldn't get the igniter to work. She couldn't get her cigarette lighter to work either. Wesley hefted the propane tank. Light as a feather.

"Duane," she said. "I thought you had this thing refilled."

Duane glanced at Crystal then returned his attention to the boobs on the boob tube, jiggling rapid fire.

"I could run to the store," Wesley offered, halfheartedly. Twenty minutes each way.

Crystal fixed her partner with a look of disgust.

High in the trees the cicadas buzzed. Loud already. By nightfall their racket would be deafening. Would she come? She wouldn't return his calls. Or, if she did, his mother wouldn't say. How much would it cost to get phone service at the cottage, or maybe one of those mobile phones like Bill's? If Lucy did come, what would he say? If they just talked, could she help him understand whether he had spent too many years alone to share himself fully now with a woman? Crystal and Duane kept arguing about the propane tank, trying to determine who was to blame. Bill was digging in the cooler for a beer; he said he had to stop drinking wine. Wesley had missed his workout today. Missed the visit he had planned to Grandpa and Granny, too.

Over by the dog lot he found a level spot and started pumping out push-ups. Soft grass cushioned his chest. He pumped out the push-ups until he was exhausted. He wrapped his fingers around a hardened triceps. He brought a hand across his chest as he flexed.

Crystal came over and stood above him, asked if he could give her a hand once he finished his exercise. She was having a good couple of days, nearly free of pain, but she could use a hand.

In the outbuilding she and Wesley found an old kettle grill. They dusted off the soot and cobwebs. Crystal found a sack of charcoal and a can of lighter fluid. They carried it over by the carport. Wesley built a pyramid of charcoal and Crystal doused it with the stinking fluid. When she brought her lighter near, a ball of flame shot up, *whomp!* as it sucked at the air. Over by the TV, Duane and Bill were both melting into the lawn furniture. A jar of moonshine had appeared on the slab between them. Bill had insisted on driving separately. Yet another burden: how to get the keys away from him. Wesley tried to make small talk with Crystal, but they'd always had trouble communicating. In silence, they breathed carbon monoxide and watched the briquettes, waiting for the corners to ash.

"So, you're feeling better this week?" Wesley asked.

"I feel like I could dance a jig." She did a little dance in her long skirt. "Maybe we should go out dancing tonight, head to that roadhouse your brother was talking up. Leave Duane here alone with the TV."

In the dog pen a chorus of howls erupted, and Wesley felt his pulse quicken. Tires crunched the gravel. He turned to watch for the car to round the house. When it did, it wasn't the white Corvette he'd hoped for. Some little rusted beater, with stickers plastered over the bumpers.

"Oh, hell yeah!" Bill shouted. "Y'all prepare to be enlightened."

A short blue man in mirror shades got out and stood by his car, taking in the scene, a scowl forming on his features. Tattoos covered his forearms, his neck.

The genuine emotion Crystal put into her welcome told Wesley how desperate she was for guests. Wesley shook the little blue man's hand, and then Crystal pointed him toward the cooler. She apologized for Duane and his taste in TV programming, then she sent Wesley to the outbuilding for another chair.

"Y'all," Bill said, "This here is my shaman, Niall. He's teaching me magic."

"I am doing nothing of the sort." The little man settled himself between Bill and Duane. The tape Duane was speed-watching came to an end and ejected itself from the VCR. Bill reached into the box behind Duane's chair for another tape.

"Here you go, Cuz. Here's a classic—*Boldfinger*."

Niall suggested an alternate title. "How about *Ejacula*?"

"No, no," Bill said. "I'm feeling *Anus and Andy*."

Some of the professional tapes were dubbed with home content, so Duane had committed to speed-watching the entire collection. Wesley would give Lucy another hour, maybe two. If she didn't show, he was out of here.

It didn't take long for the blue man to offer his critique. The porn industry, he said, was a symptom of a more pervasive malady. The deep roots of puritanism in western culture actually helped explain Hugh Hefner, Larry Flynt. They and their ilk were just exploiting our deep disaffiliation with our erotic nature. "To quote my favorite extraterrestrial," he said, "what we're witnessing is the pimping of the pleasure principle. When the object of sexual gratification becomes so diffused, when not only bodies but body parts become interchangeable, the endless series of breasts, cocks, gaping vaginas, signal a wearied quest for the sui generis—"

Duane pressed a finger to his lips and glared at the little blue man. Wesley was still trying to figure out half of what he'd said when Crystal came out of the house with a bag of tortilla chips and some of Duane's homemade salsa.

"Duane," she barked. "Turn that thing off and talk to our company. This is not what the Fourth of July is supposed to be." Crystal said she had the croquet course set up in the front yard if anybody wanted to play. And she had sparklers for when it got dark.

"Y'all do whatever you want," Duane said. "I'm going to sit right here."

"He wants to blame me because my ex-husband is a pervert. How is that my fault?" Crystal fidgeted in her seat. "It's what you don't know about a person that can hurt you the worst. I don't *think* he ever filmed the two of us together, but how can I be sure?"

"We're going to find out," Duane said. "Today."

Niall lifted his thin blue arms above his head and, standing to arch his back, pivoted to survey the backyard.

"That stand of bamboo over there," he said. "Those are some healthy stalks."

Duane mumbled how it was an endless war to keep it from taking over the property. Chainsaw, machete, riding mower. He was constantly cutting it back. Wesley remembered helping out with the chainsaw, even though he had promised his mother he would never use a chainsaw.

Along the edge of the backyard the wall of bamboo rose skyward. Niall stood nodding in that direction. He brought his hands together at his chest and bowed, then said he felt like realigning his chakras. He invited Bill to realign his chakras, too. And anyone else who was interested. "Wesley?"

Wesley said his chakras were doing just fine. Bill followed

the blue man across the backyard and left Wesley behind with Duane and Crystal. Just like any other weekend. Their lives had stalled together. But they had been young and hopeful once, as hopeful as those little boys on the other side of the house playing croquet. Wesley remembered himself and Bill and Duane as boys, biking into town on the Fourth. At Hailey Creek High School, down on that ball field, they could find a day's entertainment in a can of Crisco. Good clean fun. A greased pole with a ten-dollar bill on top. Greased pig, chased by a crowd of roughneck boys—not ever Wesley himself, as Bill and Duane had reminded him. At the sound of that pig's terror, its angry squeal, Wesley had always contented himself to stand on the sidelines and watch.

The sky had started to fill with a scrim of high, thin clouds. The light had changed. Noonday brightness gave way to the sad and fading light of late afternoon. He hadn't really expected her to show. She hadn't actually promised. If he was honest with himself, he could feel how his heartache had begun to wind itself around a core of relief.

When the neighbor boys rounded the corner of the house, Crystal pulled the extension cord out of the wall, and the TV went black. The oldest boy said they were looking to pick up a fourth to make teams. Wesley rose from his chair, and the littlest boy, freckles spreading across his cheeks, was assigned to be his partner. Wesley could tell the older boys had been picking on him—he knew all about that. The little boy looked up at Wesley with such innocent trust. The boy smiled, a new confidence showing itself. He handed a mallet to Wesley. As they marched around to the front of the house, Wesley glanced in the opposite direction. Over against that wall of bamboo, Bill and his shaman sat facing each other, their legs crossed and their arms wrapped around themselves in strange alignments.

The boy tugged at Wesley's hand and kept calling him "Mister" while explaining the many rules of the game.

"I know how to play croquet," Wesley said with more heat than he intended. "You think I don't know how to play croquet?"

32

Some serious country. Lucy smelled smoke. Road so narrow, pines growing right up to the shoulder, kudzu thick and high. And then suddenly a clearing opened in the pines. She set her foot on the brake. A clump of houses on the right. Not exactly the way Wesley had described it. Not much grand or homey about those little shotgun shacks. Out front, a group of men in sleeveless shirts, bare-chested, stood around a fire and glanced up at her. She hit the gas. If she didn't come across it soon, she was just going to turn around and drive right back to Charlotte. She didn't even know these people. Wesley's cousin or something. And no doubt Bill would be there. How awkward. And maybe Niall. Doubly awkward. But easier maybe to talk with Wesley than somewhere alone. She had to break it off clean. When he had called on the phone, she had confronted him about his mother. "That's just Mother being Mother," he had said, like that was the only reassurance Lucy needed. She had fifty dollars in her purse, the first repayment on the "loan" he'd given her. Whatever he came to believe about her, it was important to her that his mother not ever know she had taken his money without the intent to repay it.

She would earn more in tips later tonight. A big night at The Jackpot, with July 4th drink specials. Table dances, two for one. Big Sammy had lectured them all about partying too hard today. He was tired of girls dancing so drunk or coked up they couldn't walk a straight line across the stage. If they kept it up, he was going to enforce a sobriety test. Fuck that. Let *him* try to strip cold sober. But that's what she was going to do. Unless she could maybe score a line. Two or three girls owed her. But no, no, fuck, no. If she was ever going to quit, this might be her last chance. Cold turkey, going on three weeks. After overhearing Wesley's mother's speech in the garden, Lucy had driven straight to her dealer's trailer. But the minute she pulled into his dead-end road and heard the gravel crunch beneath her tires, she saw the flashing blue lights, the cop standing by the cruiser, looking her way. It fried her nerves now to remember. No way was she doing time. She needed something, though. The world was so empty—like her gut. She was constantly hungry now. Bill had complained about her habit of opening a bag of chips and leaving it half finished. She had explained how they grew stale, but that wasn't it. If there had been only one flavor, she might have reconciled herself to the piddling solace of salt and grease. But there was always a different flavor—sour cream 'n' onion, salt and vinegar, nacho cheese. And ever since giving up the nose candy, she had developed a wicked sweet tooth. Oatmeal cream pies, cinnamon twists, Twinkies, Moon Pies. Snickers, Baby Ruth, Six Million Dollar Bars. The worst kind of processed lard and chemicals. She would eat half and throw the rest in the garbage. More than once she had actually pilfered through the garbage to find the half she had thrown away. She had no self control when it came to junk food. The more she ate, the more she hated herself. If she didn't watch out, she would get as fat as her mama.

Just when she had almost given up on finding the place, there it was. Not as grand as Wesley had made it sound. White, with old plank siding. One story, but tall. Across the front lawn a stand of oak and poplar made the empty sky more distant. She turned into the gravel drive and eased her way between those massive pillars of oak. Around back she found the party. In the carport, a man slouched down in a chaise lounge, cup in hand, staring at a TV, while a woman stood by a smoking grill. A long mane of untamable hair, brown as earth, with tones of red. Lucy always did like a redhead. The woman wore a tank top and peasant skirt. Wiry strong. She had a nice shape.

There was a big blue cooler next to the man, and a smaller one near the grill, but other than this couple, not another soul in sight. Lucy let the car idle while she reconsidered. In the backyard, a small fence enclosed hounds that leapt against its sides and howled. The woman turned and smiled, and Lucy recognized her right away. Crystal Rankin, Crouse High School.

She cut the ignition and stuffed the keys in her purse, then left the purse in the car. Nobody out here in the sticks. When she closed the door and stepped toward the grill, her head swam. All she had in her stomach was an oatmeal pie and half a bag of popcorn.

The grill poured out smoke. The woman leaned over it with a pair of tongs, rearranging charcoal. Crystal Rankin, what do you know? Memory came flooding back. Crouse High School, that old brick fortress down in the holler. Crystal had been a member of the glorious senior class, when Lucy was only a freshman, so their social worlds had hardly crossed, even in a school that small. But they did cross, briefly, in 4-H. That year, Lucy had joined every after-school program she could find, just to stay away from home. How she had managed focus and sanity sufficient to pass her classes was still beyond her comprehension. It was before the mohawk, before she dropped out and ran away from home.

Since then, she had become a judge of smiles, and the one Crystal now showed her bore no stain of condescension.

"Hey there. Come join our party! Duane, *please* turn that thing off."

In the corner of the carport sat Wesley's cousin, the man from The Jackpot. He'd been loud and belligerent. Now he sat glumly staring at the TV, while Crystal manned the grill. Porn outdoors? Some of these guys were truly pathetic.

"I hope you don't mind me crashing your party." She wondered whether Crystal would recognize her.

"Shoot, no. Somebody's got to eat these ribs." Crystal lifted the lid on the red cooler, full to the brim. All that white fat. Ribs never looked good raw. "I hope you brought your appetite," Crystal said. She apologized for the delay, said Duane had forgot to refill the propane tank and she was waiting for the charcoal to get hot. She wiped her hands on her apron and took a step across the concrete toward Lucy.

"Yeah. I could eat," Lucy said, smelling the charcoal, the promise of roasting pork. As if in apology for her existence, she explained how Wesley had invited her. She wasn't sure if he had informed Crystal.

Crystal tossed her mop of wiry hair toward the front yard. "He's around there playing croquet with the neighbor kids. You want me to call him?"

"No." It was suddenly very important that this woman not believe Lucy was *with* Wesley—or Bill, or any man.

"Well, come on in here and try my fig preserves. We just now lit this charcoal. It's going to take a while yet."

Lucy could tell right away how a person looked at her, what kind of chances the two of them might have for authenticity. Most often, not much. She didn't know if it was the tattoos or maybe something deeper. Something failed and broken. Most people either took a step way back or they leaned forward, sniffing out how they might use her. Bill and Wesley, a little bit of both. Their mama, she'd stepped way the hell back, with her baby boy in her arms, like she was escaping the plague. This woman Crystal, though, she didn't need to be conned. She seemed to accept Lucy from the first instant.

Crystal got Lucy a Coke out of the blue cooler. They were headed for the door, when Bill came at a jog across the backyard.

"Hey, hey. Lucy!"

She turned and saw his beaming smile. Drunk. Not falling down drunk yet. She'd seen this phase often enough to know how he could charm, but she knew what invariably followed.

"You came. I was telling Niall you would come." He gestured across the lawn, and there was Niall, sitting in the lotus pose.

"Well," she said. "I don't have to go in till eight."

"Oh, you're dancing tonight. I didn't know. I could give you a ride. Oh yeah, you drove. Yeah. Well, maybe I'll come cheer you on."

The way he stared at her, that raw need. She searched for Crystal, but Crystal had gone in the house. "I saw your friend last night," she said.

"What's that?"

Best way to push a man away—talk about another man. "The Right Reverend."

"Kent?"

"He came into the club, thumping his Bible at me, like he was the first preacher ever to think of that. When did he get so much religion?"

"Yeah."

"I told him he only wanted to save my soul because he couldn't get in my pants."

Bill laughed nervously. "I told him about the party, but I don't really expect him to come."

"Jesus, I hope not!"

"Yeah."

"I'm going to go help Crystal. Good to see you, though." She made herself smile and spun on her heel, walked to the house.

As soon as she stepped inside, she felt the change in the air, cooler by five degrees. These old farm houses and their high ceilings. An enclosed porch led into a kitchen, where a pair of kittens stopped their rough play and stared up at her.

The smell of fresh-baked bread filled the air. A watermelon sat on the floor under the table.

"Crystal?"

"There you are." Crystal strode into the room, fastening a hoop earring. She handed Lucy a knife and asked if she would mind slicing the loaf of bread cooling on a cutting board.

It was a sharp knife. It slid right through the dense bread, still hot from the oven.

Crystal reached into the fridge for a tub of cheese and the fig preserves she had mentioned. She said she had made the cheese from goat's milk. A friend of hers over by Crouse kept goats. The figs were from her own trees. Goat cheese and figs on fresh bread—Crystal said there wasn't anything better. Lucy liked that, a woman who didn't mind bragging about her own food. They both spread the cheese and preserves in equal portions onto the dark bread and ate it standing. And my God, it was good. Crystal said what they needed was coffee—did Lucy like coffee? Yes, she did. So Crystal filled the pot with well water, and then while they waited for it to brew, and before they spoiled their appetite entirely, maybe Lucy would like to join her for a smoke. Did Lucy smoke? A little weed? Why yes, she did—on occasion.

Lucy got the tour of the farm house—ending in a bedroom, heavily draped, so that even in the middle of the day the fish inside Crystal's aquarium glowed a brilliant orange and purple. Shoved into the corner was a loveseat, so well worn it had earned the right to stay. But Crystal led her to the bed, where they sat and passed Crystal's pipe back and forth.

"I just smoke this stuff," Crystal said, "because it's the only thing that ever lets me forget the pain in my joints." She passed the pipe. "But I'm feeling pretty good today. And it's okay to party from time to time. Ain't it? It's nice to share."

"Yes." The smoke burned sweet, a different sweetness

than the figs that still coated her tongue. It satisfied a different part of Lucy's craving. This bed was maybe the softest bed she had ever felt. Firm. High. Covered by a handmade quilt in a wedding-ring pattern. She spread a hand across the cotton, softer after probably decades of wear and washing and hanging on the line.

"That's my granny's work," Crystal said.

"My Ma Maw used to quilt, too," Lucy said, remembering the frame that always took up the spare bedroom. She put her nose down and smelled the sunshine. The one thing that would make her comfort complete would be to lay her head in Crystal's lap. And so she did. She stretched out her legs on the bed and looked up at all that hair. Crystal laughed and rested her hands on both sides of Lucy's head.

"Don't go to sleep on me," she said. "We've got some more eating to do."

"You don't remember me, do you?"

"What's that?"

"Crouse High School. I was a freshman the year you graduated. You were president of the 4-H." Lucy reminisced about Crystal's speeches and Crystal's prize-winning calf.

"Minnie. She was my girl!"

"I remember how shiny her coat was. How well you kept her fed."

"She was a jersey. My uncle raised dairy cows."

It was a hard year, that freshman year, maybe the hardest in her life, and it had helped Lucy just to know there were people like Crystal in the world. How weird to think about that now—that 4-H Club and their little shamrock patches, and the little speeches Crystal made to the club, the faith she'd kept that they could all grow pure heads, hearts, hands, and health. To say that Lucy had harbored a crush on Crystal back then would be to trivialize what she had felt. But that's the best she could say it now—*I had a crush on you*—which brought a smile to Crystal's eyes. Way back then, Crystal was probably somebody with whom Lucy could have shared her nightmare. Maybe now she still could. But before she could work her way back to that dank bedroom and that man in the dark, before she could even climb the steps of that mobile home with the peeling green paint, their conversation somehow drifted to Lucy's work at The Jackpot—which she didn't try to hide—and then Crystal's offer to show her a video. Crystal said she had danced once, too, on amateur night. Maybe Lucy could provide her professional opinion of Crystal's dance steps? From there they moved on to the very broad topic of shitty men, like Crystal's first husband, the video tapes he had made, including this one Crystal wanted to show Lucy. But also she feared there were other videos, and acknowledging their possible continued existence made Crystal's breathing tighten, made her fingers tremble as they pulled through Lucy's hair.

Lucy lifted her head from Crystal's lap. "Nobody should do a thing like that to you," she said. "Some damn men think they can get away with anything. Tell me where he lives, and we'll hop in my car and go find those tapes. We'll trash that fucker's house."

Crystal averted her eyes. "I already stole what I could find. He never changed the locks on his doors." Crystal explained how she had stolen his entire library of porn and so now Duane was sitting out there on the carport with the intention of watching every single tape until he found one that showed Crystal having sex with her ex-husband.

"Shitty men," said Lucy.

"Yeah, right?" Crystal slid into a dark mood. Then she pursed her lips and made herself smile. "I smell coffee," she said.

In the kitchen they filled two heavy mugs. After smoking, they were both starving. More bread. More goat cheese. More fig preserves. They pulled two chairs close together. Thigh to thigh. Through the open kitchen window, they could hear the wails of painful sex reverberating out of a tiny TV speaker turned up loud as it would go. Crystal closed the window and stepped over to a radio on the counter beside the sink. She tuned it to a country station, some woman singer from the 70s singing about her heartbreak.

They laughed and chugged the coffee and scarfed down the little meal. A gray tabby cat sauntered into the kitchen and abruptly stopped when it saw Lucy. Its striped pelt hung from its bones. Elongated teats drooped from its belly. The cat stared at them and then, in what seemed a proprietary way, hopped up into Crystal's lap where it settled itself into a puddle. Lucy reached over and stroked its fur. She took the knife and fixed them both another piece of bread with figs and cheese.

"Crystal," she said, figs dribbling down her chin and dripping onto her skirt. "This is the best damn food I ever put in my mouth."

33

The bamboo grew so dense, it made a wall. With the crown of his head buried in the turf, Bill trusted the wall of bamboo, let his back lie against it all the way up to the heels of his bare feet, pointed skyward. Duane had griped that if he didn't constantly cut them back, the bamboo stalks would take over the yard. Bill imagined stalks erupting across the lawn, building a fortress around that house, around the two women inside. Briar Rose, Sleeping Beauty. How to fight this urge to possess a woman? He was as bad as Duane.

"How long do we have to stay here before we reach Nirvana?" Bill asked, twisting the crown of his head in the dirt, angling his eyes to the right, so that he could glimpse Niall's torso, wrapped in blue scrollwork as dense as the bamboo.

"If you keep thinking about time," Niall said, "you'll never get there."

"I'm not thinking about time. I'm thinking about my neck. This hurts!"

"Yes." The smirk in Niall's voice thickened. "Isn't that what you've been wanting?"

"To rupture a disk? No." Bill listened to Niall's steady breathing and tried to copy it, focused on the purring, the air pouring in and out. Some of that neck muscle from high school had to be there still. He only had to find it.

"Calm the mind," Niall said. "Open the soul. Release thought, release self. Imagine your ego getting lost in and among these bamboo stalks, digging down into the interconnected root system. Chant after me . . . *m-o-h-h-h*."

"*Moh?*"

"*Moh* is *Om* upside down."

They chanted, and Bill was surprised by how much it did help. He forgot about the pain in his neck. He forgot the smell of burning charcoal and his hunger. His grip on the bamboo stalks loosened. Smooth against the palms. If he closed his eyes, he could almost forget her fake smile, the way she'd stepped back when he'd stepped near. But when he opened his eyes and stared across the upside-down earth, at the oaks plunging their branches down from the world's green ceiling, at the farmhouse hanging there like a tiny bauble, his mind worked through the many ways he might be able to find a way inside.

"What do you think they're doing in there?"

Niall continued to chant the holy word.

"I mean, they've been in there how long? How long since you started teaching me how to breathe?"

"M-o-h-h-h-h-h-h." Niall grunted in irritation. "Lucy and I have been incommunicado. If she's not committed to helping herself, there's not much I can do for her."

According to Wesley, she was off the nose candy. *According to Wesley.* Man. Bill had never seen that coming. It still did not make any kind of sense, his innocent brother—look at him over there with those children—stealing his girlfriend!

"This would be a lot easier," he said, "if I hadn't discovered Duane's stash of moonshine."

"You think?"

His neck strained, wobbled. Bill straightened his spine, leaned more firmly against the wall of bamboo. Green fortress, always growing. Like the walls he built. To keep Maddie out, keep family out. Why? Was it fear? That's what Kent said. Mr. Evangelist. So, he had taken his witness to The Jackpot. That was funny—or it would be, if it weren't sad. After the incident with the truck, Kent had given up preaching at Bill.

The blood puddling in his face was starting to hurt. The pressure in his cheeks, his forehead. The world's ceiling had become unbearably heavy. Without explaining his actions, Bill let the world slip. He dropped to all fours. The instant relief was followed by instant worry. His neck froze up. His head spun.

Stumbling across the lawn toward the carport, where Duane lay sprawled in his chaise lounge in front of the TV, Bill tried to crank his head one way then the other. He couldn't tell whether the dizziness came from standing on his head or from his cousin's moonshine. Only one way to find out.

Duane grunted by way of greeting. Gone was the garrulous, joke-cracking, back-slapping good ol' boy, replaced by this seething muscle of hostility. Duane kept his eyes on the TV but lifted the Mason jar. "Did your guru get you straightened out?"

Bill rotated his head, his shoulders, stretching like Niall had taught him, hoping to release the tension. "I don't know. Do I look straighter?"

Duane shrugged.

"Where's Crystal?"

Duane nodded toward the back door. "Still in there. With that friend of yours."

The windows were dark, no light on inside as far as Bill could tell. "Should I go check on them?" he asked. Duane pressed fast forward; the VCR whined. He pressed play and the tape stopped with a *kathunk*. Some European sex fantasy involving the Eiffel Tower. Duane rummaged in the box for a new tape and leaned forward and hit the eject button. The TV switched to news. It was an update on the scandal at the White House and the ongoing battle between Clinton and Starr. Talking heads were discussing rumors of impeachment.

"Oh, look," Niall said, stepping forward to join them on the carport. "More pornography!"

The commentators moved on to news of the other women who had claimed themselves to be victims of the President. But Duane didn't wait for the rest of the news. He stuffed a new tape in the slot.

Around the corner of the house Wesley came, followed by a runt who kept talking up at him. Bill grabbed the extension cord, but Duane held up a hand to stop him.

"Little boy," Duane said. "You run along home. Your parents called. They want y'all to come home."

"We was hoping to try the ribs." The boy smiled, his face full of freckles.

"Run along home. Don't make me tell you again."

The boy's face clouded. He looked up at Wesley, but Wesley shook hands and sent him on his way.

"What about that meat?" Bill asked. If he had succeeded in realigning his chakras, they were now threatening to slip out of line, just spill into a useless heap. It was important to act. He walked over to the grill and lifted the lid. Hot coals glowed through gray ash. "We need to get those ribs on the grill pronto."

"That's Crystal's thing," Duane said.

Bill looked at the house. He couldn't go in there without totally losing all pride. He opened the red cooler. He loaded up the grill and felt better when the fat was sizzling on the coals, when the smell of roasting pork promised some sort of satisfaction today. He closed the lid to keep the heat in. It would be one last failure in a long line of failure, too much to stand, if this fire went out before the meat was done.

Under the carport the other three men gathered in a circle, stared at the TV with glazed eyes, while the machine whirred and stopped. Cocks entered vaginas long enough for Duane to make certain the latter did not belong to Crystal, and then the machine whirred again. That cardboard box contained endless hours of pornography.

Wesley turned his chair away. He said they should find some fireworks to watch. He picked up the Gastonia newspaper and started thumbing through the pages, looking for a show.

Bill felt the wad of cash thick in his pocket. He had never anticipated taking money from his brother, the way he'd been doing lately. He needed to give this wad of bills back, that's what he needed to do. He needed to pay a visit to his parents, to Grandpa and Granny, just like Wesley said, and he would certainly do that. He would. He turned up the Mason jar and swallowed the last inch of Duane's shine. Napalm. That had to be almost pure alcohol. Okay, that would be the end. He had to drive sometime later. Wesley had been trying to get his keys. Like that was going to happen. If he stopped drinking now, he could follow her to Charlotte later. He had cash money. Maybe buy her a drink or two, just to sit over a beer and have a conversation, because it seemed impossible to get her alone at this party. And what was she doing in that house so long?

A gray tabby kitten sauntered over, leaned against his ankle, walked in a circle, wrapped its tail around his shin. He lifted the kitten and carried it over to his brother's chair.

"Did you talk to her?" Bill tossed his head toward the house.

"No. Did you?"

"No." It wasn't really a lie, considering the extent of their conversation. He set his empty Mason jar down on the slab. He saw the pain in his brother's face.

"Hey, man, are you sure you're okay?"

Wesley looked over at the dark windows of the house. "I should probably go talk to her," he said, but he kept sitting there with the newspaper spread open in his lap.

Niall announced, as if anyone cared, that he would be leaving soon. Bill begged him to stay, at least for supper. At this point, observing the formalities of hospitality might be the only thing to save him from putting his head in the oven and hoping Crystal had paid the gas bill. What a beloved community.

On the TV, Duane was playing another one of Victor's seductions, by now a recognizable formula, starting with the offer of party favors (pour a drink, spread lines of coke), followed by negotiation:

Her: "Oh, no, no, ha ha, I can't do it for that."

Him: *firm, in charge*, "That's what I'm paying."

Her: "But you want to *film* it? Ha ha, no way, baby. That's going to cost you extra. A hundred extra."

Him: "Fifty."

And then the undressing. Bill had to look away. Garden or machine? No, sex was a cancer, at least it was today. This sick shit. Duane was as sick as Victor, and Bill wasn't feeling very good himself. Maybe some food in his stomach would help. The meat smelled done. He went to check the grill. He lifted a rib and bit into the thick center. Pink inside, but it tasted done.

He started forking ribs onto the platter, which he covered with foil and brought to the picnic table under the carport.

"Should I get Crystal and Lucy?"

Duane shrugged. "Crystal will come when she gets hungry enough."

Bill looked up at the house, the windows still dark. He forked more ribs onto paper plates, sprinkled piles of potato chips and passed them to Wesley, to Duane.

Niall held up a hand. "Do you, by chance, have any hummus?"

Duane glared at him, a bone between his teeth. With the greasy fingers of his other hand, he operated the remote control. The tape jerked to a stop at a scene dating surely all the way back to the 1960s, based on the hairstyles, the lack of muscle tone, the pale skin; these actors were trapped in time, still struggling decades later to achieve orgasm.

Bill settled himself beside his brother, a plate in his lap. He gnawed off big hunks of meat, bolted them down. He watched the lovers' pace slacken, watched them find their second wind. Over the noise of the TV, from inside the farmhouse, came a sudden lilting voice, a woman's voice passing through layers of wood and insulation, through glass. Whether Crystal or Lucy, he couldn't be sure. Half laughter, half song. He glanced back at the TV, its noise. He set the plate in his chair and stepped toward the door, stood holding the handle. Two voices, now he could make them out. It was a hilarity that did not include him. A private party.

The light of late afternoon poured into the mud room. From the kitchen came their laughter, clearer now. And the smell of freshly brewed coffee. He tapped lightly on the half-open kitchen door. The table was a mess. Jars sat opened, spoons plunged inside. Plates smeared with jam and cheese sat before the women. Their lips glistened. Lucy had her arm draped across Crystal's shoulders, and they were both heaving with silent laughter, the kind that leaves your belly aching with joy. No part of their pleasure was his to share.

"Um, I wanted to let you know the ribs are done."

Whether or not they heard him, he wasn't sure. Crystal started dancing in her chair to music on the radio, and Lucy smiled at her. They were a picture of freedom and grace so beautiful Bill could not bring himself to spoil it with his presence. He had to leave the room, back the way he had come and, as quick as he could, out of that house. On the carport it was the same depressing scene. On TV, the pale, long-haired couple were still going at it. God almighty, couldn't they just finish? Just come already. He wanted it out of his own body. He needed rest, he needed sleep.

"Any hummus?" Niall asked.

"There's some baked beans here." Bill lifted the lids on the beans, the slaw.

"Gastonia is shooting fireworks at nine-thirty," Wesley said without glancing up from the paper.

No more TV for Bill this evening. No more people and their appetites. No more simulacra of people, either. He walked past the dog run. The stir-crazy hounds ran in circles, leapt at the fence, like he was going to feed them or maybe even release them. Bill marched across the lawn toward the wall of bamboo and peered inside. He turned and walked a lap around the house, if only to keep moving. The worst thing he could do was sit. When he came back around the house, he walked into the drifting smoke from the grill. As he came closer, he heard the fat inside sizzling on the coals. Pigs were sentient beings. He felt the meat in his gut, felt its grease settle in a lump. There by the grill sat the can of lighter fluid. Half full. A slick of that fuel could penetrate skin, sink deep into pink fat and flesh. Only one way to kill a cancer—burn it. One flick of a lighter and *whoosh*, corruption gone, fucking incinerated. He stepped over to the can, felt it give in his grip. In his pocket was a fresh lighter, a book of matches. He lit a cigarette and breathed deep to settle his nerves, steady his resolve.

Holding the can, he stepped behind the chaise lounge, where his cousin had lazed the day away, had made them all watch along with him. Grease spread across Duane's chin, his hands. In his lap lay a paper plate, stacked with bones he had gnawed clean.

Behind Duane's chair sat the box full of plastic cartridges. Video tape, Bill had always heard, was highly combustible. He squeezed the can and soaked the tapes, the box, the stolen camcorder, too. The fluid reeked of unknown chemicals. Volatile, they instantly fouled the air. Even when Duane jumped up in shock, Bill still poured the fuel. He emptied the can until it whistled and squeaked. And while Duane tried to wrestle the matches out of his hand, Bill scratched at the little friction strip until the match popped into flame and he dropped it at his feet.

They both jumped back from the ball of fire. Black smoke. The smell of plastic burning. The smell of hair. He felt his eyelashes curling into singed balls. Duane was staring down at the fire, and Bill readied himself for blows. Duane reached into the pile and plucked out a tape on fire. The plastic case had warped from the heat. Duane waved the tape through the air, but that only fanned the flames.

"I'm sorry, man," Bill said. "I had to do it." He backed away from the smoke to catch his breath. Duane tossed the tape back into the flaming box.

"What's the matter?" said Niall, settling deeper into his chair. "You don't want to live in a world without *Ejacula*?"

Duane squatted by the fire and turned eyes clouded by intoxication on Niall. Then he looked up at Bill. "You're right, Cuz. They needed to die." The firelight playing across his features showed how his eyes softened with hurt, like it should have been his idea all along to destroy them.

Bill squatted beside him and watched them burn. He reached out a hand to place on his cousin's shoulder, but Duane pushed it away. He stood and stepped over to the VCR and pressed the eject button. The machine buzzed and pushed out the tape, which Duane grabbed and tossed into the burning box with the rest of its kind. Then he lifted the VCR off the top of the TV, yanked loose the cables, and tossed the machine on top of the fire, too. He shoved the TV, which sat atop a flimsy cart on tiny coasters. It careened across the carport until the coasters caught a crack and the cart and TV tipped over and crashed to the cement. Duane walked toward the house and yanked the screen door open so that it smacked the clapboards. After he passed through, the taut spring pulled it back to smack the jamb. Inside the house a cat squealed, and then Bill heard Duane shout, "Crystal! Crystal! Where's my claw hammer?"

Bill exchanged a look with Wesley and Niall, then hurried across the carport to the house. Before he made it to the door, he heard a heavy *thunk* and then Crystal shouting.

In the kitchen, Duane stood over the new microwave oven, which lay in the middle of the floor, its door ajar, the glass turntable describing a circle across the linoleum like a coin in a funnel.

Crystal and Lucy sat at the kitchen table over their love feast of fig jam and cheese. Duane took a meaty hand and hooked the electric blender, scooped it to the floor. He walked down the length of the counter, smashing to the floor a newfangled toaster, a food processor, an espresso machine. Metal clanged, plastic cracked. By now Crystal was on her feet and moving across the room toward him. Without a trace of the usual hitch in her gait, she sidestepped the clutter and headed for the weathered boards of the old butter churn in the corner. She reached for the dasher and in one fluid movement hurled herself across the room at Duane. She cracked him hard on the shoulder, but when she lifted the dasher to strike again he grabbed the handle and wrenched it from her hand.

Bill turned toward the sound of the screen door stretching open. Wesley stood there, taking time to wipe his feet on the mat, before stepping into the kitchen, licking his lips, eyes darting nervously. Lucy kept her seat at the table and leveled a languid look of hatred at Duane. Weaponless, Crystal started calling her man every expected bad name: *dickhead, asshole, stupid barbaric motherfucker.*

Bill stepped between them and gently reached for the dasher, which Duane still held like a club. Duane only gripped it tighter. Cornered by the sink, he stared back at them, everybody who had ganged up against him. Finally, he let Bill have the dasher and nodded once, like he should have expected this, then he stomped out of the room. Crystal shouted curses at his retreat, and now Lucy was there, taking her by the hand, but Crystal pushed Lucy away and kept up her barrage of words.

Bill was trying to catch Lucy's eye, to see what she might suggest. Maybe she could take Crystal for a ride? And then Bill and Wesley could try to talk Duane down. Somehow they needed to separate them. He heard from the living room the sound of furniture scraping against the hardwood floor, something heavy.

Crystal left the kitchen, and Bill followed her into the living room. There he found her standing over Duane, who was squatting by the console TV, hugging it to his chest.

"What the hell are you doing?" she said.

By way of response, he grunted and hugged the TV tighter, while the glowing screen flashed light against his T-shirt. He looked up at the ceiling and hefted the console from the floor, but Crystal put a hand on the top of the walnut cabinet and pressed it back down. He turned loose the TV, stood up, and shoved Crystal hard. Lucy caught her and held her back.

"Come on!" Lucy said. "He ain't worth it."

Crystal started screaming, but she let Lucy pull her out of the room and back to the kitchen.

Bill stood trying to decide whether or not he should try and say or do something to stop Duane. The last time he had chosen to act had only led to this violence. While he hesitated, Wesley stepped forward to reason with their cousin, and Duane punched him in the face. Despite all his muscle, Wesley fell hard and lay on the floor, cradling his head.

Bill squatted to help his brother, feeling his own guts turn rotten. Duane squatted again in front of the TV. He grunted with the effort, squatting low, wrapping his arms around that heavy wooden cabinet. With a defiant shout of rage, he stood up straight, the TV hugged to his chest, the tube still radiating light, and then he stumbled backward and the cord pulled taut. It unplugged and the screen went dark. The back of Duane's knee caught the coffee table, but he regained his balance and did a little dance in the middle of the floor trying to center the weight over his work boots. Slowly he moved toward the front door. Evidently he wanted the TV out of the house. The door frame was too narrow and he had to turn sideways to squeeze through.

As he was propping open the screen door with his shoulders, about to step over the threshold, Crystal came back into the room, leveling a pistol at the side of his head.

"Put down my goddamn TV," she said. "I paid for that TV. I paid for that microwave oven, too." Her whole body was jerking, and the muzzle of the pistol bounced around so violently that Bill pulled his brother backward out of its range. The gun looked ancient, maybe even a family heirloom. Her lip lifted in a snarl, and her breath came in explosive bursts. It seemed as though at any moment she might break into tears or pull the trigger.

"Now," she said, "you are going to step over there and set that TV down where it belongs. Or, I swear to God, I'm going to blow a hole in you so big, it'll fit two of my TV sets." She stepped across the room till the gun was aimed at the hollow in Duane's throat. He looked down at the revolver. She held it in both hands. Her struggle to hold the gun level was obvious not only in her face but throughout her trembling frame. The muscles in her forearms tensed with the struggle, and still the revolver jerked around like a wild animal with a powerful, angry will of its own.

Duane stood balancing the cabinet in the doorway, staring at the muzzle of the gun. He glanced around the room, his eyes briefly met Bill's, and then he stared at the revolver, as if surprised to still see it there aimed at him. The TV slipped from his grasp. He caught it with his hip. He grunted with the effort to keep it from crashing to the floor. And then he tilted forward and stumbled back into the room. His boots moved in tiny, stuttering steps across the living room, past Bill who was still cradling his brother in the middle of the floor. The heavy box seemed to pull Duane across the room, back to its spot, where he squatted again and set the thing down hard to cover the square of dust.

A long, tense moment followed. Crystal kept the revolver aimed at the back of her partner's head. Her breathing came fast and ragged, turning to angry, racking sobs.

Lucy stepped forward and pulled her close. She put a hand out for the gun. Crystal wouldn't turn it loose, but she did lower her aim at the floor. Nobody spoke. Everybody stared at Duane. He sat down on the floorboards in front of the cabinet and stared into the blank screen. His look of defiance had succumbed to a look of shame, though whether it was shame for allowing Crystal to defeat him in front of this audience or shame over the destruction he had wrought, Bill did not know.

Bill helped Wesley to his feet. His eye was already starting to swell. Through the house, Bill heard a screen door screech open and slam shut. Then footsteps. Niall put his head into the room and looked from person to person. Finally, his eyes came to rest on the gun in Crystal's fist. Niall's eyes closed. His face lifted to the ceiling. His head slowly rotated on his blue neck. He placed a finger to one nostril, like he had tried to show Bill earlier, a way to slow the breath, to calm the mind. His chest rose, and then his other nostril flared with a long exhalation.

"If you people are through murdering each other," he said, "there's another rack of ribs on the grill. So I hope you're still hungry."

34

At dusk, Wesley saw the bright light buried in the heart of his watermelon patch. As soon as the engine in his pickup coughed, sputtered, and then stopped, he could hear the crackling voice chanting Bible verses. The AM preacher's words floated through the evening air out to the unheeding melons and cornstalks and the critters hiding at the edge of the woods waiting for night to fall so they could raid the garden. Scarecrows were useless against deer and raccoons. Every year when his garden reached the ripeness of mid-summer, Wesley and his mother would stretch three hundred feet of heavy-duty extension cord through the woods from his cottage and out into the center of the watermelon patch, where they plugged in a three-hundred-watt light bulb and a cheap radio. But this year he had not been around to help her. Too preoccupied with his "woman of the night."

The dried mud crunched beneath his sneakers. He mopped the sweat from his forehead, careful with the swelling around his eye. The sweat stung, but it hurt to blot it. Too tender to try to see, so he left it shut and stared one-eyed at the bloated moon shining through the trees, then at the other horizon where the afterglow of sun was still visible, providing enough light to see where deer had trampled through a section of corn. If he believed in harvesting by the signs, a full moon meant the melon meat might already be blood red. But he hadn't driven out here tonight to harvest. After the violence at Duane's, he'd come here to seek stillness.

Instead, he found fruit swelling with ripeness, rotting in the ditch, spilling its seed. That stench. Cicadas trilling in tortured ecstasy. Tomato vines overcome by weeds. Watermelon hills that had formed straight lines in May now wandering away from any sense of order, zigzagging across red clay. Everywhere there was increase, everywhere sex, even in the radio preacher's voice. It was impossible to tell whether he bellowed out the gospel to check the entropy of weeds or if his shouts were meant to egg it all on. If you didn't listen to the preacher's words, he sounded just like a man begging a woman for love.

Black foam oozed from the ears of corn. Smut, a cancerous fungus that swelled kernels with pollution. How fast it spread.

He reached into his pocket and fingered the fifty-dollar bill she had insisted he take, smooth with the wear of many hands. After the gun, the party had collapsed into leave-taking and chaos, Lucy leading Crystal to her Corvette, Bill making too much of Wesley's eye, then determined to drive his own car. When Wesley had tried to wrestle the keys away from his brother, Lucy had stepped forward and put the fifty in Wesley's hand. She'd made a little speech about how she intended to repay him in full, the first words they had shared all afternoon.

He lifted several corn stalks that had been trampled by deer, but they wouldn't stay up on their own.

The lazy breeze shifted, and there it was. That stench, sweet-sour melon. Hot from the sun, how quickly it fermented.

Charleston Grays big as swollen wombs. Big with rain and sun.

He followed the smell to the far edge of his patch. There, a cluster of melons, their bellies rising smooth above the leaves, big with seed, bleached white by sun. They were ruined. He bent to inspect the softball-sized holes. Hornets buzzed about the opened rims. Raccoon would claw their way in. Deer would kick holes and suck the juice out.

Whatever it was, now that they had found them, they would be back for more—every night until nothing was left to save.

35

Bill opened his eyes inside the tin can he now called home. He'd been kept awake half the night by the neighbors' party, their gunshots. What little rest he had found had been plagued by nightmares, more cancer dreams involving family. Going cold turkey had fucked up his sleep. Pioneer-Land hadn't helped. It was the cheapest place he could find, this travel trailer with a busted axle. He hoped it was more than self-pity that had led him here. Every time he got close to somebody, he only caused them pain. Like Niall said, once he refused to close his eyes and came to see how he was not simply in the middle of so much suffering but was possibly the cause of it, then he had to be one evil bastard not to come to terms with his responsibility.

He threw the sleeping bag to the floor and stumbled to the sink to fill a glass with water. At least that worked. He swallowed hard and refilled the glass. He could live without A/C. And without a phone—he'd let his mobile service lapse. He could even use the port-a-potty when nature called. But he could not live without water. There was no shortage today. It was pouring rain. He had lain awake hours listening to the drumming on his camper's shell. He glanced out the window—the Mercedes was still there, its fabric top intact, the door unlocked, in case one of these fine neighbors needed to discover he had nothing for them to steal—including a driver's license.

Pioneer-Land was maybe a dozen trailers lined up at odd angles. With broken windows and sheet metal hanging loose, probably half of them wouldn't meet code. The sign on the highway had letters formed by little logs hammered onto a sheet of plywood, bleached gray by rain and sun. Today, the rain was as gray as the sign. PIONEER-LAND. Come live simply and purely. Recreate the lives of your ancestors.

It had been nearly two weeks since the DWI, and he was still waiting to hear from his lawyer about the court date. How long would he go without a license? Well, where did he need to go? All of the amenities of life could be found right here at home: the smell of stale spaghetti congealing in a bowl, the odor of raw sewage creeping through closed windows, cracked glass held shut with duct tape. The dulcet notes of domestic tranquility blended with gentle rain—*You fucking asshole! You expect me to fucking believe that fucking lie again!* So early in the morning. Like him, his neighbors never slept. He sniffed at the spaghetti. If he had a microwave, he might attempt to kill the bacteria. There was a propane stove, but after the fire at Duane's party, he avoided accelerants. He raked the spaghetti into the trash and turned on the tap, foamed up a sponge, started working through the mound of dishes piled in the sink. There lay the butcher knife. He grabbed the plastic handle, ran a thumb along the dull blade. Sore heart. How much would it hurt? One swift movement, just plunge it deep and sure. *Nah. Nah, nah, nah, nah, nah.* Not that stupid yet.

If he could only sleep. The last good rest he'd found was behind the wheel of his Mercedes, parked in the middle of a country road under a full moon. The dark shapes of cows in a pasture, so peaceful. The soft leather of the steering wheel was a perfect pillow. There had been the pistol in Crystal's hand, the shouting, Wesley trying to dig the keys out of Bill's pocket, Lucy with her hands in Crystal's hair. And then, the next thing he knew, cows. Their massive bodies at perfect rest. All that inertia. The moon was singing a lullaby. And then there was the cop with her flashlight in his face, rousing him, making him try to stand.

Mounted above the sink was a camp TV with a screen six inches across. Maybe six. Basic amenities. He turned the knob and cycled through the three channels he could pick up, looking for news, some connection to the world. The screen filled with green static. He stepped out into the rain and pivoted the antenna mounted to the side of the camper then stepped back inside, wiped the rain and mud from his toes. Static still, but better. Aging athletes in button-downs and sports jackets argued about Charlotte's new football franchise, its chances of improving its record this year. If Bill cared more about sports, maybe his life would have more meaning. Structure, at least. He had friends who couldn't understand how a guy who had excelled at sports in high school could care nothing about watching them afterward. But wasn't it obvious? What real athlete wants to sit on his ass and watch other people be athletic? Commercials. Commercials. The crime beat. As temperatures soared into the upper nineties, Gaston County became a hotbed of violence. Across the state, alcohol-related traffic deaths were up from this point last year. More than six hundred fatalities so far, nearly one third related to alcohol. She did a good job impersonating concern for human tragedy, this reporter. Very attractive, filming on location. Rain coat. Wet hair. Even on a six-inch screen, she was pretty. Talking at the camera and all of greater Charlotte. In the background, wreckage. She gestured at the crumpled hood and shattered glass. Driving too fast for the conditions. Sharp turns and wet pavement, going double the speed limit. And then, out of her mouth, the incongruous element, so wrong to hear amplified over the tinny speaker of this rented camp television, spoken by the miniscule green figure on a miniscule screen—out of the banal stream of useless information, what you had assumed to be somebody else's tragedy—a familiar name. Kent Dempsey, a self-employed Willow Winds resident, pronounced dead at the scene of the accident. A neighbor remembers the man as *never any trouble to anybody. Always had a friendly word.* The camera panned one last time to the truck, flipped on its side and scattered in pieces along the road like trash. A flock of birds. Crows? An overturned deep freezer, packages of frozen steaks, and crows digging through plastic wrappers with talons, beaks. *Next up, the story of how kindergartners make friends with skunks. Don't go away.*

Bill turned off the TV and reached into the camp refrigerator for the tray of ice cubes. His hand shook so bad that the ice rattled in the plastic cup like dice. Above the cupboard, the bottle of Beam. Three fingers left. Not enough, but enough. He dumped it onto the ice and brought it to his lips. He breathed in the oaky vapors then dumped it into the sink. The fumes filled the camper. Kent. Goddamn.

Outside, the rain had increased. It was unnaturally cool for July. He didn't know his neighbors yet, but a woman lived in the single-wide next door with children. From a distance, she looked like someone he might be able to ask for help. He could see movement through their windows, blue light flickering from a TV screen.

Broken plastic furniture was heaped into a pile beside a set of cinder block steps. He stepped up onto the cinder blocks and knocked at the trailer door. People inside were arguing. He knocked louder. A woman in a sagging T-shirt with a baby on her hip opened the door. Bill explained his need, a quick phone call. It wouldn't take more than a minute or two. A bare-chested man with a beard joined the woman. His mouth hung open, like he was drunk, or hungover, or in some other way incapacitated. The woman was trying to explain something about their telephone that Bill was having trouble understanding. Another baby wobbled over and grabbed hold of the man's pant leg, trying to climb him. The man kicked the baby off, the way you do with a dog that tries to hump your leg. The child hollered so loud Bill couldn't hear what the woman was saying. When she closed the door, he stood there in the rain. But up the road there was a convenience store and outside stood a pay phone.

Inside the booth, he leaned against the slick glass while he plugged in quarters for a long-distance call. He dialed the number and waited.

The phone rang and kept ringing. No answering machine. He slumped against the glass and let it keep ringing, so long that when she finally did answer, out of breath and a little frantic, as if she had run in from some chore outside, hearing the phone ringing over and over and expecting some emergency, Bill was not prepared for her voice and the urgency with which she could fill that one word:

"Hello!"

He breathed deeply and tried to make his tongue work.

"Hello?" she repeated. And then, the judgment and warning, "Who is this? If you keep calling here, I'm going to contact the police."

"Mother?"

"Hello? Bill?"

"I'm sorry, Mother," he said. "For everything. I'm so sorry."

THAT NIGHT, BILL WENT TO BED with a fever and chills. Underneath a thin summer quilt, he lay shivering in a half sleep, his teeth chattering. He pulled his frozen toes toward his butt for warmth—until his legs cramped and he had to surrender to the icy cold. All night long he kept seeing his father, his mother, their bodies slowly eaten by a deep blue, starless sky. Sometime early in the morning, gray light began to filter through the trailer windows. The drip of rain from the awning over the camper door came at irregular intervals.

In one of his dreams he lay curled against the wall on the edge of a king-sized bed. At the other side of the bed lay Maddie. They lay with their backs to each other, but he knew without needing to turn and look that she was there. And then he knew also that she was dying, unable to breathe. Fighting back panic, he clawed his way through a web of covers until he made it to the other side of the bed. He shook her lifeless corpse. When he brought his mouth to hers, to try and give her his own breath, he saw flies buzzing in and out, and worms on her tongue. He opened his eyes to try and forget the image. He stared out across the RV's shoddy interior—the thin paneling, the tiny sink speckled with rust, the camp TV, the camp stove, the narrow closet housing the child-sized toilet. It reeked of disinfectant. He lay awake, shivering, watching the now familiar shapes define themselves in the growing light.

The birds outside had begun to chirp and caw. A mockingbird somewhere nearby worked through its varied repertoire. The changing patterns of its notes made it difficult for Bill to return to sleep. But he was exhausted and still very cold. He needed sleep. He lay there for what seemed a long time waiting for sleep to come, for the fever to leave. When he saw the glow from across the trailer, it took him some minutes to register. Its source was the rusted sink, which had begun to suffuse a green light. It came slowly streaming out of the spigot, a thin pour of green that filled the sink and overflowed onto the floor. And the more of the stuff that poured out, the brighter it shimmered, until it collected itself into a mass of green light that stood erect, flickering more and more brightly.

Bill felt curiosity rather than fright, as if this moment were a natural part of his fever, for which the fever had prepared him. And when the figure became a man and Bill recognized that man as his friend, he felt only desperate eagerness.

"Kent," he whispered through chattering teeth.

"Yowza!" the figure said, taking a step toward the bed, trailing green pixels of flame. "Hot, hot, *hot!*"

"Kent?"

"Hey there, Big Time! How's it hanging?"

"They said you were dead."

"Dead? Who says I'm not?"

"But you're—"

"What, skinny? Hell yes, I am. You try this sauna. The weight just pours off of you. And I thought it was hot in Mexico." Kent struggled for breath and grimaced against the heat.

He was green skin and bones. The former beer belly caved inward beneath his ribcage. His penis hung limp and withered, dripping green flame. His cheekbones jutted out beneath sunken eye sockets. Green lips stretched taut over long teeth. Only the bald head, large and prominent, definitely belonged to Kent. The green figure glimmered, as if on a TV screen. Fire burbled upward inside him. Green flames bulged through his guts, pushed against his ribs, and shot out his mouth, his empty eye sockets. After every explosion, Kent would grimace with a combination of pain and pleasure. One long jet shot out the top of his head, leaving him howling ecstatic curses.

"God-toe-mighty! Holy moly! Fuck! Brother, that one *hurt!*"

Bill's eyes watered. Watching his friend burn was akin to burning himself. "Are you okay?"

"Am I *okay?* My skull cap ignites and he asks if I'm okay. Fuck no!"

"I'm sorry."

"Sorry?"

"I abandoned you. You were my only real friend. I was my best and worst self with you."

"Superlative. Hell yeah. That's what friends are for."

"I'm sorry, I fucked it up. Just like I did with Maddie. I took you for granted. I'm so fucking selfish. You were there for me, you were always there, and I was gone."

"Ah, Jeez, stop your whining. Save it for somebody who cares."

"I'm sorry, Kent."

"We had some good times, didn't we?"

The words burst from his friend's mouth in a conflagration that should have set fire to the entire trailer. Instead, they kindled a memory in Bill's brain—he and Kent were dressed up for a night on the town, leaning hungrily toward The Jackpot stage as Lucy wrapped herself around the pole, her garter full of green bills. Bill felt the alternating currents of lust and shame electrocute every inch of his flesh. When he looked up, Kent's head was bowed, and the points of his shoulders shook with mournful laughter.

"I don't have to tell you, so much of this life is spent alone." Kent took the withered cock in his hand and stretched it tight, then gave his pelvis a pathetic pump toward Bill's bed. A green torch rent a gash in his side. The blaze fed on his flesh, and when it subsided, the damage was clear. A pile of ash lay at Kent's feet. He was consuming himself right before Bill's eyes.

"When I get down to my fighting weight," Kent joked, "then I'll be ready for some higher loving." He pumped his pelvis again, and fire tore through his limbs, shooting out the stumps of his hands and feet. Flame engorged his penis and exploded out the end, spraying a bright arc across the room that he aimed toward Bill. When the eruption had spent itself, Kent stood holding the stump of his cock.

"Fuck." He gritted his teeth and glowered at Bill. He opened his mouth to speak, but the resurgent flame obscured his voice, a long monologue he seemed desperate to share. All Bill caught were two words: ". . . purify me."

In answer to Kent's plea, Bill conjured an old memory: two boys lying beneath tent canvas, whispering to each other in the high-pitched voices of pre-pubescence. Outside in the night, older voices, teenage boys calling them names—*fatso, pretty boy*, *butter lips*—and then the wet earth, a chilling flood creeping up through their sleeping bags. Bucket after bucket of cold water. "Don't pay them any mind," the young Bill said to young Kent.

"Shit," said the burning man inside the RV, leather tongue licking at lips that were baked and blistered. He nodded at the shared memory. "What I wouldn't give for some of that cool water now." As if by the magic of sympathy, the green flames abated. What was left of Kent's flesh and bone took on heft. His words rang clear.

"Listen," he said. "I don't have much time. And I hate to get all Jacob Marley on your ass, but if you haven't figured out yet that you love me, that I am your brother—I mean the full birthright—then I don't know what else to tell you."

"Don't—"

"What?"

"I should have been. . . should have been there for you."

The fire suddenly erupted again in full fury. It found a clear path through the cavity that had widened inside of Kent. He had become a chimney, and the flames shot up through him without impediment, building toward one last spectacular blaze.

"Don't do this alone," Bill pleaded. "Let me come with you!"

"You'll get your chance." Kent lifted his head as if to stare at the jets of flame spewing out his eye sockets. He let his jaw drop wide open for a long geyser of fire. "Don't worry about me, pretty boy. I was made for—"

But his words were lost in the noise of the inferno. Bill watched his friend burn.

There came a tremendous roaring and whoosh of green. Then, in an instant, the fire flickered and there came the tiny sound of fire being snuffed out, its last grab at oxygen. All that was left was silence and a puff of odorless smoke.

36

Wesley reached deep into the truck bed until he found the biggest Sugar Baby. He palmed the leathery rind, thumped it once to make sure it was ripe. Not nearly as big as some of the other melons, but it was Grandpa's favorite. An heirloom.

He knocked and then stood out on their porch and patiently waited until Granny opened the door. Whenever she worried, her head took on a bobbing motion, and this morning it seemed to have come completely unmoored.

"He won't wake up," she said. "I've tried talking to him. He needs to take his pills. He hasn't eaten any breakfast. I can't get him to take food lately. Nurse says we might have to feed him through needles. But, Wesley, he just won't wake up!"

There in the middle of the living room, he lay in the hospital bed, its mattress inclined so that his head drooped to the side. Even from across the room, Wesley could see a change in his grandfather. How long since his last visit? Two weeks? Three? How could so much have changed so quickly?

The TV blared full volume, but Grandpa slept on, his breathing labored and deep. His withered hands lay clenched at his sides. His sallow jowls were covered in thick, white stubble.

"They've got him on those painkillers," she said. "And I think that's what's making him sleep."

He was gone. Riding that raft far out to sea, he was out of their reach.

"Can't you do something?" Granny gestured toward the chair beside Grandpa's bed. "Maybe just talk to him. He

tunes me out. But he'll wake up if he knows you're here."
She bent over him and announced, "Matthew! Wake up!
Wesley is here to see you!"

Wesley was torn between wanting to let him get his rest
and wanting to help Granny get hers. She needed to see
him conscious, if only for a minute. And maybe Wesley
needed that, too. He stood by and watched as she took the
bed control in her hand and experimented with pushing the
several buttons until she had managed to raise the back rest
into a sitting position. Grandpa slid into what looked to be
an uncomfortable angle. His head dropped farther to the
side, but he slept on.

Wesley reached over the chrome rail and set the watermelon in his lap, careful not to disturb his catheter.

Like a reflex, Grandpa's gnarled hands came up to rest
on top of the melon. Then gradually they began circling it
to measure its size and pressing the rind as if checking for
ripeness. When his eyes opened, Wesley grinned.

"I brought you a watermelon, Grandpa."

He looked around himself like a man confused, trying to
find his bearings, wondering how he had come to arrive in
such a strange place. Then he focused on the melon in his
lap. "Sugar Baby," he said. "Why, it's big as a cannonball."

"Yeah, I saved out the biggest one for y'all. I remember
you used to grow these."

Grandpa nodded and stared down at the melon. He
stroked it, as if to conjure that other time. Then he let
his head fall back on his pillow and closed his eyes. His
breathing came hard and he seemed like he might cry. He
tried to lift the melon from his lap, but it was too heavy for
him, so Wesley reached down to take it away.

He cleared a space in the refrigerator for it and shouted
that it ought to be cool enough to eat by suppertime. When
he came back to the living room, Grandpa was asleep again,
breathing regular.

Granny said his bag was full and needed to be changed. The young woman they had hired to help out during the early shift had called in sick again this morning for the second time this week.

Wesley had watched his mother do this, and with his grandmother's coaching he was able to replace the bag with the spare. He emptied the full one into the toilet and then came back to join his grandmother, who had her rocker pulled up close to the blaring TV. She seemed a little calmer, now that she had seen Grandpa conscious for a few minutes.

Wesley pulled a chair over beside her and she handed him a stack of yellowed newspaper clippings, all from the "Heritage" column, which she was trying to sort.

"Oh my goodness," she said, noticing his eye for the first time. "What happened?"

"I had an accident." He was glad she hadn't seen it last week. It looked a lot better now. The swelling had disappeared, leaving only a slight purple stain.

"I thought maybe you got into a fight," she said. "Over that girl you've been sparking." She grinned up at him, and for a moment her head stopped bobbing and she looked at him askance, as if waiting for him to tell her about it. But he was so surprised, not only by the question, but by the tone in which it was asked—as if she were proud finally to be able to gossip with her favorite grandson about his girl—that Wesley just stared down at the newspaper clippings in his lap.

"Your mother tells me the two of you have been spending a lot of time together," she said. "I thought maybe you had some important news for us." She glanced over at her comatose partner.

"No," Wesley said. "No news." What could his mother possibly have said? Whatever it was, Granny had evidently heard it in a positive light.

"Actually," Wesley said, "we broke up."

"Ohhh." She moaned like she had been wounded, like strength was draining from her body. "That's terrible! I'm so sorry to hear that."

He was afraid she might cry. And for a moment, he felt himself on the verge of tears. There was something on the TV news about driving fatalities, but Wesley tuned it out. He scooted closer to Granny. She sat absentmindedly gazing across the room at Grandpa.

The backs of her hands were a patchwork of age spots. The veins were blue and raised, her knuckles swollen knots. He tried to picture that hand young and supple, an instrument of flirtation. It was hard to imagine his grandparents when they were kids, courting. They had never been one of those old couples that moon over each other. As long as he could remember, they had slept in separate beds. He couldn't recall a single instance of them holding hands. But they must have, once.

He reached out and took her hand in his own. Not in the usual way. Not with the reassuring pat to the back of the hand or the perfunctory squeeze. He took hold of her with the possessiveness of a worried lover. And she returned his grip with a strength that surprised him. He took her misshapen claw in both of his hands and brought it to his lips. He tasted the skin and smoothed the wrinkles out against his cheek.

"Oh, Daddy," she whined, looking Wesley in the eyes, and he wasn't sure who she was talking to. "Oh, Daddy, please," she repeated. "Don't go!"

37

At the graveyard, Bill felt the coffin grow suddenly heavier, when Wesley abandoned his role as pallbearer and rushed to help Granny from the hearse. That left Bill and Duane to hold up one side as they slid the casket out of the back and carried it to the pit under the green canopy.

It was the slowest of death marches. They followed behind Granny, who leaned heavily on Wesley's arm. Wesley held the black parasol high to keep her out of the worst of the heat. Finally, they entered the shade of the burial tent. As soon as the minister opened his mouth, Granny broke down. Sitting in the folding chair next to hers, Wesley pulled her tight to his side and whispered into her ear until her sobbing stopped. The old woman sat staring up at Wesley like he was the most beautiful boy in the world. And at that moment, he was.

Bill sat beside his mother and let the film of tears wash down his face. Try as he might, he could not stop himself. Mother reached for his hand and clutched it tight. She was forcing herself to smile. It was her father, but she was being the strong one, as she had always been. Bill had reached the age of seventeen before he learned of the girl child she had lost between the two boys who had lived. As long as he could remember, she had been a cancer survivor.

Despite the many tears, Grandpa's funeral was a celebration of the man they were about to put in the ground. Everyone in the family had always held up Grandpa's long life as an ideal full of joy and health, to which they all aspired and not a soul hoped to match.

Besides Granny, who varied between fits of weeping and long vacant stares, the only person who seemed to be taking it really hard—to the point of becoming antisocial—was Duane. Throughout the graveside service, Duane stood off by himself, out among the gravestones under the broiling sun. And later, at Aunt Rachel's house, while everyone else was crammed shoulder to shoulder inside, some younger folks standing while they ate off paper plates, Duane took his lunch out to the front yard and sat leaning against an old blasted hickory that provided little shade. That's where Bill joined him.

"You doing all right?" he asked.

Duane shook his head.

Bill put an arm around his shoulder and jostled him slightly. "I know you were close to him."

"No, I wasn't. Not for a long time. Probably not since I was a boy. He never did like my daddy, and I think he didn't especially care for me. But I did worship the man. Still do. He had everything I ever wanted for myself."

Bill nodded.

"You know Crystal left me." Duane took off his suit jacket and tossed it onto the lawn.

"No. I'm sorry to hear that."

"That girlfriend of yours came over and loaded her up while I was away from the house. I passed them in the driveway. In one of them U-hauls. I didn't chase after them. But now I'm wishing I had. I don't have the slightest idea where Crystal is. She hasn't called. And if her family knows, they're not telling. I just want to tell her I've decided to change. I've been going to AA. You probably didn't know that either."

"No. Well, good luck. If there's anything I can do to help, let me know. I'm on the wagon myself. So I know what you're going through."

"Do you wake up in the middle of the night angry?"

"Bad dreams."

"I just don't have no patience. But I'm working on it. I am. The meetings are helping. I'm glad to be sober."

"Me too. Most of the time. There were moments there today by the grave that I wished real bad I wasn't."

"I know what you mean."

But Grandpa's funeral had been a lot easier to get through than the one earlier in the week, the one to which he had not been invited. Kent had always had a bad habit of driving too fast when he was hurt. How much of that hurt was Bill's fault? And the booze? Bill should have been the one in that cruel ditch. Who passes out behind the wheel but has the sense to put the car in park first? How lucky for Bill that the cop found him before he woke.

IN THE FOLLOWING WEEKS, Wesley helped Bill get his life together, mostly by providing another generous loan and frequent transportation. Wesley's truck was having transmission problems, so Bill let him drive the Mercedes. The car wasn't doing Bill any good. And he had started worrying about the Mercedes parked out at Pioneer Land. After somebody broke into the camper Bill was renting, Wesley helped him move out of the trailer park into an efficiency apartment in South Charlotte.

Wesley sat with him in court, while Bill received the good news of a shortened license suspension and community service. Bill worked out his time in a homeless shelter, where he learned just how privileged he was, lucky to have most of the teeth in his head, for starters. Lucky that when he was down and out and broke he had family who could spot him a loan, a place to sleep. But what really surprised him was how most of these people, at least the ones he got to know, still desperately clung to hope of a better life.

The day he met Woodrow, they compared tattoos. By the end of Bill's shift, they had stepped out behind the shelter, by the dumpster, and taken their shirts off. Woodrow was proud of his tattoos, which were, indeed, the most attractive aspect of the surface he presented to the world. He looked sixty, at least, and his scrawny frame was covered in abundant gray hair and more than one scar, including a single smooth line that ran down his ribcage. Under the dumpster, a half-full quart bottle of Colt 45 had lodged against one of the wheels. They both looked at it longer than they should have. Woodrow was the first to look up. He put back on his old frayed shirt, fastened the buttons down the front.

"You know, Bill," he said, "whenever I feel the itch, I remember where I'm at."

"Where's that, Woodrow?"

"Earth."

"Earth?"

"That's right. Best place in the solar system. And I really, really don't want to fuck it all up."

AT WESLEY'S THIRTIETH BIRTHDAY PARTY, an argument arose concerning the ingredients Mother had used for his cake. Wesley was helping her set the table, and Bill heard his brother asking how much butter she had used, how much sugar.

"Good lord!" Bill shouted from the living room. "The woman bakes you a cake and all you do is complain."

"I wasn't complaining," Wesley mumbled. "I only wanted to know what was in it."

"So you won't ruin that girlish figure." He grinned at his father, who lay on his back in his recliner pushing the buttons on the remote control, not even listening, maybe not hearing them at all. Bill looked across the room until his father looked back at him.

"Did she bake you a cake?" Bill asked. "She didn't bake me a cake."

"Oh, I eat too many of her sweets." Daddy patted his belly and smiled, then looked back at the TV.

Bill desperately needed to find some new magic, and this seemed as good a place to look as any. Over three weeks now without a drop to drink, and he was still feeling very, very dry. He'd become a caffeine and sugar addict. On his fourth cup of coffee today, and he was jonesing hard for that birthday cake.

They waited for Wesley's new girlfriend to arrive before they lit the candles. Mariah was the daughter of one of the women in Mother's circle at church. According to Mother, Mariah and Wesley had become quite attached. An attractive woman, she was a good deal older than Wesley. But not too old to bear children, if that's what they wanted. If they hurried. It was clear in an instant that she had taken Wesley in hand. After they had finished their cake—after Bill served himself a second helping—Mariah started asking about the Mercedes. What would Bill want for it if Wesley were interested in buying? How many miles were on it? Had it ever been wrecked? Reflecting on what he owed his brother, Bill said he would be happy for Wesley to take over the payments.

Full of birthday cake, they moved to the living room to watch the evening news. The headline was a report about the possibility of a long-awaited stock market correction. Bill mumbled something about media euphemisms, letting his mind spiral into fears planted there by Niall: malevolent aliens and intergalactic real estate deals. If the shit did hit the fan, this countryside might be the best place to hole up. And they would need his help. If Bill had nothing else to contribute but his fading youth, he would at least give them that. Mother and Daddy were not old yet, but it would not be long before they were. The cancer could return at any moment, to strike any one of them. There was no more time left to waste.

Daddy eased back in the recliner, still staring at the TV, listening to the dire predictions about Dow Jones. "Our money's going to get to where it ain't worth nothing," he said through the bristles of his mustache. "What would happen if we had another Depression?"

"Back in our day," Mother said, "nearly everybody could go back home. Everybody was connected with the farm and the land. They had something in the smokehouse and something in the jars. You could go back. But now there's nowhere to go. Everybody's parents are living in condos in Florida. If something were to happen—"

"There won't be nowhere to run," Mariah said and reached for Wesley's hand.

"There won't be no food. No shelter," Mother said. "The basics won't be there."

Next up on the news was a clip from the President's recent speech about his mistress. He admitted his errors but then quickly started talking about the future. *Now it is time—in fact, it is past time—to move on. We have important work to do, real opportunities to seize, real problems to solve.* Was that possible—to move on? Bill had to hope so. He wanted to be inspired by the President's words. But he had a hard time now believing the man's performance. And what about his own performance?

"I never trusted him," Mariah chimed in. "And he never apologized to that girl or her family. He didn't mention anything at all about the other women he groped. What about them?"

"Amen," Mother said.

Bill excused himself. In the bathroom where he had entered puberty—like falling into a vat of acid laced with morphine—the walls were still pink. At thirteen why had he believed the simple act of pleasure, the suddenly new and disturbingly alien atmosphere of lust, had forfeited his soul to hellfire? Nobody had told him explicitly so. Had they? Well, maybe some of those revival preachers. However it came about, Bill had so convinced himself that he would burn eternally—if he could not stop touching himself—that one night he had decided he must save his brother a similar fate. Bill had entered nine-year-old Wesley's bedroom and announced that the Rapture would begin that very night, precisely at midnight, that Wesley should not delay but prepare his soul. What voice had whispered that date and time, Bill never knew. Wesley had looked up from his paint-by-numbers, confused but not sufficiently alarmed to tell Mother or Daddy. He had no doubt already learned that sometimes Bill said and did really stupid shit.

And this morning Bill sought out that same bedroom, which his mother had occupied ever since Wesley had returned from his two years at junior college and moved into the cottage in the woods. She suffered from insomnia and had found that she slept much better in a room of her own. But she had left Wesley's childhood crafts and trophies and plaques on the walls—until this morning. She and Wesley were busy emptying shelves and transferring the universe of knickknacks to cardboard boxes. They filled boxes with Boy Scout awards, school projects, model planes, drawings of superheroes, an unfired clay bust of Abraham Lincoln. Mother looked up at Bill.

"So," he said, "you finally decided to dismantle the shrine."

"Well, I've been needing some shelf space for my books and things," she said, a note of sadness in her voice. "And, I didn't want Wesley's treasures to get mixed up and lost. I thought he might want to keep them somewhere safe."

38

The ink factory was changing shifts, and before Bill could correct him, Wesley guided the Mercedes straight through visitors' parking and into the production lot, where men in blue uniforms were coming and going. When Bill had called Max to follow up on any new leads, he'd heard how the old man had ejected in his golden parachute and that Anne Compson, their OSHA specialist, had been promoted to plant manager. And when Bill had spoken to Anne, she hadn't minced words. The ax was falling left and right, she said. They were slashing budgets, paying her half what Max had made. She essentially offered Bill a job over the phone—in quality control. He would have been insulted if he weren't so desperate. So, here he was today to discuss the details, such as salary and her need to be clear that he would be expected to work many Saturdays. No laying out of work on the weekend to go golfing.

The air in the parking lot was sweet, any volatile emissions masked by the syrup of magnolia blossoms. Dark, glossy leaves clattered in the breeze.

Melons, two deep, filled the trunk. Wesley had offered Bill several as gifts for him to give to friends. So, Bill picked out a long, white Charleston Gray and hoisted it to his shoulder. Hopefully Anne liked watermelon.

He leaned through the passenger window. "I'm not sure how long this will take."

"I'll be right here." Wesley eased down in the driver's seat, a book on frontier architecture open in his lap.

Bill walked up the steps by the loading dock and into the back end of the factory, into a familiar landscape of pipes and vats and mixers blending pigment with binder, the low hum of machinery in gear, the whir of fans struggling to clear the air of alcohol and toluene. This still wasn't such a bad place to be. Behind him, the steady chime of a forklift—then Lamar pulled up and shut off the engine. He hopped down from his perch, extending a brown hand.

"You came back to see me, baby. I was about to give up on you."

"Yeah, Lamar, I couldn't keep myself away from you."

Lamar's hands went to the red bandana around his neck, an unconscious habit. Bill watched how the older man straightened the fabric so that it covered the discolored skin, the knots of flesh. Bill could never look at Lamar without sobering up, remembering that this place was a bomb with a short fuse, liable to explode into flames at any moment. And, yet, even though the older man had gained such knowledge firsthand, it did not prevent him from celebrating his own combustible flesh with every kind of adornment: the red bandana, gold bracelets hanging heavy from his wrists. Lamar's spicy cologne overpowered the current of solvent fumes that blew past them.

"You coming back to work?" Lamar asked. "For real?"

"Well, that's what I'm here to find out. I have a meeting with Anne."

"Mm hmm. That woman never stops. They got her working 'round the clock. Look at her eyes. I don't know if she sleeps. You be good to her."

"I'll try my best." They shared a smile, but not a broad one. This rough humor of men, it could get both of them in trouble now. Bill asked about layoffs in the plant, and Lamar explained how, so far, production had been spared the cuts that had hit the lab and the office. But everybody was still holding their breath.

"It's lucky any of us are still here," Lamar said.

"Why's that?"

"They didn't tell you? Man!" He shook his head.

"Sometimes people around here act like they don't have a lick of sense."

"What happened?"

"A batch of cotton caught fire."

"Good Lord. Big?"

"Tank number two. Nitrocellulose-B. You know how hot that shit gets."

Bill looked up at the mezzanine and noticed the soot covering the walls and the paint that had bubbled off of the cement blocks. "Holy moly! How many people got hurt?"

"We got lucky. Some fool on third shift. No grounding cable. Lighting a cigarette, can you believe that? I hear Manuel is a hero. He put it out all by himself. Flames shooting up to the ceiling."

"Good Lord."

"Some people don't have no business in here."

A group of men were coming from the locker room—pulling on plastic hair nets, stuffing in ear plugs. Still almost all of the black people Bill knew worked in this factory or in the adjacent lab; that much hadn't changed. Without even trying to deny his whiteness, was there anything he had learned that would help him be of use, or, if not of use, at least authentic?

Several of the men stopped to nod at Bill, to ask "What's up?" before they clocked in. He noticed how they exchanged looks, snuck glances at his neck. Sooner or later he would have to tell his story, but not today. Lamar acted like he hadn't noticed the tattoo. And now his eyes fixed on the melon Bill carried on his shoulder, which was getting heavier by the minute.

"Did you bring that for me?"

Lamar didn't smile. The question sounded almost hostile.

"Well," Bill said, feeling the double bind tighten. Yes or no, neither seemed a fit answer. "You like watermelon?" He brought the melon down from his shoulder, as if to offer it, and its waxy skin slipped through his fingers. He fumbled and caught it before it burst on the concrete floor.

"Careful with that thing." Lamar said. "Could be dangerous."

"Did you grow it?" Jerome challenged, as if he was sure that Bill, the paper-pusher, big boss man, couldn't possibly know anything about growing watermelons.

"My brother grew this one. Y'all got a knife around here somewheres?"

"Might be," Jerome said. "I can't stand no watermelon. Too mushy. You bring in some cantaloupe, now, I'll chow down."

Lamar relieved Bill of his burden and carried the melon to the production break room, where he left it on the bench of the picnic table. When he came back, the other men were punching their time cards and heading to their posts.

Lamar winked and nodded at Bill's neck. "What you got there?"

"Had a little fun."

"Mm hmm. I see that."

"Maybe I should have worn a tie." But he'd figured if he were interviewing for a position in quality control, a tie might send the wrong message. Nobody in Q.C. ever wore a tie.

Lamar reached for the red bandana at his own neck and removed the slide. He handed the length of red fabric, like a live flame, out to Bill. "You want to borrow this? For your big interview?" He lifted his chin and measured Bill with a questioning glance. "If you don't mind a little sweat."

Bill had never seen Lamar without a bandana, and now his old scars revealed themselves more fully. Bill had heard the stories of how twenty years ago fire in the north wing had seared a tree into Lamar's back. And now Bill saw for himself how the upper branches wrapped around his throat in hard, pink lumps.

"I've got a dozen of these things in my locker," Lamar said, still holding the bandana out to Bill.

So, how could he say no?

WHEN WESLEY DROPPED BILL OFF at his apartment, there seemed a finality about their parting. Bill had a job now. And he had his work at the shelter. He was beginning to figure out the bus routes. He was thinking of buying a bicycle. And Wesley had a woman now who organized his social calendar.

Considering the many hours they had spent in each other's company over the course of the summer, it seemed they should have learned better how to speak their minds. With the exception of several late-night heart-to-hearts, most of them ones Bill could barely remember, they had not made an awful lot of progress talking with each other.

"Hey, I want you to know how much I appreciate all your help." Bill leaned through the passenger window of the Mercedes and watched his brother sitting behind the wheel, staring out through the windshield. The black eye was gone, leaving only the slightest discoloration underneath. "I don't know what I would have done if you hadn't taken me in," Bill said. "And the money. I'll pay you back, I swear, as soon as I start drawing a regular paycheck."

Wesley nodded, but it seemed like he wasn't really listening. "I been meaning to say," Wesley began. "I been meaning to tell you I'm sorry—for what happened with Lucy. I behaved badly. I'm sorry."

Bill stuck his head deeper into the car. "I'm the one who brought her to your house. I believe that dance was on me."

Wesley turned and looked him in the face. He leaned across the seat and reached out a hand. Before Bill could bring his own hand up to shake, Wesley took hold of Bill's arm, around the biceps, and squeezed tight. His grip was a vice. Over the summer, through those many hot evenings stuck in Wesley's cottage, most nights even sharing a bed, this was the first time Wesley had reached out and deliberately touched him.

"You been pumping my weights while I wasn't around?" he said.

"Yeah, right. That's what I need to do."

"I hear you. Come around sometime. I'll teach you how to sweat."

Bill turned to go. He was halfway across the parking lot, pulling out the keys to his apartment, when he heard the Mercedes purr and Wesley pulled up beside him, rolled down the window, and spat on the pavement.

"I meant to tell you," he said. "About Grandpa. One day after you and me visited, he got to reminiscing with me about his year in Jacksonville when he was a young man. He told me to tell you to have a big time in the city. Said he nearly turned city rat himself."

[Hear the author's thoughts on the challenges of writing about sexuality by visiting Fugitive Views, Southern Fried Karma's YouTube channel.]

Part V

39

The following weekend, still battling to grab hold of his life, Bill found himself seated before a white linen tablecloth, with candles and heavy flatware. He was trying to act normal, under control. But by the time the main course arrived, he felt himself floating somewhere above his body, looking down at the white linen, glancing nervously at Maddie and watching his friends across the table, Blake and Samantha, getting smashed without him. He heard himself tell them a string of amusing anecdotes about the last few months, and they laughed so hard that people at other tables began to stare. He could not stop, even though he feared that with every story, he was losing any chance he might have with Maddie. He kept glancing furtively at her, while she sat distracted, staring out across the restaurant.

He told them about waking up drunk with his first tattoo, and about selling steaks to the trailer parks. He told about Niall's apocalyptic vision of intergalactic real estate deals. When he finally got around to the story of how his virgin brother had stolen his hooker girlfriend, he glanced over at Maddie again and waited in vain for her to offer a reaction. If the two of them were going to have anything together—friendship, even—he had to be honest from the start, and this was the easiest way for him to tell it, trying to make it funny. But halfway through the confession, he realized his mistake: they should have met somewhere in private.

Because they had been members of the same pledge class, Blake had been trying for years to get Bill more involved in alumni activities, inviting him on golf weekends, offering him football tickets. He meant well. Blake wanted everybody to be a big happy family. He'd seemed authentically distressed by the news of Bill and Maddie's separation. So, when Blake had called to say that he'd spoken to Maddie and that he thought she might be receptive to the idea of a double date, Bill had called her and she had, shockingly, accepted the invitation to dinner. He hadn't yet brought up her boyfriend. All things in due time. Maddie met the three of them at the restaurant, and from the moment they were seated, conversation was dominated by the happily married couple, who had started out drinking double martinis and switched to red wine when the appetizers arrived. After dinner they moved on to whiskey sours.

"I want to see his tattoos." Samantha leaned drunkenly across the table. "You can show us *something*, can't you? Come on, loosen that tie. I'm eventually going to see them all, honey. Whet my appetite." She reached for the button on his cuff, and he forced a laugh and pulled his hand free. He and Samantha had always flirted. Whenever he saw her at a party, he could count on her to create an atmosphere of expectancy. But tonight when she leaned across the table to flirt, he smelled the whiskey on her breath and thought only of how much he would love to grab her drink and chug it.

"You passed out behind the wheel? Just parked your Mercedes in the middle of some country road?" Blake couldn't stop laughing. "You never change. You're a lucky one. I would have wrapped it around a telephone pole. So, what did the cop say? When she put her flashlight in your face and saw you snoring?"

"I don't remember." His hands were shaking again, and he put them under the table on his lap. The comedy had gone too far. Maddie would never take him seriously. But it didn't seem to matter to her. And to him, these were only words. With a few drinks, it would have been hilarious. There was nothing in the world more glamorous than a drunk's vision of his own life. If he were not mourning Kent's death, and if he had not nearly caused his own death or that of another driver, he would have ordered a four-liquor cocktail and chugged it, anything to make the dinner conversation seem less sad and pointless. Was this what he had to look forward to in a life of sobriety—pretending that he cared at all that the pasta he shoved into his mouth was *al dente*, taking his golf game too seriously, securing a mortgage on as many square feet as he could afford?

Maddie had let her hair grow. She wore no makeup, or very little. No base, for once, so he could see her face, skin that had been damaged by teenage acne but that was still tender and translucent and beautiful to see. And she had gained weight, which was a relief. Fuller in the arms and breasts and neck. She had cheeks again. He kept waiting for a smile to blossom, but after all his jokes she remained glum and indifferent.

Bill had known that Blake would eventually bring the conversation around to the fraternity. It surprised him that he waited as long as he did. Blake filled him in on the fall fundraiser for permanent housing. He was the chairman of the committee and he wanted Bill's help. He said Bill had the ability like no one else to remind the alumni of the reasons they had pledged Gamma Omicron in the first place.

"I really haven't been active since graduation."

"I know." Blake spoke through a mouthful of pasta. "That's why your being on the committee would be such a coup. You'd breathe life into the thing. Remember the time you and The Bug shrink-wrapped Cranshaw to his bed? Remember that?"

"Maybe?"

"All the guys remember that. Every time we meet, some-body brings up your name. I really want you in on this thing. We'll only meet maybe . . . once a month? Come on, say yes. For the brotherhood."

"Thanks for asking. I'll think about it. I will." He watched Blake carefully wind the strands of spaghetti around his fork and open his mouth wide to keep the sauce away from his blonde mustache. Something about mustaches unnerved Bill. Blake was one of the brothers who had come to both of Bill's weddings. He had been a faithful friend, even if their lives had never interpenetrated very deeply, which was no fault of Blake's. The sadness that fueled Samantha's heavy drinking was all too clear. Beneath the surface of their happy marriage, Bill had long suspected trouble. He had also sensed in Blake the need of a confidant and had done little to help.

"Permanent housing is so important," Blake said. "If the chapter stands a chance this time around, we have to have it. Even if Kent hadn't bankrupted us, housing always would have posed a problem. The chapter might still have folded."

A wave of nausea swept across Bill. Piccolo Italia was a small, intimate restaurant, and the tables suddenly seemed too close together, the dining room too noisy. He felt the need to point out that Kent had paid the money back, but of course, the damage had been done.

"Poor Kent." Blake shook his head. "It's tragic, isn't it? When we heard, I told Samantha that was no accident. I felt responsible somehow."

"How's that?"

"Of course, I don't mean personally responsible. I only mean that I guess all of us are responsible in ways we can never realize."

"How could you have been responsible?"

"I don't know. I could have stayed in touch. The money he stole, it was just money." Blake wound the pasta around his fork. "Bill, that's why the fraternity is so important to me. I mean, I know Kent was a wildcard. But it could happen to any of us, to you or me—without a community of friends to hold us down to earth, to make us feel connected."

"He was my good friend." Bill felt a space yawning open inside himself. "I worked with him this summer. He helped me out. We grew up together."

"Boy Scouts or something, right?"

"Yeah. We were Scouts." He excused himself and went to the bathroom. He closed the stall door behind himself and stood looking down at the water inside the bowl. Somebody had scrawled graffiti on the wall, even in this nice restaurant. *For discreet sex, call*—but the phone number was smudged out. His bile rose and spilled. He leaned over the toilet and it kept coming, until he had thrown up his meal. At the sink he washed out his mouth, but he still felt the burn in his throat, in his gut, like flames had seared his insides.

When he came back to the table there was an awkward moment. Maddie said she had to get up early for work. Everybody else agreed: one more day, Friday, then the weekend, except for Bill, who was working Saturday, a fact he didn't bother to mention. Blake told Bill that he would call him about being on the committee, though the enthusiasm was gone from his voice.

After saying good-bye to their friends, Bill convinced Maddie to stay out later. They walked down the street to the Cajun Queen, a New Orleans-style restaurant in a historic, two-story brick house. They sat upstairs near the bar at a table by the wall where they could look out at the traffic passing below. Behind that plaster wall, in the main dining room, the house band blasted Dixieland jazz. He and Maddie used to come here to drink Hurricanes and listen to those horns.

He anxiously worked his fingers through the colored plastic beads hanging in front of the window and wished he could have just one drink. He could not trust himself to say the right words. He had to think too hard about every sentence.

"So, I'm working for Anne now. Quality Control. At least I have my hands in ink again."

"I'm sorry to hear about your friend," she said.

"Thanks."

"And I'm sorry I was no fun at dinner. I just really can't stand those two. They're so damn condescending." She sipped her Club soda. He wondered if it was for his sake that she wasn't having a drink.

"I appreciate your coming out tonight, Maddie. I really do. It's great to see you again."

She looked out across the dining room, like she might at any moment excuse herself and leave the restaurant without explaining.

"So, your boyfriend didn't mind your meeting me?"

The anger in her eyes let him know this was the wrong approach.

"I'm sorry. I didn't mean to pry."

"I'd like to put the house on the market," she said. "Before the summer is entirely gone."

"Okay."

"You never liked the neighborhood."

"That's true." Still, selling the house was like the final goodbye to the years they had spent together.

"It was always twice the house you and I needed."

"True."

"I thought you'd be happy."

The words hung there between them as they sipped their sodas and listened to the bright horns in the other room.

"So," he began. "You've heard about my summer. How was yours?" He nervously chewed chunks of ice.

"There's a lot we need to talk about. Sorry I've been so hard to reach. It sounds like you've been working hard to punish me."

He tried to read her emotions and could not. "It's over now," he said. "Look at me." He pulled down his collar, rolled up his sleeve. "I've got this shit all over me. I don't know what happened, but I'm over it."

"Uh huh."

"I know you don't believe me. I don't expect you to, not

right away. But I'll show you, if you give me another chance. I just want us to be friends. I've been such a lousy friend to you." He waited for some response. "You're looking good," he said, to fill the silence. "You've gained a little weight and it looks really good on you." He wasn't sure whether she could take that as a compliment, but suddenly her eyes brightened and a hiccup of laughter escaped from her, which she fought to control.

She smiled, and whispered, "I'm pregnant."

Throughout dinner, he had been sneaking glances at her skin—now he had to look away. In the next room the trumpet held a high C that cut right through him. There was no possibility the baby could be his.

"Why didn't you tell me?"

"It didn't really concern you."

"Well, congratulations." He felt his world sink yet another level lower. Of all the sucker punches he had prepared himself for, he had not anticipated this one. And, yet, he understood that he should celebrate her happiness. He remembered her and Anthony at the Renaissance Fair and how content they had been together, how easily he had made her laugh.

"What kind of plans have the two of you made?" he asked, trying his best not to make this about him and his loss. Maddie was having a baby.

"Why would you assume I've made such plans?"

"I suppose by now Anthony has left his wife."

"No, he hasn't. I'm not sure what he ever told her about me. I think maybe they have some sort of arrangement." She laid her head heavily against the wall and tried to control her breathing which had become ragged.

Bill reached across the table to stroke her hand, a gesture she ignored.

"Do you still love him?" He pulled his hand back into his lap and tried to resist the dizziness that had swept over him.

She kneaded the back of her neck and watched the cars out on the street. "It's funny how quickly you can forget somebody after they hurt you so bad." She stared across the table.

He remembered how when they were first married Maddie had wanted a baby, and he hadn't been ready. Then, by the time he suggested the idea, they both knew it was only his desperate gambit to win back what he had already lost.

"How far along?"

"Two months. Anthony doesn't even know. I'm not telling him. I haven't told anyone yet. You're the first."

"You're going to keep it?"

"Yes. I need somebody. Somebody I can build a future with. I've got a good job now."

"Congratulations. I'm excited for you—on both accounts."

"Really, Bill?"

"You will be a magnificent mother. Any child you bring into this world will be as brilliant as she is beautiful."

"You're so full of shit."

"I'm entirely serious. That is one lucky girl—or boy. Now, tell me about the new job."

"It's with NationsBank, in investment. The starting salary isn't quite what I'd hoped for, but there's a lot of potential to move up."

"NationsBank?"

"I've never worked for a company near that size. It's a little intimidating. But I'm excited."

Every impulse he felt to speak he fought against. The resentment he harbored against NationsBank for downsizing his own career, his admittedly wild notions about that monolith, that monument to mammon and its potential alliance with an alien takeover, he just ate those words.

"I'm a little nervous, I'll admit," she said. "About starting a career and becoming a mother at the same time. I haven't told H.R., or anyone at work, not yet. I want them to see I'm capable first. I want to know it myself."

"Well. I only hope you'll let me help. Please. I would be honored to help."

She measured him with a glance, and he felt he had come up lacking. He shook a Marlboro Light from its pack. Since he had stopped drinking, he was up to two packs a day. Then he caught her tired glare.

"Oh, sorry." He slipped the lighter back into his pocket. "Sorry, I wasn't thinking."

She wore that look of fatigue he had seen so often, the many times she'd had to instruct him in the basics of civilized living.

"I don't feel pregnant yet," she said. "I mean I've had some mild nausea, but if I hadn't missed my period, I'd have no idea that another life is growing inside me. I dreamed the other night that I was fat. Huge. There was so much of me, all I would ever need. I woke up laughing."

Bill's dreams lately had all been nightmares, filled with rotting flesh and burning friends. So, he let himself be buoyed up by her hopeful augury. He remembered a time, a year ago or more, taking a long bath with her in warm water, her breasts in his hands, her body lying soapy on top of him. He had been so contented in that bath water, unable to tell where his body stopped and hers began.

"I mean that about wanting to help," he said. "I know you have no reason to trust me, but I hope you'll give me a chance anyway. Anything I can do in the coming months, and afterward, just, please, let me know." He laid a palm on his chest, covering the whorls of blue that showed through his open collar. The entire evening he had been terrified that sooner or later she would bring up the D word.

She stood up and looked over his shoulder out the window. "I'm sorry, but I need to go."

"So, what are we going to do? Are you going to let me see you?"

"Yes. I want us to be friends again, too. You're right, I still don't trust you. And I'm sure you feel the same about me. But we'll see. We should talk more soon, about selling the house."

She offered him a ride home. He said he did want to show her his new, meager apartment, but tonight he needed to walk. This anxiety that had been rising within him, for days now, the only things that might dispel it were booze or vigorous exercise. She let him kiss her on the cheek and then he was on his way, jogging down Seventh Street until he had to walk, overcome by a fit of coughing. He opened the pack of Marlboro Lights and counted them, then put the carton back in his pocket. It wasn't just the cigarettes causing this tightening in his chest.

Across the street, Independence Park was lit up for young men to shoot hoops late into the night. He could hear their shit-talking. This was his city now, too. The cheap apartment he rented was within biking distance of work, walking distance to a park. He wanted to believe it wasn't too late to sweat himself back into shape. But this tightening in the chest, this headache, the burning in his lungs, they said otherwise.

He took a left onto Hawthorne and hiked uphill past the hospital. He kept navigating a now familiar route until, when he crested the hill, the skyline assaulted him. In the center of all that light, the NationsBank Tower stood like a glowing castle, bright against a dark sky. He and Maddie differed on one fundamental point: he believed a city was not the best place to raise a child. The kid would discover the city soon enough. But, of course, it wasn't his child. He could foresee the argument—assuming she did let him be involved—the moment when he pushed his opinion on one of any number of matters—nutrition, TV, day care—and she could simply choose to shut him out.

His apartment lay about a mile, maybe two miles, away. At this quick pace he could make that distance in no time— taking Queens southward and striding beneath the massive oaks that towered over some of the oldest mansions in town. Instead, he found himself heading in the opposite direction, crossing a parking lot, stepping down a side street that led back toward downtown past desperate people without homes except whatever makeshift shelter they could manage for the night. Even when a bed was available, within walking distance, where Bill's new colleagues provided a warm, dry mattress, a hot meal, Bill understood too completely the inability of these citizens to give up whatever substance kept them on the streets.

If he wasn't mistaken, this road would take him straight out to Arlington Avenue and Way of the Flesh. In fact, it dumped him right in front of The Jackpot and its bright lights, the line of men waiting to be let inside. Cash from his first paycheck lay folded in his wallet. A stack of twenties. She was surely dancing tonight. Thursday nights were always busy. He averted his eyes from the neon pot of gold and lengthened his stride. The boisterous voices of young men faded behind him, and just as fast the buzz of anticipation faded, the hope that he might get a lift, however temporary, out of the depression that was steadily securing its grip. Instead of remembering her dancing on that purple stage, he thought of Kent, sitting in the shadows beside him, watching her, both of them getting very drunk.

He was having trouble mourning his friend in a way that seemed proper. As early as he could remember, his parents had regularly taken him out to the local funeral parlors. There they had waited in line to look at a body lying in a casket, and afterward they'd stood around with the other friends and family of the deceased. It was difficult now to be

The Skin Artist 359

denied even this simplest consolation, access to the circle of mourners, which Kent's family had decided to limit to family. Evidently, his mother was tired of seeing her son become a public spectacle, first the embezzlement and flight to Mexico, and now this gruesome car crash on the evening news.

When Kent's mother had answered the door, she had refused even to let Bill inside. She stood there, filling up the doorway of her double-wide. She looked down the steps, and he thought to himself how much older she looked than he remembered.

"Don't you think you people have caused my son enough hurt?" she said.

"Mrs. Dempsey, I'm Bill Becker." He held the store-bought lasagna out toward her, but she made no move to take it. "You remember me. Kent and I were in the Scouts. We were in college together."

"I know who you are."

He saw the two boys clinging to her skirt. Kent's nephews? Dressed in their hand-me-down Sunday clothes. From the long summer of selling steaks, he was used to the mistrustful stares of children following him down the front steps of mobile homes. Burning with shame, he carried the lasagna away. There was nothing he could have said to those two boys to win their trust.

So, now on this starry night, working his way through the maze of streets to the inner city, Bill still needed to talk with somebody who knew Kent and missed him. If there were Gammas who had respected Kent, Bill didn't know them. Niall knew Kent only through Bill's stories about him, and in those stories Bill had pandered to Niall's sardonic wit, leading the artist to view Kent as, at best, a sort of Quixote. Bill was obligated to set the record straight, to tell a new story, whatever that was.

As soon as he came to the bottom of the hill, a young woman across the street made eye contact and thrust out her hip. He didn't want to make assumptions, but that makeup, that very short skirt, communicated a level of desperation you saw on this street late at night. He felt the urge to cross the street and offer her money, for a meal, or for cocaine, or for whatever she thought she needed, but instead he looked away and lengthened his stride. He could see the sign glowing up ahead, the vertical rectangle with red neon letters spelling out TATTOO. The sign burned all night and day, but you felt it best at night. At night, that sign worked its own mojo. The door stood wide open as always. Niall said an open door left an invitation in the mind of anyone who walked by. It wasn't just for business; he did it to mess with people who ordinarily wouldn't even consider a tattoo.

There was a phone booth on the corner and a loose brick at his feet. He could rent a cab to the suburbs and go bash that fucker Anthony's head in. Damn him for treating Maddie the way he had, for getting her with child and not even sticking around long enough to know it. The sleazy lawyer. Bill stood on the curb, his lungs burning, and stared across at the word in red neon. He knew that he did not deserve this righteousness. He placed a hand on his chest, over the wings beneath his shirt. It was a good thing, he must remember, a wonderful thing that had happened. He could be a daddy to Maddie's child. Or an "uncle." Anything other than the angry ex-husband. He did not want to miss this opportunity, the way he had missed being there when his father had needed him. Not to compare the treatment of cancer to childbirth, but both events transformed the body in ways nobody should ever have to experience without a loving community.

When he crossed the street, he felt how the vibe pouring out that door had changed. The paranoid energy of the thrash guitar Niall played through the tinny speaker of a transistor radio had been replaced by Nashville twang. On the greasy pavement, in front of the dumpster out front, a pair of gray tabby cats fought over some sort of carcass. A chicken? Another cat leapt up out of the dumpster and walked along its edge, eyeing Bill warily.

Inside, everything had changed. The shop was impeccably clean, with the atmosphere of an Indian tea house. Niall's posters were gone from the walls—gone was the chaos of tacked-up Polaroids, the Sistine Chapel pinned to the ceiling. In their place hung long batik sheets to cover the dingy sheetrock. Framed prints were evenly spaced: pen-and-ink drawings, photographs of skin art. On the air, a scent of freshly brewed coffee.

"I'll be right there," came her voice from the storage room in back. When she stepped through the doorway, hesitation spread across her face. "Can I help you?"

"Lucy."

She had chopped her hair off, and her ears were full of new silver piercings. She went about straightening the equipment laid out on the bench beside the barber's chair there in the center of the room, the one artifact Bill recognized.

"What do you want?" she asked, her back still squared to him. Across her shoulders spread the top branches, leaves tipped golden with fire. The couple standing beneath the tree were hidden by her shirt, but he knew they were there.

"Well, I came by to tell Niall—"

"He's not here. Obviously." She explained how Niall had been invited to work for a shop in New York City. "To hear him tell it," she said, "he will be working on nobody but celebrities."

"So, you . . . you—"

"I took over the lease. And his business."

"Oh!" Bill flipped through a booklet of stencils displayed on the counter. "Are these your designs? You never showed me—"

"You never asked."

Willowy figures. An angry angularity. But there was serenity there if you looked long enough.

"I stopped by to tell Niall about Kent."

She nodded, and a hard look came over her face, like she was being accused. "I was real sorry to hear," she said.

A car pulled up out front, and in through the open doorway stepped Crystal in blue hospital scrubs, carrying a paper sack bearing grease stains and the Krispy Kreme logo. The cats followed her inside.

"Hey there," she said, apprehension clear in her voice.

They made small talk. Crystal explained her scrubs—she was on her way to work the night shift at a local hospital, she didn't say which one. Bill knew better than to speak of Duane, even the good news that he was off the bottle. When Duane's name finally did come up, it was Crystal asking Bill to please not mention he'd seen her.

"If he does that," Lucy said, "he knows I'll come kick his ass." She reached for Crystal's hand and held on tight. Crystal looked down at her sneakers. She stepped through the curtains to the rear of the shop and a moment later came back, her arms loaded with a box of supplies. She gave Lucy a kiss, promised to call when she had a chance, and before she could break free and head out the door, Lucy pulled her close for a long, hungry embrace.

When Crystal drove away, Lucy turned her back to Bill again, resuming her house cleaning, and he realized the right thing to do was take his leave. And he would. But so long as he stood this close to her, it felt physically impossible to make himself widen the distance. Standing among the order she had created eased the pain in his chest, even if he was only a spectator. He feared stepping back into that night.

He stepped over to the barber chair and leaned back into the padding, feeling the familiar crinkle of Naugahyde.

"How's business?"

She said business was slow but picking up. There was an unmistakable edge to her voice, fending off inquiries of a more personal sort. He closed his eyes and tried to steady his breathing.

"Look," she said, and when he opened his eyes, he saw her leaning over him, close. He recalled that first morning in this chair, when she had stood right there in the same spot, with a crooked grin and crazed eyes, the whole room spinning.

"Look," she repeated, "I can't see you."

"Hey, I think I've figured that out." He tried to laugh. "You two are beautiful together. And I don't mean that in some sick, voyeuristic way." One of Crystal's cats scurried by and he scooped it up, began stroking its fur.

"No. You don't understand," she said, slowly, patiently. "I can't *see* you. Literally."

"Oh. Okay."

"You've got friends," she said. "A good family. A wife. You don't need me."

"Well. Okay. Okay." The cat lurched out of his hands and stepped languidly over to Lucy, where it weaved itself in and out of her ankles. Bill leaned forward, tried to think of some fitting words for farewell. What came instead was his best sales pitch.

"I've been thinking of getting one last tattoo. I don't want to cover myself. No offense! They look perfect on you. But, well, I sort of drifted into each of these images by accident, you know. I like best the butterfly you picked out for me, but—"

"You picked that. Not me."

"Well, with your guidance. But I was unconscious, remember?" He wanted something significant. Niall was always talking about meaningful imagery, the importance of design, of placement, of deliberate choice.

"What did you have in mind?" Her eyes hardened.

"Well, those stencils of yours are gorgeous. Really. But,

well, it would need to be something personal, you know."

"I have a customer coming in an hour. The design would have to be very simple. Maybe a flower?" She smirked and waited.

No, not a flower. He already had a rose. He didn't want to turn into a walking greenhouse. No more flowers or insects or vegetables. Nothing dead. No conventionally religious iconography. Then it came to him: a simple cross, the one Kent had seen in the sky, that constellation down in Mexico. Five starbursts. He took her pencil and pad and made a crude sketch.

"Where?"

Bill felt his cheeks. He slapped his face, experimenting with the sting.

"I'd never do that," she said.

"No? Me neither. But somewhere significant." He adjusted the chair so that he could lie down on his stomach. He pulled up his shirt and unbuckled his belt. When he started tugging at his waist band, he hesitated. Earlier this evening, running late for dinner, unable to find fresh underwear, he had dug into the hamper to recycle a pair. He hadn't even bothered to test their smell, and now it was too late. He pulled his pants down to his ankles, pulled his dubious underwear down, too.

"Southern cheeks," he said, his forehead pressed against the Naugahyde. "Fitting location for a southern cross."

She sighed. If it was a look of disgust that crossed her face, he was glad he didn't see it. She adjusted the level on the power supply, and the gun came buzzing to life.

"You better tip well," she said.

BILL LEFT WAY OF THE FLESH, knowing full well he would not be allowed to return. His ass burned with every step he took. His own private stigmata. But there was a comfort in that pain. In the hands of the right artist, there was an addictive comfort in the ritual of desecrating the flesh. Like the most intimate sex, like religion when it really moved him, like a dangerous family dinner, feeling ink injected beneath the skin let him know, at least for the moment, that he was alive and vulnerable. He left the parlor with a secret beneath his clothes. The barrier of skin had just been broken. He passed the people on the street and suspected that he might have things in common with them.

On the way home, he walked by a twenty-four-hour convenience store with a buzzing neon sign in its window advertising COLD BEER. He stood for a moment and watched it flicker before he turned away and hobbled across the street. He passed through an alley that was narrow and dark. The stretch of sky framed by the walls of the buildings was filled with stars. He felt the five novae that had blazed to life searing his ass, connecting him more fully to the cosmos. A path of light flowed behind the brighter stars up there, and he could not be certain whether he was seeing the Milky Way or only the glow from the city. Like the flickering beer sign and that red TATTOO and most of the neon in town, Charlotte's skyline burned all night long, promising fulfillment, progress, magic . . . love? And, despite the scripture Kent had come to quote so frequently, Bill did not want to believe that it was all a lie, that it was better to pluck out both eyes than eternally to burn with desire.

When he came to the edge of the street, his foot shifted beneath him and then he smelled the asphalt. He looked down at his footprint and at the tar on his loafer. He stepped back onto the sidewalk and looked around for a way to cross the freshly paved road. For a second he was lost. Everything here looked new, changed. Then, just above an apartment rooftop he spied the sliver of a moon, its horns pointed up. And, by instinct, he knew the way home.

[Visit Southern Fried Karma's YouTube channel, Fugitive Views, to hear the author's thoughts on Adam and Eve.]

Acknowledgments

I am indebted to the amazing team at SFK Press, especially Pinckney Benedict, April Ford, Cade Leebron, and Steve McCondichie. What a gift your careful reading and support of this project has been to me! Thanks, also, to Eleanor Burden, Nicole Byrne, Olivia M. Croom, Emery Duffey, Amanda Dyar, Alison McCondichie, and A.M. O'Malley & Grant Miller.

I remain humbled that the following writers, whom I have long revered, generously gave of their time to read the manuscript and offer their insights: Fred Chappell, Clyde Edgerton, Eric Gansworth, Randall Kenan, Dale Ray Phillips, Lee Smith, and Leah Stewart. I want to thank, also, several early readers for their ideas and encouragement: Betina Entzminger, Kristen Jastremski, Michael Jastremski, and Dave VanHook. I am grateful to Chip Anderson, whose conceptual drawings of Bill's tattoos helped me to see them more clearly, to artist Daniel Scannell and his colleagues at Oculo Visitant Gallery, to Brett Bowman, Charles Bullock, and all my colleagues at SUNY Oneonta, the Sewanee Writers' Conference, and the Thomas Wolfe Society. I remain grateful to my family—in North Carolina, New York, and elsewhere—especially my parents, my brother, my children, and my wife of twenty years, Kim Jastremski, for her patience, enduring love, and her always clear eye for prose.

About the Author

George Hovis is a native of Gaston County, North Carolina. Before becoming a writer and teacher, he worked as a process chemist at several ink factories in Charlotte. His stories and essays have appeared widely, most recently in *The Carolina Quarterly*, *The Fourth River*, and *North Carolina Literary Review*. A Pushcart Prize nominee, he earned a PhD from the University of North Carolina at Chapel Hill and has attended the Sewanee Writers' Conference. He currently lives with his wife and their two children in Upstate New York, where he is a professor of English at SUNY Oneonta.

SHARE YOUR THOUGHTS

Want to help make *The Skin Artist* a bestselling novel? Consider leaving an honest review on Goodreads, your personal author website or blog, and anywhere else readers go for recommendations. It's our priority at SFK Press to publish books for readers to enjoy, and our authors appreciate and value your feedback.

Our Southern Fried Guarantee

If you wouldn't enthusiastically recommend one of our books with a 4- or 5-star rating to a friend, then the next story is on us. We believe that much in the stories we're telling. Simply email us at **pr@sfkmultimedia.com**.

You Know About Our Bi-Monthly Zine?

Would you like your unpublished prose, poetry, or visual art featured in *The New Southern Fugitives*? A bi-monthly zine that's free to readers and subscribers and pays contributors:

$100 for book reviews, essays, short stories
$40 for flash/micro fiction
$40 for poetry
$40 for photography & visual art

Visit NewSouthernFugitives.com/Submit for more information.

THE NEW
Southern Fugitives

SFK
PRESS

Also by SFK Press

A Body's Just as Dead, Cathy Adams

The Banshee of Machrae, Sonja Condit

Amidst This Fading Light, Rebecca Davis

American Judas, Mickey Dubrow

A Curious Matter of Men with Wings, F. Rutledge Hammes

Lying for a Living, Steve McCondichie

The Parlor Girl's Guide, Steve McCondichie

Hardscrabble Road, George Weinstein

Aftermath, George Weinstein

The Five Destinies of Carlos Moreno, George Weinstein

The Caretaker, George Weinstein

RIPPLES, Evan Williams